Special Delivery

♦ ♦ ♦

Steven Mark Sachs

Durban House

Copyright © 2008, Steven Mark Sachs

All rights reserved. No part of this book may be used or reproduced in any manner whatsoever without the written permission of the Publisher.

Printed in the United States of America.

For information address:
Durban House Press, Inc.
5001 LBJ Freeway, Suite 700, Dallas, Texas 75244

Library of Congress Cataloging-in-Publication Data
Sachs, Steven Mark, 1950 -

Special Delivery / Steven Mark Sachs

Library of Congress Control Number: 2007943817

p. cm.

ISBN: 0-9800067-6-7
978-0-9800067-6-6

First Edition

10 9 8 7 6 5 4 3 2 1

Visit our Web site at
http://www.durbanhouse.com

Acknowledgments

I am grateful to Bob Middlemiss, Jennifer Adkins, Walter Doniger, Robert Jaffe, MD, Alexander Viduetsky, MD, PhD, and John Lewis, all of whom helped enhance *Special Delivery* with incomparable, valuable expertise.

Special Delivery is a work of fiction. Any resemblance of names or characters within this book to real persons, living or dead, is coincidental.

Prelude

    The castle tower is frigid. An eerie stillness is cast over the vast Romanian moor. Fog coils beyond the balcony, beckoning the countess to emerge. Little disturbs the foul odors infesting the castle walls, but the countess' nostrils do not flare. She presses herself against the railing, peering out into the fog, seeking the village. She hears the muffled neigh of a horse, the fog-dampened shouts of farmers readying their crude 17th-century equipment for a day's toil. But it is the women she listens for, the women...
    Their cries are hard to discern, snatches of despair inside the fog. Her eyes widen in primal response to persistent hungers. It is time.

One

The phone's faint electronic warble signaled another job coming in. Things became still in the stuffy room, and everyone looked up.

As she listened through the receiver, Sharona Gomez stiffened in her chair. All eight eyes watching her knew that there was some urgency to this call. This wasn't just a request for bathing a quad or for taking some codger out for a turn in the park.

The desk's hollow recesses magnified the scratching, slipping sound of Sharona's pencil as she captured all the details on her two-part, yellow assignment sheet. As she nodded her head, Sharona closed the conversation with "No problem."

She had limited foresight.

When Sharona hung up, she turned to Lisbath, who rose automatically, like a child ready to receive Holy Communion for the hundredth time.

"Mrs. Blücher sounds ripe, Lisbath. Better get out there pretty fast."

"Certainly," said Lisbath.

As Lisbath accepted the top copy of the sheet, her quite substantial derrière wiggled just a little, an involuntary dance of triumph that always secretly irritated her seated competitors. They eyed each other in shared disgust and just a bit of relief as the nurse-midwife moved slowly out the door to prepare for her task.

When people call a nursing registry, they visualize something like a bright white, gleaming, sterile nurse vending machine. But the reality of Dickinson's Nurse Registry Service, now nestled in the chilly throes of January, was much cozier.

The place was a comfortable, converted home on Fairfield Avenue near Spruce Street in Bridgeport, Connecticut. There were three old couches and four stuffed chairs, scattered magazines, a worn brown carpet, and a coffee maker forced to pump out its homey fragrance unendingly. The Millennium 2004 multi-line phone and e-mail unit, with its flashing buttons and metallic black casing, was the only truly modern item in the place. A fragrant blend of coffee, old wood, worn upholstery and competing inexpensive colognes made for a remarkable sensory environment.

"Hey, everybody," said Susie, the youngest member of the crew. She pointed through the curtains. "Look outside. Manoff's got new vans. Cool!"

On either side of the wooden building housing Dickinson's were two other former single-family houses that had also been outfitted for small businesses. One was an Internet web design establishment busy twenty-four hours a day, and the other housed a whitewashed janitorial service. Manoff's Housekeeping had apparently just upgraded their fleet.

Across the street was a large apartment complex. From time to time some of the kids would come over to Sharona's to raid the large donut box Sharona replenished every day.

Even though they could just as well stay home and wait for a call or a page to get to work, there was a core group who found Dickinson's a kind of social center. They were usually relaxing on the couches, flipping through old issues of *National Geographic* or *Nurse* magazine. For most of them—particularly the single ones—Dickinson's generated a sense of belonging and even of family.

Today's assortment of regulars included Karen Stade, who used to work for Doc Stowage until his untimely death in a bowling accident; Wanda Pettridge, a true "old school" nurse who still insisted on wearing her cap and pin even while at rest; and Susie Rime, a youthful born-again Christian with the perky demeanor of inexperience. Susie's bright turquoise stethoscope hung on her Hyundai's rear-view mirror, announcing to everyone her recent nursing school graduation.

Lisbath Milliken had spent most of the morning there too, absolutely filling her favorite armchair. As usual, she had been humming "Tie a Yellow Ribbon" lightly to herself, tapping her wide fingers on her lap, and nodding her head slightly. Her sunglasses hung onto her purse strap by their thick temples.

Lisbath was an anachronism. She always wore a cream-colored apron trimmed with white lace and ties and sporting three pockets. She had sewn an extra stethoscope pocket onto the bib of each of her aprons; it looked awkward when that top pocket was filled with black tubing and metal. No matter; Lisbath was a functionalist, and whatever worked, worked.

She was in her mid-fifties. Her light brown hair was just beginning to gray. It was always bunned perfectly. Whenever she spoke or tilted her head downward, her lowest chin barely touched the apron bib's starched, white lace crown.

Lisbath was a nurse-midwife—one of a diminishing breed. Her job was to deliver babies, and she did it with aplomb. She usually worked right in the new mother's home, without the presence of a doctor or other medical personnel. She was trained, competent, reassuring and matronly. That was why she got so much work. Nurse Milliken had delivered close to 700 babies in her almost four decades of nursing, and there had been very few problems along the way. At least very few that had ever surfaced.

Boss Lady Sharona Gomez sat at her desk fielding calls and sucking coffee through sugar cubes all day long. Her ability to round up the troops and to soothe irritated doctors and rest home personnel directors was legendary, and Sharona needed these skills almost constantly.

Sharona was a tall woman with a self-assured carriage, lean

legs, and only a slight flare in her hips. Her obvious personal power was counterbalanced by a face so feminine and strikingly pretty that even women would do a double-take when she entered a room. She had medium-length brown hair cut in a simple style. Her smooth bangs dangled over large, deep brown eyes. Her flawless skin was like that of a girl half her thirty-two years.

♦ ♦ ♦

Lisbath drove the two miles to her place at Yankee Pines Apartments in Bridgeport while the newest country-western tune, "Puzzle of Broken Hearts," crept out through her car windows. She passed wet roofs and an irregular spate of umbrellas: black, bouncing mushrooms growing five feet above the ground. Despite its being overcast, Lisbath wore her sunglasses as usual.

In the Connecticut winter, Lisbath always kept the windows shut tight to keep out blustery winds. Her 1986 Ford was heavy enough to resist all but January's strongest drafts, but its shocks were in bad shape, so when the car pulled to a stop in the parking lot just off Howard Court, it waddled just a little like Lisbath's victory dance. The woman never noticed.

"Time to move, move, move," Lisbath said to herself.

She went straight to the elevator without checking her mail. Lisbath tapped the dingy "3" button with her pudgy finger and headed up to her modest third-floor apartment with the serene determination of a medical professional gearing up for her calling. The elevator doors were opening too slowly, like a yawning, screeching mechanical mouth. A sense of urgency about her, Lisbath shouldered the rubber bumper into the side of the door to speed things up.

Even before Lisbath covered the short distance down the hallway to her apartment door, Lad was wagging his tail wildly, scratching at the inside of the door, and yelping in his combination of unfocused joy and anticipation of a good meal. He wanted to see if she had brought him what he needed. And of course, he wanted to see Mommy, too.

Lad was a cross-breed of some kind. Even vets had trouble identifying his canine heritage. A foot and a half tall at the shoulder, the black-and-white mutt weighed sixty-five pounds. The only color to him was his left rear leg, which was mostly yellow.

When Lisbath opened the door, Lad leapt happily onto her. "No, Laddie! Get down! Mustn't soil Mommy's uniform. I've got to go out to work, and when I come back, Laddie will have a special treat!"

Lad obeyed, but stuck close to Lisbath's side as if tethered.

Lisbath had spent the better part of the morning drinking coffee at Dickinson's, so she headed directly for the bathroom and didn't bother to shut Lad out. She lifted her uniform skirt and apron carefully to minimize wrinkling and brought down her tent-size panties.

After scrubbing her hands and forearms extra carefully, Lisbath went to her supply closet, spun the combination lock she had had installed the very day she moved in, and eased the door open. A strong chemical pungency billowed out into the hallway. Before her lay many of the tools and materials of her trade as well as a group of large shelved jars and other special paraphernalia of her own design.

Surgical and examination equipment was laid out in orderly fashion in the metal drawers of a gleaming, four-foot-high, cherry-red Craftsman tool cabinet. As she slid each drawer open with a smooth, deft tug, the gliding roller bearings rumbled softly. There were sterile packages of cutting blades, clamps, speculums, tubes, wires, lots of odd-shaped metal instruments, and other pieces made to address the body.

On the shelves, each row of four-inch-diameter jars was restrained by an industry-standard metal wire running the width of the cabinet, fastened to stretch across about 2/3 of the way to the top of the evenly-sized containers.

Most of the jars held liquids as colorless as water. In others resided a brownish, thick liquid suggesting they were full of brine. Two jars near the rear contained a blackened, congealed fluid.

At the far left was a jar with something deeply, unevenly brown and roughly cylindrical floating in the amber suspension. The solid object was three or four inches long, with one end butting against the top of the jar and the lower portion leaning against the side as the unit tried to float out of the stringy fluid. Its diameter varied irregularly between that of a quarter and that of a fifty-cent piece. A casual observer might think the jar held a branch or root or, God forbid, a penis ripped from its living mooring and jabbed into its glass prison before it could bleed out all the way. The alien cylinder seemed to have been bruised, and sported what appeared to be torn tissues issuing from the lower end.

Many of the jars were unlabeled, but this special one had a piece of aging masking tape with *S067980702* carefully printed in paling black letters. Lisbath's memento. Lisbath's prize.

The nurse turned her attention to the matters at hand and selected a wide array of tools for the upcoming birth. She took each equipment packet and placed it carefully in a large carpetbag covered with a fading, magenta flowered design. The simple, musty smell one would have expected from the old bag was absent, and in its place was a diluted disinfectant odor mixed with something unmistakably organic but not easily identified.

Lisbath thought the flowered bag reflected at once her seriousness as well as her professionalism. These days, most nurse midwives also brought clear plastic goggles to help avoid splashed-blood-to-eye contact. What with AIDS and other blood-borne diseases, one couldn't be too careful. But Lisbath wasn't worried and had never added even one pair of goggles to her supply cache.

A portable fetal heart monitor sat on the floor in its own metallic case. As was her habit, Lisbath put it outside the closet door to be doubly sure she would take it when she left.

To her right was a low painted shelf with some equipment her nursing colleagues would not associate with midwifery. Lisbath selected a metal-clad, expensive Thermos bottle which had been airing out in a plastic tray, as well as a couple of black trash bags. She took them from the shelf and placed these things atop the shining Craftsman cabinet.

Lad, who was watching all this preparation, began to respond the moment he saw the metal gleam of the vacuum bottle. Led by its wildly oscillating tail, his rear end did its own quick version of the Milliken triumph dance.

Lisbath rolled the Thermos and the extra bags in a long, thin red towel and inserted the irregular, bullet-shaped packet into the bottom and off to the side in the carpetbag. She tucked the ends around the bottom; nothing of the package's contents remained visible.

On her way out, Lisbath paused a moment to pat her dog's head. "See you soon, my little Laddie."

She sang her little tune to him:

Treats a-comin', treats a-comin'
Mommy does as Mommy should;
Treats a-comin', treats a-comin'
Mommy brings it sweet and good!

Lisbath left the apartment humming as Lad literally spun with anticipation.

Two

The winds scurrying over the New England roads had died down somewhat, but nature's exchange for this temporary respite was a darkening sky. Lisbath's Ford made its way south toward the Blücher house on Frank Street.

The radio was on as always, this time turned down low. Lisbath wasn't really paying attention to its news break. She was softly humming "Rock-a-Bye Baby," a mild grin on her face. She was visualizing the baby plunging from a pine tree's highest bough, the infant plummeting past lower branches that slice into its skin as it flies down, tumbling out of the cradle, throwing sprays of blood from its flailing limbs as it heads earthward, dumbfounded and in incomprehensible pain. Lisbath bit the smile out of her cheek and very deliberately returned her attention to the radio and the road.

Spinning the volume knob with the fleshy side of her right palm in a fast, practiced sweep, Lisbath could now hear the country-western station's news break finally terminating. She hated the news, especially featuring that bitchy "Big T" local reporter, preferring the comfort of her familiar, tell-it-like-it-is music. She also hated reading the articles written by Big T in the *Bridgeport Informant* newspaper. And how did that T woman get so famous that she did both radio and newspaper? The fact is, Bridgeport was in many ways a small, small town.

Since this was Sunday, radio stations spewed forth their required weekly sixty minutes of Public Service Announcements in batches.

"Just fifty cents a day will feed these pitifully hungry, needy Ethiopian children," the has-been actress mewed. "They didn't ask to be born, they didn't ask for your help. They don't know how to ask. We need to do this for them. Folks, with God's help and your generous dollars . . ."

Lisbath's mind wandered. Poor, hungry children. She thought of her own childhood, accessing misty, vague, incomplete images …

Lisbath was on her mama's lap, leaning toward the kitchen table and drinking out of a tiny cup. Her older sister Deborah was slurping soggy cornflakes out of a chipped bowl.

Abruptly, Mama grabbed the milk cup out of Lisbath's hand. The child was destined to be a big girl, and she was still very hungry, but Mama felt she had had enough. Lisbath began to cry, and Mama was confused. Mama was careful not to overfeed the girl. Like goldfish; you feed them too much and you can hurt them.

Hail began smashing onto the Ford's rooftop and windshield. It made a jarring racket, yanking Lisbath back to driving awareness. A soaked, frightened mutt tore by the front of the car, and a startled Lisbath slammed on the brakes, almost causing a skid. There were no other cars around, so she just sat there for a moment, letting her pulse drop down into the double digits.

After regaining her bearings, Lisbath realized that she was just a couple of blocks from the Blücher house on Frank Street. She rounded the corner and made her way down a treed lane that scratched at the pummeling winter sky with thousands of leafless, pointed fingers.

Rock-a-bye baby
On the tree top
When the bough breaks . . .

Lisbath pulled up right into the driveway, knowing that nobody would be leaving while she was still there. She put her sunglasses on the rear-view mirror, brought two satchels and the fetal heart monitor out from the trunk, slammed the lid with her elbow, and trundled to the front door.

The screen was pulled to, and the door behind it was wide open since Lisbath was expected. With certitude and aplomb, Lisbath opened the screen without knocking and was stopped immediately by Erich Blücher, the agitated father-to-be. He and Lisbath had never met since he had always been at work during Lisbath's prenatal visits with Mrs. Blücher.

Erich's approach was quite direct and powerful. His Austrian accent was thick and, to Lisbath, foreboding.

"Miss Milliken, I am Erich Blücher. We have been waiting here many minutes for you. Ilse is from Old Country and to her is the midwife normal. But to me, I am not so sure. What if there is problem? You are *not* Doktor, no?"

Lisbath was used to this kind of questioning. It was usually the dads. Overprotective, ignorant, always in her way. The men always reminded her of the pig doctors: directing, demanding, questioning her skill and knowledge. Didn't they know? Why couldn't they understand what she had been through?

Lisbath did not feel appreciated by the so-called "stronger sex." They couldn't appreciate anything *woman-to-woman*.

But she had to tolerate them.

Lisbath stiffened and lowered her equipment and bags very slowly. As they settled, the bags made a crunching sound on the wooden floor. She brought herself to her full 5'5" of height, but the irritation running through her made Lisbath seem a couple of inches taller.

"Mr. Blücher, I am a licensed nurse-midwife. I have been doing this fine work for about forty years, and I am *very good* at it. Your wife trusts me. *Thousands* of wives trust me. Now either you step out of my way or you'll need to call an ambulance to take Ilse to the hospital *right now*. Which will it be? Well? *Well?*"

Blücher was not used to being challenged in this way, especially not by an American woman. His face reddened. But, like Lisbath, he was a pragmatist. Lisbath's logic was insurmountable, and Ilse was beginning to scream bloody murder in the bedroom.

"All right, Miss Milliken. I ask you to take your best care of my wife and son."

"How do you know it'll be a son?" Lisbath snapped. "Ilse's records show no ultrasound and no amniocentesis, even though I advised both on my initial examination."

Two peals of thunder failed to break Erich's stern, determined concentration.

"I will only have sons. Please, now, get to work."

Lisbath could not fathom the audacity of this bastard, but she had work to do, and that was that. She lifted her equipment bags and scurried into the bedroom, cursing under her breath. Ilse was clutching the bed sheets so hard that one of her fingernails had already broken. Mrs. Blücher was sweating heavily and in apparent agony; Lisbath's arrival did not seem to comfort her. *Poor dear*, thought Lisbath.

"Hello, Ilse. Nice to see you again." Lisbath smiled her professional smile, distant and a little too toothy to convey sincerity. An exhausted Ilse just stared at her, temporarily motionless save irregular, frightened breathing, as she waited for the next dreadful contraction.

"I'll just set up right next to the bed and everything will be all right. Okay?"

Ilse said nothing. She started to drool a little, and Lisbath's thoughts flashed briefly back to watching *The Exorcist* for the first of her eight viewings. Ilse gasped as a new surprise contraction grabbed at her from inside her own body. Her back arched.

Lisbath was searching for an electrical outlet for the fetal heart monitor when Erich strutted through the doorway. The nurse saw him from the corner of her eye, and her blood pressure upped a notch.

"Mr. Blücher, please leave. I must set up and you are distracting me." Outside the house, the hail continued to fall, punctuated by lightning flashes close enough to light up the room.

"*Aber* I will be present during my son's birth." Thunder shook the lace curtains and Lisbath's eyes gleamed as if lit from deep inside.

"Yes, yes. In good time. I will call you in. Close the door behind you and ask anyone else to wait outside! Boil lots of water and have it ready." Erich felt like he was in the Austrian military again, and he didn't like it.

"Fine!" Blücher stormed out briskly, and Lisbath could almost hear the asshole's heels click together as the door latch caught. Ilse was in her own delirious world of agony, totally out of tune with the repartee around her. She wanted the pain to stop. She wanted her body to re-form from its grotesque, misshapen bulb to something Erich would find attractive again. Ilse wanted with every straining fiber of her being to get comfortable after all these draining, screaming hours. She wanted the child *out. Right now.*

Lisbath set to work placing large towels, each with a blue stripe down the middle, upon every available horizontal surface around the bed. A complete array at arm's reach meant good, fast, responsive nursing.

As she unpacked, Lisbath laid out each piece of equipment carefully and methodically. Like a dentist hiding the startlingly severe long needle as she reaches around your jaw to insert and twist, Lisbath positioned her own cutting, clamping, puncturing, restraining, and pinching equipment just out of Ilse's line of sight. She placed a sterile towel over each row of gleaming, waiting tools lest the family members who would witness the birth soil anything.

"Almost ready, my dear," said Lisbath as she positioned the fetal heart monitor's sensor belts around Ilse's bulging abdomen. Ilse's vision of the rectangular blue box of plastic-encased electronics strapped to her wiggling flesh made for an absurd picture. It was a common sight for Lisbath just the same.

The nurse-midwife switched on the monitor, and the fast heartbeat sound offered reassurance that the fetus was strong and getting ready for its grand entrance. Contractions for the moment were quiescent. The tracing tape began to snake out of the monitor unit.

"Hear that monitor, Ilse? That's your baby! It sounds very, very good."

Ilse finally zoned in. "I'm glad, Mrs. Milliken. I want to get this over with."

"Call me Lisbath, Ilse. You know we have to let nature take her course. But I'll tell you, *woman-to-woman*, it shouldn't be too long."

"*Danken sie Gott.*"

The slightly overheated nurse-midwife continued her preparations, making two trips out to the kitchen and the linen closet during five minutes of fast-paced setup activities. While Ilse was staring vacantly out the window at the lightning flashes, Lisbath carefully unwrapped and placed the Thermos bottle and trash bags under the bed. She tapped them with her toes to get a feel for their exact location and to ensure that she would not kick them during her birth support activities.

The touch and slight metallic "tink" sound of the lightly-kicked Thermos gave Lisbath a swift, brief and enjoyable labial shudder. She smiled and squatted ever so slightly. She was ready.

Ilse screamed.

From the sound of it, Ilse was ready too.

Lisbath went to Ilse's face and wiped it with a washcloth dipped in the cool water she had placed in one of the kidney-shaped steel basins.

"That feels good. Thank you."

Lisbath smiled and moved to position Ilse on the bed, with her legs spread and the covers drawn back to her hips. Commencing the exam, Lisbath inserted a vaginal speculum of her own design and peered inside. There was now enough cervical dilation to call in the troops.

"You may enter now," Lisbath called toward the door. Four people spilled into the room instantly, with Helmut, the Blüchers' retarded but exquisitely agile child, leading the pack. He had apparently been leaning on the old door, looking through its large keyhole, waiting for the signal to come in.

Everyone gathered around the bed. Aunt Genya put her arms lovingly but firmly around Helmut and restrained him near the head of the bed. It was not right to have Helmut stare at his mother's private parts. Ilse's best friend went right to Ilse's side and began to stroke her forehead with great care. Lisbath approved with a nod of her head, then turned her attention immediately back to the business at hand.

Erich entered and stationed himself at the far wall, a little dumbfounded at the experience. Several minutes later when the baby began to crown, Mr. Blücher put on his glasses, the better to see his next son emerge.

His mother's screams became increasingly intense and pitiful, and Helmut began to lose his already limited composure. In a flurry of incomprehension, Helmut covered his ears, grinding his puny hands into them as if scrunching an infuriated, biting insect before it could complete its frightening midnight attack. Helmut buried his shaking head in Aunt Genya's abdomen. Finally, the boy began to writhe and scream, producing a ghostly duet with his mother's unabashed yowls. Aunt Genya dragged the overwhelmed child out of the room and everyone relaxed noticeably.

The family dog tried to barrel through the door, but Erich put a stop to that immediately. Still, as Lisbath's anger about the dog's intrusion began to subside, her thoughts turned to her little Laddie.

In her mind's eye, she saw him hopping happily into her ample lap, his tail wagging so hard it actually stung as it hit her belly rhythmically. But she tolerated—even enjoyed—the pain.

Lisbath saw herself smiling broadly, her face made wet with Laddie's lapping tongue. She petted the pup vigorously, and with each pat his tail went faster and faster.

Mommy rose from the chair. Lad's eyes sparkled as they followed her into the kitchen and to the refrigerator. The industrial green tiling on the walls shone brightly, like the walkway to a morgue.

As Lisbath reached for the refrigerator's old lever handle, Laddie went ballistic. The dog began running in circles, yelping randomly, urinating tiny drops involuntarily, and shaking in an ecstatic, benign violence only a dog in unbridled bliss can exhibit. He began scratching, scrabbling wildly on the linoleum. It sounded like a stiff scrub brush attacking concrete, with the uneven, relentless vigor of a criminal vainly trying to remove the blood traces after a fresh murder.

Mrs. Blücher's wrenching screams tore Lisbath out of her reverie. The birth-mother was foaming at the mouth, her saliva spraying left and right as she flailed her head, unintentionally aiming her painful shouts all about the room.

"Take it easy, Mama. Now, push. PUSH!"

The baby's head began to peek through, and Lisbath ran her fingers between the baby's skull and its labial restraints, kind of breaking the seal. The head was covered with white, ricotta-like slime mixed with spats of blood and a little clear fluid.

"Push! PUSH! NOW!"

Everyone in attendance was panting in time with Mrs. Blücher. It was a comical sight made somber by the mother-to-be's painful cries.

After several bouts of pushing and relaxing, the baby began to emerge very rapidly. Everyone crowded around for the presentation. "Give her room, now. Everyone back now. NOW!" As the baby's head emerged fully, Lisbath reached under the bed and brought out the black plastic trash bag. A brief look of confusion shot across the onlookers. A plastic bag? Not a body bag, surely!

But one defers to an expert in any field, so everyone found themselves dismissing the bag's appearance as part of the ritual and returned their attention to the newest Blücher being pulled out of its mother.

As the birth progressed, Nurse Milliken continued reaching under the bed for equipment, but the participants' focus was all on the now screaming little girl still attached to its mother by the umbilicus.

Nurse Milliken kept close in front of Mrs. Blücher's opening, but from the side it almost appeared that Lisbath licked her fingers a couple of times during the birthing process. She would immediately wipe her forehead and then her mouth with her forearm, so whatever she was really doing was essentially inconspicuous.

The baby was entirely out now, and Milliken double-clamped the umbilicus, cut it, wiped the baby off with two towels, and sat her on her mother. Out of the corner of her eye, Lisbath could see Herr Blücher grimace as he spied the lack of a penis on his new prize. No new boy today.

Mrs. Blücher was crying with relief and joy and that maternal pleasure no man can really appreciate. Everyone crowded in around her as Lisbath and her bag o' tricks receded into the bathroom.

◆ ◆ ◆

In short order, Lisbath emerged crisp, clean, nurseworthy and drooling imperceptibly. She approached Mrs. Blücher.

"Mama, you did well. Baby is beautiful! Now, I'll be back for a postpartum check in three days. Call me if anything seems unusual. Okay?"

Erich broke in: "Unusual? There is something wrong? Tell me, and tell me now!"

"No, no, Herr Blücher. Everything appears perfect. We still

must have mother and baby checked soon after birthing. You understand."

Patriarch Blücher did *not* understand. Why have a midwife if a doctor had to be involved later? *Inefficient*. But that didn't matter. He would comply. This was how things were done. Never take chances with family. Never.

Lisbath Milliken was done with this birthing. She packed up, methodically and unobtrusively, including placing the afterbirth in its plastic container. She became merely a shadow servant amidst the warm glee of family surrounding the new baby.

◆ ◆ ◆

Milliken spun the On/Off/Volume knob on her car radio 180 degrees to halfway on. This was loud enough to drown out the traffic and tire noise, but not glaringly offensive like those damn teenagers driving by her apartment window after midnight every weekend. Predictable guitar chord progressions and the country-western twang gave Lisbath peace as she pulled away from the curb in front of the Blüchers'. She flipped on her windshield wipers to squeegee off the last hour's downpour.

When she reached Olde Towne Road, Nurse Milliken turned right. She drove about 250 yards down the pebbly, unimproved surface, appreciatively aware that it wasn't a state road and therefore was traveled only infrequently. Lisbath wanted privacy. Although she was exhausted, this trek to solitude wasn't for rest, but instead for her special feast.

Once she rounded a curve, Lisbath checked her rearview mirror and satisfied herself that she was alone, not followed, and out of sight of the main highway. Nobody would come by here accidentally. This place was good and safe enough, yet she drove another fifty yards, then pulled off to the right shoulder. A final glance in the rearview mirror, the front window, and all around assured Lisbath that this was a good place. She took off her sunglasses and hung them on the rearview mirror.

As she reached from the gearshift around in an arc to the back of the car, Lisbath's ample arm flapped as it struck the top of the front bench seat. She didn't notice the sting. She grabbed the black semicircular handles of the carpetbag and heaved it over the seat back. The special luggage thudded into place beside her, and Lisbath began a slow, joyous squirm.

Three

The following morning, young Susie Rime was tapping her fingers on her knees as she sat on Dickinson's front porch. She was waiting for Sharona to open up for the day. Her New Christian music was on so loud that nearby Lisbath could hear a tinny version of it seeping out of Susie's headphones.

"You'll ruin your hearing that way, young lady," Lisbath admonished as she shook her thick finger in Susie's direction.

Susie didn't bother to remove her headphones, but she knew full well what Lisbath was saying. Nurse Milliken was always trying to play mother to the rest of the nurses. Susie just smiled and nodded her head in time with the music.

As Milliken was about to press her point, Sharona pulled up and parked her station wagon right in front of Dickinson's. Everyone considered the prime parking spot in front of the door as Sharona's. She could watch her car all day, and besides, she was the owner.

Sharona took her steel clipboard off the passenger seat, locked her car, and strode quickly to the registry's front door. Most of the usual clan had already arrived. A few were already on assignment, and there was always the cadre who chose to remain at home to wait for the call to work.

Karen pulled up in her old Datsun B-210 just as Sharona opened the door. She put The Club on her right-hand drive, small-bumper English model steering wheel and trotted in.

Sharona's clipboard was filled with assignments. Her habit was to call the answering service from her cell phone enroute to Dickinson's so she could dispatch her nurses as soon as she arrived in the morning.

"Come on into the back for a second, Lisbath, okay?" asked Sharona. This place was reserved for private conferences and the occasional nap on the cot.

If Lisbath was surprised, she hid it well. She followed Sharona through the door, and Wanda efficiently took the seat at the desk to cover for Sharona.

"Lisbath, this is no big deal, but do you remember that a few days ago you saw two patients? One was that Audlin woman? You picked up the extra job even though it wasn't a midwifery call because I was short-handed that early in the morning."

"Sure. She was pretty bad off. I advised her to see her doc ASAP. She needed more than a nurse."

"And the other one you saw was Mrs. Smithson."

"Yes. And?"

Sharona got serious. "Mrs. Smithson had her postpartum check and was found to have real low BP and an elevated temp. Dr. Gold's office asked for any background we may have on her. Did you notice anything? Was she extra pallid or a heavy bleeder or something?"

Lisbath's heart skipped a beat, and she reddened ever so slightly.

"No, Sharona. Nothing. Poor dear." She frowned. "Anything else?"

"Dr. Gold's office also reported nausea and vertigo. The doc doesn't think that it's related to the anemia; they're doing some other tests."

"Okay, boss. Well, let me know what they find." Lisbath put her hands into her apron pockets. They made little, invisible fists. "Sharona, why'd you really call me back here? You could have told me about Mrs. Smithson's postpartum check in the outer office, right?"

Sharona pressed her lovely lips together for a moment.

"When the doctor's office called to tell me about the patient's nausea and vertigo, there was something in the nurse's voice. I don't know—like they were worried more than they should be, or they expected to see something in your report about precipitating factors and they didn't. Something. I can't put my finger on it, and nobody actually said anything out of the ordinary, but I've learned to trust my feelings, and this feels *off* somehow." Her beautiful face was solemn with concern. "Are you sure there's nothing atypical here?"

Sharona's voice was supportive—even protective. Her troops were golden, and she would trust all her nurses with her own life, if need be.

Lisbath answered, "Nothing at all, Sharona. Ms. Smithson was an unremarkable patient."

But Lisbath was confused. Did she mess up? And what would account for the vertigo and nausea? She was silently reviewing the Smithson case and the earlier Audlin visit with not a little trepidation.

"Lisbath, are you okay? You look like your mind's off somewhere else. Did you hear the stuff I've been saying?"

"Of course. I'm just thinking back to the birth. Nothing out of the ordinary. Oh, well!" Lisbath raised her hands in an "I give up" gesture.

Both walked back into the main office. Sharona went right to her desk, and Lisbath went to pour a cup of the coffee Susie had put up before leaving for her day's assignment.

As Sharona began to descend into her seat, her phone rang. She took a deep breath and answered the phone.

"Dickinson's. May I help you?"

"Hi, Tweedles!"

"Who is ... is this *Barbara*?"

"Who else?"

Sharona started to smile so wide her eyes crinkled. She couldn't have asked for a nicer break from the tension.

"Hey, Barb! I haven't heard 'Tweedles' for eons!"

"Three whole years, girl."

"Oh, come on!" said Sharona. "Could it really be three years?"

"We haven't talked since Jeff and I split up. That was March three years ago."

"No kidding." Sharona paused. "Isn't it stupid that my best friend would live less than fifty miles away and we can't even get it together enough to meet for coffee for three whole years?"

"You know, Sharona, that's the price of being a pro."

Sharona owned Dickinson's, but she was a businesswoman, not a nurse. Her mother had been, but when her mother described her day-to-day work—dealing with sick people, having to act so subservient to doctors, being stereotyped in a "girlie" profession—these things did not appeal to Sharona. Still, every day as a child Sharona would hear about Doctor this or hospital that or patient so-and-so.

Her father had owned a small grocery store and was often consumed with business. He would talk over the dinner table about new promotions he was thinking of creating, or about his employees, and very often about making money.

With nursing in her blood but having more of a business bent, Sharona decided just before graduating high school that she wanted to combine the two. So when she enrolled at Connecticut State University, she selected a health administration major.

Barbara Yoge and Sharona had met the first day at school. They were both health ad. majors at that time, which was twelve years ago. Less than six months after their graduation, both were earning a good living in the field.

Professionals sometimes get so busy that they don't have much time for the social part of life, and both Sharona and Barbara were victims of that trap. Neither had much time for friends beyond the people at work, so this call from Sharona's college roomie was especially welcome.

"Hey, Barb. How's the hospital?" asked Sharona.

Barbara was assistant director of the Blue Cross hospital and medical offices in Hartford, about forty miles north of Bridgeport. She had secured that job within two months of graduating CSU.

Barbara didn't really want to talk shop, but she respected Sharona's honest question. "Well, Tweedles, the short story is that the head of neurology just got Parkinson's. It's kind of ironic, and he's really a nice man, but we're having a hell of a time getting him to quit. And we can't really name a replacement without starting a political war here."

"Oh, man, Barb. Sorry to hear about it."

"Yeah. Well, that's *not* why I called, you know."

"Still, I'm always here to listen to whatever's going on," said Sharona. "You're almost the only one I have to talk to. I can't tell you how important you are to me."

"That's sweet. Well, speaking of speaking, how about we get together for some wine and cheese? Trader Joe's just got in the best Chardonnay I've ever tasted, and I want to share a bottle with you."

"I'm not sure I really have time, Barb. I need to be open…"

"*Sharona!*"

Sharona leaned back in her chair and smiled.

"You know, you're right. I need a break, and I really would love to see you."

"Tweedles, I'll come down there. That'll save you some time. Maybe we can meet at Bunnell's pond dam over in Beardsley park. That place is so beautiful. And it reminds me of when we would take our one-day vacations when we were studying. We'll have a picnic right by the bridge. Unless it's too cold. Gotta dress warm. Okay?"

"Sounds wonderful. If the weather's bad, we'll just go to my place. I live less than ten minutes from there."

"Great! When can we arrange it? I'm already dreaming," said Barbara.

Sharona and Barbara worked out the details, giggling like little girls about to go to the county fair.

◆ ◆ ◆

Linda Boating was hanging over her toilet bowl, vomiting the last few brown drops before the dry heaves would set in. Her enlarged, pregnant abdomen fit neatly into the curve of the toilet's lower front face, and it was apparent that she had been in that position for well over an hour.

Her straggly, blonde hair, moist with the perspiration of illness, flapped at her ears as her head bobbed mercilessly and irregularly over the bowl. She had long ago lost the strength to reach up to the handle to flush her effluent away. On top of all this, Linda was getting over the flu, having been reamed out by a series of antibiotics. She was in a drastically weakened state.

Out in the front room, her husband Bob was watching TV and drinking his fifth Budweiser of the evening, trying to get the pitiful sound of his poor wife out of his head. She'd been like this for over two weeks, and the Boatings were frankly too stupid to know she should have been hospitalized long ago. "You just have morning sickness all day long, don't you?" the ignorant McDonald's assistant manager would say. "Or maybe it's that flu."

Linda was almost too weak to talk. "When's that nurse coming, Bob? The baby's ripping me up inside. My stomach is so sore!"

"Oh, shit!" Bob said to himself. In his drunken haze, he had forgotten all about calling for the appointment.

"She's very busy, honey. They don't know when she can make it."

Linda was getting angry; her tolerance was paper-thin and getting thinner as she felt increasingly ill.

"Then get someone *else*, Bob. Please. If I could get to the phone, I'd call myself."

"Sure, honey. Right away. Can I get you anything?"

"Just make the damn call."

Bob went sheepishly to the phone and got out the phone book. He had written the Dickinson's Registry number down under

"Baby," so his alcohol-ridden research took him an extra couple of minutes.

He finally found the number and had to dial twice, his fingers stumbling over the numbers the first time.

"Dickinson's. This is Sharona. May I help you?"

The snappy greeting sobered Bob up a bit.

"Hi. Yes, hi. This is Linda Boating's husband. We was supposed to ask for a nurse a few days ago, and we need one bad now. My wife's pregnant, and she's been throwing up for two weeks, and she just had the flu, and her friend said to ask for Elizabeth or something."

Sharona heard raspy dry heaves as well as a cheerful parakeet chirping away in the background.

"Please hold one moment, Mr. Boating."

"'Kay." He slobbered on his goatee.

Sharona checked her records and came up empty.

"Mr. Boating, do you have a doctor's referral? I don't see your name here."

"No. We just want Elizabeth, okay?" His patience had almost vanished as well.

"Yes, *okay*, Mr. Boating. Just relax. We do have a Lisbath, and I'll send her out as soon as she comes back from lunch."

"Thanks. Sorry, Miss. . . this is just really hard to take."

"What's your wife's doctor's name?"

His eyes tracked the game on TV. "Uh, check with me later. I gotta get off now."

"Okay, Mr. Boating. But we'll need to know some time today. 'Bye."

Bob and Sharona put down their phones simultaneously, but Sharona's receiver landed on the cradle the very first time.

♦ ♦ ♦

Lisbath came in from lunch while Sharona was in the bathroom. She sat down on the couch, picked up a *Time* magazine, and started reading the cover story.

The sound of the paper towel dispenser meant Sharona was coming out.

"Lisbath, I've got one for you."

Lisbath held up her right index finger, signaling Sharona to wait a moment while she finished reading her paragraph. As one of the tenured Dickinson's agents, Nurse Milliken had a certain stature Sharona accepted.

Susie had come in and was on the couch nearest Sharona's desk. She looked almost jealously at Lisbath. Seems Nurse Milliken always got first call.

Lisbath got up, straightened her apron and victory-waddled over to Sharona's desk. "What's her name, love?"

"Linda. Linda Boating. She's been vomiting for two weeks and we don't know how far along she is. Her husband's there. He sounds like a dork. They asked for you by name, Lisbath. Some friend of Mrs. Boating knows you."

"Okay. Thanks, Sharona. Can I have the slip?"

"Sure. Keep an eye on Mr. Dork, okay?"

Lisbath just winked and scanned the slip: 1405 Tennessee Street. Not a very wholesome part of town. Trailer parks, disheveled buildings, lots of transients.

💧 💧 💧

Lisbath fought her way through the fetid cloud of alcohol breath Bob had belched up during the last few minutes. He was adorned with at least a two-day growth of stubbly beard, thongs, and a T-shirt sporting huge, yellowed underarms.

As soon as she made it ten feet into the house, Lisbath steeled herself against the cloying stench of vomit that filled her nostrils.

Linda was splayed out on the bathroom floor, head resting on her forearm, her green chenille robe off one shoulder and wrapped partly around her legs. The toilet bowl was foul.

Mrs. Boating looked up upon seeing the white hospital shoes with the thick stumps covered by white hose sticking out of them.

"Hello, Linda. I'm Nurse-midwife Milliken. You poor dear. May I help you up?"

Linda raised her left hand limply, and Lisbath clamped Mrs. Boating above the wrist and above the elbow. She eased her patient up slowly and wrapped her arm around Mrs. Boating's waist when it was accessible. Lisbath began to lead the woman from the bathroom over to the unkempt bed. Linda stumbled toward it, and Lisbath made sure Mrs. Boating's descent was easy.

Her abdomen was significantly distended and low; she could easily be in her ninth month. Her pallid complexion, puffy red eyes, and slight shaking indicated something more than mere pregnancy was controlling her body. She appeared to be perhaps twenty-five to twenty-eight years old.

"Linda, how long have you been pregnant?"

"Seems like forever."

"So you don't know exactly when you got pregnant? Do you remember when you missed your period for the first time?"

"Do you know what it's like to be taken over and over every single day? God! I thought that would slow down after we were married. Bob said it was my wifely duty, you know, and I never said no. But I was bleeding all the time. *All* the time. Sometimes it was thicker or heavier, and I guess that's when I had my period, but I don't know. I just don't *know*."

Linda began to whimper.

As Lisbath listened to this blood talk, she began getting wet. She fantasized about blood flowing vaginally and labially and from other secret places. She wondered about the Boating flavor and fragrance.

"Have you taken your temperature over the last few days?" asked Lisbath.

Linda shook her head. "Uh-uh. We ain't got no thermometer."

Lisbath determined that her temp was 101.1.

"Mrs. Boating, you should be in the hospital."

"We can't afford to be in no hospital. You can take care of me, can't you?"

"We'll do what we can, Linda. I promise to take special care of you. We all know, *woman-to-woman*, how hard life can be."

Lisbath's favorite phrase—"*woman-to-woman*"—always felt to her like she was cleaving fully and almost secretly to her moms. Like she excluded the rest of the world from the two of them, creating the specialness that a nurse-midwife and her charge needed to experience.

Lisbath completed her exam and left her contact number with Mrs. Boating. Nurse Milliken knew the baby would come soon. She reiterated her recommendation that Linda should go to a hospital, but it fell on deaf ears.

As Lisbath was walking out of the bedroom, Bob quickly punched off the VCR. Before he did, Lisbath saw it clearly showing a naked couple making babies very, very actively.

"Mr. Boating, are you employed?"

"What's it to you?"

"Please tell me if you have an income."

"I'll have you know I'm in management. Assistant manager of the McDonald's, if you must know."

"You should contact the Department of Social Services to find out if your family may be eligible for health and hospitalization benefits."

Boating just stared at the empty TV screen, remote control poised in one hand, the other over his crotch. He asked nothing about his wife as Lisbath let herself out.

Four

Lad nuzzled Lisbath's nose absentmindedly and lapped at the corner of her mouth as she snored and drooled in her dark bedroom. Distant lightning flashes illuminated the small room.

The brash ring of Lisbath's Princess phone jarred her awake and shook Lad from his reverie. Lisbath saw that it was still dark. She felt exhausted, but a midwife's work is a twenty-four-hour commitment.

"Miss Milliken here," she croaked into the phone. "Who's calling?"

"Lisbath, it's Sharona. I'm sorry to bother you, but I just got a call and the patient you saw yesterday—Mrs. Boating—is having contractions."

Lisbath looked at her clock radio and noted that it was just after 4:00 a.m. A shameful hour, but nature didn't wait for anyone.

"Okay, Sharona. I'll get there."

"Thanks, Lisbath. You're a trooper. Let me know how it went when you're done."

"Okay, I will. You know, *woman-to-woman*, our work is never done." She yawned. "Now you get some sleep."

"I can always count on you, Lisbath. Thanks. Bye, dear."

💧 💧 💧

It took quite a few tries to get her old Ford to turn over in the winter's sub-zero temperatures, but the car finally roared to life. White, foggy plumes of condensation and exhaust flowed into the still of the frozen night as Lisbath settled in for the drive. The car wobbled as the nurse shifted this way and that until her rear cheeks found their well-worn indentations.

A siren wailed off in the distance, but sounds carried so far in the cold, unpopulated air that it could have been two or a hundred blocks away.

In fact, the ambulance was three-quarters of a mile distant, on final approach to Queen of Angels Hospital. It shut down its siren as it pulled softly into the driveway. The machine came to a quick stop, then backed up to the Emergency receiving door as its wet tires scrunched over the smoothed, painted pavement.

This was a slow time, so a nurse and an orderly who had heard the approaching siren were already at the electric sliding door, ready to assist the entry of whatever poor soul was being brought in. As soon as the ambulance's brake lights went out, the white-clad orderly pulled the chrome handle and pivoted the wide, copper-colored rear door open.

It revealed a deathly ill woman tended by a hunched-over ambulance attendant. She was panting and quite red. Her breathing was fast and light. There was no I.V. running, though, and this would make for a fast and easy egress.

As the gurney slid out of the ambulance and unfolded, Mrs. Blücher began to cry in well-deserved self-pity. Tears and mucus mixed.

Erich's VW screeched to a halt right next to the ambulance. Fortunately, he didn't have his newborn with him. Aunt Genya had come over as soon as she heard that Ilse was so ill. When the ambulance had arrived back at the house, Erich had left the baby and Helmut in her care.

The distraught husband hurried toward the hospital door to tend to his wife. The thick veins on his forehead were pulsating visibly.

SPECIAL DELIVERY

◆ ◆ ◆

When Nurse Milliken arrived at the Boating household, she was surprised to see Bob Boating almost sober. He had on a clean wife-beater tank top, shoes, and had even shaved. Her opinion of Bob Boating notched all the way up to sniveling ne'er-do-well.

Mrs. Boating was on the bed, holding her abdomen, moaning softly. She looked more disheveled than she had during Lisbath's very recent visit. Sick as a dog and about to burst.

"Hello, dear. How far apart are your contractions?"

"Four or five minutes. I don't know."

"That's fine. Let's get to work."

Lisbath began laying out her equipment. She openly spread two large, black trash bags below the bed. She placed her Thermos atop the bags and went about the rest of her business.

There were two other women in the house whose presence Lisbath hadn't detected when she came in. This didn't bode well for Lisbath's plans. They sauntered into the bedroom, reeking of putrid tobacco and cheap perfume.

"Mr. Boating, who are these people? I wasn't informed about this." Nurse Milliken didn't even look them in the eye as she directed her inquiry to Bob.

"Gertie and Fay are gonna watch. They's our neighbors. They's good people."

Lisbath was immediately taken aback. She thought to herself, *This fool involved in my birth process? With an audience, no less? And then I couldn't collect my spoils. Nothing for me; nothing for Laddie. No. No. NO NO NO!*

"I'm sorry, Mr. Boating, but this will be a complicated procedure. I cannot allow anything that may compromise the mother's or the baby's safety. You and these women need to leave."

The nurse stared viciously into the nystagmic eyes of her cowering foe. Gertie and Fay were flabbergasted and began reaching nervously for their cigarettes to help them cope.

Bob Boating looked like a sad puppy that had just lost its rubber teething bone. It was obvious even to him that there wasn't time to call in anyone new, and this Nurse Milliken seemed to know her shit, anyway.

"Okay, you win. Deliver the damn baby alone. I'm gonna have myself a drink."

"Me three," hacked Fay's cigarette-ravaged voice box.

♦ ♦ ♦

Mostly because she was almost unconscious, Mrs. Blücher wasn't the least bit fazed by her gurney's rough ride from the ambulance to the emergency room's reception area. Erich noticed her writhing body bouncing up and down irregularly as the wheeled bed was brought to the automatic door and parked.

The triage nurse took Ilse's vital signs and decided quickly that the patient needed a doctor's attention stat. She helped the ambulance attendants bring Mrs. Blücher's gurney into ER Room 3, assisted in transitioning her to the bed, and drew the curtains around her in a loud, jangling swish.

Erich remained outside the ER doors, peering through the small rectangle of glass and gritting his teeth. Once his wife disappeared into the room, Herr Blücher found a seat in the waiting room as far from the blaring TV as he could get. Several children bounced from chair to chair, their mother oblivious to their racket. After all, this was an Oprah rerun. Thoughts of Daddy's bleeding ulcer dissipated in the woman as the TV hostess continued her diatribe on weight loss.

In just over five minutes, Dr. D'Angostino trudged into Room 3. Maria D'Angostino was clearly tired—wiped out, even—but she still preserved her professional demeanor.

After a quick look at her paperwork, the doctor washed her hands and turned to Ilse. "Hello, Mrs. Blucker. I'm Dr. D'Angostino. I'm just going to check you out for a moment, okay?"

Ilse was almost delirious, barely even aware of her hospital surroundings.

Dr. D'Angostino began her exam at the patient's head, working her way over Mrs. Blücher's body, using all her senses to divine what was wrong.

"Did you have a baby recently, Mrs. Blucker?"

"Y... yes, doctor."

"Fine."

The physician observed a fever of 104°, low BP, abdominal tenderness on palpation, a pallid complexion, some hyperventilation, no vaginal odors suggestive of bacterial or fungal infection, and obvious, probably temporary cognitive compromise.

"We're just going to run some tests, Mrs. Blucker. Just relax for a while, and I will let you know what we find as soon as we know something."

Ilse Blücher just stared into space, tired, dizzy, and uncomprehending.

Five

A small child kicked the ball into the large, yellow ring painted on the blacktop. The ball barely missed the raven-haired girl's thin calves as it boinged to the ground behind her. Mandy the Dodgeball Queen chuckled with delight and pride that she hadn't been tagged "out" yet. The tall, lanky eleven-year-old had unusual coordination despite her body's recent growth spurt.

As she turned to face her next challenger, Mandy's knees were surprised by the light sting of rubber against her skin.

"Oh, phooey!" she exclaimed, much to the pleasure of the five other girls stationed around the circle. The Dodgeball Queen took her minor defeat in stride. She stepped out of the ring and began to remove her white cashmere sweater, revealing a pure white blouse underneath. Jumping out of the way of a ball for an intense two minutes had overheated her.

"Eeeeioou! What stinks?" asked one of the girls. The heating body lying mostly hidden beside the curb was beginning to release its decomposition stench to the moving air. The odor was sickening, made all the worse because all the girls were breathing hard from the active dodgeball game.

Despite the offensiveness of the smell, like flies being instinctively drawn to a dung heap, the gaggle of schoolgirls all moved toward the source. They pinched their noses melodramatically as they approached the chain-link fence dividing the play yard from the sidewalk outside the school perimeter. Most of the kids could see a dark flowered material rising just above the curb's edge.

Still charged with the adrenaline of her game, Mandy ran over to the teacher on playground duty. "Mrs. Bowles, Mrs. Bowles! Come smell!"

"What?"

"It stinks! Come look!" Mandy pointed to the crowd of girls glued almost involuntarily to the fence, each of whose nose now stuck through its own hole.

Mrs. Bowles knew something was up, thinking as she walked that it was probably a run-over cat in the street. Young girls didn't need to be staring at such a distasteful thing.

"Girls, come away now," she shouted. "Go sit on the benches until the bell rings."

Voices yelled out in protest.

"Go to the benches, *now*." Mrs. Bowles used her authority voice this time as she pointed toward the benches. The girls knew to obey. They moved over to the bench area and sat watching the fence.

Being about a foot taller than any of the girls, Mrs. Bowles had a fuller view of what used to be Terry Audlin now lying lifelessly in the gutter. As Mrs. Bowles scanned the long, brown hair and the one hand stretched toward the center of the street, it was immediately evident that this was a person. Bowles did not yet know that the person was a corpse.

"My God," she said as much to herself as she could. Then she turned to the peanut gallery. "Girls, stay there. Nobody move. Mandy, you're in charge. *Nobody moves, okay?*"

"Sure, Mrs. Bowles."

The girls' eyes widened on the adult's activities.

The teacher ran toward the gate, reaching into her smock's large pocket for the padlock key. She was nervous, and it was difficult to get the key into the keyhole. After a few seconds' fumbling, she unlocked the thing, let it drop by its chain, and threw the gate open. She shuffled quickly, hands at shoulder level, toward the object of everyone's attention.

As she got closer, Mrs. Bowles saw that it was the body of a woman almost completely face down in the gutter. Bowles was frightened, but she still had the presence of mind to yell, "Are you all right?" There was no response.

She decided to sweep the woman's hair back with her shoe. She did so gingerly, not wanting to contact the skin in any way. Not wanting to have any bugs creep onto her feet, either.

The side of the woman's face and her neck were covered in a mottled red rash, like she'd been spattered with a small can of paint.

The woman was surely dead: there was no motion, no breathing. Her one visible open eye was staring straight down to the asphalt.

The teacher was startled and disgusted to see the body's tongue. It looked like a fat, milk-drenched strawberry extending from the corpse's puffed lips. Flies were moving freely, seeking out choice spots to plant maggots.

The girls on the play yard saw supervisor Bowles shriek "She's dead!" and fall to the ground in a true faint. A flurry of flies rose like black, buzzing smog, then re-settled quickly. All the children began screaming, got up, and ran for the principal's office.

🌢 🌢 🌢

County Coroner Dr. Bill Pelt's black suit seemed to absorb the bright, flashing lights from the fire department ambulance and the two police cars. The vehicles were all parked askew near the curb by the body.

Pelt had been called in once the paramedics had determined that there was neither pulse nor breathing in the red corpse occupying the gutter. He hammered his temperature probe into Mrs. Audlin's liver to determine time of death. The metallic instrument stuck out from the woman's abdomen like a silver arrow. After a couple of minutes, Dr. Pelt took his reading, withdrew the shaft, and wiped it off. He held up a couple of gloved fingers toward the removal service men, indicating that the body would be ready for them in just a couple of minutes.

They shook their heads and began to don their gloves and plastic masks. They waited with a practiced patience.

As Dr. Pelt recorded his temperature readings, a red sports car screeched to a halt just down the street. A striking woman dressed professionally but looking somewhat haggard popped out of the car. A couple of the neighbors eventually recognized her as reporter Constance Teitelmeier, otherwise known as "Big T." She had a steno pad, a pencil, and an attitude, and she carried all of them in a whirlwind of energy.

"What's goin' on, guys?" asked Big T.

Everyone working the scene knew her. Five years ago Big T had somehow conned her way into both doing the evening news and writing for the local paper. Whatever she thought was news became news. Whether it was newsworthy or not.

"So far just a body," said Pelt.

"Why's she so red?" asked Big T.

"Don't know yet. Looks like a rash. And her external temp seems to be supra-ambient. We'll have to keep her body quarantined until I know for sure."

"Supra what?"

"She seems to be warmer than her surroundings. We normally don't measure external temperature, but I can feel her radiating a little. It doesn't make much sense yet since her internal temperature suggests she's been dead for at least six or seven hours."

"I'm going to follow you to the morgue," resolved Big T.

Dr. Pelt didn't particularly like the level of interest reporter Teitelmeier was already showing, and the corners of his mouth tightened. His preliminary hypothesis about what had happened with his newest patient was something he wanted to keep to himself. He wanted to be wrong about the circumstances of Ms. Audlin's death. That way, a citywide panic could be averted.

◆ ◆ ◆

Back in the schoolroom, all the girls in the sixth grade class were clustered together, their chairs drawn into a tight circle. They were buzzing with juicy, fresh gossip. The children had been told to wait there while their parents were being called. The school officials thought that their seeing the teacher drop into a faint—and seeing even the edge of a dead body—were sufficiently traumatic to send them all home early to be with their families. It was the principal's plan to bring in a crisis management team for the next day, but for now, the kids should be with their parents.

Mr. Plantine, who had a free period after recess, had been assigned to sit in and be the girls' custodian until all the parents had come to the room to get their children. Ordinarily the school nurse would have been there, but she was busy ministering to the recovering Mrs. Bowles.

Plantine just sat at the desk, letting the girls chatter at will.

Always independent in her interactions with other children, Mandy Shapiro was leading the girls' conversation. She offered, "My poppy sees dead people all the time!"

"Oooohhh, Mandy!" mouthed all the girls huddled around her. Several of them put their hands over their mouths.

"He goes to funerals about every week," said the Dodgeball Queen.

"Why?" asked several of the girls.

"At a funeral, a man like my poppy talks to everyone. It's part of his job. He tells them about the person who died. And he helps them pray to God and stuff like that."

Mandy was now lecturing the girls, teaching them as she had seen her rabbi father do with adults many times. She was in her element. Even at eleven years old, Mandy Shapiro showed natural leadership and a demeanor that seemed to surpass that of all of her classmates. She bore this difference without condescension, though, so the girls looked up to her rather than hated her.

The first of the parents began to arrive and infuse the room with their concern. Still, all the kids were fascinated by the story of death, and none of them budged.

"Did you ever see a dead person?" one of Mandy's classmates asked her. The kids were all pop-eyed, waiting for the gory answer.

Mandy looked away. "Today," she said. "Just today."

Six

Perhaps because she was so sick, Linda Boating had been in labor throughout the day and into the evening. Mandy Shapiro was beside the Boating house, up on her tiptoes and hidden from any outsider's view by dense oleander. She peered through cheap lace curtains into the bedroom window.

She had been drawn to the neighbor's across-the-tracks house by the blood-curdling shrieks she'd heard as she was walking down the block. Nobody could possibly resist checking out sounds like that; it's like trying to ignore an ambulance speeding by with its lights and siren blaring.

The child was focused on a fat lady wearing a cream apron and white shoes and white stockings. From the rear, Mandy's head was a bobbing, shining sphere of evenly-parted, perfectly black hair just above the windowsill.

The object of Mandy's innocent spying was leaning over Mrs. Boating, and Mrs. Boating had started a fresh scream.

The young girl's eyes widened as Linda Boating's stretching vaginal lips were revealed. Mandy had to pee real bad, but she forced herself to hold it. This was just too good to pass up. She bounced up and down on the balls of her feet, and this helped hold her water.

Linda Boating's water was another story. In a startling gush of body fluids the likes of which Mandy had never imagined, clearish liquid came spilling out. Milliken held a silver bowl beneath the vaginal os, collecting and treasuring the effluent.

"What's happening to me? Did I lose the baby?"

"Oh no, Linda. Your water just broke. It usually happens before I arrive, but it was just fine that it happened now, *woman-to-woman*."

No sound softer than a scream would make it through the closed window, so Mandy wasn't privy to this explanation. But the girl did see the nurse take the basin to one side and wipe up Mrs. Boating's perineal area. Mandy was mesmerized. She could not feel her calves screaming complaints as they continued to shove her eyes above the windowsill.

On the La-Z-Boy recliner in the living room, Bob was telling Gertie and Fay about how much he hated that cunt nurse who wouldn't let him in to see his own kid's birth.

Fay sucked on her cigarette hard and fast, commiserating. She turned her head to cough up phlegm. Gertie was biting her smoke-yellowed nails; her focus was on the childbirth screams coming from the bedroom.

As the birth progressed, despite Linda's apparent illness, everything went textbook-perfectly. From her vantage point, Mandy's attention soaked up every move, every muffled sound, every inch of birthing procedure. It would be an event she would never, ever forget.

As Lisbath continued her work, the monotonous, predictable sequence of rubbing, cleaning, testing, and relaxing allowed the nurse-midwife's mind to wander like that of an assembly line worker who's got her technique down pat. The stiff, whisk-broom sound of Lad's nails on the kitchen linoleum crept again into her thinking.

Slowly and carefully, Lisbath drew the refrigerator door open. The dim light revealed a paper bag on the bottom left shelf at the rear; it was apparently wrapped around some kind of cylinder. Lisbath's shortdog.

She brought out the package and removed a beaker. It had a partially opaque, stretched plastic sheet drawn over its wide, lipped mouth. The labware's masking tape label said S073961125.

The beaker contained a semi-coagulated, deep red-purple liquid. And it was blood. Rich, nutritious, cool, slightly gummy blood. Its coppery aroma was very light since the mass had been refrigerated, and it had an overscent of onion from the loosely-wrapped vegetable resting near it on the lower refrigerator shelf.

Milliken placed the beaker on the kitchen counter and reached into the cabinet for Lad's special bowl. It had been given to the pair by her apartment manager, Joanie Perkins, a dog lover from way back.

Lisbath pulled a tablespoon from the nearest drawer, slid it into the dark mass, and removed a shimmering dollop about the size of a golf ball. She plopped the chunk into the center of the dog bowl as droplets splattered onto the kitchen counter. Lad leapt toward the counter. He began whimpering. Lisbath smiled. She took the bowl off the counter and placed it carefully on her pet's food mat. Lad jumped down and ran, nails clicking, skidding, to the dream meal. Lad sank his canines into the bloodball.

When Lisbath regained real-time attention, she found that her autopilot had done its work well. She put the new baby on her mother's chest, wrapped in swaddling clothes and crying quality screams.

Deliberately out of Mrs. Boating's line of sight, Lisbath brought up the silver-bullet Thermos. She unscrewed the top and placed the tube beneath the clamped umbilicus. Lisbath manipulated the hemostat to open just enough for a small flow. No squirting, no splashing; that wouldn't do at all.

The blood leaked into the Thermos, some spilling onto Lisbath's hand and forearm. Crouched below mattress level, Lisbath licked the precious fluid off her arm with a look of pure ecstasy. She managed the Thermos and umbilicus so nothing else was lost.

Then she went to the bathroom to clean up. Alone in there,

she placed each finger in her mouth in turn, licking every morsel. Her eyes closed tightly, and the corners of her mouth turned up just slightly in a self-satisfying grin that she believed was entirely private.

Lisbath was in heaven. This flavor was so much richer than she had ever tasted. Why? Because Mrs. Boating was ill? That was *sick*! Perhaps, then, because of the taste of victory when she got rid of the audience? Maybe it had something to do with the mother's state of dehydration, making for an exquisitely more concentrated blood.

As Lisbath was musing, Mandy became increasingly confused. She could see into the bathroom as the nurse hadn't closed the door. She had witnessed virtually all of the nurse-midwife's bloody antics, and it created a superbly strange feeling for her. The young girl became honestly frightened and released a small, inadvertent shriek.

What was this? Was this how a birth was done? Licking another woman's blood was okay? And what was that horrible rope thing hanging out of Mrs. Boating, anyhow? Was Mrs. Boating really a man? Is that what a man-penis looked like? What was it doing there when the baby was being born? And all the blood—all the *blood*!

The girl bit her lower lip as Lisbath spun around, orienting to the strange, distant yelp she thought she might have heard from the other room. But Mandy was already two steps ahead of Lisbath. The eleven-year-old knew instinctively that something was deeply wrong, even if these were grown-up things she couldn't really acknowledge. The child had taken off running toward home, crying without comprehension, scared and wanting the safety of Mommy and Poppy. Her eyes streamed tears as her feet slapped the sidewalk in a frightened staccato that split the cold, dark winter morning.

So Lisbath saw nothing but the mottled green of the oleander outside the window.

Quickly rolling the Thermos into the bags, Lisbath rose and took another confirming look at mother and daughter. Weak as she was, Linda smiled at Lisbath and hugged her baby.

"She's a lovely baby girl, Mrs. Boating. I'll let the others in now, if that's okay."

"Just Bob. Please. I'm not up to anybody else."

"Sure, dearie. I understand. *woman-to-woman*."

Milliken let the memory of that strange sound fade to oblivion. It must have been nothing—nothing at all.

🌢 🌢 🌢

Out of some sense of spite or perhaps apology, Lisbath stopped at the McDonald's of which Mr. Boating was the assistant manager for her celebration meal.

After getting her food, the tired nurse drove to a familiar neighborhood. She shut down the car, made her fast visual sweep to ensure privacy, removed her sunglasses, then rapidly ripped open the brown McDonald's bag and dug in, her practiced fingertips hitting the hot fries first. Appetizers.

As she chomped on the steamy, industrial cholesterol sticks, Lisbath began to hum between her hard-working teeth:

Rock-a-bye baby
On the tree top
When the bough breaks . . .

The nurse visualized an infant tumbling helplessly down to the ground, on impact bleeding all that precious fluid into a waiting, parched Mother Earth. Lisbath felt a kinship with Mother Earth.

As the song's imagery worked its way through her thoughts, and as the salt on the fries worked its way into her hypothalamus, Lisbath's thirst became overwhelming. She almost twisted her back reaching for the Thermos hiding in her special bag.

The top zipper was tremendous and thick, and its tab was fully one inch in width. It reminded Lisbath of the closure of a body bag. She expectantly pinched the tab and began to slide the zipper open with unusual strength and gusto. Many years of use had smoothed all its surfaces, and the bag revealed its contents almost silently and with just a hint of vibration.

Lisbath furtively unrolled the satanic tube below dashboard level. She unscrewed the top so fast it went spinning to the passenger-side floor. Immediately a thick, coppery smell wafted from the Thermos' neck deep into Lisbath's soul. Her eyes fluttered and her heart began to patter faster and faster. Lisbath's grip almost began to waver as her excitement intensified. The scent played the strings of Lisbath's genetic memory; her entire body resonated to the sanguine fragrance.

Grabbing the Thermos with both hands to steady its path, Nurse Milliken brought the gleaming tube's mouth slowly to her lips. She groaned repeatedly.

It began to rain, each tiny drop making a soft tapping sound on the windshield. Lisbath was grateful for the additional camouflage on the windows.

An old Karmann-Ghia came chortling down the road on its way to a farmhouse two miles further along, but by this time Lisbath was oblivious to anything but the dense, sloshing, semi-congealed liquid in the Thermos. The fortyish, longhaired VW driver glanced at Lisbath but just assumed that she was about to have her soup for a late lunch. He downshifted and passed her by. Lisbath never knew it.

Now that her initial craving was satisfied, Lisbath could begin to relish her catch more effectively. Taking two French fries at a time, she dunked them in blood. Ketchup was so very passé.

Seven

Lad was scratching at the door and panting as Lisbath wearily climbed the flight of stairs to her apartment. The lady of the house shot straight for the bathroom, bringing her carpetbag and other paraphernalia with her.

Lad had grown increasingly excited and impatient during his mistress' potty time, especially because she sang to him through the door:

Treats a-comin', treats a-comin'
Mommy does as Mommy should;
Treats a-comin', treats a-comin'
Mommy makes it sweet and good!

When she opened the door, Lad jumped up, bouncing off her chest with his scrabbling paws.

"Yes, my little Laddie. Mommy has your very special treat, indeed!"

Lisbath's tone of voice let him know that it would be mere moments before his version of manna would grace his bowl. He began nudging the bowl in random directions.

Lisbath unrolled the Thermos from its protective bag, opened it carefully, and reached into a kitchen drawer for a long-handled plastic spoon she had saved from a 7-11 Smoothie. It reached deep into the Thermos, and she brought out a glob of the best eatin' this side of El Paso (she knew she had heard a line something like that in a CW song recently). Placing the Thermos on the counter, Lisbath lowered the morsel into Lad's bowl. He was wagging his tail so hard and was so out of control that he peed several bright yellow drops onto the kitchen linoleum.

Suddenly, out of Lad came a frightening snarl Lisbath had heard only rarely. Something more than canine—something keen and raspy with very high tones at the same time. He dropped his head into the bowl and lapped up the chunk. But something was different here. Instead of swallowing it or even making a pretense of chewing, Lad seemed to run the bloodball over his teeth with his tongue. As he did this, an otherworldly whine eased out of his nostrils, and his eyes were shut tight.

Lisbath now moved to the locked closet, spun the combination, and opened the door. Paying no attention to the formaldehyde-like smell, she reached back to a special shelf. The shelf held several liter-sized jars with screw caps. She selected one, opened it, sniffed to ensure it was pure, and took a wide-lumen funnel from the rear of a lower shelf. Carefully, Lisbath poured the remainder of the Thermos' contents into the funnel, then into the jar.

Once the jar was full, the nurse capped it tightly and brought the funnel to the kitchen sink. She reached into a drawer and took out a roll of masking tape and a black, small Marks-A-Lot. Lisbath printed in block letters: *S182000112*.

💧 💧 💧

Dr. D'Angostino entered Ilse Blücher's room over an hour after her blood had been drawn. The doctor looked tired; ER duty always takes its toll. She scooted the wheeled stool over to Ilse's bedside, sat down on the black, round pad, and placed her hand on Ilse's arm.

"Mrs. Blucker?"

Ilse had been on the verge of unconsciousness, but she oriented to Dr. D'Angostino's presence.

Scanning the patient's chart, Dr. D'Angostino said, "Our tests are inconclusive right now. We don't really know what's wrong with you. You do have a pretty high fever of 104, but your lungs are clear and your heart sounds okay. Since we're not sure what is wrong, we're going to do some more extensive tests. I'm going to admit you to the hospital tonight, Ilse, mostly because your fever is so high. Don't worry. We'll keep an eye on you."

Ilse's head lolled to the side as she felt a wave of nausea roll over her.

♦ ♦ ♦

Ilse had fallen asleep quickly after the doctor left, but she stirred out of her slumber when Erich entered the room and came to her side.

"*Mien liebschen! Wie sind du?*"

"Erich. Where am I? Is this a hospital?"

"*Ja, liebschen.* You were brought here last night. Don't you remember?"

Ilse became frightened. "Where is the baby? WHERE IS SHE?" Ilse began to cough.

"At home with Genya. Don't worry; she will be fine. Tell me: How are you feeling?" He felt her forehead with the back of his hand, and it seemed almost burning hot.

Dr. D'Angostino's knuckle rapping on the open door caused Erich's head to turn. Herr Blücher was glad that he wouldn't have to wait very long to hear about the test results.

"How are we this morning?" asked Dr. D'Angostino as she stepped into the room. She was smiling that professional smile that conveyed practice but not necessarily warmth or joy. And of course, in Erich's eyes, she was still a woman and therefore an inferior doctor.

Erich stepped back to make room for her. Ilse, who had no

recollection of ever seeing this woman, just waited and wondered what was to happen next. She felt weak and vulnerable and scared. She had reason to be.

"Mrs. Blucker, Mr. Blucker, I need to ask you a few questions. Do I understand correctly that you had your baby at home with a midwife?"

"I *knew* we shouldn't have done it. I *knew* it!" Erich was moving toward her, becoming livid. His fists were white with pressure. "That bitch-woman did something wrong, didn't she, Doctor?"

Ilse's fear was now reaching deeper. It began to crawl within her abdomen like a parasite.

"Please calm down, please." Dr. D'Angostino was almost pleading. "We still have many things to learn, and I need the answers to my questions. Who was the midwife?"

"She was a nurse. . . Elizabeth or Lisbath or something like that. We got her from an agency," said Ilse. Giving this information provided her with some sense of control over the situation; she began to put her fear in check.

"Doctor, that woman was from Dickinson's," said Erich. "I did not like her from the beginning. Do you know her?"

"No, Mr. Blucker. But my office will be contacting her for more information."

"It is *Blücher*," said Erich.

"Fine. Now, Mr. and Mrs. Blücher, please tell me this: Was anyone ill in the house either during the birth or during the few days before the birth?"

"What has that to do with my wife? She is a good, clean woman."

"Yes. Of course. But was anyone ill during perhaps the week before the birth?"

"Not that I know of," said Erich. "Ilse?"

"No. Nobody."

"Did the midwife cough or look ill?"

Eric became red as an Austrian beet. Just thinking that the nurse might have hurt his wife made his blood boil. But he had not noticed any signs of illness.

"No," said Erich. "Why do you ask this?"

"Our tests show that Mrs. Blücher has septicemia. I need to examine her. Mr. Blücher, please step outside. I will call you in when I am done."

"What is septicemia?"

The doctor hesitated for a moment, then sighed. She knew that this man would have to have an answer, even if somewhat premature, or he would never leave the doctor alone to do her work.

"Blood poisoning."

"She was POISONED?"

"Not likely. It rarely works that way. When I complete my examination I may have more answers for you. *Please* step outside."

Erich squeezed Ilse's arm and forced a smile. Dr. D'Angostino motioned for Erich to move back, and as the worried husband did so, the physician drew the curtain around Ilse's bed. A moment later, the bright room-examination lights snapped on.

Herr Blücher stepped out into the swirling hospital smells of alcohol, urine and vomit, and walked deliberately toward the elevator. Despite the cool hallway, he began to perspire heavily.

Dr. D'Angostino took a much more detailed history from the woman. She then went through her standard intake exam and found nothing remarkable. But now it was time to play her hunch.

She had Mrs. Blücher open her legs for the internal, and she inserted a hand-warmed speculum extra gently. Not only had this woman given birth recently, but Dr. D'Angostino was suspicious of what she might find in her vagina and uterus.

"Mmmmm, yes" said the doctor as she peered in with a flashlight. She inserted a specimen probe and worked it through Ilse's sore cervix. As she did so, Ilse jumped and let out a little scream. She bit her lip very, very hard and grabbed the sheets with both hands.

"Sorry, Mrs. Blucker. I know this is uncomfortable, but it is necessary. I'll be done in just a few seconds."

She withdrew the probe and stared at it for several seconds.

The gob of intensely red tissue with tiny white speckles told a story the lab would eventually confirm. At this point, though, medical ethics dictated that the doctor say nothing prior to getting the new lab results.

"You may put your legs down, Mrs. Blucker." As she did so, Dr. D'Angostino brought the covers down past her feet.

Ilse sighed as she adjusted her legs. She hoped she would never have to go through anything like this again. Her insides hurt far beyond what she had expected from the exam. It felt like a white-hot iron had been poked repeatedly into her stomach, and that it had left behind simmering chunks of rough metal and charcoal which continued to burn and eat away at her insides.

Eight

The streetlight shone on the two boys exchanging places every few seconds. Jim and Perry were taking turns balancing on the yellow fire hydrant on the corner of Alfred and Curson. The hydrant's top nut was slippery, but the two pint-size athletes were intent on staying on as long as they could.

"Rodeo riders on bulls only have to stay on for eight seconds. Watch me do longer," Jimmy bragged.

"That's no bull, you idiot!"

"So what? Bulls aren't slippery."

"Are!"

"Are not!"

Jim's attention was elsewhere as he tumbled to the sidewalk, caroming off the extended control nut with his free foot just in time to save his knee. As he got up he wiped some of the brownish puddle splash off his forearm.

Perry was getting ready to mount the yellow bovine enemy when he heard the rat-tat-tat of running little feet. He spun around. Jim's gaze followed.

Half a block away the Jewish kid was running in their direction. She was impressively fast. As Mandy got closer, the boys heard her crying and, closer still, saw her wet, red face.

"Hey! Wait a minute, Mandy! Where're you going?" screeched Perry.

Mandy blurted back, "Shut up! Shut up! *Shut up!*" She was just a few feet from the boys now, and not slowing down.

"Hey! Whatsa matter? Get scared by a ghost?"

As Mandy began to pass the boys, Perry thumped her shoulder to throw her off balance. The tall, lithe girl sprawled onto the grass runner near the fire hydrant and began screaming and crying like she was in great pain. Then she got up, shaking her head, sniffling. The girl's emotions in overdrive, all she could think to do was to strike out. Mandy started punching, battering in the direction of the boys. She really couldn't see much detail through her tears, but her clenched fists achieved purchase over half the time as she screamed and hit and shook uncontrollably. Her pummeling was incomprehensible to the stunned boys.

"What are you doing, Mandy? You nuts?"

Mandy was running out of energy, but not of fear and bewilderment. "Get away from me, you meanies! I have to go home! Get away!"

She continued to hit and slash randomly, working off steam and generating more at the same time.

Jim grabbed Mandy's right upper arm and pulled it hard toward him. Perry latched onto the girl's left forearm. Mandy resisted for a few seconds, then let her knees buckle, crumpling toward the ground. The dead weight became overwhelming for the boys, and they dropped to their knees after her. The three of them made a hodgepodge, spindly pile of tired, mixed-up kids, each trying in vain to make sense of what the moment held.

Mandy's crying got increasingly boisterous—a crescendo of fear and childish misunderstanding that became more frightening to her and to the boys as it became louder and louder.

Jim became insistent. "Mandy, stop. STOP! Did you get hurt? Whatsa matter?"

The child began to calm down little by little, perhaps because that was all she could do. The boys' grip was tight, and she could barely move, let alone flail.

"It was horrible. HORRIBLE! I can't. . . I don't know! A monster!"

The boys were glued to every word.

"Monster? You saw a MONSTER? Where? How big was it? Is it coming here? Is it CHASING YOU?"

"*She's* a monster. That nurse."

"What nurse? Were you at the doctor's?"

"That nurse. With Mrs. Boating. She. . ."

Mandy broke into another crying fit, mumbling something the boys couldn't make out at all. They loosened their grip slightly.

"Is Mrs. Boating sick?"

"No, stupid! She's having a baby!"

The signal had changed a block south, and two cars drove by, one right after the other, completely oblivious to the drama unfolding on the sidewalk.

"The baby came out a monster? *COOL!*"

"The nurse. She's a monster. She drank. . . she drank. . ."

Mandy started to drool involuntarily as she spat out her frightened words.

"She drank the blood! SHE DRANK THE BLOOD! OOOOOHHHHH! GOD! She drank the *BLOOD!*"

Both boys had their eyes open as if they were getting electric shocks. They visualized a nurse drinking blood from a glass, from a cup, from the mouth of the pregnant lady. They couldn't really reconcile the image Mandy had just foisted on them, but she sure had their attention.

"Blood? Are you sure? Where'd she get it? Did the monster have fangs? Was she big and hairy?"

"Oh, you idiots. Let me go. LET ME GO! I gotta go home."

Mandy writhed with so much surprising force that both boys let go at the same time. As soon as she was free, the girl got up and started running again, not even bothering to brush off her skirt.

Perry and Jim just looked at each other, then after Mandy. They sat on the wet pavement squinting foolishly as they tried to imagine what that crazy girl had been talking about.

◆ ◆ ◆

The elder Shapiros were relaxing before dinner. The hot food had been placed in the microwave awaiting its revivification, the chalah was on the table on its pure-white plate with a towel over it, the butter dish was covered and pristinely clean on the table, and two casserole place mats rested silently on center stage.

Papa read his newspaper in his favorite leather chair, and Mama read her book. No television broke the warm, family atmosphere. A sense of peace and gentility permeated the scene. This was Family in its true sense.

Mandy burst through the front door and headed directly upstairs to her room. Her steps echoed loudly through the storage area beneath the stairwell.

She had her own bathroom, all made up in pink and lace, and Mandy went to the sink and began to wash vigorously—her face, her hands, her neck, her forearms—over and over and over again. This was not primping, but rather like the furious hygienic cleansing of a freshly raped girl trying in vain to erase forever the ugliness and stickiness of the crime.

Mandy's mother Selma had heard the girl come in and called up the stairway. "Mandy, we're waiting dinner on you. Wash up and come down right now."

"Mama, not now, okay?" was Mandy's warbly reply.

"You come now, Mandy. I'm turning on the microwave."

From upstairs, Mandy heard the whooshing fan and electronic noises as their re-heated dinner was coming back to life. When Mama said "now," she meant Now.

The girl was scared. Could she tell her parents? Part of her fear came from having to admit that she was spying on her neighbors, but that was nothing compared to trying to tell them what she had seen.

Mandy wiped her face and hands, straightened her skirt, made an abortive attempt to look completely presentable, and went downstairs. For the first time since she was a toddler, Mandy used the smooth banister as a crutch.

And Mama noticed.

"What's wrong, dear?"

"Ah, nothing, Mama."

"Something is *wrong*, Mandy. What happened?"

Mandy reached the dining room table and sat demurely if shakily.

"Mama, I can't say." She turned her eyes downward at her place setting.

Papa had been hearing this interchange and would have none of it.

"Mandy, you tell us what happened. Did somebody hurt you? Are you all right?" Rabbi Shapiro's agitation was out of character. He was concerned; maybe frightened for his daughter.

"Yes, Papa. I mean no, Papa. Nobody hurt me. Nothing happened."

"You mustn't lie to your father," Mama said. "It's a sin."

Mandy's lips shut so tightly it looked like a thin white line of paint had been laid down where they met. The line was made all the brighter since it lay under her increasingly bright, pink cheeks.

Papa became more intense. He put his hand down uncharacteristically hard on the white, lace-trimmed tablecloth. "Mandy, you must tell us what happened." He rose up slightly in his seat. "You must tell us *now*."

"The nurse at Mrs. Boating's. I don't know. It was *icky*. She was doing Mrs. Boating's baby. Having the baby. She . . . she . . . the blood, Mama! The BLOOD!"

"What? What blood? What are you talking about?" There is always some blood at a birth, but *die kinder* shouldn't be there to see it. It is for the adults, the doctor. Not for her *maidlach*.

Mandy began to cry and rub her eyes. Mama went over to her and knelt on the floor beside her child's chair. Papa's jaw tightened. His eyes narrowed. It was the middle of January, it was cold, the cheap bastard hadn't turned on the heat, and he was perspiring through his white shirt all the same.

The microwave went "ding," and nobody noticed. The Shapiro elders were so involved with their daughter Mandy's stress that their focus totally excluded their surroundings. They didn't pay attention to their dinner now cooling in the microwave, and they lost all vestiges of hunger.

"Mandy, what happened!?" shouted Mr. Shapiro. As he became more agitated and confused, the rabbi lapsed back to the broken English pronunciations he had used when he had first come to the United States.

"Papa, I don't know. *I don't know!* I saw something terrible. It's so *bad*, Papa. I can't tell you!"

Selma Shapiro stiffened as she resolved to get to the bottom of this mystery. "Mandy, whatever it was—*whatever it was*—it's okay. You are here with your family. We will take care of you. You are safe, *maidlach*. Everything is okay.

"Now, what did you *see*?"

Papa was glad Mama had taken over. He just wanted to know—to observe.

"The woman with Mrs. Boating. She . . . she took—she drank the blood. MAMA, SHE DRANK THE BLOOD!"

"*Drank* the *blood*? What are you talking about?" asked the incredulous rebbetsin.

"Mama, the woman—the nurse—she licked and drank the blood coming out of Mrs. Boating's baby—no, not the baby—the place where the baby came out!"

Mrs. Shapiro was far beyond shocked. Her eyes had narrowed, her brain was racing, and she shook as she tried to hold and comfort her poor daughter.

"Tell me more, Mandy. Mama needs to know." The matron squeezed her daughter's hand; both of their hands were warm and perspiring slightly.

Papa Shapiro was there but not there. This seemed to be a true mother-daughter moment, and the patriarch simply stayed in the background.

"Mama, it's hard to talk." The girl inhaled in small jerks, clearly on the verge of crying. "It was so ugly. So scary!"

Mrs. Shapiro simply squeezed Mandy's hand a little harder and assumed her listening posture. Mandy knew she wasn't going to get out of this: she had to say something. And so she gave out what she could. It emerged slowly, her words like fudge being pulled out of a sticky box.

"The … the woman? The nurse? I think she was doing weird things. Mama, she would look around the room and then move her tongue all over her hands and her arms. Like she had been eating an ice cream that melted. But, Mama, it wasn't ice cream! It was blood from the lady!"

"*Gott im Himmel*," prayed Mama.

"Mama, is that right? Do people do that? I never, ever saw anything like that. Tell me it's okay, Mama!"

Selma Shapiro knew damn well it wasn't okay, but this wasn't the time to let her frightened, overwhelmed daughter know. She just held Mandy reassuringly, rocking slightly.

The rabbi needed to break the tension. He sat down on the bed next to his wife and placed his palm on Mandy's forehead. The only thing he could think of was to say, "Mandy, you can sleep now. We will take care of this. You will be okay. God will make everything right, my baby."

Slowly, both parents moved toward understanding and, more importantly, belief. They saw the picture. They accepted Mandy's story completely. The couple's eyes met and they nodded slowly to each other. Mandy was, after all, a Good Girl and would not make something like this up.

The inhumanity of the image grew on them as they pictured increasingly more vividly the scene Mandy had painted through her horror-ridden tears. Their daughter needed to be consoled, to be brought back to a semblance of normalcy and calm. But that wasn't all.

Something had to be done.

Nine

Sharona picked up the phone expecting it to be a call for another nurse assignment. She already had her pen ready, her pretty profile cocked to cradle the phone.

"Dickinson's. May I help you?"

"May I speak with the records clerk, please?"

"This is Sharona Gomez. I'm the owner. Can I help you?"

"Yes. This is Dr. Gold's office calling. Do you have a patient named Lucinda Smithson?"

"The name sounds familiar," answered Sharona.

"Would you check your records, please?"

"Sure. Please hold on for a moment."

Sharona looked through the filing cabinet behind her and got the Smithson file. She reviewed that Lucinda was the mom Lisbath had taken care of about a week ago, and that she had become ill.

Sharona punched the hold button. "Hello? Could you identify yourself again for me please?"

"Yes. This is Phyllis from Dr. Coop Gold's office. Is Ms. Smithson in fact your patient?"

"We do have a Ms. Smithson. She's Nurse Milliken's patient. As a matter of fact, I have a record that your office called us a few days ago to ask about her. What's going on?"

"Dr. Gold has admitted Ms. Smithson to Mercy General, and he wants to ask your Nurse Milliken some questions." She continued,

"Is she there now? Can you get her on the phone for me?"

"Not right now. She's out on a call. Is this urgent?"

"Please have her get in touch with us."

"No problem, Phyllis. May I have your number?"

After she hung up, Sharona thought over the conversation. She began to hear between the lines. Sharona's concern grew as she realized that a call like that from a doctor's office is extremely rare; in fact, it was downright threatening. And this was their second call about the same patient. As issues of liability, ethics, and potential claims of malpractice began to roll around in her head, they started to bang at its insides. It was aspirin time.

🝏 🝏 🝏

Once Lisbath did make it into work the day after the Boating birth, Sharona caught her eye immediately.

Sharona said, "Hi, Lisbath. A couple of things. First, I've had two calls from a Dr. Gold's office about your patient Lucinda Smithson. She's been admitted. Here's the message. Please give him a call."

Sharona handed Lisbath the call slip. Lisbath had a quick look and slid it into her pocket while nodding her head. Lisbath didn't want to pursue this with Dr. Gold; it felt threatening. She would put off the call as long as she could. And she'd put irritating doctor out of her mind for now.

Sharona continued. "Now, Lisbath, dear, we've got another hard one for you. Look at this message Wanda took late yesterday."

Nurse Milliken scanned the message. In the *Comments* section of the pink form, it said "Obesity complic; no travel; doc no housecall."

"Ready for some tough work, dearie?" asked Sharona.

"*Always.*"

Lisbath's victory waddle bumped the in-box on Sharona's desk, and it was okay. Sharona's headache had begun to subside and she felt a little better overall.

SPECIAL DELIVERY

♦ ♦ ♦

Oooh, this winter weather, Lisbath thought to herself. She was fully stocked with supplies and enroute to La-TaKeisha Jeffers' filthy tenement apartment on 103rd St.

Her car rambled all over the road, splashing from pothole to pothole as she entered the poor side of town. It seemed like the street maintenance got worse as the area got poorer.

Lisbath had trouble reading the apartment houses' addresses through the rain-mottled side window, but eventually she found the broken-down building housing her quarry. It had five garbage-strewn, deteriorating wooden steps leading from the sidewalk up to a graffitied door.

She inserted her car between a trashed old Cadillac and a drenched motorcycle up to its transmission in oily, filthy rainwater. Lisbath planned her egress via the passenger's side so she wouldn't have to step into the calf-deep water while she was being pelted with hail.

Nurse Milliken decided to sit tight for a little while. Maybe the hail would stop. She mused about how such an apparently poor mother could get Public Assistance to authorize a nurse-midwife rather than going the traditional County Hospital route. Milliken guessed that it was the Squeaky Wheel effect. She was wrong.

Despite the pounding of the rain on her roof and windshield and the thunder's noise and vibration scaring the roaches into their hiding places, Lisbath heard the unmistakable scream of labor emanating from an upper-floor window.

She'd have to get out of the car now, and damn the torpedoes.

Lisbath slid over to the passenger side, leaving a humid, massive indentation just behind the steering wheel. She reached over the seat back and brought the carpetbag to the edge of the front seat. Lisbath opened the door and shot (to the extent that a 285-pound, 5'5" woman can shoot) out of the car and up the steps. Lisbath was in gear.

She climbed the interior stairwells, dragging her carpetbag and huffing and puffing by the time she began the second flight. Fortunately, Ms. Jeffers' apartment was on 3, so Nurse Milliken took less than ninety seconds to catch her breath.

Although the slip said 3E, Lisbath didn't really need the information. The screaming clearly came from there. Milliken knocked forcefully and got an immediate response.

"Mrs. Jeffers, I'm Nurse-midwife Milliken. May I come in?"

"Git in!"

Milliken was used to being greeted at the door by an appreciative, distraught family member, but apparently this time would be different. No matter. She could handle almost anything.

She reached for the doorknob and turned it. The knob gave unevenly as rust partially impeded its rotation.

When the door opened, Lisbath was astounded by the raw stench billowing out almost palpably from the tiny apartment. Eyes tearing slightly, yet boldly dedicated to her profession, Lisbath made her way into the room and stopped dead in her tracks. Now she knew from whence the smell arose. Beached on a sagging king-size bed taking up fully half the apartment's floor space was the truly huge La-TaKeisha Jeffers' hulk. No less than 625 pounds unclothed, La-TaKeisha was a sweating, swearing mother-to-be who *could not* get out of bed. No wonder the docs wouldn't come to her.

Lisbath had her challenge, but she also had a blood source unrivaled in her experience. She wished she'd brought another Thermos or perhaps a bucket. And no family around to observe! A special kind of heaven and hell, and Milliken was in the middle of it.

"Ooooooaaaahhhhhh!" yelled La-TaKeisha as her baby forced additional cervical dilation. Her chins sloshed as she screamed. The hairs sticking out of the dime-sized mole on one chin wiggled as rapidly as a bee's wings.

"Well, let's take a look at you." Lisbath began to set up, opened all the windows as wide as she could, and ran some water for lavage.

"Mmmmmmmohmaaaah! This gonna be big!"

SPECIAL DELIVERY

As Milliken worked, she hummed absentmindedly. Her voice was country-western, but in a rare moment, her thoughts were in the gutter. What kind of man would inseminate this human meat? What would that quasi-sexual congress have been like? Had he slipped off from sweat? Had La-TaKeisha agreed to grant her favors in exchange for the promise of a couple of meals?

No more time for that. Nurse Milliken's exam showed a normal cervix with nine centimeters' dilation. Ms. Jeffers was close, her water had broken long ago, and Lisbath needed to brace for work.

One of the first orders of business was to separate the legs far enough to allow the newborn an exit route. At the same time, Lisbath brought out her Thermos and placed it at the foot of the bed, far beyond the mountain of carcass over which La-TaKeisha could never see.

Almost immediately, La-TaKeisha's offspring began to make its way out of her. It was clear to Lisbath that La-TaKeisha was a multipara—a mother who had given birth before. Many times.

"How many other children have you had, Mrs. Jeffers?"

"Too many, too many! They's next door."

Lisbath was glad they were next door.

Little Ma-Chondra, as she would be called, slid out like cooked giblets from hot turkey. She was healthy, loud, wiggling, and quite a prize indeed.

Milliken immediately went to work on the umbilicus. The double clamping and cutting was fast and practiced. She pointed both sheared ends down toward the Thermos mouth and waited a few moments for her liquid prizes to accumulate. Mama was relieved enough not to care what was happening at that moment.

As soon as Nurse Milliken had her take, she wiped the newborn down, aspirated her nasal passages, applied the silver nitrate, assigned a high five-minute APGAR of nine, and placed the baby in the undulating, moist crease between La-TaKeisha's upper chest and her chins. She smiled and said, "Mrs. Jeffers, she is perfect! What a great job you did!"

La-TaKeisha was in heaven. Lisbath left her in matronly bliss while she concentrated on collecting all the extra solids and liquids she could. As she collected, Lisbath bounced up and down almost imperceptibly.

The nurse-midwife brought out a jar with a blank piece of tape across its front. It contained some clear liquid, some of which almost sloshed out when the nurse-midwife unscrewed the top. She sliced a four-inch piece of umbilicus and placed it in a jar that was already primed with formalin solution. On the jar's blank masking tape label she wrote *S082000212*. This would join her closet collection shortly.

For just a moment, black marker in hand, Lisbath paused. She squinted and shook her head slightly, her eyes roving, unfocused. The smallest, concerned frown passed through her forehead, then it was gone. She was herself again.

Like a trick-or-treater on Halloween, Milliken unrolled another black trash bag and held it beneath Ms. Jeffers' ample birth canal. Smiling broadly, she simply waited for the juicy afterbirth and its liquid chaperones to glide into her possession.

Ten

Chili's hot pink miniskirt painted a startling swath of bright color. The handcuffed prostitute swished through the police station's complex stench of spilled beer and the street. Vice was bringing Chili in for the second time this week; she was all too familiar with where to go, when to sit, what to say, and what not to say.

"You fuckers gotta stop *hassling* me! Go out and catch some goddamn *real* bad guys, okay?"

"Come on, Chili. You know the drill. What's your address tonight?" asked the cop.

Margaret "Chili" Fontaine folded her thin, black arms in front of her and shoved them down below her ample breasts. Her back stiffened. This was an orchestrated act of defiance that did little more than bulge her 44D's about two more inches above her cheap yellow halter top's scooped neckline. The pair wiggled, indicators of Chili's impatience and frustration. Her butt scrunched in the chair, creating just enough bottom friction to make an inadvertent farting sound. Her dimples deepened.

"Honey, you talk to me or you'll spend the next couple o' weeks with your soul sisters downstairs."

Phones rang in the background and a couple of men's voices laughed raucously through the lieutenant's internal office window.

"Listen, big-shot Mr. Policeman, I got as much right on the street as you do. You make 'em feel bad, I make 'em feel good. So leave me the fuck *alone*."

"Chili, cut the shit or I'll just throw you downstairs myself. Let's get this over with."

In the next room, Detective-Sergeant Judd Stevenson reached for the ringing phone on his desk. He was just out of line-up, his shift just getting under way, and he was about as fresh as he'd ever be. Picking up the phone in a police station was kind of like batting open a sinister piñata, waiting for hell to spatter out in all directions.

Through the handset, Stevenson heard a heavily accented voice: "Is this the detectives?"

The sergeant heard whimpering in the background. He toyed with the department-issue black pen on his desk as he began to focus on the task at hand.

"Yes, sir. I am Detective-Sergeant Stevenson."

"Listen: My daughter saw something. . ." The rabbi's voice trailed off in a blend of uncertainty and shock.

"Your daughter? So what happened to your daughter?"

Stevenson began tapping the pen on his yellow pad, making a random pattern of black tick marks.

"No, no. Mandy saw a woman do something ungodly. At a neighbor's so very, very near to where we live."

The detective wanted his caller to get to the point. He had lots to do. Prank call? Maybe.

"Who is this? Identify yourself."

"I am Rabbi Chaim Shapiro. We live at 352 North Alfred Street. But this is not about me. This concerns what my daughter saw."

"She witnessed a crime?"

"Yes. Such a crime!"

"You can come into the station and make a report. Send your daughter in."

"No, officer. She is too shaken and fragile. Can't you take the information on the telephone? Something *must* be done."

Stevenson's pen tapped faster and faster, making darker, thicker tick marks, reflecting his declining mood and increasing intolerance.

"Okay, okay. What did she say she saw? Can you just put the

SPECIAL DELIVERY

girl on the phone, rabbi?"

"Wait."

The detective heard Rabbi and Mrs. Shapiro's animated, muffled conversation through the earpiece. He heard what sounded like a shriek, then the rabbi's hand sliding loudly off the mouthpiece to reestablish communication.

"Detective, Mandy is frightened and will not speak to strangers about this. She told me that a woman was . . . was . . . *oy, vay* . . . was doing something with blood."

"Blood? Whose blood? When? Where?"

"Please, sir. Slow down. This is very difficult."

The rabbi turned to his wife. "*Liebschen*, take Mandy up to bed. Comfort her. I will take care of this."

Selma put her arm around a badly shaking Mandy, and both headed toward the staircase. Their steps were uneven, lumbering. Mandy's eyes were pressed tightly together in a futile attempt to shut out the new, disgusting visual memories that would haunt her in later life.

"Detective, my daughter saw one woman taking the blood of another. Or touching it. Or *licking* it. Something like that. This is not God's way. You must find out about this."

"Did your daughter say she witnessed a murder?"

"No. It was a *birth*. You know, the young child, she said it was 'icky.' But there must have been much more to it. Mandy does not make up stories."

Stevenson thought instantly that he had a nut case on the other end of the line. Still, he needed to collect enough information to dismiss the call if he could.

"Where did this happen?" asked Stevenson. He sounded bored.

"She was at the window of one of our neighbors. I don't know the people. Mandy says they live somewhere on Tennessee Street. Near Curson, I think."

"That's not much to go on."

"My daughter also said something about a boat or a ship."

Detective Stevenson was now sure he was dealing with a nut case.

"Well, we'll look into it. Call again if she sees anything else."

"Yes. I will. Thank you."

Stevenson hung up without ceremony, shook his head, deliberately forgot everything he had just heard, and went to do an in-and-out at the coffee machine and bathroom. Low triumph intensified the wiggle in her butt as the released Chili Fontaine brushed indignantly by Stevenson on her way back to the street.

♦ ♦ ♦

Perry's black-and-blue arms and filthy shirt caught his mom's attention right away.

"Little man, what happened to you? Did you fall again?"

"No, Mom. Just playing. Leave me alone, okay?"

"Playing where?"

"At the corner. On the fire hydrant."

The boy began to climb the stairs to his bedroom two at a time. Mama would have none of it.

"Perry, that really looks bad. Come down here. Now."

The sheepish boy trudged back down the stairs toward his mother, but he wasn't too worried. Mom seemed concerned rather than pissed off, so things would probably be all right.

Melissa Clark grabbed Perry's wrists and lifted them, holding her son's forearms up for inspection. She twisted him around to the light and squinted hard. What she saw scared and irritated her. This was, after all, only Mrs. Clark's first child. She hadn't yet been steeled to the sundry, unavoidable horrors of child rearing.

"What's this? How did you get hurt?"

"Oh, *Mom*! We were just playing! On the fire hydrant. It doesn't even hurt!"

"Young man, you have to be *careful*. Who was with you?"

"Just Jimmy. And Mandy came by."

"Mandy? Was she playing on the fire hydrant? I always thought she was such a do-nothing girl."

"No, Mom. She just ran by and was crying."

"Did you hurt her? DID YOU HURT HER? I told you over and over again to leave the girls alone. WHAT DID YOU DO?"

"Nothing, Mom. She was just scared of something she saw."

"Did she see you fall?"

"Mom, it wasn't us she was scared of. She saw some kind of blood monster or something. Some nurse or something dead or bleeding or I don't know what."

Mrs. Clark's eyes rolled up into her head. Another monster. Too much TV for these damn kids.

"Go get washed up for dinner, little man."

"That's where I was going in the first place. *Geez!*"

Melissa went over to her stove, shaking her head. A motherly grin crept onto her face as steam rose to warm it from the boiling pot of softening spaghetti.

💧 💧 💧

"What did the police say?"

"Selma, I think maybe they did not take me seriously. These men are so hard, *Liebschen*. Sometimes they cannot see the way. God sets them apart in some way."

The rabbi asked, "How is Mandy?"

"She seems exhausted, but she didn't fall asleep. Something is really bothering her, Chaim. This is not normal. I'm worried."

"Yes. We will all sleep on this. Tomorrow morning, we will decide what to do."

"I love you, Rabbi."

Two sad smiles met each other in the unspoken communication only a husband and wife can truly share.

Selma put the dishes away and the two headed up to bed much earlier than usual.

Mandy's dreams finally came. They were insidiously frightening, and would be for years to come.

♦ ♦ ♦

Right after finishing his spaghetti dinner, Perry said, "Mom, I want to go to bed, okay?"

Perry had never actually asked to go to bed. He liked tricking his mom into letting him stay up as late as possible. He always liked watching the adult shows on TV with his mom. He just wanted to be close to her and paid virtually no attention to the programs themselves unless they had sex or violence.

"You want to go to bed? So early?"

"Mom, that stuff Mandy said; I don't know. It kinda makes me sick. I don't want to think about it. She was really scared. Not like seeing a spider or anything. Like the way Willy Tufts looked when he saw his dog get run over last year."

"Sure, little man. Sleep safe, okay?"

Perry kissed his mom on the cheek and headed for the bathroom.

The boy's words and his discomfort ate into Melissa's thinking throughout the night, causing her to toss and turn, scrunch her eyes, bang the pillow. Her head swam with images of infants, nurse's caps, blood, and tiny coffins.

At 4:00 a.m. she couldn't stand it anymore. In the bleary-eyed fog of sleeplessness and confusion, she reached over to the nightstand and picked up the phone.

Then she slammed it down again. "What the hell am I doing?" she thought. "Who am I going to call? What business is it of mine, anyway?"

Then she heard her son sobbing in his bedroom. That was something he almost never did, so it felt very, very significant to her. Perry's muffled sounds made Mother Melissa feel almost guilty that she had dismissed Perry's stories as if they'd been tripe. On some subconscious level, the experience bothered the boy, and her son's going through this was eating away at her as well.

Melissa went to Perry's room and held her precious son. She

hummed his favorite bedtime tune, and he was asleep in a couple of minutes. She would talk to him in the morning to give him a chance to get everything off his chest. For now, his rest was important.

With more conviction, and more awake now, Melissa firmed up her decision to do something about what her son had heard. Second-hand information, sure. But Perry was a good boy and a smart one. He never misrepresented his experiences to his mom as far as she knew. Besides, what did she have to lose? If the police thought she was out of her mind, so what? They weren't going to arrest her. And if what Mandy had said was even half true, there was something eerily weird going on, and somebody needed to look into it.

Her lips pressed against each other as she lifted the phone and dialed 911.

Eleven

Lisbath went down to her car after the Jeffers birth and was relieved to find the old Ford intact. In this neighborhood, a no-loss event was something to be appreciated.

She headed back home to the Yankee Pines apartments with her cache. She was happy but exhausted. The woman always immersed herself in her work. With tremendous La-TaKeisha, the immersion was quite literal and in fact unavoidable.

It was 6:20 p.m. when Lisbath pulled into the carport. Her Ford had failing power brakes, and Lisbath barely had enough leg strength to stop the vehicle. The intensity of her work usually left Lisbath feeling as drained as a marathon runner at the end of a race, and tonight was no exception.

Fortunately, the yellow, illuminated elevator button was able to spirit the nurse and her accoutrements to the third floor. She virtually tumbled out of the elevator with all her equipment bags in tow.

As Milliken opened her apartment door, Lad sped through. That was okay with Mommy. Let him take his walk alone tonight. Lisbath put a small block of wood at the foot of the stairwell's security door so the pet could get back to her apartment door. She would leave some dog food and a special red treat on the kitchen floor, ready for Lad's return.

Lisbath was absolutely ravenous for blood, and her well-earned meal was almost violently sloppy. She threw the fine red glops into her mouth. Her breathing was rapid and shallow. As she ate, she began to relax and to breathe more normally.

After her fine meal, Lisbath was exhausted but more herself again. Too tired to clean up the kitchen, she bathed, let Lad in from his walk, and retired to bed.

Yankee Pines was finally quiet. The kids who normally played in the hallway outside her door were long gone, and from the sound of it, the couple above her who usually argued all evening were silently watching some kind of game show.

But the peace of her building left Lisbath with nothing to focus upon; no noise to complain to her ceiling about. So she was forced to spend her pre-sleep moments with herself, and that's where the trouble began.

Lying in bed, Lisbath visualized her day-to-day existence. Events tracked behind her eyes. She saw herself killing time at Dickinson's, waiting for an assignment. Driving to and from the store. Walking Lad. Those things were painless.

Blood that had splashed onto the kitchen counter while Lisbath was preparing Lad's treat produced a strong scent. It wafted into Lisbath's bedroom. She could not help but think about the blood. About what amounted to theft of body fluids from her precious moms. Lisbath felt at once justified and villainous. Vulgar. How could she do such a thing?

Perhaps it was Lisbath's increasing maturity that brought these troubling thoughts to the surface of her thinking. She had been taking the vital blood prizes for so many years, but only in the last few months had she become concerned about her supply. On top of these scary thoughts, her health had been dwindling little by little. She felt like she was getting old.

Lisbath's psyche was becoming awash in the mixture of the kitchen's blood scent and the mounting secretions of her pineal gland, the pea-shaped bundle of tissue tucked away near the middle of her brain. Lisbath felt the inexorable, exquisite terrors coming on again, and her bizarre musings about her patients' blood and placental fluids were just the beginning. She became angry and nauseated, but most of all, fearful. Lisbath hated these bouts of frightful thoughts and dreams, but they were inevitable, she knew, and the devil must have been performing the orchestration. She could not resist.

Her body began small, uncoordinated twitches—myoclonic jerks everyone has from time to time; but now in Lisbath a barrage of fast jolts made her prone body do a bizarre dance beneath the sheets. Saliva coated her mouth as groans and tiny cries, all too familiar, primal and ancient, escaped her.

Lisbath's eyes squeezed shut. She froze in anticipation. Then, as had happened so may times before, her consciousness was transported 400 years into the past in a scene as relentlessly vivid as genetic memory.

She tasted dank fog, then its wraiths were around her, drawing her in, and to her dying shame she wanted to be there. Not at Dickinson's, not driving her car. These vestigial images cartwheeled away into the void…

There was a primitive table. Its rough, thick legs supported a chipped plank acting as a tabletop. This uneven surface was covered with handmade flaxen cloth with a stubbly surface and irregular, bland coloration.

Upon this table was a setting for one. A rough-hewn cup and bowl rested before her as she surveyed her land. The countess had patience, but her hungers were growing. For the past fortnight she had been growing weary; growing visibly old. She needed her Fountain of Youth again. As she needed every month.

The crude stool that supported her remarkable weight dipped slightly as one of its three legs dug bluntly into the soil. The lady's leg moved outward for stability, and she groaned under her breath.

As the winds began their eastward trek over the countryside, the otherwise beautiful and outdoorsy scent of pine mixed uncomfortably with the stenches of rotting flesh and feces.

A low rumble off to the east broke the moment's stillness as tranquility began to give way to growing, joyous anticipation. Casting her eyes just over the east hill and toward the sunrise, the lady saw what looked like light steam rising from a slowly boiling pot.

The thick sound became almost palpable under her curled toes, and the countess watched the stirred fog mingle with the rays of the surfacing sun. Waves of gossamer pink and red eddies just over the rise heralded the arrival of her sinister procession.

The intensifying ground thunder was made by heavy oxen hooves. The beasts were drawing a large cart rolling and tilting over the rutted ground. It had large, wooden wheels. Above the cart's platform was a cage made of closely-spaced branches, each as thick as a man's arm. The wooden bars were lashed together with many tight leather straps. They had been soaked in a crude mucilage to ensure their solidity and impenetrability. Still, one could see sadly colorful snatches of the inhabitants between the branches.

Three manservants marched gracelessly before the cart, and five more brought up the rear. They had made this trek every month, always on the morning after the full moon, when the countess would become weak. Each functionary knew his role well. The ceremony had taken place monthly since 1587, so, despite its repugnance, most of these practiced serfs could go through its foul choreography without retching.

The rolling, thumping cage held thirteen women from the surrounding village. Most had been stripped practically naked during their struggles to escape. Their high-pitched, pitiful screams drew attention from all over the countryside. Onlookers, whether miles away or assembled and praying beside the road, shed tears of pity. But they could do nothing within sight of the dirge to stop the outrage—nothing to reduce either the impact or the inevitability of the inhuman experiences each girl was about to face.

The night before, under cover of darkness, the countess' thugs had moved through the outskirts of the village, capturing the girls one by one.

The men would first use their torches to look for adult family members. If the invaders found any, they would bludgeon them, usually in their sleep, to ensure that no one provided any resistance. This activity usually awakened the girl prey, who would begin screaming as she saw her mother and father lying bloody on their beds.

Virtually all of these young girls were simple villagers, destined to make babies and their farmer husbands happy and comfortable over the years. Their dreams were of hay piles and giggling children playing happily by the fire; of drawing water from the well and cuddling with their future families until the candles flickered out.

The countess would terminate those dreams, replacing them with living nightmares.

As the chorus of wails became audible over the hooves' rhythmic thunder, the corners of the countess' mouth jerked upward slightly and without her knowledge. The lady's tongue swept slowly across her lower teeth while her nostrils flared. Her mouth became increasingly lubricated with her pumping saliva. Even in the morning's chill, she began to perspire lightly as her cart of prey crested the rise. She squirmed on the stool, and the pressure caused by her underthings' catching on the seat's surface made her excitement intensify even further.

"Halt!" yelled the slavemaster as he raised his powerful forearm. The rolling prison's slavemaster was called Derek Holdar. He was experienced and hardened to the ways of the countess. Holdar drew back firmly on the ropes, tightening their purchase on the oxen throats. The beasts were sluggish to respond, and the procession slowed in uncoordinated fashion as the grunts began to subside.

Finally, as the dust settled, all movement ceased save the frantic motions of the Thirteen of Month.

The countess raised her steel-blue eyes to review her supply of whimpering victims. What she saw pleased her, and she sat back on her stool to regard the catch as a proud fisherman would beam over the ones that didn't get away.

In the cage were three red-haired women, one of whom was plump and shivering. Her chins wobbled uncontrollably as she bit the inside of her ample cheeks and felt woe far beyond any prior ken. The other two red-haired victims were fine specimens—strong and fighting and obviously unaware of their fates. Irish blood coursed through their temporarily engorged veins.

Five black-haired creatures were in the group, all of whom were dressed in dirty peasant garb. Most stared blankly out from between the wooden bars and either hummed or wailed with no palpable show of facial emotion.

Three women had been trampled beneath the rest of the poor souls. The countess knew they were there; she could see the twitching feet of one of them and the hair of the other spewing out over the floor, through the bars and down toward the mud.

Another two victims rounded out the group. The taller, yellow-haired beauty reached at least a regal 18 hand, and her counterpart, only half the first's height and with no remaining raiment, appeared to be sweet and innocent. As she sobbed, her breasts jiggled pitifully beneath runnels of mucus and tears.

To the countess, all these women were merely meat. Sources of pleasurable fluids and experiences: as transiently discardable as freshly picked chicken carcasses. And just as cheap.

"*We begin!*" was the countess' command. Her head tilted slightly as her ceremony began to engage.

Milliken gnashed her teeth as the intensifying horror terminated her dream. When she would finally awaken, the nurse would feel exhausted and strangely unsettled, yet absent of any lingering awareness of the dream's burgeoning, horrific content.

Twelve

Eight years ago, Detective George Haberdeen of the Connecticut PD had been nicknamed "The G-Man" by his superior officer, Detective Sergeant Judd Stevenson. The name hadn't been based on George's first name, nor particularly on his job. Nor was it created to reflect Haberdeen's impressively hulking 6'5" frame. Suggesting a hunk with a crew cut, square jaw, and a sparkling, professional demeanor, "G-Man" was actually a tongue-in-cheek moniker. Haberdeen was an unabashed slob.

It was about ten minutes before his 4:30 a.m. "lunch" time and he wanted most urgently to get the hell out of there. The thing he most wanted not to happen, happened. His phone rang.

"Shit," he said. He looked around for someone on whom to pawn the call, but everyone else was either on the phone or out of the cramped six-person office.

"Bridgeport PD, Detective Haberdeen." He sounded tired; unexcited.

"Hello, officer. Listen: I'm not really sure I should be calling, especially at this hour... but there's something really wrong."

"Who is this?"

"Oh, I'm sorry. This is Melissa Clark."

"Where are you calling from?" This was a standard question even though the police-enhanced caller-ID display on his phone had the phone number, address, and name of the phone service subscriber displayed prominently.

"I'm at home. Last night. . . well, I guess it's really just a few hours ago. . . my son Perry told me about something very strange, and I'm concerned."

Haberdeen thought to himself: *Get to the point, lady.* But he said, "Yes, go on."

"Well, Perry was playing last night and a neighborhood girl came by and said she saw some terrible things and it's very upsetting. Perry's upset and now I am too."

"Was the girl hurt?"

"No, it's not *like* that. She—her name is Mandy—she said she saw something *bloody* last night. And a nurse was involved somehow."

Melissa's voice began to crack and get louder as she spoke. Her own blood was pumping harder and faster as her involvement in her son's troubles began to infuse the mother with a blend of sympathy and anger.

Haberdeen doodled as he listened almost absentmindedly to this woman. As he did, Detective Sergeant Stevenson came in and sat across from him.

Stevenson listened as Haberdeen said, "Okay, lady. Calm down. Now what's this about a nurse and blood? The little girl said what? Or was it your son?"

Earlier that evening Stevenson had fielded the rabbi's call, and Haberdeen's comments to his caller sounded like they might be related. Maybe that rabbi wasn't as out to lunch as he'd sounded. Or maybe this was all getting blown way out of proportion. Either way, the detective sergeant felt obligated to step in and deal with it.

"Hey, G-Man. What's the call about?"

Haberdeen held up a sit-tight-for-a-second index finger.

"Ma'am, I'm going to need to put you on hold for a moment. I'll get right back to you."

"All right. I'll wait." *You bet you will, honey*, thought Haberdeen as he hit the hold button.

"Hey, Judd, what's up?" It was unusual for a superior to ask about a phone call; it seemed to the G-Man that they usually wanted to avoid as much work as possible.

"George, what's this?" He pointed to the flashing hold button.

"Some woman says her son's upset because another kid saw some blood."

"Did you say something about a nurse?"

"Yeah. I don't know. The girl saw a nurse and some blood or something. Sounds like crap to me."

"Just leave the call on hold. I'm going to take it in my office."

"Sure thing, Judd. I'm going to lunch. The call's all yours."

Stevenson put the receiver to his ear and hit the flashing button.

"This is Detective Sergeant Stevenson. Can I help you?"

"I think I was just talking to someone else."

"Yes. I'm taking over the call. What's the story?"

"I *already* told the other man." Melissa was getting impatient.

"I'm better when I get it first-hand. Now what happened?"

Melissa resigned herself to having to go through it all again. She gave Stevenson all the detail she had about Perry's story and about her own increasing concern.

The detective picked his teeth as he got as much information as he could. Stevenson told Ms. Clark that he would be looking into it, ended the call, and put his feet up on his desk. Papers crinkled under his size 12's.

Perry's mom did feel better—like someone had actually paid attention to her—and went into her son's room to reassure him. When she got to the doorway, she listened carefully and heard nary a whisper. The faint buzz of his electronic football clock overpowered Perry's mild inspirations. He must have been asleep, she thought. Thank God. Let sleeping boys lie.

Melissa went to bed herself and was out like a light within two minutes.

So is this just another nut case? thought Detective Sergeant Stevenson. What's the big deal about a nurse and blood? They go together like cops and guns.

But two independent calls about the same thing within twelve hours suggested something more. Years ago in a psychology class, Judd Stevenson had learned about Gestalt theory, where "the whole is greater than the sum of its parts." And in his police work over the decades, he'd often found loud rings of truth in that Gestalt dictum.

Because the sergeant was handling an unusually large number of other cases, and because he believed this could end up being absolutely benign (and therefore a potential waste of time), Stevenson decided to assign it to the G-Man. He was just back from his vacation and was ripe to handle the inquiry.

Haberdeen and his girlfriend had spent the past month touring the good old USA in his rusting motor home. Stevenson, in a charitable mood this week, thought he would simply assign a technical officer to make a few initial inquiry calls, then drop the straightforward file into Haberdeen's lap. The sergeant figured this case would be an uncomplicated one, so this was a great way to make his pal George's return to police work nice and easy.

Wrong-o.

♦ ♦ ♦

The G-Man had received the case matter-of-factly. After his early morning lunch, he sat his immense frame down in his creaking wooden chair and began to settle in. He opened the file and made a few immediate decisions.

Haberdeen knew from Stevenson that two calls had come in from children—actually, parents of the children—concerning some unusual observations during what was obviously a home birth. It was the redundancy of the complaints and certainly not their apparent substance that had motivated his superior Stevenson to assign the case out. One weird complaint usually goes straight to the circular file, but two complaints on the same target sometimes add up.

Haberdeen made some notes:

SPECIAL DELIVERY

1. Who was the woman giving birth?
2. Who was the nurse?
3. When did the kid see all this?
4. Why would any of this get reported?
5. Missed the waterfalls along the Columbia River. Maybe next time.

At 9:30 a.m. Haberdeen's first call was to the boy's mother, Melissa Clark. She had had a serious talk with her son Perry the morning after his tumultuous night, and Mom had gotten lots of details. Haberdeen learned from Melissa that it was Mrs. Boating on Tennessee Street who had had the baby. Melissa didn't have Boating's phone number, but that was no problem for a cop. They could get anything on anybody. Haberdeen decided to call the Boatings as soon as he hung up with Melissa.

"Hello. This is Detective Haberdeen from the Bridgeport Police. Is this Mr. Boating?"

"Yeah." Bob the Slob Boating had had *lots* of calls from the police throughout his life. He wasn't particularly shaken.

"Mr. Boating, this is about your wife's in-home birth."

"The police are calling about that? What the fuck's wrong with having a baby at home? What's your problem?"

"No, sir. No. I need to ask you some things about the nurse that carried out the procedure."

"Cunt."

"I'll need a little more than that, sir."

"Waddya on to her for? She do something?"

The G-Man could tell that Bob was well into a six-pack. "Mr. Boating, did you observe anything unusual during the nurse's work?"

"She treated me and my neighbors like shit."

"I need to know if she did anything to your wife."

"Well, shit, yes! She pulled the baby."

"How do you mean?"

"The nurse was in there with Linda when the baby came, and

she took care of it. Pulled it out. Cleaned up. Like that." He beer-belched into the back of his paw.

"Did you see anything unusual with blood?"

"What? Blood?"

"Yes. Did the nurse do anything unusual with blood?"

"How should I know? I ain't no nurse."

"Okay. Just tell me everything you saw the nurse do."

"Nothing but kick us out of the room."

This guy was no help at all.

"May I speak to your wife?"

"She's sick." This was more to avoid having to get up than to protect his poor ill wife.

"Mr. Boating, this is important."

"All right. Hold your horses."

Boating put his beer down and rolled forward on his recliner. He got up slowly and brought the cordless phone handset into the bedroom. Bob held the receiver to his wife's ear.

"The cops want to talk to you, baby," said Bob.

Linda was lying almost unconscious and drooling. The baby's crib next to the bed was filthy, but the bouncing newborn seemed content to chew on her blanket.

"Mrs. Boating?" Haberdeen prodded her slightly through the phone. "Mrs. Boating? May I talk to you for a moment?"

Groggy and weak, Linda dragged her eyes open. As they came into focus, she asked, "Bob, honey? Bob? What's going on?"

"Mrs. Boating, I'm Detective Haberdeen from the police. I want to talk to you about the nurse who worked on you. You aren't in any trouble; neither is your husband."

Bob just stood there, staring into space, holding the phone to his wife's ear.

Linda Boating began to understand, but only barely.

"You're from the police?"

"Yes. I need to talk you about the nurse who took care of you when you had your baby."

"Hold on a minute."

Mrs. Boating looked at Bob with a "What the hell are you doing this to me for?" expression. He just shrugged and continued pressing the phone to her ear.

"What?" she asked into the phone.

"Mrs. Boating, we are investigating the nurse who birthed your child. You know who I'm talking about, right?"

"The woman from Dickinson's?"

"Dickinson's?" asked Haberdeen.

"The service Bob called. I don't remember the nurse's name exactly—I was so sick. I think it was Elizabeth. But she came from Dickinson's. I trust Dickinson's."

Haberdeen made a note of the name.

"Okay, Mrs. Boating. Did the nurse do anything unusual?"

"Unusual? What are you talking about?"

"Specifically with blood."

"God, I don't know. She did spend a lot of time down there after my baby was born, but I figured she was just doing her job."

"What's a lot of time?"

"I don't know. Maybe fifteen minutes or so. I don't know."

Haberdeen didn't know if that was unusually long or short or normal, but he wrote it down anyway.

"Mrs. Boating, was there anything else unusual about the nurse's behavior? Anything at all. Anything related to blood?"

"She gave me the baby and that's all I cared about. Listen, mister, I'm not feeling good. I need to get off the phone." Linda looked pathetic.

"Okay. If you think of anything, please call Bridgeport Police and just ask for the detectives."

Another virtually useless call. This was going nowhere fast. Was fifteen minutes a lot of time? Who knew?

Thirteen

Haberdeen left the station, drove fast, and pulled up to Dickinson's. He had to re-check the address because the building looked more like a boarding house than a nurse registry. Lace curtains on the window belied the medical purpose of the establishment.

There was a Chevy station wagon parked out front and a young lady sitting out on the wooden steps reading a paperback and smoking a cigarette. She was hacking and coughing as if on death's door. Surely this couldn't be a nurse, could it?

He sat in his unmarked black car for a while munching on some pretzels. The G-Man was checking out the foot traffic with his electric adjustable rearview mirrors.

About three minutes into the G-Man's snack surveillance time, a young woman bounded through Dickinson's glass-paned door. She had a bright turquoise stethoscope bouncing around her neck and carried a bag sized somewhere between a purse and a briefcase. It became evident that this really was Dickinson's, and his stereotypes of the nursing profession were adjusted accordingly.

Detective Haberdeen pulled his Milliken file out from between the seats, brushed some of the salt off his tie, shirt, and pants, and reviewed the file's top summary sheet as prepared by one of the PD's on-the-ball desk people:

14 JANUARY 1730 HOURS GIRL MANDY SHAPIRO

SPECIAL DELIVERY

REPORTED VIA PARENTS SEEING A NURSE DOING SOMETHING WITH BLOOD DURING BIRTH OF NEIGHBOR LINDA BOATING'S CHILD. WAS HOME BIRTH/DELIVERY. SHAPIRO TOLD STORY TO BOY PERRY CLARK. 15 JANUARY 0430 HOURS MELISSA CLARK—MOTHER—CALLED 911 RE: SAME INCIDENT.

BOATING'S NURSE IS EMPLOYED DICKINSON'S REGISTRY 1323 FAIRCHILD AVE BRIDGEPORT CT 06604 (203) 555-4911.

//15 JANUARY 0847 HOURS PER JDS, BPD

Out in his car, Detective Haberdeen began to think about what he was doing there. Why had he been given this assignment? Not much of this made sense. Children misinterpret things all the time. Hell, he made stuff up all the time when he was a kid. And patients get sick constantly. That's what makes them patients, after all. Then again, it wasn't the G-Man's task to question his orders, and he almost enjoyed the cushy-job break he assumed this assignment would ultimately provide.

Earlier that day, Haberdeen had talked to one Sergeant Lemon, who had called the Queen of Angels emergency room to check on a stabbing victim. The detective happened to hear about a woman named Ilse Blücher who had been admitted. The sick woman had just recently had a home birth—pretty unusual these days. And the attending medico was an employee of none other than Dickinson's.

Rotating toward the door, G-Man Haberdeen squeezed his elbows inward in the standard check for his shoulder holster and wallet. He didn't expect any trouble at all, but this motion was S.O.P. for him since a frightening experience he'd had four years ago: What was supposed to be a simple donut-and-coffee run had turned into a physical confrontation with a knife-yielding druggie dirtbag in a 7-11.

Haberdeen stepped out of the car, hit the lock button, shut the door, and walked briskly up the steps to Dickinson's front door. It was slightly ajar, so he let himself in.

All the women oriented immediately to this tall stranger. Nurses and cops are a frequent pair, and all of them knew immediately what he was. A glance under his jacket simply reaffirmed his police status.

Sharona was at her station, and the detective knew from the "Ms. Gomez" nameplate on her desk that she ran the show. He couldn't help notice that she was good looking, too. But that wouldn't soften him.

"Good day, sir. May I help you?" asked Sharona.

The G-Man was direct. "Yes. I'm Detective George Haberdeen, Bridgeport PD." He brought out his wallet-badge and flashed it matter-of-factly. "Do you have a nurse named Elizabeth employed here?"

Every ear in the place tuned in.

"Is she okay? Is she in trouble?" asked Sharona.

"I take it you have an Elizabeth employed here, then. This is just routine."

"Detective, I am Sharona Gomez. I own Dickinson's. I need to know what's going on. Is Lisbath okay? Do we have a problem? Why the police?"

"What is the nurse's full name?"

"Lisbath Milliken. She's a nurse-midwife. One of the finest. Why are you asking about her?"

"Like I said, just routine."

"Will you join me back here, please?" As the large, pulsing Vein of Concern began to throb visibly in the middle of her forehead, Sharona motioned toward the door to her private conference room and got up. It was more of a demand than a question. Her wooden chair squeaked loudly as she rose, but nobody registered it. The G-Man pursed his lips, nodded his head, and followed.

Maintaining her professional demeanor, Sharona closed the door and faced the detective. She motioned for him to sit down, and she seated herself across the small table from him.

"Mr. Aberdeen . . ."

"*Haberdeen*, ma'am."

"Yes, Mr. Haberdeen. We deal with people's lives here, just like you do. I need to hear more than simply that your inquiry is 'routine.' You wouldn't be here—at my place of business, which is my heart and soul—if something weren't amiss, and I'm assuming that Lisbath is physically okay or you would have said something already. Now, please, what's going on?" She folded her hands under her chin, elbows on the table.

"Ms. Gomez. This is an official police investigation and I am not at liberty to discuss its details at this time. That's all I can say right now."

"Then what do I say to my staff? Everyone in the room heard you. Gossip will travel like wildfire, Mr. Haberdeen. And when do I get to find out what is really going on?"

"Let me ask you about a few things, Ms. Gomez. First, did Ms. Milliken have a patient named Blücher? And if so, when was the last time they were together?"

"I don't have that information in here, Detective. I'll need to check my files and get back to you."

Haberdeen was getting a little ticked by what seemed like delaying tactics. Sharona was actually just buying time so she could figure out what to do. This police visit could mean big trouble for Dickinson's, and that was scary.

The G-Man became more insistent. "This is information that I need, Miss. Now, I can get it from you here, or it can be subpoenaed while we're waiting at the station. Which will it be?"

"Very well. Just wait here!"

Sharona went out to the filing cabinet in the front office. Even though she had already recognized the Blücher patient's name, she thought she'd better have the formal file for reference when she returned to that meanie in the other room. The G-Man just took a seat and waited calmly. *Nobody fucks with the police*, he thought.

Gomez returned in less than a minute with a file in hand. "Yes, Detective Aahberdeen. Mrs. Blücher is a current patient of Ms. Milliken's. Lisbath's last visit with her was . . . let's see . . . looks like it was on the 8th of January. Okay?"

Haberdeen brought his notepad out of his jacket's inner breast pocket, flipped over its black cover, and took his time writing himself a note. "And what was the purpose of that last visit?"

"Just *routine*," Sharona said as she pursed her lips slightly. She felt so damn smart.

"What specifically was the interaction between nurse and client, Ms. Gomez?"

"Our files aren't that detailed, Detective. The nurses are professionals; we just keep track of whom they see, when they saw them, how much time they spent, and generally what the purpose of the visit was. The rest is in the medical record written by the nurse him or herself."

She continued. "Mr. Haberdeen, we're basically a brokering service here. A nurse needs a job, we get a call for a nurse, and we put them together. That's it. We are not responsible for the nurse's actions."

"That remains to be seen."

"Good-*bye*, Mr. Haberdeen." Poor Sharona's thin fingers were starting to shake. She was fighting a real battle between anger and fear, and her graceful fingers shaking like antennae were broadcasting her stress.

"We'll be in touch."

She reddened and her eyes crimped, but she said nothing. G-Man let himself out of the makeshift conference room and strutted past the peanut gallery of nurses. The detective nodded darkly with a cop's self-assurance as he slipped his notepad back into his breast pocket and left the building. He brushed past the still-smoking nurse on the steps and waved the toxic cigarette gases out of his path.

Inside, Sharona Gomez was really scared. "Bastard," she said.

The word sped past her lips, a solid puff of intensity.

Susie Rime had heard the sound of the G-Man opening the door and had glanced up and back from her front-step stoop. She had seen the detective's shoulder holster and gun butt flash under his arm as the winter winds slapped his rumpled suit jacket back. He was putting his wide-brimmed fedora on when Susie addressed him.

"Are you from the police?" Susie asked.

G-Man Haberdeen, irritated with the whole scene and hungry to boot, turned and answered curtly, "Yeah." Then he turned back toward the sidewalk.

"So, why'd you come here?"

"Routine business."

Susie had been jealous of Lisbath's privileges since she got herself listed at Dickinson's, and she saw an opening for revenge. She began a fishing expedition that paid off immediately.

"You didn't come here to talk about Lisbath, did you?"

Haberdeen's interest piqued real fast. His eyes widened at this unforeseen opportunity.

"Do you know something about her?" asked the G-Man.

"I know lots about her. I think there's something wrong with that woman. She doesn't talk much to anybody, and Sharona is always giving her the best jobs. How can anyone make any money around here with her around? She's a *bitch*." Susie shook her head and squinted; she flicked her cigarette butt out toward the street and her small breasts jiggled under her white tank top. "And you should see the way she acts when she gets an assignment. She just jumps right up and flaunts it. It makes me *sick*."

The G-Man had seen the green eyes of jealousy before, and this looked like a classic case. Which meant that this girl's testimony was going to be fundamentally useless. A waste of time.

"Thanks, honey. I'll keep it in mind." The detective was about to have an earlier lunch than he had expected.

"She hurts her patients, too," Susie said. Haberdeen's heart rate went up ten percent. He turned to face Susie.

"What do you mean?" he asked.

"I know she does. I heard Sharona talking to the hospital about one of her moms," said Susie.

"Her moms?"

"Lisbath's a midwife. She handles home births."

"Go on, honey."

"Well, one of them's incapacitated and the diagnosis is inconclusive."

This kid started sounding like a nurse real fast. Haberdeen's faith in the value of this interview was rising.

As a south wind kicked up, the sky began to sprinkle tiny bits of ice. The pellets crunched underfoot as the two of them moved under the overhang on the porch, toward the corner where there were no windows.

"They can't figure out what's wrong with her?" Haberdeen asked.

"Not last I heard. Of course, I don't get reports or anything. I just heard Sharona on the phone with somebody."

"What's the patient's name?"

"I don't know. I just know she's one of Lisbath's. I *told* you she was a … bitch!" Susie felt the satisfaction of a whistle-blower saving the world.

"Can you get me more information?" asked the G-Man.

"Like what?"

"Like the patient's name, where she is, when she was admitted, what the diagnosis is now, where she lives, who. . ."

Susie Rime realized she was getting in deeper than she wanted. All she had wanted to do was to get Lisbath in trouble. She didn't want a detective assignment. And she was scared, too. Scared of Lisbath's possible retribution, scared that Sharona might get mad that she had shared essentially confidential information with an outsider (but he was a policeman, right?), scared that she might lose her job and not be able to make her Hyundai payments and lose her car.

"Wait a minute! I'm not a policewoman, I'm a nurse! I can't do all that!"

Haberdeen needed the information. When a cop wants info, he'll go to any length to get it.

"Do you mean you want to obstruct my official investigation? This is police business, young lady. You want to go downtown with me? We can talk there, you know."

Oh, shitties, thought Nurse Susie Rime. *Now I've done it.*

Dickinson's door opened with a squeak, and Sharona peered around it to see Susie and the G-Man talking at the end of the porch.

"Nurse Rime," said Sharona, "I need you in here right this minute."

Saved by the bell, Susie thought. She turned toward the door. Haberdeen grabbed her upper arm like a kindergarten teacher would grab a recalcitrant child. His immense hand easily encircled ninety percent of her arm, and her white sleeve ground into her skin beneath his thick fingers.

Susie Rime looked up at his tall frame with fear in her eyes. He didn't give a shit.

"You're hurting me!"

He spoke just softly enough to remain below Sharona's threshold. "Sorry. Do you want to come downtown with me, or can I count on you?"

"Okay. I'll help."

"How can I contact you? Will you call me at the station?"

"Let's *go*!" said Sharona. The supervisor was exerting all the pressure she could, but the fear of police reprisals had Rime's attention in a tight grip.

"Yes, yes. I'll call you."

"Tomorrow."

"Yes. Tomorrow."

"Say nothing to Gomez. This is a police investigation. Don't screw it up, girlie."

"Uh, okay." Susie Rime shuddered. A little girl under the thumb of the government. Fear began its insidious trek through her thinking, and it had much, much further to go.

Haberdeen gave the young nurse his card, released his grip, and stepped smartly past Sharona onto the steps. He headed toward his car down the crunchy hail-carpeted thoroughfare without turning around.

As Susie Rime watched the detective's figure recede down the street, she felt satisfied that she had finally spilled the beans on Nurse Milliken. But she had a vague, nagging inkling that now she was trapped in an ugly web of her own making.

Susie's eyes began to fill with tears. They rolled down her cheeks as she moved haltingly toward the office's screen door.

Fourteen

Rabbi and Rebbetsin Shapiro were more playing with their breakfast eggs than eating them. Both of them looked haggard.

"Selma, I don't know what to do. Mandy must go to school."

"But Chaim, she is in no shape to do anything. The poor child! She barely comes out of her room. How can she go to school?" Mrs. Shapiro pursed her lips together as she reached for her cooling coffee cup.

"She must not miss her education because of this. It is not right."

"Since the day she saw that horrible woman she's been sick."

"You didn't tell me she was sick! Now we have more problems?" Chaim's patience was wearing thin. Far from at his best, his thinking was not as sharp as usual.

"Oh, Chaim, don't take me so literally. She's emotionally sick. She cries all the time. I don't know what to do either, my fine husband." She dipped her head and raised her eyebrows slightly.

"We must trust in God."

"God is moving too slowly for me," said the Rebbetsin. "I want you to call the police again."

"But Selma! They know who I am. They will call me if they need information or if they find anything."

"Oh, papa. You are naïve. You must call them now. Maybe some good news will help our Mandy's mood."

"Fine. If it will make you happy."

"It will make you happy too, Chaim."

Both smiled, but there was still something missing.

"Papa?" Mrs. Shapiro asked.

"Yes, my dearest."

"Do you think maybe we need someone to talk to Mandy?"

"What?"

"Maybe a child psychologist?"

"*Feh*! No psychologist! God will take care of this."

"May it be soon," Selma prayed aloud.

The rabbi went into his study to make the phone call. He sank down in his old leather chair and dialed 911.

"Emergency 911 operator—what are you reporting?"

"I need to speak to the detective."

"What are you reporting, sir?" The operator was insistent and assertive, as she needed to be.

"No, not reporting. Let me speak with the detectives, please."

"Detective division is at 203-555-8744. 911 is for emergency calls only. Good-bye." The operator released the line abruptly.

The rabbi was sad and nervous and atypically unsure of himself. He wrote the number down and went to get a glass of water before dialing the detectives' direct line.

Haberdeen's phone rang. "Haberdeen. Detectives," he answered.

"Detective, this is Rabbi Shapiro. You remember?"

Haberdeen knew instantly. And he knew that the rabbi was virtually useless to him and would no doubt prove more of an irritant than anything else. But the G-Man began thinking about the daughter Mandy. He hadn't yet interviewed her directly; Haberdeen had decided to wait a while, hoping the kid would be more apt to communicate after the shock was further in the past. Her story—that of an actual eyewitness—should strengthen the rationale behind the nurse's arrest. He pressed the receiver hard to his ear.

"Yes, I remember. Listen, Rabbi. I *need* to talk to your daughter."

"I'm afraid that's impossible, detective. She is in a bad way."

"Rabbi, I need to talk to her. It has become important police business."

This seemed odd to Mr. Shapiro. Why all of a sudden did this detective need to talk to Mandy? Was his call this incredibly serendipitous?

"Detective, if it is so important, why didn't you ask before?"

What the fuck is it his business what and when I ask something? thought Haberdeen. But G-Man realized that he wouldn't get anywhere arguing with the man—especially one who was as used to being in control as the detective was himself. He decided to tone it down.

"Rabbi, things have developed very quickly just recently. I was going to need to talk to your daughter within a day or two. Doing it now would be best."

"You don't mean you need me to bring her down to the station?"

"No. Not necessary. Please just put her on the phone for a couple of minutes."

"Wait. Let me talk to Selma."

"Selma who?"

"My wife."

"Oh, okay. Fine."

The rabbi put the phone down and went into the kitchen.

Selma was at the kitchen table, nursing her coffee.

"Chaim, what did the police say?"

"They're still on the phone."

"Why?"

"They want to talk to Mandy." He shrugged his shoulders.

"She can't talk to them."

"I know, I know, dearest. But sooner or later she will need to talk to them. And maybe it will give her a sense of helping to steer her own fate if she talks with the detective."

Selma thought about it for a moment. She had not considered that a talk with the police could actually be therapeutic for their very fragile daughter. Mostly just to get it over with, she acquiesced.

"Okay, Chaim. I'll get her. The study telephone?"

"No. Bring the cordless phone up to her room and then leave her alone with it. We must let her be her own person now. Perhaps with one of us around she would be less forthcoming. This is no time for hesitancy."

"But Chaim! She will need our support while she is on the phone. It will frighten her!"

"She will take the call alone." The rabbi was firm, the rebbetsin knew it, and that was the end of the discussion.

"All right. I'll take her the phone."

The rabbi nodded and headed for the study.

"Detective," Mr. Shapiro said into the receiver, "my daughter Mandy will be on the line in just a moment. You must be gentle with her. Do you understand? She is under a lot of stress."

"Yes. No problem. I just need some information from . . ."

"Yes?" Mandy's voice came on to the line. It was weak and high and child-like.

"Mandy," said the rabbi, "we have the Detective Haberdeen on the phone. He needs to ask you some things. Will you be all right?"

"I . . . I don't know, Papa. This scares me!"

Mama grabbed the phone from her daughter's hand. "Chaim! You heard? She is frightened. This is not going to work. I do not want her on the phone with this man!"

Shit, thought Haberdeen. *Just what I need. A family argument with me in the middle.*

"Mrs. Shapiro, this is Detective Haberdeen. I just need to talk to your daughter for a couple of minutes. I have already promised your husband that I would take care to be gentle with her. Please allow her to speak to me."

Haberdeen felt kind of like a fool, basically begging to talk to a child. But the situation demanded it, and police were nothing if not functionalists.

"Selma," said the rabbi, "give her the phone."

There was a brief silence followed by the rubbing of bedclothes on the receiver. Then Mandy spoke up.

"Hello? This is Mandy Shapiro."

"Hello, Miss Shapiro. This is Detective Haberdeen. I know you're not feeling well and I just need to ask you a few questions, okay?"

"Yes, sir." Mandy was being as tough and brave as she could under the circumstances.

"Miss Shapiro, I understand that you saw something at another house a couple of days ago. That you saw a nurse do something. Do you know what I am talking about?"

"Yes. Over at the boat house. I mean the Boating house. We just call it the boat house."

"Good. I need to ask you a few questions about what you saw."

Mandy was getting scared. But her mother, standing in the bedroom doorway, slowly nodded her head. It was okay to talk to this man—to give him the information he needed.

"What do you want to know?"

"What did the nurse look like?"

"Fat."

"How else did she look?"

"She looked like that fat lady on an old movie we saw on TV. She was on a big boat that sank. It was called *Poison Adventure* or something."

"Mmmm." Haberdeen had to think about that—he wasn't much of a movie buff, but that movie—*The Poseidon Adventure*—had been advertised to death several years ago. He realized that the girl was talking about Shelly Winters. Yes, he thought. That was a pretty good physical description of Lisbath Milliken. He felt like he was making progress.

"Good, Miss Shapiro." Mandy heard sirens in the background through the receiver. She had almost forgotten that she was talking to a policeman. Haberdeen's calling her "Miss" made Mandy even more uncomfortable.

"Now think carefully. Did you see the nurse hurt Mrs. Boating?"

"I don't know if she was hurting her! Sometimes Mrs. Boating would yell. But I thought everyone having a baby was supposed to yell."

"Of course. But could you tell if the nurse was actually doing something to Mrs. Boating?" Haberdeen realized the foolish vagueness of his question as soon as it got all the way out of his mouth, but it was blood under the bridge, so to speak.

"She was doing lots of things."

"Like what?"

"I don't know, mister. I mostly saw her back. Her arms moved a lot. And she used lots of towels."

Selma Shapiro was motionless, focused on her daughter, soaking up every inch of information. This was the most she had heard about the experience herself, for she had been too protective of Mandy's state of mind to risk stirring her daughter up by asking challenging or very direct questions.

"Okay. Now tell me about anything you saw that was unusual. Anything weird."

This question shook Mandy. Up to this point things had been pretty easy. She had felt virtually no anxiety about remembering anything so far. But now she had to think of the gross stuff. The stuff that had sent her screaming down the street that night.

She paused.

Haberdeen kept his mouth shut.

Finally, the girl worked up enough courage to tell.

"Mister, it was the blood!"

"The blood?"

"The blood! That nurse—she was …"

"Go on. What was the nurse doing? With the blood?"

"I . . . I can't. I can't *tell*." Mandy was becoming visibly upset, and Mrs. Shapiro went in to sit beside her. Mama didn't care if Papa had said to leave her alone. Her little girl was in trouble, and maternal instincts are always unstoppably stronger than any other.

She took the phone from Mandy "Don't worry, dear. You don't have to say anything more. It's all right."

Haberdeen's voice wafted up from the earpiece. "Miss Shapiro? Hello? What about the blood and the nurse?" Haberdeen was on the verge of getting what he wanted. He could almost taste the blood, so to speak.

Selma put the receiver to her ear. "Detective, this is Mrs. Shapiro. I don't want Mandy to suffer. You'll just have to do your job in some other way."

"Mrs. Shapiro, I must learn what happened. We believe a crime may have been committed. Let me talk to your daughter. Put her on. Now."

"I said 'No,' Detective." She thought for a moment. "I'll tell you what. I know you must find these things out. I will talk to Mandy and call you with whatever I learn."

"It's much better if I do the interro. . . if I ask your daughter the questions."

"Do you want me to call you later or not?" Shapiro was losing her composure as the detective was approaching the threshold of her temper.

"Yes. Okay. Do you have the number?"

"Nine-one-one, right? Everybody knows that."

"No, I want you to have my direct line. Do you have something to write on?"

"No. Listen: I need to get off the phone." She had reached her limit. "I will call you, or maybe Chaim will be calling. Good-bye." She hung up immediately. And hard. She gave Haberdeen no opportunity to reply.

The G-Man rolled his eyes. This was becoming one of his most frustrating cases. Hell of a way to start up on the job right after a vacation.

Mandy was shaking and shocked. Mrs. Shapiro knew that this wasn't the time to pursue the information that detective wanted.

"Mandy, you go back to sleep now." She almost said *We'll talk later*, but thought better of it. Why make the girl dread waking up? Mandy needed soothing rest, and Selma Shapiro was going to see to it that her precious and fragile daughter got it.

Mandy seemed grateful for the respite. She kissed her mother on the cheek and got under the covers. She was asleep before Mama had closed the door on her way out.

Mrs. Shapiro went downstairs to a waiting Chaim.

"So how did it go?" he asked.

"I cut the detective off. Mandy was becoming agitated."

"Woman! I wanted to get this over with. Now he'll be calling again and again."

"No, dear. Relax. I told him I'd talk to Mandy and call him with whatever I learned."

"You're going to talk to her? I thought you said it would be too painful for her."

"Better me than that brash policeman."

The rabbi thought for a moment.

"You're right. As usual." Chaim opened his arms, inviting his wife in. "Let's go into the living room."

They held each other for a moment, quiet and in love. Both felt a strange mixture of strength and weakness in the face of this situation. They had active faith that God would help the Shapiro family through all of this. Both said silent prayers before releasing their hug.

Five hours later, Mandy still had not stirred from her bedroom. On her worst days she would linger in bed, awake and hungry but without the emotional strength to drag herself out of bed and join her parents. But today Mama needed to talk to her, so Mrs. Shapiro came upstairs with a snack on a tray.

Selma knocked quietly on the child's bedroom door. "Mandy?"

"Yes, Mama."

"I have a snack for you. You had no lunch. I'm coming in."

Mrs. Shapiro put the tray on the bedside table and sat down next to Mandy. She put her hand on the girl's arm and gave her a slight smile. Mandy always loved seeing her mother smile; it warmed her to the core. But this afternoon, that core would rather have stayed cool.

"Mandy, aren't you hungry?"

"No, Mama."

"Baby, I must ask you about that nurse."

"No, Mama. Please. I hate thinking about that."

"Listen, dear. I must find out a little to tell that detective. This way he will not call again."

Secretly, Selma wanted to know for her own edification too. But "blaming" it on the detective was still reasonably honest and gave the inquiry a veneer of additional importance.

"Okay, Mama. If you must."

"Yes, Mandy. Baby, what happened with the nurse?"

"You want to know about the blood, right?"

"Yes. I need to know." She squeezed Mandy's arm just a little harder, giving physical support for the girl's emotional state.

"Mama, the nurse was putting the blood in a Thermos bottle."

"What? What Thermos bottle? How?"

"The blood came from a . . . a . . ."

"You can say it. You can say anything to your mother."

Selma saw tears well up in Mandy's eyes. She almost began crying herself. But this was too significant to ignore.

"What do you need to say, my baby? It is all right to say what happened, I promise you."

"Mama, the nurse was holding a . . . a *penis*. Blood came out of the penis into the Thermos. Mama, it was *terrible*!"

Selma was flabbergasted to hear such a word come out of her daughter's mouth, but she had to mask her reaction. She stiffened a little and acted as much as possible like it was just a word. Still, she was visibly shaken.

"A penis? How could that be?"

"I don't know, Mama. I *told* you I didn't want to say. It was long and coming out of Mrs. Boating—from between her legs—and blood was coming out. Mama, I don't understand!"

Mandy began crying hard, and Mrs. Shapiro leaned over to hold her tightly. The girl felt some comfort smelling her mother's special scent and feeling her supporting arms around her. But the child's ordeal wasn't over yet.

It took a moment for Selma to realize that the child was talking about the umbilicus. Mama decided it would be too much, at least at this time, to explain any of it to her daughter.

"What else, honey? Did you see anything else?"

Sounds of the radio's news program wafted up the steps. The Palestinians and the Israelis were at it again.

"Yes, Mama." Mandy took some sheet and brought it up to her cheeks to dry her tears.

"What else?"

"Mama, the nurse went into the bathroom and licked the blood."

"What do you mean, she licked the blood?"

"It was all over her arm and her fingers, and she licked it off. Mama, she didn't wash it off—she licked it off. Mama, it was so *gross*!"

Mrs. Shapiro rarely felt ill, but with this image she began to feel her lunch making its way back up. She believed her daughter implicitly, and the pictures she was seeing in her head were filthy, ungodly, and insanely sick. She was almost afraid to ask for more, but she bore up to her responsibility.

"What else, Mandy?" She hoped to God there wasn't anything else.

"Mama, when she was sucking on her fingers I couldn't stand it. I ran. I ran home."

"So you didn't see anything else?"

"No."

"You remember nothing else?"

"No, Mama. On my way home I was stopped by two boys. They were kind of mean. But I told them what I saw and I got away from them."

"Did the boys hurt you?"

"Oh, no, Mama. I just didn't like them."

"What did they do to you?"

"I told you, Mama. Nothing. Please leave me alone!" The girl began crying harder and harder, and the rebbetsin knew that it was time to stop.

"Of course, Mandy. We will not talk of this anymore now. I love you. You did not do anything wrong." Mandy's crying was letting up somewhat. "Now you can feel better because you got it off your chest. Do you understand?"

"Yes, Mama. I feel a little better."

"Have your food, my baby. Come downstairs when you feel better. We love you, Mandy. Now eat, eat. You will be all right. I promise."

"Okay, Mama. Thank you. I'll come down in a little while." She dried up the last of her tears and put her head back down on the pillow. Mandy curled up, put her thumb in her mouth, and began to suck lightly and rhythmically.

Fifteen

Haberdeen was in his office chair, not yet convinced that there was anything worth investigation. Was this case a puzzle worthy of a professional, or just a bunch of meaningless, fruitless coincidences wasting his time?

On the one hand, he was aware of two separate complaints concerning this Milliken character. But these were second-hand, reported by the parents of a couple of local kids.

On the other hand, that Gomez bitch's actions reeked of a cover-up. The G-Man thought about Sharona's *esprit de corps* in talking about her nurses and their normal procedures. He interpreted her inability to share information as deliberate resistance.

The G-Man was on to something, but he really didn't know it. Neither did Sharona Gomez. Yet.

What most bothered Haberdeen about all this—what really ground away at the very base of this experienced detective's brain—was the fact that one Mrs. Ilse Blücher had been in the Queen of Angels emergency room just days ago. That she was one of Lisbath Milliken's patients, and that she had an odd set of symptoms.

As he pondered, the G-Man's stomach reminded him that he hadn't eaten for several hours. The pretzels didn't count. He decided to grab his bag lunch from the refrigerator in the locker room and headed back to his desk for a well-deserved peanut butter and jelly sandwich and some Fritos.

The G-Man's phone rang. He waited for two more rings to give himself time to clear his mouth, then picked up the receiver.

He answered with a hint of sandwich still interfering with his enunciation: "Detective Haberdeen."

"George, it's Judd. Can you come into my office?"

"Sure. Be there in a minute."

He opened the metal-and-glass door. Stevenson was on the phone, so the G-Man seated himself in front of his desk and started picking his teeth with his fingernail.

"Okay," said Stevenson into the phone. "Get back to me within twenty-four hours." He hung up and swung around to face Haberdeen.

"Well, G-Man, how was your time off? Do some more touring?"

"Yeah, Judd. All over the place. Went with my girlfriend. What's up?" His answer was curt because he wanted to get back to his sandwich, but a detective can't just get up and leave when speaking to his superior officer.

"One of the police commissioners goes to the same temple that Rabbi Shapiro handles. So I get the call to see what's happening. Fucking rabbi is telling everybody about it. I don't need this shit. Find out what's going on and let me know right away. You got anything else going?"

"Nothing big. I just got back, remember?"

"Let's make this one priority one, okay?"

"Sure, Sarge. No problem." Haberdeen thought this was crap, but the politicos do wield their own kind of power, and when the sergeant says something is important, it's important. No matter how unimportant it is.

The G-Man got up and left Judd's office. He was a little angry that this small-potatoes case had gotten dropped on him as a high priority task the same day he came back from vacation. It reminded him of the kind of pussy assignment he'd gotten early in his detective career, when nobody really trusted his judgment. He had always felt resentment that right after they'd hired him as a full detective, he still had to check in with the sergeant before actually making each arrest. A couple of years later when he had finally earned the trust and respect of his superior officers, he'd often think back to the early days—his "boot camp" on the job, as he called it—and figure he'd let any novices coming up through the ranks under *him* have the benefit of the doubt.

But a job's a job. Haberdeen needed to give his full attention to this bullshit case, and he'd do it. He went back to his desk to begin to think. And eat.

♦ ♦ ♦

George Haberdeen's girlfriend Lisa Kristine Ipple had moved from Houston, Texas to Bridgeport, Connecticut to escape stresses between herself and her parents. At twenty-three years of age—and shortly before her decision to leave—Lisa had become pregnant. She hadn't felt like she was ready to have a baby, and the guy who had fathered the kid was a deadbeat musician who had stopped calling her once he learned that she was with child. Lisa Ipple was an independent thinker often at odds with the rest of her family. Despite the repercussions she knew would ensue, she decided to have an abortion.

Lisa calculatedly told her family about it after the fact. The entire course of events, from the pregnancy to the abortion itself, had been a bad experience for everyone concerned. It was especially so for her parents. Their Southern Baptist background forbade not only fornication, but the sin of abortion as well, and they let her know about it daily. Almost hourly. That whole scene was a major motivator for Lisa's emigration out of the Lone Star State. She really needed to get away.

Lisa had always liked the highly expressive style of people from the Eastern seaboard, so she decided on a whim that she would take her chances in the Connecticut area. She'd saved enough for an airplane ticket and a couple of months' rent, and her independent demeanor put her on an airplane just as soon as she felt healthy enough to tolerate the flight.

Lisa needed a job fast. She'd seen a Denny's coffee shop through the bus window as she left Connecticut's Sikorski airport, and decided to go by there and give them a shot. She got the job. She figured maybe her accent helped.

Over a couple of years at Denny's she grew more experienced and became a fixture there. But Lisa felt unfulfilled. When she turned twenty-five she decided to get more educated. She enrolled at the nearby Minion Valley Community College. Lisa had seen some programs on Jane Goodall and was so impressed that she decided to take courses in anthropology.

After a while, Lisa's lack of contentment extended beyond the intellectual. While she could go to school and mix with people who interested her, the coffee shop job near the airport became taxing. She realized that the tips were paltry and the clientele were mostly dirty, exhausted travelers with short tempers and very, very messy kids.

That's when she applied for a job at the Ports O'Call Diner, a twenty-four-hour coffee shop downtown and almost directly across the street from the Bridgeport police station. Lisa was hired on the spot since she was willing to take graveyard and had experience. Besides, she was a good looker, and that never hurt.

Lisa had considered Haberdeen to be a Good Joe ever since the first time he ordered a 4:45 a.m. coffee and donut from her. She had been working there about two weeks. Things were slow at "the POC" that night. When she brought him the sugar-dusted donut, the G-Man had his thumbs under his jaw and was holding his fingers straight out. His eyes were closed and his face was so red it was obvious he was holding his breath. He was hiccupping with little chirping sounds. Lisa ringed the donut on his index finger and started to laugh. George's eyes popped open and he joined in. That rare laughter coming out of a supposedly hard-boiled detective moved some hormones around in Haberdeen. And in Lisa too.

Lisa had perfectly straight, long brown hair that complemented her smooth, light complexion. She was quite slender, but her ample breasts and slightly flared hips gave her the stance of a magazine model. Despite her independence, Lisa was an informal kind of girl, but on the few occasions when she wore heels, she turned heads. More often than not, though, when she was off work, Lisa wore jeans and a loose t-shirt, and invariably one of perhaps thirty pairs of tennis shoes she had cached in her apartment.

The G-Man liked Lisa's independence as well as her fine looks, and the couple had hit it off right away. Within a couple of weeks they were sharing a bed from time to time. The sex was a little awkward since George's pot belly extended almost a foot in front of him, but he was a strong man and could achieve almost any position despite his prominent stomach. They made do.

The two of them liked to go to sleep spoon style, with Lisa behind George, her breasts massaging the G-Man's back. He'd read her dirty jokes while she held him tight with her arms and long legs.

Lisa had become pregnant after just a few weeks of overnighters. Neither of them was ready to get married, and George had tried to talk Lisa into having an abortion. Because she had already gone through that terrible experience in Texas three years ago, Lisa insisted on having the baby this time. George promised to chip in to help support the two of them.

That promise had been made four and a half months ago. The relationship between Lisa and George had matured; they were more used to each other. Most of their times together were smooth and easy, almost like a married couple.

They were going out on the town tonight, and George was thinking about where to go for dinner. He visualized her slipping behind a table at a restaurant with both hands directly in front of her abdomen. Since she'd gotten pregnant, she always did this to protect her baby.

George began to muse about the baby, and it struck him that Lisa's pregnancy could be used to advantage in his pursuit of information about Lisbath Milliken. Maybe Lisa could act as a confederate for the PD. Maybe she could act as if she were considering a home birth. She could interview Milliken and perhaps get some information from the woman.

It sounded good to him, but he had a hard time figuring out how to approach his girlfriend with this proposal. That was especially true since her pregnancy had been unplanned and a source of some stress between them. Still, maybe she'd want to help catch a dirtbag nurse. No way to tell without asking.

George finally decided to take Lisa out to dinner at Bottom Burners, a chili place just outside of the city. He pulled up to her apartment building just as it was getting dark. The winds were blustery and cold, but there was no apparent threat of rain.

"Hi, baby," Lisa said as she opened the cheap apartment door. She was rested and smiling, and her belly bulged a bit into her purple stretch pants. Her long brown hair was still wet from her shower.

"Lisa, you're beautiful. How's our boy?"

"You don't know it's a boy! Why do you always say that?" This was a little game they played pretty much every time they got together. It never got old.

"Can't teach a girl to play football, can I?" Both of them smiled.

They kissed hello with a melodramatic pop. George went to sit down on the couch, and Lisa went to the kitchen to get him a beer. He smiled as he snapped its top open. Lisa had stopped drinking as soon as she learned she was pregnant; she had just brought water for herself.

"So chili tonight, huh?" asked Lisa. Both of them liked the stuff, and Bottom Burners was the best around. You could tell them how hot you wanted it, and they'd spice it to taste right there at your table.

"Yeah, Lisa." George became uneasy, but he had to get this over with. "Lisa, I've got to ask you something."

"Okay. What?"

The G-Man hesitated. He still hadn't put together exactly what words to use to ask his girlfriend to do police work. It was an awkward moment.

"Uh, Lisa, we've got an interesting case at work."

"You always have interesting cases. So does everyone else. You know I hear about them all the time at the diner. So what's up?"

George let out a long, halting breath. Lisa knew something was wrong. She stiffened in anticipation.

"Baby, we've got information about a nurse who might've gone bad, and we could really use ... use your help with this."

"What? How could you use my help? You know I'm not a cop." Lisa started to squish around on the couch, as if she had just sat on some Vaseline by accident.

"Of course not, baby. Nobody's asking you to be a cop. There isn't any danger or risk or anything. But I need someone to play like they may want the suspect's services. She's not exactly a nurse—she's a nurse-midwife. She delivers babies. So you can see how perfect you'd be for this."

"What could I possibly do? I'm not having no midwife deliver my baby! That's stuff from the middle ages, George. This is too weird!"

"We just want you to act like you're interested. You don't need to let her touch you or anything. Just talk to her. Like playing a part. That's all."

George continued. "I mean, you don't have to do it, but so what? It might be fun." He was sophomorically unconvincing.

"*We* want you to act like you're interested? Jesus, George. You sound like a cop."

George stifled his automatic "I *am* a cop" answer; that would be counterproductive.

Lisa said, "I don't know. What's supposed to be wrong with this woman? It *is* a woman, isn't it? Not a guy nurse?"

"Yeah, sure it's a woman. And... it's got something to do with blood."

"*Blood?*" Lisa felt like someone had just dropped her into a freezing swimming pool. She had instant visions of having her own blood drawn, poisoned, and reinserted into her and her baby's bloodstream. She visualized IV tubes with sharp, long needles and red liquids streaming into her otherwise healthy body; of her baby flailing around in her womb, thrashing involuntarily with spasms of pain.

She began to sweat.

George saw her entire mood change real fast. He had never seen her this way: perspiring, clammy, her brow crunched down hard and her eyes darting aimlessly into space.

"Listen, baby. Don't worry. You don't have to do anything."

"Fucking right I don't."

"Hey, let's go eat," the G-Man said, wanting to appease his girlfriend. He felt guilty for even mentioning the subject.

His timing sucked.

"I'm not hungry. I feel sick."

"Oh, baby. I'm sorry. Here, lie down on my big lap, okay? We'll just sit for a while."

After a few seconds, Lisa said, "Shoot, I guess I'm okay. Let me go to the bathroom. I need to dry my hair. We can leave in a few minutes."

"Great. Sure. Whenever you're ready, baby." George took a long draught of his beer and slowly sat back on the couch, watching her.

He was glad things hadn't gotten any worse.

♦ ♦ ♦

The dinner at Bottom Burners was a little strained and their conversation was superficial. They talked about the weather, Lisa's sister's new job with the New York Department of Sanitation, the HBO special both had wanted to see but missed anyway, and other nothings. The only real positive moment was when George complimented Lisa's sweeping hairstyle—something new she had created in the bathroom just before leaving the apartment. The food was atypically mediocre. Lisa hit a piece of gristle, and that ended dinner.

The ride home was silent. Both of them pretty much listened to the winds buffeting George's car and lived in their own worlds of thought. Not surprisingly, both were thinking about the same thing: the nurse-midwife case.

When they got to Lisa's apartment, they went back to the couch, each divining the other's wavelength.

Lisa was softening. "Honey, what would you really want me to do with this nurse woman?"

"You mean you're considering doing it? Oh, baby! Oh, that's great!"

"I haven't said 'yes' yet. I'm just thinking about it." George felt lots of relief real fast.

"Lisa, it would be easy. Just call the woman and talk to her like you're thinking of having a home birth. That's all. Just pay attention to what she says and how she does whatever she does, then let me know. And if she charges, the department will pay for it, of course."

"That's it? That's *really* all?"

"Well, I really can't say yet. There's a small chance that you'd have to give a deposition or maybe tell what you heard in court. That's just if we find any actionable facts."

"Actionable facts?"

"Just a fancy way to say that if we find that the woman seems to be breaking any laws, we'll have to move against her," George said. "And if not, no harm done."

"Well, maybe." Lisa was quiet for a few moments, then said, "Maybe I'll do it to get an insane woman off the streets. Or something like that."

"Oh, this is great, Lisa. Thanks."

"Okay, big guy."

Sixteen

Lisbath Milliken at home was a peaceful, quiet woman. She went about her daily ablutions as rituals, partly because of her nursing training and partly because washing could cleanse her of more than dirt and dead skin. Each day she would wipe down her counters, her cupboard doors, and her entire bathroom. The kitchen floor was particularly important to her, and she would scrub it, often on hands and knees, at the very least twice a week. She often had country music playing softly in the background, and she would sway slightly with the more rhythmic pieces.

During her home hours, Lisbath would often drift to her highly-polished third-floor window and stare out over Bridgeport. She would squint to obliterate the old wooden and concrete buildings, seeing instead the tops of trees and the ever-changing sky. Her window focus would sometimes shift to her own reflection. Seeing into her own eyes always made Lisbath uncomfortable, yet she did not know why. Then would come the inevitable urge to clean and scrub and disinfect her immaculate apartment.

Sometimes when she gazed out the window, she would have brief episodes of feeling unpleasantly different. Her head would shake just a bit, and her eyes would squint. Her hand might move to the window's edge for no reason at all. Or she might kneel, or turn slowly. These actions were frightening to Lisbath, but they passed quickly and seemed to do no harm. As soon as they were over, Lisbath moved her thinking back to the more pleasant things about her: her clean apartment, the wonderful sky, and of course, Lad's company.

Many of her free hours would be spent communing with Lad as he lay on her lap. Lisbath was sure that, even as a dog, Lad could purr. She would sing old country-western ballads to him. She would reassure him. And she looked to Lad for reassurance. Lisbath felt safe with Lad: connected. Complete.

Now it was early morning, and winter's loud declarations reminded Lisbath that Thursday's heritage was the name for thunder. Outside, the skies crashed and illuminated violently. Every window in her apartment building shuddered, making a racket like falling, empty aluminum cans. No one in Bridgeport needed an alarm clock for help waking up this particular morning. It was Lisbath's day off, but trooper that she was, the nurse-midwife never slept in. Rain or shine, she was up early and alert.

Lisbath rolled out of bed and found Lad, tail wagging, already waiting for her at the foot of her bed. He needed to be let out more than he needed to eat, but either one would have been welcome.

She decided to let the animal out first. She went to the door and opened it just wide enough for Lad to make his exit while protecting her privacy (after all, she didn't even have her robe on). She stuck her head out far enough to confirm that the door stop was holding the stairs entryway open enough for Lad to squeeze his way in. The ground floor door swung freely both ways, so he could get in and out.

Lad scampered out of the apartment. Lisbath smiled to herself and shut the door quietly. He'd be back just a little lighter within a few minutes. Good dog.

Lisbath took care of her toilet, then went to the kitchen. With the refrigerator door open wide, she surveyed her stores. She was shocked to see that she had only a couple of beakers of her favorite fluid—her life's blood, so to speak—left in the door. The stuff in the closet wasn't for day-to-day consumption, so it didn't count.

SPECIAL DELIVERY

This wouldn't do at all. This was barely enough for her and Laddie to last the week, and that was on minimum rations.

She reached for one of the beakers and peeled back its stretchy film cover. She inhaled deeply, a little irritated that the refrigeration reduced the depth of fragrance. As the red and white cells parted reluctantly with some of their bouquet, flashes of Lisbath's night terrors jabbed behind her closed eyes. She became rattled, almost dropping the precious beaker. She grabbed the beaker with both hands and replaced it carefully on the refrigerator shelf. Lisbath felt a little stunned and a little weakened. This would not do.

Something had to be done.

🜆 🜆 🜆

Lisbath sat down to recuperate and was feeling better in just a few minutes. She heard Lad rearing up on his haunches, scratching on the apartment door. The rhythm was a familiar one to Nurse Milliken, and she enjoyed it. Lad was dedicated to her. He was a one-woman dog, so to speak. She needed no husband, no roommate, no other soul with whom to commune. Lad was her other half. Yet he was a half that exhibited a daunting independence.

Lisbath let the dog in. Lad made his way to his three bowls and found dry, uninteresting food in one. Water was in another, and nothing but a brown stain ringed the third. He lapped up a bit of water and raised his head toward Lisbath. It was clear what he wanted—what he yearned for. The dog's look carried with it something more—some powerful imperative beyond a simple desire for a treat. Lisbath felt this in her bones and in her brain. The animal's communication was pervasive and caused her to shudder. Lad growled soundlessly, and Lisbath received it with sadness and an edge of terror. It felt like the recurring dream on the moors, but this was real and here and now.

Lad circled the bowls slowly three times. The uneven clicking of his nails on the linoleum was sinister; a pecking against the grain of Lisbath's sanity. Lisbath closed her robe more tightly around her and stared at Lad's motions, transfixed, as if by a hypnotist's swinging pocket watch.

Lisbath knew that if a blood meal did not make its way into his third bowl, Lad would become increasingly weaker. And angrier. Lad acted very strangely whenever he went for several days without his red sustenance. The animal's odd behaviors—like gnawing on his own paws to the point of rupturing his skin while eying Lisbath's stumpy legs—often frightened Lisbath, and it was a fear she would do almost anything to avoid.

Tears began to form in Lad's eyes. They were tears of fear and of self-pity that a normal dog would not produce. On some unspoken level, Lisbath knew that they were even more tears of anger. The animal was approaching a limit of some kind, and Lisbath did not want that limit to be reached under any circumstances.

As Lisbath stared—connected, really—she too began to whimper. Her tears were not of self-pity but rather of guilt and matronly sadness. She was failing her little Laddie, and that hurt bad.

But she was terrified by him as well.

Dickinson's registry's phone assignments for nurse-midwives had dwindled precipitously the last few weeks. Lisbath would still get the odd post-op follow-up call or doc's office fill-in assignment, so she made enough money.

But she wasn't in it for the money. Lisbath's need for blood—for both herself and for Lad—was deeply real. It wasn't some weirdo whim or just a disgusting antisocial quirk. Lisbath Milliken actually, fundamentally, and vitally *needed* blood, and not just any blood.

And she was running out.

Lisbath needed nurse-midwife assignments, or she'd have to do something drastic and heretofore unconscionable.

An unwitting victim of her own maternal sadness, Lisbath knelt down to the hound. She took a large kibble of dry food and moistened it by swishing it around in Lad's water bowl. She then offered the soggy morsel to Lad by putting it right in front of his

SPECIAL DELIVERY

muzzle, wiggling it beneath his drying nose. She had hoped to assuage his hunger, to assuage her own guilt, with this inadequate peace offering.

In what appeared initially to be an attempt to console Mommy, Lad licked the wetted morsel. But then he lunged toward it, snapping his teeth down on the clump and upon the surprised fingers holding it.

Lisbath yelled, "Ouch!" but the animal held his muzzle's grip on her fingers for several seconds. The silent growl became louder. He began a very slow side-to-side motion, like a shark thrashing its prey. His eyes narrowed as he looked at Lisbath. His grip remained firm and painful.

Suddenly, his jaws simply opened wide and he backed away. Lisbath was stunned; Lad had never done anything like this before, and she was deeply confused. To have her own Laddie turn on her was a foul surprise. Still, it was understandable. Maybe.

The dog then simply turned away and walked slowly to his resting spot.

Like the family rape victim trying foolishly to console her incestuous father, Lisbath began to bawl quietly, crushing the dog food over the bowl for Lad as much as she could between her bloody, weakened fingers. She thought and thought about what to do—how to remedy this paucity of sustenance and its sinister implications.

She needed to go to Dickinson's. Day off or not, she *needed* to go.

Lisbath bandaged her fingers together and then she was ready to leave. She knelt again by Lad, stroking and petting him gingerly. Supportively. Carefully.

"Laddie, Mommy knows. She knows. Don't worry. Mommy knows. She won't let you down."

She continued her solace in her special song:

Treats a-comin' . . .

A very soft growl again. Tears formed in Lisbath's eyes as she continued her song.

Treats a'comin'
Mommy does as Mommy should . . .

Her voice trailed off as she was descending the steps toward the first floor of her apartment building. Her phone rang, but it was out of earshot. It was Dickinson's. She would be relieved once she got there.

🌢 🌢 🌢

Wanda Pettridge looked up from her magazine when she heard the door open.

"Hi, Lisbath. Thought you were off today."

"Hello, Wanda. I am off. But I thought I might be able to pick up a little extra work anyway."

Sharona came out of the bathroom, drying her hands with a paper towel. She saw Lisbath immediately. "Lisbath! I'm glad you're here. Did you get my message? And what's wrong with your hand?"

"It's nothing, dear. Just a cut. When did you call?"

"Less than a half hour ago. I sure wish you'd carry a pager."

"Must have been after I left. And you know I don't like those pager things. They're so impersonal. Do you have something for me?"

"Yes. We have a new midwife call. But I've got to talk to you first."

"About what?"

"Come on in," said Sharona as she gestured to her conference room.

Lisbath frowned, but at the same time her interest was piqued. She went into the room and sat down. Sharona came in with a small folder and began talking immediately.

"Lisbath, one of your patients has been admitted to Mercy General."

"Okay. Who?"

Sharona pulled a slip out of the folder. "Lucinda Smithson."

"Too bad."

"Well, yes," said Sharona. "Her doctor asked you to call. It's Coop Gold."

"Never heard of him." There was a small shudder in Lisbath's voice.

"Well, you need to call him. Here's his number. His front-office nurse is a woman named Phyllis."

"Okay, I'll call. But why did we have to come into the conference room for this, Sharona?"

"Well, for one thing, Phyllis's call sounded stressed. I thought you might not want our colleagues out there to hear that one of your patients had to be hospitalized."

"That's nice of you, Sharona. *Woman-to-woman*, it was the right thing to do, you know? But her hospitalization wouldn't mean I did anything wrong, now would it?"

"Of course not, " Sharona continued, sounding foreboding. "There's something else."

Lisbath's head was pointing down, but her eyebrows popped up. "What might that be?" she asked.

"A detective was here asking about you."

"*What?*" Lisbath squeaked. Every fiber in her body began to vibrate like an out-of-tune harp.

"Yes. A man named Haberdeen."

"What did he want? Why did he ask?" Bloody, secret visions cavorted in Lisbath's mind's eye.

"Actually, he just wanted to know about you. Kind of non-specific."

"What in God's name does that mean? Sharona, you can't just leave me hanging like this!" Lisbath's fear began to build. Her eyes darted nowhere in particular as she tensed her jaw.

"I'm sorry, dear. That's all I have. I don't guess I need to tell you anything about P's and Q's, do I?"

"Are you *threatening* me, Sharona?"

"No, of course not, dear. It's just best that we all protect our investment here. Know what I mean?"

Without saying another word, Sharona rose and went to the door. Lisbath followed. She wasn't satisfied, and her churning insides reminded her of it obtrusively during the next several hours.

Sharona went back to her desk and picked up some papers. She studied them with caricatured intensity, an obvious attempt to terminate the conversation.

"Here's the info on your call." Sharona handed Lisbath a couple of slips of paper stapled together. She asked, "You can go now, can't you?"

Lisbath scanned the information. "Yes. She's local. Unmarried and pregnant." Uncomfortable with Sharona for the moment, Lisbath turned instead to her colleagues around the rest of the room. "There's more and more of that these days, isn't it the truth?"

All of the nurses in Dickinson's nodded.

♦ ♦ ♦

Since this was a first consult, Lisbath only needed minimal equipment: latex gloves, a stethoscope, a sphygmomanometer, a thermometer, a few other examination goodies, and a note pad. She always kept a separate "fast-response" kit in her trunk so she could travel directly to her new patients without having to stop at home.

It was the first day in a long time when the sun had finally begun to shine, and it became so clear outside that the sun's rays were almost blinding.

Lisbath squinted through the glare on her windshield to find the address. It was an apartment building in a poorer part of town, and the young lady—one Lisa Ipple—lived on the first floor. Lisbath could see the "4" nailed to the door as soon as she walked up to the building.

She walked up deliberately and professionally. Two young children, perhaps four or five years old, stopped their mud play long enough to eye the fat woman curiously. The one nearer Lisbath chewed her morsel of mud absentmindedly.

Lisbath gave the children a quick grin and rapped on Lisa's door three times in quick succession. In about twenty seconds, a thirtyish lady with nicely-combed brown hair opened the door.

Lisbath didn't wait for an inquiry.

"Good morning. I am Nurse Milliken from Dickinson's Registry. Are you Lisa Ipple?"

"Yes. I'm glad you're here. Please come in."

Lisa's simple apartment was clean and well-kept, yet it had a lived-in appearance. It was an older apartment building, and it was obvious that Ms. Ipple had not been the first tenant. There was the faint fragrance of coffee and soap. A tinny radio in what must have been the bedroom was playing morning news.

"Please sit down, Ms. Milliken."

"Call me Lisbath, dear."

"Okay, Lisbath. Can I offer you anything? I can make instant coffee."

"No thanks. So. . . how far along are we, Lisa?"

"Not quite five months."

"Uh-huh. Have you seen your regular doctor or perhaps an obstetrician?"

"Well. . . yes, yes I have. He just assumed I'd be having my baby in the hospital. But I've been talking to some of my girlfriends, you know? Everybody's going natural, if you know what I mean. So I'm thinking about having the baby here, or maybe at Gina's house."

"Gina?"

"Yes. Gina Motto is one of my best friends. She lives in a great home in the Hill area. Maybe I'll have the baby there."

Lisbath became an advisor. "Well, it's a little early to make that decision as yet. Have you ever had a child before?"

Lisa hadn't expected this question. She had not thought about the abortion she had had in Texas, weeks before moving to Connecticut, for a long time. All of a sudden the risks she was taking and the added stress she would experience during this deception began to surface and grow in her thinking. Lisa's ruse felt like it was beginning to trap her rather than her quarry.

So now what was Lisa supposed to do? She really hadn't rehearsed how this interview should go. What was she supposed to find out? What kind of fake commitments was she expected to make? She felt increasingly uncomfortable, awkward, and confused. Lisbath went on happily and routinely.

"Ms. Ipple, I need to know if you have had a child before. Multiparas—women who are not first-timers—need different care, and their timelines are different."

"Oh, sorry, Ms. Milliken. Well, to be honest, I was pregnant once, but I didn't carry it through."

"What happened? Were there problems?"

"No, not problems. I just didn't want the baby. Oh, what I mean is, the baby wasn't planned, and at that time in my life I couldn't afford a child. Couldn't afford it financially and couldn't afford the time and attention a baby would take."

"Did you have a D&C?" asked Lisbath.

"Yes. The abortion was in Texas about three years ago."

"Any problems? Complications?"

"No. Not except for the people who were protesting outside the clinic. God, I didn't need that at all."

"Yes, dear. *Woman-to-woman*, I know what you mean. We all make our choices. So this time you're going to bring your child to full term?"

"Y-yes. This time I'm going through with it."

"You're not married?"

"No. Does that matter?" Lisa was getting closer to her limits of tolerance, and her face reddened a little. Challenges like this just tilted the scales in a bad direction.

"Of course not, dear. Of course not. It makes no difference at all."

All of a sudden a loud thump hit Lisa's door. It startled both of the women. It was followed immediately by loud crying—shrieking, really—from one of the mud eaters who had followed Lisbath's entry to Lisa's place.

"It's just the kids from a couple of doors down. Even though they're girls, they play like little boys. Very rough. I sure hope my baby doesn't act like that."

The crying stopped almost immediately, so neither woman felt obligated to go out and have a look. A few seconds later they heard giggling from both the kids waft through the thin apartment door.

"Ms. Ipple, do you work?" asked Milliken.

"Yes. I waitress graveyard shift most of the time. Why do you ask?"

"I just want to get a full picture of you, dear. It's part of doing my job right. I need to relate to you *woman-to-woman*, if you know what I mean. Not like you're just somebody off the street."

Lisa thought this was unusual language, and her who-is-this-woman antennae were vibrating a little.

Lisa continued her investigatory task. "So Ms. Milliken, what's it like? It couldn't be anything like my abortion, could it?" Lisa began to play intelligent, finding a way to divine whatever oddness or information she could from this unknowing police suspect.

"Of course that would depend on your abortion experience, but, no, dear, it should be completely different. The main thing here —the main difference with a home birth assisted by a midwife—is the intimacy. Nothing can compare with being home or perhaps at your best friend's house when you give birth to your child. It's a beautiful experience."

"But isn't it kind of dangerous? I mean, it's not a hospital. What if something goes wrong? There's no doctor. No ambulance, no emergency equipment, no anything!" Lisa was actually beginning to get a little excited. Frightened. Her role-playing was improving, but her mood was not.

"Not to worry, dear. *Woman-to-woman*, I've been doing this for longer than you've been on this green earth. Never had a problem. Listen. Why don't you call me Lisbath. And may I call you Lisa?"

"Okay, sure, Lisbath. But tell the truth. You never had a problem? Never?" This was the time for Lisa to remove the knife from the sheath. "Not once? Didn't anybody ever have a breech delivery or get too much anesthetic or get sick or anything?"

"Slow down—calm down, Lisa. We always do a very thorough pre-delivery check. If it looks like the birth could be any kind of problem, we always have a back-up plan to go to the hospital long before the baby crowns.

"And we have special ambulance numbers, just in case, where they truly come immediately. Not like 911, where you could wait forever. But listen, dear. I can take care of virtually anything anyway. A hospital birth—it just loses the specialness, if you know what I mean."

"Isn't it messy?" asked Lisa.

Lisbath said, "Not to worry, Lisa. I truly do this all the time. I clean everything up. *Every last drop!*"

"What about drugs?"

"Lisa, dear, home births with nurse-midwives are done naturally. Have you taken Lamaze yet?"

Lisa was feeling caught in her own trap again. "I didn't think about that."

"The Lamaze method lets you give your child birth without exposing it to unnatural chemicals in the process. It really is the best way."

"But what if it really hurts?"

"Lisa, women have been giving birth for tens of thousands of years. We've only had anesthesia for a short time, relatively speaking. All women can give birth without drugs, with or without Lamaze. It's a very, very natural act."

Lisa became frightened—dumbfounded. She thought of having her baby squeeze out of her, ripping her perineum, crying and flailing and tearing her insides out, with no hope of pain relief for Mommy Lisa. She saw herself bloodying the sheets, screaming, enveloped in fear, helpless. Her eyes darted fast from side to side, and Lisbath could see that this was one scared mom-to-be.

Then Lisa thought to herself, *Why is this woman so very insistent that she execute the birth? Is this desperation? Something's wrong here.* Lisa couldn't put her finger on it, and nothing seemed truly extraordinary or illegal, but something was definitely not Kosher.

"Ms. Milliken, I have to think about this. To tell you the truth, it's a little scary. You know that when I called your company I hadn't decided really whether or not I was going to have a midwife. I have to think about it. Thanks for coming, though."

Lisa felt like she probably should have tried to get more information from the midwife, but she was really shaken. Her abdomen actually hurt; maybe this was hurting the baby, too. Besides, this wasn't a job she was doing. It was a favor for a friend. And she truly didn't need all this extra stress.

Lisbath was internally furious but outwardly still The Professional Nurse. This was the very first time in all her nursing career that she felt she was getting the full brush-off. Right when she is most desperate, this girl—this blue-collar worker waitress—lets Lisbath know in so many words that even when the girl eventually delivers, there'll be no blood for Lisbath. She had to try to think of a way to reverse this bad trend.

"Lisa, dear. It will be absolutely fine. And I *want* you to think about it," Lisbath lied. "I'm going to give you my personal, home number. I want you to call me when you've made up your mind, and we'll talk about it."

"Sure, okay." Lisa sounded—and was—rather unsure of herself. Here she was, at once vulnerable and empowered, at once honest and dishonest. This was the first time she could remember since childhood ever trying to trick anyone. Her psychological sustenance was that she was doing this to protect other women—pregnant or otherwise—whom Lisbath Milliken might harm in some way. It made the effort worth it.

Still, had she really learned anything? Enough? Did she "have the goods" on the nurse-midwife? Or was she just about to come away with essentially nothing—just the thought that Ms. Milliken was odd in her ways and surprisingly desperate?

Lisa would have to leave that to George. He would either be happy and proud of her work, or he'd be let down. But either way Lisa would feel that she had done her job.

Lisa thought: *It* is *over now, isn't it?*

Seventeen

Lisbath drove home from Lisa's in a cold drizzle. It was so dark that she didn't even put on her sunglasses. The sun had abandoned the town. The weather and Milliken's mood made a perfect match.

She got into her apartment, went to the bathroom, gave Lad a dog biscuit, let him out, and slumped down by her phone. She knew she had to return that Dr. Gold's call soon, and she figured this was the time to get it over with.

Gold's office phone was answered on the second ring.

"Doctor's office." The voice sounded a bit rushed.

"Hello. This is Nurse Lisbath Milliken. I am returning Dr. Gold's call."

"Oh yes, Ms. Milliken. I'll get him. I think he's free. I'm putting you on hold."

After a few seconds, a strong, deep male voice boomed over the phone.

"Hello. Nurse Milliken?"

"Yes."

"This is Dr. Gold. I am treating our patient Lucinda Smithson."

"Yes?"

"What was her prepartum condition?"

"She was fine. If she had been ill, I would have insisted on a hospital birthing. With an obstetrician, of course."

"I see. Well, she's one sick woman now. I've admitted her to Mercy General. She has a fever over 100 and a white count in the 20,000 range. I suspect something from the birth process itself contributed. Did she give you any history of sensitivity to antibiotics or anything else unusual? She seemed hesitant to give me the full picture."

"Nothing, doctor." Lisbath's threat antennae began a mild vibration.

"What meds was she on?"

"None she told me about. I had her taking a pack of prenatal-mix vitamins daily; that's all."

"Well, all right. Let me know if you remember anything."

"Certainly, Doctor. Please give her my best."

"Surely. Good-bye."

Well, that wasn't bad, thought Lisbath. She wondered what might be wrong with the woman. Surely her bloodletting wouldn't have caused any problem or infection.

One can't get personally involved in every single case, can one?

🞄 🞄 🞄

After her high-stress interview with Lisbath, Lisa decided late in the afternoon that she wanted to wait until the next day to "report" to George about what she had learned. She needed to sort out her feelings and her observations. To cool off. The fact is, Lisa wasn't really sure what she had learned and what she hadn't.

Lisa's night was almost completely sleepless. She had nightmares of wiggling groups of babies spewing forth serially and in clumps from her vagina, spilling her blood and other organs all over her bed. Her abdomen was cramping and undulating visibly during these multiple births. Like having the worst period of her life even though she wasn't menstruating.

Throughout her dreams, the infants scratched at each other with their soft nails and were tangled helplessly in their irregular web of umbilici. All this as Nurse Milliken laughed sinisterly at Lisa from the bed's splattered, soggy foot. The demonic nurse threw her head back in a wicked gesture of triumph and alignment with Hades' minions.

Lisa was as apt to follow her intuition as her logic, and she knew deep down inside that one Nurse Lisbath Milliken was bad news. It was unimportant that nothing really damning had come of her conversation the day before. This bitch was going to bite the dust if Lisa had anything to do with it. Lisa's stomach was raw from the burning juices that were pumped out during her dream sessions last night. This punctuated her growing emotional conviction that Milliken was going down.

Lisa decided to try to meet with George as soon as she could. She wanted to get her "report" over with—to wash her hands of the whole thing—to normalize her life. Just a couple of days helping out the police and look what it had done to her! *This was definitely not worth it.*

She dialed the direct line into the detectives.

"Detective bureau, Harris."

"Hi, Herb. This is Lisa. Is George there?"

"Sure, hon. He's over at the posters. I'll get him."

"Thanks. Say hello to Jane, okay?"

"Yeah, sure." Detective Harris put Lisa on hold and shouted over the din. "Hey, George. Lisa's on 2."

The G-Man got out a fresh sheet of paper, punched line 2, and picked up the receiver.

"Hi, baby. How'd it go?"

Lisa was often irritated at the G-Man's directness. No social "How are you today" or "Did you sleep well?" from him. Just direct and to-the-point. Of course, that's how cops are. She needed someone to bitch to about her horrible night, but George wasn't going to be the one. Lisa decided she would call one of her friends—maybe Gina or perhaps Brancie—later.

"George, sometimes I wish you'd actually *talk* to me."

"Baby, what do you think I'm doing? What do you mean?" The G-Man wasn't being defensive; he was simply clueless.

"Oh, forget it, Detective Haberdeen."

"Lisa, did you talk to that Milliken woman?"

"Yes, yes I did. George, there's something wrong with her. She's weird."

"Can you be any more specific, baby? 'Weird' doesn't stand up too well in police reports."

"What do you want me to say?"

Okay, here we go, thought George. *I'm going to have to coax it out of her.* "Please tell me anything unusual she said. Did she mention anything about blood? Did she say anything about her other patients? Did she say anything that would be related to breaking the law?"

"George, you know that I don't know all the law."

"I know, baby. Just tell me what you can." His teeth ground silently.

"Well . . . she really didn't say anything. I mean, we just talked. She told me that it would be safe, and that if anything looked bad then the birth would be at the hospital instead of at home."

"I don't understand."

"She was trying to let me know that everything was safe. She said she always does a big-deal pre-birth checkout, and if anything was wrong, she'd be sure that the birth was at a hospital."

"She checked you out? Did she touch you?"

"No, no. I told her I was just thinking about it. She didn't examine me or anything."

"So what else? You must have gotten more than that. What did she say about blood? Blood seems to be a major league player in this case, you know."

"George, I'm not a damn detective, and you know it." Lisa was getting angry. "Listen: I had a really shitty night, and it was because of that Milliken bitch."

"What did she do to you?"

"She didn't do nothing to me. I just got scared and had some scary dreams."

"Oh, that's nothing. Just dreams."

"Bullshit, George! What are you saying? That my dreams don't matter to you? That I don't matter to you? Why the *hell* do you think I went through all of this?"

"You *do* matter to me, baby. Really you do."

"Yeah, right." Lisa hung up hard and started to cry. Her hormones were working overtime, and in the context of last night's nightmares, it was all just too much.

George didn't understand why she was so mad, so he turned his attention to the matter at hand. He felt almost cheated—that Lisa had come up with virtually nothing about the case. Nothing to go on.

Haberdeen pulled out his Milliken file. He needed to find the name of Lisbath's patient—the one who had been admitted to Queen of Angels. Last he heard her diagnosis had not been completed.

The G-Man dialed Queen of Angels. He got the hospital's automated greeting: "*Thank you for calling Queen of Angels. If this is an emergency, hang up and dial 911. Otherwise, for a patient's room, dial 1; for the lab, dial 2; for emergency, dial 3; for . . .*" G-Man just hit "O" assuming that it'd get him to the operator. It did.

"Hospital operator. May I help you?"

"This is the Bridgeport Police. I need information on one of your patients."

"Hold on. I'll connect you." The crappy music started, and Haberdeen felt around in his desk drawer for a pencil. He only had to wait about ten seconds on the line.

"Information desk."

"This is Detective Haberdeen of the Bridgeport PD. I need information about one of your patients—one Ilse Blücher."

"Sir, this is the information desk."

"I know. I want information on Mrs. Blücher."

"Sir, I'm just a volunteer at the information desk. I can help you with directions to the hospital if you wish."

"Shit." The G-Man hung up hard, irritated at the incompetence he ran across on a daily basis. He re-dialed the hospital, and as soon as the recording began, he once again hit "O."

"Hospital operator. May I help you?"

"This is the police. First, do NOT send this call to the information desk. Do you understand? I need confidential information about one of your patients, and the information desk does NOT have that information. Transfer me to someone who does." G-Man had had his fill of incompetence. He was, after all, The Police.

"Sir, when someone asks for information, I transfer them to the information desk. Would you like to speak with them?"

"NO! Send me to the head of the hospital."

"The business office is closed. They are only open Monday through Friday, 9:30 to 5:30."

"Christ, lady. Send me to the main doctor."

"I'll send your call to Medical Records."

"Fine."

Haberdeen was getting his way, the operator was taking care of business, and at least at this juncture there was progress.

"Medical Records," said the recently post-pubescent voice at the other end of the line. It was about as obviously gay as the men-women of *La Cage au Folles*. No question.

"This is Bridgeport PD. Do you still have an Ilse Blücher at the hospital?"

"You need to talk to Patient Information. I'll transfer you."

"STOP. DO NOT TRANSFER ME. Do you have an Ilse Blücher there or not?"

"I don't know. All I do is work with patient files. And how do I know you are who you say you are?"

Shit. He had dealt with roadblocks like this in the past, but today it was particularly irritating. He demanded, "Let me talk to your supervisor."

"Mrs. Chung?"

"I don't care who the hell it is. Let me talk to her."

"Okay, okay. Don't get so *excited*. Sheeeesh!"

Haberdeen heard some muffled discussion; the receiver was obviously pressing against the boy's palm as he talked to someone.

There was a break of several seconds. Then: "Hello. This is Joy Chung. I am the Medical Records Supervisor. May I help you?"

"Yes. Haberdeen of Bridgeport PD. Do or did you have an Ilse Blücher in the hospital?" G-Man was becoming as desperate as he was angry.

"Sir, what is your badge number?"

Haberdeen, in all his anger, recognized the professionalism of Ms. Chung. He knew that this was going to take a few extra minutes, but at least he was finally talking with a competent.

"Badge D1446. Please be fast."

"Yes sir. I'll be back on the line momentarily."

G-Man knew that Chung was calling the department to confirm that he was a legitimate police officer. That was okay. He doodled and thought and waited. The delay was just shy of two minutes.

"Detective Haberdeen, please repeat your question. I will help you any way I can."

"First, I need to know if you have or had one Ilse Blücher at your hospital."

"Yes, we do." Chung had sent her clerk to pull the file even before she called the PD for verification of Haberdeen's status.

"Is she still there?"

"Yes." Chung, an experienced, certified MR supervisor, knew that she could answer direct questions but could not volunteer any information other than the patient's location in the hospital. Information beyond direct answers and location information could destroy a court case and were the purview of the primary doctor, anyway.

"Is she the patient of a nurse-midwife named Lisbath Milliken?"

"Yes."

"Does Milliken still see her?"

Chung took a few seconds to leaf through the file. "There are no notes to that effect. However, sir, you must be aware that the nursing notes and other contemporaneous notes and plans about her stay remain with the floor supervisor while the patient is a resident at this institution."

"You mean you don't have the whole picture?"

"Precisely. You need to talk to the floor supervisor. Ms. Blücher is in 5A, so the 5 South supervisor should be able to help you. Do you want me to transfer?"

"Yes. But what's the direct line, in case I need to call later?"

"Five South is at extension 5101."

"Good. Please transfer me."

"As you wish, sir."

The phone line went directly to boring music, and was finally answered by what sounded like a Filipino boy. "Five South. Can I help you?"

"Are you the floor supervisor?"

"No, sir. I am the wing secretary. Do you need the supervisor?"

"Either her or Patient Ilse Blücher's nurse."

"They are different people, sir. Which do you need?"

"Christ, man, just give me the one you see first."

The line went directly to hold as Frank Amargo rolled his chair over to Supervisor Linda Neaton. She was on the phone, saw his urgency, and put the caller on hold.

"Linda, there's a mean man on the phone asking for the supervisor."

"Okay, I'll be there in a minute." Linda had been talking to Joy Chung, who had called her to warn her that Haberdeen's call was imminent. She finished the call, took her sweet time in making a few final notes in her wing log, pulled the red three-ring binder marked "Blücher" from the rotating carousel of patient files, finally picked up the phone, and punched the flashing line.

"This is Supervisor Neaton."

"Haberdeen of the Bridgeport PD. I've already been verified by your Miss Chung. I need information on Ilse Blücher. Please get her file."

"I have it here, Detective. What do you need?"

"Is she well enough to talk?"

This kind of information wasn't in the file, and Neaton would have to ask Penny Arrow, Blücher's nurse for this shift. "Please hold on a minute." She put G-Man on hold without waiting for his acknowledgement. Linda took a walk to 512, where Nurse Arrow was making bed B in anticipation of a new arrival on her way from check-in.

"Penny, is Ilse Blücher up to a police interview?"

"God! Did she do something wrong?"

"I don't think so. But the police want to talk to her about something. Is she up to it?"

"Well, today's the first time she actually asked for breakfast, and she's been on the phone for a couple of hours. I think she's probably okay for it even though she still looks real sick. Do you think we need to check with Dr. D'Angostino? She hasn't even prescribed anything beyond the ringer IV drip, some Tylenol, and icing every four hours for her fever. I don't think she knows what's going on yet, so she may not want visitors."

"No. We don't need to call her. Ms. Blücher's chart doesn't say anything about visitor limitations, and it's a cop, anyway. Thanks. I'll leave you to your sheets."

"Thanks a bunch, Linda."

Neaton went back to the nurse's station and picked up her phone. "Detective—what did you say your name was?"

"Haberdeen, Ma'am. Is Blücher communicable?"

"You mean 'communicative,' and we don't know yet. But the doctor hasn't quarantined her room. And yes, she is able to talk. Do you want me to tell her you're on the line?"

"No. I'll be in later for a personal interview. But I have more questions for you. First, tell me about Lisbath Milliken."

"Who?"

"Blücher's nurse. Or nurse-midwife."

"Oh, of course. Lisbath Milliken. Ilse was actually admitted under Dr. D'Angostino's authority. We have a courtesy call out to Milliken, though."

"Courtesy call? You mean letting her know that her patient is in the hospital?"

"Yes."

"So what's she like?"

"Ms. Milliken?"

"Yes. What's she like?"

"Well, Detective, she's rather overweight, but her uniform is always nice and clean."

"No, no. I don't care what she looks like. What does she do? Does she act strange? Do lots of her patients get admitted? Did you ever see her work a patient?"

"That's quite a barrage of questions, officer. Do we have a problem here?"

"I don't know yet. Tell me if Milliken acts odd when she's around blood."

"*What?*"

"You heard me. And this is confidential. Police business. So how does she act around blood?"

Nurse Supervisor Neaton was taken aback. What was all this? It sounded like the detective didn't really care about the patient. It was Milliken who was under investigation. Weird, but intriguing at the same time.

"Detective, I've only seen Nurse Milliken a couple of times. I've seen her look over a chart and walk into the patient's room. That's all. The examinations are personal—between care provider and the patient, unless someone asks for extra help. I'm afraid I can't tell you anything."

"Well, do lots of her patients get admitted?"

"Not on this wing. I can only remember maybe two during the past five years I've worked here."

The G-Man knew then and there that he had his work cut out for him. This was going to be time consuming, and he began liking this assignment less and less.

"Okay, Ms. Neaton. I'll be over there later. Let your staff know to expect me and to be forthcoming, but do not under any circumstances reveal the purpose of my visit. Do you understand?"

"Certainly, sir."

"Later, then." Haberdeen hung up and began making cryptic notes about his conversation. The G-Man was facing much more busywork than he wanted on a path that he believed would lead nowhere. He would be proven wrong.

Linda Neaton, meanwhile, went to the cafeteria for a cup of coffee and laced it with twice her normal sugar load. When she went back to her floor, she decided to take a more detailed look at the Blücher notebook. Frank had already replaced it into its carousel holder, so Linda removed it and took it to her desk.

The results of lab tests showed that Mrs. Blücher had a *Strep* infection that had not only infested her reproductive area, but had actually entered her blood as well.

Eighteen

As she sat at her daughter's bedside, Selma Shapiro put her cool hand on young Mandy's forehead. "Everything will be okay, Mandy," she said. "You are safe and we are safe, and that's all that matters."

Freezing rain outside beat against the bedroom window, but the house heat was turned up and everyone was physically comfortable.

"Thank you, Mama," said Mandy as she lay stiff on the bed. The girl felt little reassurance from her mother since her suffering germinated within her own private memory, and not in some corporeal boogeyman who might be stopped by Papa or the police or maybe by God.

Mandy had been suffering for several days now, reliving her foul visions of Linda Boating's birth event. She showed classic symptoms of Post-Traumatic Stress Disorder, but her parents did not or would not understand that. As far as they were concerned, Mandy had seen something that scared her, and once enough time passed after the event, the girl should pull through just fine. Yes, they had called the police. But that should finish the matter. They had executed their civil responsibility. *Finish*. They wanted to wash their hands of it.

"Mama, it was really scary!" said Mandy as she turned to face her good mother.

"Okay, Mandy. Tell me about it. What did you really see? Are you ready to talk?"

"I think I need to tell somebody."

"Well, tell me, then, dear. Tell me everything. It will be all right."

Selma had expected Mandy to talk about looking through the window at Linda Boating's birth experience—the event that had occasioned the rabbi's call to the police. But Mandy's internal horrors had their roots even before that.

"Mama, that dead woman at the school! She was right there! And I *smelled* her! It was so . . . ugly! *Sickening!*"

Rebbetsin Shapiro had forgotten the episode at the playground where the children all smelled the corpse at the curb just outside the playground fence. That had paled in the mother's memory compared to the birth Mandy had witnessed, but apparently the girl was fixating on that horrible image as well.

"Yes, yes, Mandy. It will be all right. It was a natural thing. Yes, it is scary the first time, but it is okay and it is natural."

"It is natural for someone to be dead at the school? In the gutter?" Mandy was wide-eyed, so needy of reassurance.

"God moves in his own ways, my heart. That poor woman is now at peace, *kein nehora*."

This experience was nevertheless the minor of the two memories eating away at the vulnerable girl. She continued.

"Mama, that's not all. *Oh, Mama! I'm so scared!*"

"Come, come, my Mandy." Selma put her arms around her daughter. "Tell me. Get it all out. I am here and we are safe. Get it out of your system."

After a few seconds, Mandy strengthened. She removed her mother's arms from around her and carefully, firmly placed them on her mother's lap.

She began to recount every detail, beginning with her hearing the screams coming out of the Boating house. She described them so vividly that Mama put her hand over her own mouth and crinkled her brow in a gesture of almost-disbelief.

Mandy continued her story: She recounted her sneaking up to the window and seeing the nurse handle the baby and lick the blood over and over. Mother Shapiro did her best to stifle her gasps and cover her shock, but Mandy could see through her mother's weak attempts to remain aloof. Actually, Mandy got a small charge out of frightening her mother, mostly because it legitimized her own horror. *Yes*, she thought, *it is normal and okay for me to be so scared about this.*

When story time was over, Mandy was so exhausted that Mama told her to take a nap.

Selma went downstairs to tell the rabbi all the details. Both shook their heads in disbelief and pity. For Mandy and for that poor Mrs. Boating. As tears moistened the white tablecloth, they joined hands and prayed.

🩸 🩸 🩸

. Lisbath was so irritated on her way home from her virtually abortive interview with Lisa Ipple that she almost hit a parked car as she drove down Spruce Street. She felt like a time-share salesperson who had just spent a solid two hours pitching a couple who just flipped her off and left.

That little bitch, she thought. *Who does she think she is, having me come over and then sniveling away from employing my expert services?*

On a deeper psychological level, Lisbath was bemoaning the apparent loss of Lisa Ipple as a potential blood source. In earlier days, Lisbath was swimming in available blood. Lots of clients, lots of opportunities, with blood flowing freely. But now it was as if the rich woman had suddenly become poor, and she could afford to let none of the vital red liquid slip through her fingers.

She was frightened to the core and beginning to feel active deterioration of her mental faculties. Slips of memory. Inattention while walking and driving. Misunderstanding what people were saying to her.

Too, her terrible dreams began insinuating themselves during some of her more stressful waking moments. She would be late for an appointment and see oxcarts impede her car's path. A baby's cry in a department store would transmute to the horrified scream of a tortured peasant. The smell of her car would from one moment to the next become fetid, like earth saturated with old body fluids.

As Lisbath went to bed on the night of the Ipple fiasco, she became increasingly depressed. She heard Lad scrabbling about in the next room. Her stomach growled noticeably despite her having had a full dinner. Lisbath's body was revolting against her as well—reacting as if it were in drug withdrawal. Most frightening were the small shaking motions evident in both her arms and legs that became more intense at night. She knew on some unspoken level that all of these symptoms were related to her sharply reduced blood intake.

Feeling more alone than ever and scared that she was on a one-way road to an early death, Lisbath hoped that sleep would give her some respite from these searing stressors.

She was wrong.

Lisbath sped down the dark shaft of unconsciousness as if lubricated. Her sufferings forced her back involuntarily to the ancient scene about which she had recently dreamt, rejoining the sordid festivities as an observer and in some way as a spiritual participant.

The countess had just announced the commencement of her rituals, and immediately each servant drifted toward his position. Most of the entourage trudged to a shack some twenty yards distant from the lady's seat. One serf, wearing a grimy brown hat shaped like a bent cylinder, removed the peg securing the primitive latch. He drew the door open and motioned for the rest of the group to enter.

The weak man-slaves began dragging stained, heavy crucifixes toward the clearing in front of the countess' table. The crucifix tails followed tracks in the dirt that had been worn in over the years.

As the crucifixes emerged from the shack, several of the caged women began intense screaming. Their vague ideas of what was to come were beginning to solidify, and fear began careening wildly through their bodies like rats trapped in a tumbling maze of cats and knives.

Another serf brought forth two burlap sacks and set them on the earth beside the lady's stool. From the smaller sack he removed an irregular chunk of cheese, dried meat of some sort wrapped in stained oilcloth, an empty pitcher of over a half gallon's capacity, an apple, and a plank which had been smoothed over with tallow and brine. The serf placed each item on her table as the sovereign's salivary glands began their day's work in earnest.

The larger sack was apparently filled with some kind of equipment. It clanked and thudded as the servant put it beside the table.

The countess placed her hands on the table, pursed her lips, dipped her head momentarily, and then sat erect. This was the signal that she was ready for the initial parade.

Derek the slavemaster moved toward the cage as the chorus of screams intensified. A few of the women were clawing the remaining bark off the bars, oblivious to the shards of wood lodging beneath their fingernails. The raw, animal fear coursing through their veins motivated desperate measures that seemed almost random and certainly fruitless.

A small serf met Derek at the cage's door and inserted the iron key into the lock. The lock opened swiftly, and all the women cowered at the opposite side of the rolling cage. Most were whimpering, some were screaming, some were facing forward in terror and others were burying their faces in the perspiring, shaking backs of others.

The slavemaster's long, hairy arm groped thickly through

the opening, not caring which flesh it grabbed first. A peasant named Eva's futile attempts to scramble through the wall of frightened womanhood plastered to the cage's far wall fell victim to his grasp. Derek tore her out of the cage as splinters accumulated under her thrashing feet.

Two servants clad identically in wrinkled green aprons dragged Eva to a position before the countess. The new slave's fetal position was unacceptable, so the pair began to lift and spread her for her ladyship to view.

Each man took one wrist and lifted. As she was brought up, Eva's brown hair began to flail, and the woman started to kick and scream. Her displayers grabbed her ankles, brought them down hard on the packed, moist dirt, and stood her on her feet.

The captive began to curse the countess in a low but quite loud, broken voice, and the serf on her right rammed his fist across her mouth. Blood began to flow rapidly down her chin and onto her torn peasant blouse, curling over her breast and eventually sliding haltingly down her abdomen.

"Show me more!" demanded the countess. She shifted her position slightly.

With a perceptible gleam in his eye, Derek clomped over to the spread-eagle victim and grabbed the front of her blouse. He looked toward the countess, who gave him an immediate nod of approval.

As he jerked the material down, it tore across the back of Eva's neck. Derek's rough ring sliced an angled, reddening path from the area between the girl's breasts down to the top of her skirt.

The slavemaster tore the blouse to the side as he stepped back, refusing to let go. Eva's struggling resistance intensified, but it only served to jiggle her one exposed breast wildly from side to side. The woman had mothered and suckled three children over the past five years, and her breasts sagged and wobbled like an old man's shaved scrotum.

"No! Do not lead with this one!" yelled the irritated noble. Her first was always to be plump, firm, and packed with luscious fluids. "Derek, why such a poor, poor choice? Do you not value your position, my boy?"

The slavemaster felt fear and anger at the same time. All the years he had taken care of the countess' whims, he had done so deferentially and with care. But he was getting old and, despite his earlier fantasies, Derek believed that his countess would never acquiesce to his sophomoric advances. He had started not to care, and this lack of vigor and ardor was becoming problematic.

Over the years, the countess had seen Derek's wishes in his eyes and in his postures, and it was laughable to her. But it wasn't politic to let on that her aging puppy would soon be discarded like an old shoe, particularly when he knew the rituals so well. Especially since all the other slaves and serfs feared him deep into their bones. Derek was useful and at the same time ridiculous.

"Yes, M'Lady. I will find you a good one. I am sorry." He bowed as he backed away, deferentially facing the countess for several rearward steps.

Returning slowly to the cage, the slavemaster shoved a long stick hard through the bars. He scattered the collection with the flailing stick as one would poke through a sack of coins in search of the shiniest one.

"Lie down, bitches!" he screamed. Most of the women dropped immediately to the floor, but two of them remained standing. It was clear defiance, and this angered the slavemaster. But it piqued his interest as well.

One of the two was a red-haired beauty with fine breasts and deep pink lips. Ghial's legs were strong as they pressed her body away from the slavemaster. Seeing this and her remarkable musculature led to Derek's choice of Ghial as his prime subject.

He pointed his wooden probe at her as in later centuries his descendants would point rifles at their prey. Ghial oriented like a stunned deer. Her stare transmuted slowly from unstable, riveting fear back to the defiance she had felt moments ago. True hopelessness had emboldened her.

Derek grinned as Ghial's hand began to reach for the end of his stick. She folded her fingers around it and the slave-master began to pull her toward him, a staring fish caught on his terrible fishing pole.

As Ghial began to emerge from the cage, the remaining women cackled among themselves like feeding birds disturbed from their meal by the scent of a snake. This frightened cacophony was punctuated by nervous laughter and whimpering.

Despite the girl's apparent compliance, an obedient serf bound Ghial's hands behind her back. Derek led her to the display area as the countess looked up from her food.

"Better, my boy," said the countess as she began her survey.

Ghial had planted her feet firmly on the dirt and had resolved to deny the countess even the smallest satisfaction of a whimper.

Foolish girl.

Somehow, even in her unconsciousness, Lisbath knew that the girl's throat would burn hellishly by morning's end. Her sleep moved almost grudgingly away from the countess' arena and toward more pedantic imagery. Lisbath's waking this morning would still find her bathed in sweat, but at least she would not be sick to her stomach.

Nineteen

G-Man Haberdeen couldn't predict when Ilse Blücher would be released from the hospital, and he wanted to interview her ASAP anyway. He decided to head over to Queen of Angels to talk to her there. Right after his afternoon coffee break.

He reviewed his notes from his talk with that bitch Gomez at the registry and the phone call that eventually got him hooked up with Ms. Neaton. He thought about the no-payoff setup with his girlfriend Lisa. It seemed like that whole thing was a waste of time.

Still, fresh from his caffeine buzz and mere hours from quitting time, the G-Man was actually in a pretty good mood. He snapped into a parking spot right by the Queen's emergency entrance red zone but left enough room for arriving ambulances to back up to the sliding glass doors.

Haberdeen even waved and cracked something like a smile to the admitting clerk as he sauntered through the ER waiting room. He walked right through the middle of a waiting family whose drunken patriarch, now being examined by the doc in charge, had blundered out of a second-story window.

He took the elevator to the fifth floor. As he turned the corridor's corner, Haberdeen saw the nurse's station with its donated flower pots, innumerable files, multi-line phones, and wheeled, ergonomic chairs. He went directly to 5A and was displeased to see that Mrs. Blücher's room was only semi-private. There was an old woman with a softly beeping IV sleeping in bed 5B near the window. This could interfere with his interview, so before Mrs. Blücher could see him, the G-Man went out to the nurses' station to ask some questions.

In his police-brusque fashion, Haberdeen asked, "Is the floor supervisor here?"

The male Filipino ward clerk answered, "I am the clerk. What do you need, sir? Can I help you?"

"Listen: I need to speak with . . ." he pulled his black flip-notebook out of his shirt pocket and riffled the pages to the last one with anything written on it ". . . Miss Neaton."

"She is in her office. I'll get her, sir."

The clerk got up and walked to the rear of the island-like station. He knocked on the one closed door and entered through it almost immediately. In less than ten seconds, a handsome, brown-haired woman in a nurse's uniform and blue sweater followed him out.

"I'm Linda Neaton. Are you Detective Haberdeen?" She hoped he was. She wanted to sink her teeth into this story.

"Yes. I need to speak to Mrs. Blücher, but there's another lady in the room. Can you get her out?"

"A visitor?"

"No, no. In the next bed."

"Well, no, sir, we can't do that. She is a patient with the same rights that Mrs. Blücher has."

Haberdeen said, "I need to talk to Blücher alone. Can you set it up for me?"

"Well, I really can't. Neither patient is ambulatory."

"Shit."

"Wait a minute. Was Mrs. Pope sleeping?"

"You mean the old woman? Yes."

"Then you really don't have anything to worry about. She's on enough medication to keep a horse dead asleep during an earthquake."

"Okay, okay. Good. By the way, do you have anything new on Mrs. Blücher's condition?"

"We got some test results back, but the doc hasn't been in to interpret them."

"She's got a doctor and a nurse-midwife?" asked Haberdeen.

"Yes, remember? Dr. D'Angostino is the one who admitted her. Nurse-midwives don't admit their own patients."

"Okay. Please ask D'Angostino to call me when he gets in."

"It's a 'she.' And I can ask."

"What?" Haberdeen didn't understand the implied hesitation.

"Dr. D'Angostino doesn't like cops. She complains about them every chance she gets. It's 50-50 whether she'll call you or not. You'd better plan on calling *her*. You know how doctors are."

Haberdeen made himself a note to follow up with this Dr. D'Angostino and walked back to 5A. When he got to the door, he noticed that Frau Blücher was reading a magazine. *Good. She's up*, he thought. The detective didn't notice that the magazine was upside-down.

"Mrs. Blücher? I need to talk to you."

She had been staring intently at a magazine picture of an ocean liner in distress. Hearing Haberdeen, she snapped her head up and saw a huge man with his hands on his hips. She was startled by this blunt approach. Haberdeen immediately had her full but very bleary-eyed attention. She was shaken and confused.

"*Ya?*" she asked.

"Mrs. Blücher, I am Detective Haberdeen from the police. I need to ask you some questions."

This was severely confusing for the lady. What was a policeman doing here—in a hospital—asking her questions? What could she tell him? Maybe something was wrong with Erich!

"My husband? Is something wrong *mit* my husband?"

"No, no, Mrs. Blücher. Nothing like that. I need to ask you about Nurse Milliken."

More confusing than ever. Milliken wasn't a criminal—she'd

brought the Blücher child into the world! What was all this?

"I don't understand," said Mrs. Blücher.

"Do you know who she is? Lisbath Milliken?"

"Of course. She delivered *mein* baby." Ilse was stressed, and the Austrian language bled through.

Haberdeen said, "Good. When she was delivering your baby, did she do anything unusual?"

"How would I know? I was on my back giving birth! How can you ask such a question? *Was machst du?*"

"Mrs. Blücher, I'm interested in anything—anything at all. Did you see anything you did not expect?"

Ilse was beginning to calm down a bit and to think more clearly. "Well, maybe. When I looked up once down between my legs, the nurse had blood on her face. I thought, I did not know blood would splash so much! But what do I know? I am no nurse."

Haberdeen's mind began to spin. He had never heard of anything like this. It was the first true anomaly he'd picked up in all his interviews. Of course, this could just be a simple splash. But it was consistent with part of the rabbi's daughter's story. Things began to click in his thinking. He made a note in his pad.

"Tell me more about the blood on her face, please."

"I don't know. It was just something I did not expect. She seemed to lick her lips *und* maybe her fingers. Maybe I saw wrong. I was in pain *und nur* waiting for my baby."

Haberdeen's fingers were flying, scribbling everything as verbatim as he could manage. His concentration was intense. "What else did you see? Was there blood on her mask?"

"She did not wear a mask. She was very natural," said the weakening Mrs. Blücher.

"Was there blood somewhere else?"

"Now, please, mister. This is making me sick. Leave me alone. I don't feel so good. That's all I saw except my baby. My baby is all right, yes?"

"I have no idea, Mrs. Blücher. You'll have to ask the nurse. I am just asking about the nurse who worked with you. Thank you for your time. Good-bye."

Haberdeen pivoted around and left without ceremony.

Ilse turned on her side, silently cursed her developing headache, and shut her eyes hard.

◆ ◆ ◆

Maybe Judd was right, thought Haberdeen during his ride back to the station. *There may be more to this than meets the eye.*

With no medical knowledge at all, the detective's first step was to find out whether what the Blücher woman had reported was unusual or not. Since his notes included the name of Dr. D'Angostino as Ilse Blücher's admitting physician, he decided to make contact ASAP. After a fast pit stop to the police station's men's room, Haberdeen went straight to his desk and picked up the phone to call her.

Maria D'Angostino had been a physician for 40 of her 66 years of life. She was a mildly religious woman—always wore a crucifix and went to church regularly—yet she had a mean streak. Some said she was secretly vicious to other doctors whom she didn't like, but those charges were never openly discussed. Her close-cropped gray hair was always pinned down with several thick, black bobby pins that looked like tiny worms making their way randomly through her hair.

Haberdeen's phone call was answered by the doc's front-office woman. Her voice was very calm. "Dr. D'Angostino's office."

"This is Detective Haberdeen of Bridgeport PD. I need to speak to Dr. D'Angostino."

"She's with a patient. May I take a—one minute—yes, yes, she is just done. I'll see if she can talk now." Haberdeen could hear the patient thanking the doctor in the background. D'Angostino was sliding her stethoscope back into her white lab coat's tremendous pocket as she saw her secretary's gesture.

"This is Dr. D'Angostino. I understand you have a question about a nurse. This is a one-doctor-plus-front-office operation; I don't *have* a nurse." Haberdeen picked up a very slight accent.

"No, Doctor. I need to ask you about a Lisbath Milliken, a nurse-midwife. Do you know who I'm talking about?"

Dr. D'Angostino knew immediately. Bridgeport had only a couple of these rare specialists. D'Angostino thought of them as throwbacks to caveman days. She always imagined women squatting in the fields with another peasant catching the baby and wiping it off with straw. An unglamorous image, to be sure.

"Yes. As a matter of fact, one of her patients is under my care at this time. This happens sometimes when a doctor is not in charge." D'Angostino knew from the G-Man's tone that he was a cop. Despite her distaste for the police, the physician didn't feel she needed any other verification before releasing basic information.

"I know she's one of yours. She's in Q of A. Ilse Blücher." Haberdeen continued. "What's this Milliken like?"

"I've only run across her a couple of times, but my office did put in a call to her just after I admitted Ms. Blücher. She seemed to know what she was doing. But she has the same limits any nurse has. What's the connection?"

"Doctor, are you aware of anything unusual about this woman? Either now or in the past?"

Dr. D'Angostino thought for a moment while Haberdeen folded and unfolded a paper clip over his desk. "Nothing that I know of. She's quite officious, you know. But for a medical person who works essentially independently like she does, this is really *de rigueur*."

"*De* what?" Haberdeen's formal education had ended a week before his clumsy trudge across the high school stage.

"Just normal. Par for the course. Listen, Detective. Is that all you need? I've got patients waiting."

"No, ma'am. Just one more thing. When a woman gives birth, how often does blood come out? How often does it splash onto the face of the doctor? Or the nurse?"

"Blood flows commonly during birth. The smarter OB/GYN's wear plastic over their operating room booties to keep the stuff from getting in their shoes. It can get all over the floor. But it doesn't really *splash* or *shoot* unless they forget to double-clamp the umbilicus. No, the chances are remote. A tiny stream may escape during the umbilical cut, but it's standard practice to cover the lightly pressurized segment before piercing it. It's really nothing. Negligible."

The G-Man interrupted. "How much is negligible? A teaspoon? A quart? How much? And how far could it squirt?"

"These are odd questions, Detective. Anyway, unless it's really a botched job, we're talking about a few cc's. Maybe a few tablespoons at most."

"*And how far could it squirt?*" Haberdeen was relentless. But that was his job.

"Perhaps a meter in the most extreme of circumstances. But that's about as common as a man becoming pregnant. Why are you asking?"

"The nurse reportedly had a face full of blood, and it was allegedly all over her arms, too. Is that normal?"

"Absolutely not. Are you sure about this?"

"No, ma'am. Just checking my sources and information, that's all. And, oh, I need to ask one more thing: Does a doctor or nurse wear a mask when doing a birth?"

"S.O.P. these days is to don a mask as well as plastic protective glasses. Just in case there is a fluid splash. They dress just like you see the paramedics decked out when they're servicing a really bad car accident."

"What would justify someone not wearing a mask?"

"I wouldn't expect to see anyone without a mask except maybe in some developing country with primitive medical standards. It's just not done."

"Thank you, Doctor. I hope I can call on you again if I need to. And if you think of anything or run across anything about Milliken, please call me here at the station.

"And by the way," Haberdeen continued, "this is a confidential investigation. Ms. Milliken must know nothing of it. Okay?"

"Fine. I need to get to my patients now. Good-bye." Her accent seemed to thicken as her patience wore thin. D'Angostino hung up without waiting for a response from the cop.

Arrivaderci, thought Haberdeen as he tossed the remains of the paper clip onto his desk.

Twenty

Something stinks, Haberdeen thought to himself as he pulled away from the Taco Bell and headed back to the police station. He wasn't referring to the six fragrant items in his steaming lunch bag, either.

The G-Man went over what he had so far. First, there were the two separate calls to the station about the Milliken woman. These carried only moderate weight because both were second-hand information, and ultimately from kids at that. Still, the Shapiro girl seemed to be reasonably accurate in her report of Milliken's activities at the Boating birth.

He reviewed mentally his exchange with that self-serving bitch Gomez. He and she got along like oil and water, and Gomez was the oil that slipped all around his questions. But this result didn't cut either way, really. Was she covering for Milliken, or was she just watching her own company's ass? Or maybe she really didn't know anything. The Gomez question still remained open.

Haberdeen had enlisted the covert aid of one of Gomez's troops. He still hadn't called in his cards with that that little Susie Rime nurse who was on the steps at Dickinson's. The veiled threats he had made if she didn't help out would fade with time, so Haberdeen thought he needed to activate this confederate ASAP. He'd call her before the end of the day.

It struck Haberdeen as elementary that if the Milliken suspect (yes, she had finally gained *suspect* status in his thinking) was one of the bad guys, then she probably did the dirties with more than just one of her clients. As he turned into the driveway of the police parking garage, he decided to check on some of the woman's other recent birth mothers. He'd look into that right after his Mexican food gobblefest.

Even though it was just forming, the icing on this particular cake was Blücher's verbal report of blood all over Nurse Milliken's face and arms. Dr. D'Angostino's report implied that such an event would have been a "remote" occurrence. The G-Man was committed firmly to finding out just how remote this scene was in Lisbath's questionable wake of birth jobs.

As he slipped into one of the officer parking spaces, Haberdeen hit the parking berm a little harder than usual—a sure sign of deep concentration. It was okay; nobody saw the bang, anyway, and the car really was a junker. The G-Man lifted his lunch and his Tabasco bottle, then lurched out the door.

He walked toward his desk and began to remove his overcoat. "You're working that Milliken case, right, G-Man?" asked Officer Humberto Moraga.

"Yeah. I'm right in the middle of it."

"Health department guys came by a couple of hours ago and wanted to talk to Stevenson. They said something about blood."

This piqued Haberdeen's interest nicely. "What did Stevenson say?"

"When he finally got in he told 'em that you were working a nurse-midwife case. He said you need to call them."

"After the tacos, Beaner."

As Moraga saw and smelled the Taco Bell bag, he got excited. "Hey, man! You brought me lunch?"

"No way, José. All for me."

"Pleeez, *Señor*. I am but a poor starving public servant."

Haberdeen dug into his bag and threw Humberto a squishy bean burrito.

Immediately upon his return from a productive bathroom visit, Haberdeen called the number on the State of Connecticut

Health Department business card. It was for the local Bridgeport office. He asked for and was connected directly to Deputy Peters.

"Peters."

"This is Detective Haberdeen of the Bridgeport PD. You came by today?"

"Yes, Detective. Hold on a minute." Peters opened his briefcase and brought out the file.

"Here's the background. We received an Infocard from a Dr. Coop Gold, who practices in Bridgeport. As you probably know, in certain circumstances a doctor must send us one of these Infocards—like in the case of gunshot wounds."

"Yeah," answered Haberdeen. He knew all about them.

"Well, another condition requiring an Infocard is when a woman has a temp of 100.4° or higher and certain other symptoms within ten days postpartum. That means after birth."

"Go on." Haberdeen picked his teeth.

"Dr. Gold has a patient named Smithson—Lucinda AKA Cindy Smithson—who met these criteria four days ago. The kicker is that Smithson had a nurse-midwife at her in-home birth. That's pretty unusual these days even though nurse-midwives are a legitimate segment of the medical community."

Dr. Peters continued. "Anyway, Smithson's been admitted to Sisters of Mercy on the east side. I checked this morning. She's up to 101° and she's septicemic with *Streptococcus pyogenes*."

"What the fuck does that mean?" Haberdeen didn't mince words with anybody. He needed his information in a way he could understand it.

"Well, Detective, it means that she's a very sick woman. More significantly, it means that she's got puerperal fever. That's what they used to call 'childbed fever' because it was passed inadvertently from woman to woman—by the midwives."

"And?" The G-Man was getting antsy; this technical stuff didn't help him at all, but the midwife reference was very intriguing. He sat up just a little straighter.

"We thought it was all but wiped out decades ago. Like when people learned to wash their hands after treating a sick person. It's from the same bacterium that carried scarlet fever when that was in vogue."

In vogue, thought Haberdeen. *Christ.*

"Normally we wouldn't involve the police. It's not like someone is doing anything illegal. But in this case we've got confluent factors." Peters shifted the phone to his other ear and removed a pre-addressed, postage-paid pink card from the file on his desk. "We got another Infocard a week ago from a doc working out of County General. One La-TaKeisha Jeffers showed up with the same symptoms."

"Don't tell me," said Haberdeen. "Nurse-midwife Lisbath Milliken."

"Bingo, Detective."

"Okay. Pretty meaty. Peters, what else can you tell me? I need anything you've got."

"Right now, nothing," said Peters. "We just put this all together. I'm planning to take a trip to the registry out of which Milliken works to get more on her."

"Hold your horses, Peters. I'm on this, and I don't need any jurisdiction wars. How about staying out of it for a couple of days and let me do my job."

"Sure, sure, Detective. I've got plenty to do without spending time on this. But you need to know that this has the potential to hurt lots of people. Can you imagine an outbreak of scarlet fever in Connecticut? That's what we're facing. So I need you to keep in touch with me daily. *Daily*. Got that?"

"No prob."

Peters continued, "And I have to deal with the hospitals about this. But I'll keep it as low-key as I can. I'll leave the registry and the nurse-midwife to you for now."

"Okay. Deal. I'll call you tomorrow."

"I need to count on that," stressed Peters.

"I *said* I'd call you tomorrow." Haberdeen was a little irritated, but he was too excited about all this new information to waste time getting into a pissing contest with this health department deputy.

"Talk to you then," said Peters as he hung up.

Haberdeen made some fast, weighty notes on a yellow pad.

🝆 🝆 🝆

La-TaKeisha Jeffers was lying on a makeshift bed in the first-floor ER isolation room at County General. The staff had placed six mattresses on the infrequently-polished floor in a 3x2 configuration, then covered them with industrial-strength plastic sheeting and several layers of linens. Five orderlies had rolled the blimp-like new mother onto this pad from the fork lift pallet upon which she had been delivered to the facility. They had to drag the pallet along the ER admitting floor until it was before the sliding-glass door of Isolation.

Two of the nurses had read recently about the case of one Michael Hebranko at New York's St. Luke's-Roosevelt Hospital. They were discussing the article that said that he had been removed from his apartment through a window by a crane, and that the 1,100-pounder had also been brought to the hospital on a forklift. As they talked, they stared toward La-TaKeisha's compound.

Normally a patient being admitted to County is taken directly to one of the wards on floors 3 through 6, but there was no way the 625-plus pound, wildly thrashing and screaming Ms. Jeffers could be loaded onto anything but the freight elevator, and a trip from the ER isolation room across the hospital to the freight lift was incomprehensible. So there she lay, sick, disgusting, loud, and sick like a hippo with fiery, melting innards.

The young ER clerk was assigned to go by the room once each hour with a can of Ozium air freshener and a pail. This despite the fact that the isolation door was kept closed.

Ms. Jeffers' assigned physician, Dr. Salah El-Kareem, had sent in the pink Infocard to County Health once he saw suspicious vital signs on her chart and the *Strep* report arising from a vaginal smear. In his original medical training in the Arab countries, puerperal fever was slightly more common, but this case was still remarkable and of course a necessarily reportable event.

♦ ♦ ♦

So what the hell is all of this? G-Man thought to himself. *What would allegedly licking blood (or at least having it all over one's face) have to do with a disease? What's the Milliken link here?*

It was just about time to talk to the woman herself. But not before he laid a little groundwork.

Haberdeen asked one of the more experienced female police dispatchers to call Dickinson's, act like one of Susie Rime's friends, and to ask for the girl. He didn't want Gomez to know what was going on, yet he needed to develop this Nurse Rime—to cash in his cards—right now.

The dispatcher called the registry. Nurse Rime happened to be in, and Sharona just handed her the phone without a second thought.

"Hello, Susie. I'm from the Bridgeport Police Department and this is a confidential call. Can anyone hear your part of this conversation?"

All of a sudden, Susie's uncomfortable reaction to Haberdeen's powerful solicitation at the registry a few days ago flooded her with fear. She turned red as a vial of fresh blood. Fortunately, Sharona was staring at printed staffing tables on her desk and didn't see Rime's flushing reaction.

Susie really didn't know what to do. She felt violated or trapped; she had promised that big detective that she'd help—she felt accurately like she had been forced into it—but she didn't really want to comply. Now she figured she had no choice.

"Hold on a second," she said into the receiver. "Sharona, can I take this call in your meeting room?"

"Sure, dear."

"I'm going to change phones. Hold on a minute." Susie put the call on hold, walked into the meeting room, closed the door quietly, punched the flashing line, and picked up the receiver.

"Okay, I'm on. What do you want? Are you working for that detective?"

"I'm calling on behalf of Detective George Haberdeen. Hold on a moment and I'll put him on the line."

Oh, great.

"Susie? This is Detective Haberdeen. Do you remember?"

"Yes." She shook her head. This wasn't going to be good.

"I've got a job for you. An important one," the G-Man said forcefully.

Susie leaned back against the desk.

"I need you to get into the registry's records. I need the names, addresses, and phone numbers of every one of Lisbath Milliken's clients for the past six months. And I need the stuff fast. Can you get that for me?"

Susie knew she could do it, but she wasn't sure whether or not it was ethical. She held on silently for just a little too long for Haberdeen's patience.

"Listen, Miss Rime. We had an agreement—you made an agreement with the law. And this is the time that I need you to execute your agreement. Now, when will I get those records?"

Susie's relative naïveté had created the original opening for the bully cop to coerce her into spying for him, and she was no better off now than she was at their original meeting. She felt she had no choice, and figured that anything was ethical as long as it was for the police, anyway.

"Okay. I'll get them. I don't know when; it depends on who's around."

"I need them within a day. Got it?"

"I'll try."

"Where does Milliken live?"

"I don't know her address. I've never been to her place."

"Then you need to get that for me too." The G-Man knew he could find out easily with the information he as a cop had at hand, but he wanted to stress his control over this girl.

"Oh, man! Do I have to? That's such a . . . wait a minute! I know that she lives in the Yankee Pines apartments somewhere in Bridgeport! She said that once, and it seemed funny to me that she would live in an apartment building with a name. Corny."

"That's good enough for me; I can find her. Now, what's your home number? And if you have a pager, I'll need that too."

She gave them, feeling reluctant.

"Call me the moment the stuff's in your hands. And this absolutely must be *confidential*. You need my number too. Got a pencil?"

Susie opened the conference room desk drawer and found one rolling around. She grabbed a piece of scratch paper. "What's the number?" she asked. She felt defeated, but at the same time she felt oddly empowered as an Agent of the Police.

♦ ♦ ♦

Haberdeen sat at his desk, planning his interrogation strategy for Milliken. Detective-sergeant Stevenson walked by and stared at his subordinate for a moment. He threw the latest issue of the newspaper onto Haberdeen's desk. The G-Man was startled.

"Feast your eyes, G-Man," said Stevenson. Haberdeen picked up the paper as Stevenson continued toward his own office.

On the front page, left column, was an article by reporter Big T. She had squeezed it out of the information she was able to glean from Coroner Pelt. She had written it right after Pelt performed the autopsy on the woman who was dead in the gutter at the school. The piece was predictably sensationalistic.

SCARLET FEVER IN OUR MIDST!
Epidemic Threatens Connecticut Seaboard; No Link to Terrorism

By Constance Teitelmeier

Bridgeport County Coroner William Pelt revealed today that Ms. Terry Audlin, the woman found dead beside Juniper Elementary School, had been the victim of scarlet fever, also known in years past as The Red Death.

The beet-red corpse was lying in the gutter beside the school. Its smell led playing children to alert school authorities.

Playground supervisor Francine Bowles fainted at the sight of the body.

Coroner Pelt pronounced the body dead at the scene. Later at the morgue, an autopsy revealed that Ms. Audlin's body was riddled with scarlet fever.

When asked if others might be threatened by this dread disease, the coroner admitted that scarlet fever has the ability to spread like wildfire under the right conditions.

Asked if terrorism might be responsible for Audlin's infection, the coroner stated that it was "extremely unlikely" since the disease is normally transmitted through physical touch or caught because of unsterile medical techniques.

Precautions the public should take include staying away from anyone with an obvious strawberry-colored rash.

"Shit," said Haberdeen as he threw down the paper. He didn't need to read any further. "We're going to get calls for weeks on this."

Then the possible connection hit him. That Smithson woman had that *Strep* something that was related to scarlet fever. And the Jeffers woman has the same thing. Now this Audlin corpse reportedly died of Scarlet.

Crap.

Haberdeen scribbled some notes on his next fresh notepad page, then an additional fast but important note on the very last page of his notepad—the page he reserved for follow-up tasks. It read,

AUDLIN—NEWSPAPER—MILLIKEN PT?

He stuffed the paper's front page into his top middle drawer and suited up for his confrontation with Lisbath.

Twenty-One

The G-Man's technique when cultivating a suspect was to make an initial approach with light-to-moderate threats, then watch and wait for the suspect to mess up. He decided that this should work well with Milliken, even though he wasn't really sure exactly what her crimes might be.

He left the station at 7:15 p.m. Sunday night, drove at a leisurely pace, stopped on the way to talk with one of his buddies in a black-and-white, and arrived at the Yankee Pines apartments in a light drizzle at about 7:55. The mailboxes near the front door all had apartment numbers and surnames; Milliken was in 304. The elevator ride was noisy with the rattle of cold cables, and the rising box was noticeably humid.

Despite his being a large man, Haberdeen could walk quietly when needed. He padded over to 304 and just listened. Through the door he heard a country-western variety show on the TV and a couple of yaps of what was probably a small dog. No conversation, no whistling teapots, no microwave timers, no yelling kids. So far, so good.

Knowing that he would be fully in control of this interview, Haberdeen felt a sense of calm about him. He was breathing very slowly and comfortably.

He knocked firmly on the door. Lisbath was startled; she rarely had visitors, and certainly never had had one unannounced at night. She pulled her robe tight over her bulk and just sat still. Haberdeen's second set of knocks were harder, faster, and louder. Milliken couldn't ignore them.

"Yes?" she asked as she walked toward the door. Yankee Pines, built in the older days of trust-your-neighbor and the good old boys, had neither security chains nor peepholes for the apartment doors. So Milliken's only clues as to who this "late night" visitor was were auditory.

"Lisbath Milliken?"

She was shaken. A strange voice, yet it knew her name. Not just the last name on the mailbox; her actual name. At night. Unannounced. Haberdeen's technique was already beginning to pay off.

"Who is it? What do you want?"

"Miss Milliken, I am Detective Haberdeen of the police. May I speak with you?" Professional; clear; temporarily non-threatening.

The police? Lisbath thought to herself. Millions of thoughts jangled through her head. But this man was standing outside the door, and he wasn't going away. Even though they had already been talking through the door, the G-Man knocked again. It was very scary for Lisbath. She felt rushed and out of control.

Lad was right there, right now. He was barking and scratching at the inside of the door. He projected comfort and control to Lisbath. But not really enough to get her to calm down.

"All right. One moment." She took a second to try to compose herself. Visions of jail bars and blood and restraints and public hangings flew through her head as she reached for the brass doorknob.

"Miss Milliken, I need you to restrain your dog."

"Lad? He won't hurt you."

"Restrain the dog before you open the door, please." Haberdeen's voice was forceful.

"Gracious! *Okay, okay.*" Lisbath was happy for the additional few seconds of privacy as she began to lead Lad into the bedroom. Lad had resisted initially, glaring at her with eyes that flashed briefly red. She heard a growl from Lad that had not come through the dog's throat. For a moment, Lisbath was motionless, a statue of a woman walking a dog in her own apartment. Then Lad decided to go along with the temporary sequestration and entered the bedroom of his own free will. Lisbath closed the door quietly. She did not want to disturb Lad any more than she already had.

She went over and turned off the TV, then walked with tiny, delaying steps over to the door. "Laddie's locked up," she said as Lisbath opened her castle to the attacking knight. Haberdeen ran a quick visual survey/inventory of the apartment as soon as he gained entrance. Lisbath's place had few pictures; those that did grace the walls had mostly old, pastoral scenes. The furniture was from the thirties or forties, but it was clean. Crisp, white linen covers lay over the arms of the soft chairs and the couch. There was an old 19" TV with no apparent remote. The radio, with a seventies analog tuner, was set to the only country station in the Bridgeport area. The bedroom door was closed with a whining dog behind it.

Haberdeen peered through the entrance to the kitchen and noted that there appeared to be no dishes on the counter. The odors he picked up were disinfectant, dog hair, and cinnamon.

Lisbath sat down first, then spoke. "Have a seat, Mr. Haberdeen." She gestured to the thick, gray-upholstered chair. Lisbath had seated herself on her favorite spot on the couch, as was evident from its indentations.

As he had learned to do whenever he was in dark pants, Haberdeen swept the chair with his hand before seating himself. He had picked up enough pet hair in his day to make this grooming trick a reflex.

Despite her bulk, Nurse Milliken sat up with impeccable posture, as if she were in a straight-back chair. Haberdeen saw it as a reflection of her feeling stressed, and he was smiling inwardly as he anticipated an easy time with the interview. The fact was that Lisbath's stiffened posture was actually the prim nurse's normal public comportment.

Haberdeen opened his notebook to a fresh page and scribbled

the date, time, location, and suspect Milliken's name. He then leaned back. In a move calculated to suggest the superiority of his role as The Police, G-Man Haberdeen deliberately let his shoe bang the coffee table as he crossed his legs. He noticed that there were nursing magazines and *Reader's Digest* issues stacked neatly on the two corners nearest him.

The detective's actions and body language said, *This is my show and you are under my control.* All of this was standard choreography for what the police call an "interview" but which translates functionally as a suspect's interrogation.

"Miss Milliken, I understand you are a nurse-midwife. Is that correct?" (Haberdeen knew full well she was, but this technique got the suspect talking, answering easy questions, and in the rhythm of question/fast response.)

"Yes, sir," Lisbath answered respectfully. *This man is really a dolt,* she thought.

"And that you work for Dickinson's Nurse Registry. Is that correct?"

"Well, sir, I don't actually work for them, *per se.* They solicit and obtain employment for me—broker my nursing services, so to speak. As a result, they take a percentage of my income."

This was really getting off track for Haberdeen. He wasn't interested in the business relationship. Still, the woman was talking rather easily, and this boded well for the remainder of the interview.

"Fine. Now, tell me who your current clients are."

"That's privileged information." Lisbath's posture moved from stiff to virtually catatonic, and her bowels took their first steps toward full roil.

"Miss, I came here to get information I need. I can get it here if you cooperate, or I can have you come with me to the station and give it to me there. Once again, who are your clients?"

Haberdeen waited. The dog produced a strange whine behind the door, then fell silent.

Milliken began to simmer, but at the same time to divine more of the G-Man's purpose. She decided she'd better answer, but she was not happy about it.

"Well, it depends on what you mean by 'current.' I have helped hundreds of women over the years, and from time to time they will call me again to help out or maybe for some advice. And while most of my charges are pregnant, I am from time to time called upon to provide nursing in other areas."

The bitch is being cagey now, thought Haberdeen. *This may not be a walk in the park after all.*

"Come on, lady. I mean who are you working for now? Which pregnant women are paying you to do your services for them?"

"Well," said Milliken as her dander began its rise, "why don't you just get that from Dickinson's if you know so much?"

The G-Man had far too much practice being put on the defensive to let this suspect get the better of him, especially during *his* interview. He asked, "Do you want to get your coat?"

Without another word, Milliken went to her table and brought a very small three-ring binder. She provided this intruder with the information, and he wrote down every detail. Only after getting this basic information did Haberdeen's teeth begin to appear sharpened.

"Miss Milliken, there are other clients who reportedly are yours but who you didn't include. Do you or do you not service Ms. Blücher and Ms. Boating?"

"Yes, Mr. Haberdeen. But they are not current clients—that's why I did not include them in the list. They have already had their babies."

Lisbath was furious. *Where the hell did this man get those names? What business is it of his?*

Her "already had their babies" ploy was fruitless. "Ms. Milliken, I have information that both of these women are now ill. Why are they sick?"

"Linda Boating was sick even before I got to her. And she is no longer my charge; the birth is over, and it is the *birth* that I do, Mr. Haberdeen. That is *all* I do, *Mr. Haberdeen.*" Lisbath's voice was getting louder with each word; her increasing stress and irritation were easily obvious.

She continued, "Mrs. Blücher? No, I didn't know she was sick. Because I'm *done* with her. Do you understand?" Lisbath's blood pressure was rising.

Lad was now making a loud scratching sound and was growling at the inside of the bedroom door, and Milliken felt somewhat distracted. "It's all right, Laddie," she called toward the closed door. "Mommy's fine."

The G-Man ignored the dog. "Do you or did you have a patient named. . ." he checked his notebook for what he had scrawled about the newspaper article ". . . Terry Audlin?"

"Terry? Well, yes. I suppose I did." Lisbath was forthcoming with this because she had not taken any blood from Ms. Audlin. There hadn't been any time to do it. So she saw no harm in this minor acquiescence.

Her sizzle moved up a notch. "Are you just going to ask me about every patient I have had? What is this?"

"Miss Milliken, let's talk about your work with Linda Boating. You admitted that you did her birth."

"Admitted? *Ad-mitted*? Mr. Haberdeen, a birth is a beautiful, natural thing." Her chins wobbled as she spat indignation. "How can you talk like that to me? What is your problem?" Lisbath was becoming genuinely livid as this man was moving closer to her secrets and being disrespectful and negative all the while.

"Okay, lady. Cut the histrionics." Haberdeen had been doing the local paper's crossword puzzle last weekend and just knew he'd have the chance to use this gem sometime soon. He stiffened in his chair. "Miss Milliken, what happened when Mrs. Boating gave birth?"

"Are you asking me for a medical report? You can read that in her file. I'm *sure* you already have a copy of her file." The *you son-of-a-bitch* that ended the sentence was silent.

"No, not a medical report exactly. Now, let's get down to it." Haberdeen's technique would involve asking initially indirect, open-ended questions. To give the suspect enough rope to hang herself.

"What happened that normally wouldn't happen? What was unusual? What went *wrong*?" he asked.

"*Nothing* went wrong!" screamed Milliken. "The birth was normal, the newborn was healthy, and I don't know what you're *talking* about. Why are you here, anyway? What gives you the right to be here and ask me these horrid questions?"

Lisbath's mind was racing. *How could he know? How could anyone know?* For the last forty years she had always made very, very sure that nobody was watching as she took her warm, red spoils. New conflicts she had to hide grew within Lisbath with frightening rapidity.

"Listen, Milliken." Haberdeen spoke forcefully, his breathing as completely controlled as a stage actor's. "We know about the blood." Of course, the G-Man had only a vague inkling about it, but it was standard interrogation technique to drop a hint implying that the authorities knew everything and watch the suspect squirm and wait for him to fill in the blanks. Seeing this one squirm was going to be fun.

"What in Heaven's name do you mean?" yelled Lisbath. She sprayed hair-thin, jittering streams of saliva as she spoke. "There is always blood at a birth, Detective. Don't try to tell me you have trouble understanding that!"

"Miss Milliken, we have information that you ingested blood at the birth. That you licked the substance deliberately." There. He'd said it. Now for the second barrel:

"And we have a witness."

The beans were spilled, and they splattered all over the floor and scared the shit out of Milliken and caused most of her composure to come crashing down.

Even though Lisbath had seen it coming, she was temporarily dumbfounded by the accusation that hit so very hard and dead center. Her normally greasy underarms became particularly slippery. She flushed as her own precious red liquid rushed into the tiny capillaries all over her puffy cheeks. Last night's dinner was involuntarily tugging downward toward her temporarily clean, white underpants. Lisbath's mind was a jumble of anxiety and ineffectuality.

"Well, Milliken?" shot Haberdeen. "What do you have to say for yourself?" He shifted forward, leaning menacingly as he put one fist on his knee and the other on the coffee table. "Let's have it!"

Lad picked up mean odors from under the door, and his excellent hearing perceived a threat to Mommy. He began to bark and scratch the door violently. His intrusive dog sounds had absolutely no effect on either of the warring humans in the other room.

"I . . . I . . . I don't . . . I don't know what you're talking about!" lied Lisbath. "How can you say such a thing? What proof have you?" Lisbath's emotions were beginning to transmute from fear to anger. What did this stupid man know? How could he begin to fathom what was right—what was important—what was necessary and good and vital? What right did he have to insinuate himself into her life?

"Get out of here!" Lisbath shouted. "You have no right here. I've heard enough from you. Leave. Leave now!" She pointed toward the door, fingertip quivering.

The G-Man had a decision to make. He could continue his interrogation here and now with this out-of-control screamer, he could arrest her and take her in against her will for questioning, or he could temporarily abandon his interview. It was pretty obvious that continuing the questioning at this point would be fruitless.

He chose Door Number 3.

"Miss Milliken, I will be in touch. Do not leave Bridgeport for any reason. Do you understand?"

Lisbath understood on some objective level but had trouble truly fathoming what was happening. "But what if I get an assignment from . . ."

"If you leave town you will become a fugitive and will be arrested," Haberdeen said with deafening finality. He had had it up to here talking with this fat dirtbag.

A FUGITIVE! Lisbath thought. Never in her life had she even come close to running a red light, stealing a paper clip, or *anything*. This was *outrageous*.

But before she could say anything, Haberdeen had stood up and was already heading for the door.

Lad's barking had intensified to a feverish pitch; the neighbors were certain the poor animal was being butchered alive. His extreme roars broke through Lisbath's consciousness and she almost permitted herself to open the bedroom door and let Lad have at the mean man walking out. Almost.

When Lisbath let Lad out, the loyal dog first ran at the door. He bumped against it and knew it was closed. He then jumped to his mistress. Lisbath plopped down on the couch as tears filled her staring eyes. The eyes were fixed on her crisp nurse's cap on the desk. Lad nuzzled her, and Lisbath's hand unconsciously petted the canine who was all but purring.

Lisbath wasn't purring. Lisbath was hurting. Bad.

And she was scheming. Lisbath Milliken was reflexively beginning to draw upon some ancient, frightening karma that had lain dormant for innumerable lifetimes.

Twenty-two

As Lisbath went to bed that Sunday night, several things were troubling her. She hadn't had a day as stressful as this in some time, and the tension and strain made her feel like a lump of lead as she dropped her head to the pillow.

She went over and over every word that had passed between that bastard Haberdeen and herself. *Fugitive*, she thought. *Get your coat. We have a witness.*

She couldn't stand it. Lisbath needed to go somewhere out of this searing consciousness. All of a sudden, the nurse-midwife began to break down. To cry. The world was not treating her fairly, and she had nobody to turn to—not even Lad—for help. She was a woman alone, strangely cursed to pursue blood, and damned for doing it. She was having vicious, frightening nightmares that seemed so real she almost looked for dirt on her sheets upon her return to consciousness. Sometimes her body would be taken over by something, then it would let her go for no apparent reason. Her sister had never been supportive, her father was dead, her mother was dead too for all she knew, and she could call none of her fellow nurses at Dickinson's true friends.

Lisbath needed love food. For most women, chocolate did the deed. But not for Lisbath Milliken.

She decided to get out of bed, go to the refrigerator, and secure a small dollop of her red treasure, just to let it roll around in her mouth and let it dissolve. As she opened the door, Lad immediately scrabbled up to her and began panting.

Lisbath faced down toward the dog. "No, not this time, Laddie. This one's just for me."

Lad began to vibrate and put off enormous heat—enough for Lisbath to feel it on her bare legs. She felt nausea inundate her. Immediately she knew the resolution: Give Lad some, and he would leave her in peace. "Yes, Laddie. Of course," she said.

She took a teaspoonful of the congealed blood from a Tupperware container and placed it in Lad's blood bowl. He attacked it. Like a dog biscuit, it seemed to be enough. Temporarily.

She then took a second dollop with the same teaspoon, slid the stuff under her tongue, tossed the spoon into the sink, and went to bed.

As her salivary enzymes began their work taking some of the precious liquid apart, its unmistakable fragrance wound around her mouth and nostrils and brain. Lisbath's body returned to bed, yet she did not seem to be commanding her limbs. This time, however, it felt good to relinquish control to that strange force.

Automatically, unavoidably, and relentlessly, she fell toward a foul sleep instigated by the blood's life-fragrance. The dreams that seemed so real—such a part of her—began their onslaught.

Lisbath perceived that the area around the countess was heating up. The encroaching, blaring sun was insinuating itself over the ceremonial grounds. Every captured soul in the wooden cage was watching her future fate unfold in the person of the rebellious Ghial.

Vassals tore at her raiment and at her flesh. Ghial had been chosen as the next demonstratée. Her rebellious attitude would ultimately intensify the flames of terror about to lick at her every nerve.

She stood there almost immobile, but her eyes winced involuntarily at each scrabbling assault.

SPECIAL DELIVERY

"Stretch her!" was the countess' command.

Immediately, the two servants closest to the supply sack brought forth ropes the girth of a thumb. Each fastened his rope around one of Ghial's wrists. Derek the slavemaster then cut the original bindings, freeing the poor girl's wrists to be separated by pulls on the newer ropes.

The men placed themselves perhaps three paces on either side of Ghial and began to twist and pull on their ropes. This made the woman's arms rotate in the direction of twist, and at the same time pulled her arms sideways, at shoulder height, as if she were about to be drawn and quartered. Or at least halved.

Ghial's eyes widened as she was stretched. She had never experienced nor expected such an insult to her body, and the increasing strain on her shoulder joints was deeply uncomfortable and in fact moving into painful.

The countess was pleased with the progress of her ceremony and oblivious to the continued shouts and screams of the remaining captives.

As her torturers continued twisting their ropes, Ghial's skin about her shoulders was becoming very, very taut. Her armpits became frighteningly deep as her shoulder and upper arm musculature was insulted with pressures, pulls, and twisting stresses. After a moment, the slavemaster Derek Holdar nodded to pair of serfs and they held fast, watching the tears roll down the young girl's face and seeing her breasts rise and fall with her fast but labored breathing.

Finally, the countess rose. The moment she threw back her stool, the screaming mass in the cage became silent except for the collective gasp that portended the countess' next move.

The noble strode slowly and deliberately toward her prey and, despite the lady's bulk, her movements were fluid and purposeful. She moved to a point directly before Ghial and stared into the girl's face. The countess was looking for fear or at least loathing to spice her moment, but the defiant redhead gave only occasional winces of pain as her upper arms began to separate from their sockets.

The countess now brought out a fine dagger from a sheath hidden in her bodice. The weapon had a carved, ivory handle with images of snakes and ruby-eyed dragons in deep relief. The handle's animal decorations were worn down from years of use. In some of the knife's crevices there was encrusted, brown blood from past employments. There was no thumb guard on the knife, but the blade had a long and deep blood gutter much more pronounced than any other nobleman's dagger had ever included.

"Twist!" ordered the countess, and the rope handlers rotated another couple of turns on their tethers. As they did so, Ghial's eyes filled quickly with tears, and she began to bite her lip and tilt her head back. This excited the countess even more, and the ceremony was clearly progressing as it should.

With the dagger blade glinting in the fully-surfaced sun, the countess moved the finely-sharpened point toward the margin between Ghial's armpit and the beginning of her breast. The soft skin in that area was shimmering with perspiration and nervous, involuntarily shaking. The girl's eyes were bulging as they followed the progress of the dagger's point toward her smooth, heretofore unsullied flesh.

The countess held the dagger at that sweet margin, then readjusted the angle to point the dagger upward and inward toward Ghial's throat. The sovereign smiled, squatted slightly, and in one quick, deft move, thrust the dagger deep into Ghial's flesh, piercing skin and muscle so deeply that metal almost hit bone.

Ghial's scream was blistering and heart-rending. Her body had been penetrated in the painful underarm crevice that was being twisted and pulled; she was degraded and splayed and lost all will to defy her captors in one searing moment of pain.

It took fully four seconds before the blood began to run, but run it did. The countess had sliced a small artery somewhere deep in Ghial's joint, and as it spewed its pressured contents into the new cut space, the artery began to empty the girl.

The rough entry wound first seeped and in a few intensifying seconds had literally started to throw fresh, pulsing blood out of the girl. It came out the dagger's deepening line in Ghial's skin, and as it did, the countess brought her licking mouth to the new feeding hole. The noblewoman dropped to her knees and, as she did so, the serfs dragged Ghial's arms down toward her. The countess's tongue pulsated in her red mouth, and the servants arranged the bleeding girl's arm-hold directly over their mistress. Rising just inches, the countess placed her extruded lips over the slice and bit down. Ghial screamed. The countess began to suck unabashedly, biting at the same time but not enough to restrict the blood flow.

As she sucked, the countess moved her hand between her own thick legs and pressed rhythmically for several seconds, adding sick and monstrous dimensions to her sacrilege.

"Loosen your grips!" mumbled the lady through dripping spills of blood and flesh. The serfs immediately let loose of their ropes, and as they did so, the blood flow from the arteries was freed, and the severed human tubes spat blood like fire hoses.

The countess let the blood fill her gaping mouth; let the increasing flow spill out over her cheeks and all over her face and neck and body. She was becoming warmer with the blood's temperature, but, more importantly, she was becoming hungrier for more. More flavors, more screams, more power to be derived from the young, vivacious womanhood she had so long ago left behind.

She began not only to drink but to suck, gorging herself as it slathered all over her gobbling face and neck. But she

stopped abruptly. *Don't want to spoil our appetite, do we?*
"Good, my boys. Now, the rest."

They abandoned Ghial, leaving her to whimper and bleed alone. She became nothing but refuse in this demon's ménage.

All the servants moved en masse toward the cage. As they approached, the captive women's screams became insane: shouted words without meaning or definition: souls praying and admonishing and begging for humane treatment: pathos personified.

They dragged the women out, one by one. Each was tethered about the neck after her hands were tied; she was then brought to the crucifixion area a few yards behind the display clearing where Ghial lay bleeding.

Each victim was first hit on the side of the head with a leather bag containing a heavy rock. They were hit hard and viciously on the skull, like cattle slammed unconscious by the sledgehammer before they are butchered. But these women were deliberately left conscious. The countess needed to hear their screams—needed to perceive their pain in all its glory as she had her way with their bodies and their body fluids.

One black-haired woman, Magenalene, bled much more than the others. She was placed over the horizontal crucifix, drooling unknowingly, and tied to the wooden stand at the neck, over her shoulders, at her wrists, on her waist, and at her ankles. After this initial lashing, Magenalene's fingers were each hammered with crude iron nails, palms open, into the far extents of the crucifix's wooden crossbars. Her remaining clothes were summarily torn off. All the serfs near her began slapping viciously hard at the bottoms of her feet, her vaginal lips, her stomach, her breasts, and her eyes.

The countess looked on with glee. Yet the true horrors had barely begun.

One of the slaves heaved a foul mixture of cold, filthy water, urine, tallow, and oil from a leather sack over Magenalene's face to ensure that she was conscious, stinking, and aware of what was about to befall her. Her head began to loll from side to side, and she was nauseated as her crucifix was raised so quickly to the vertical.

The wooden torture-stand was sunk into an oft-used bracing hole a few feet from the countess and fully two cubits deep. Magenalene hung there, wet, sweating, fearful to the bone, with blood accumulating under the skin just over each tight leather stricture and draining from her head and brain.

The countess had decided to focus today's festivities on this one. She was fresh, still conscious, not too rebellious, and frightened enough to add gonadal spice to the entire afternoon.

In the meantime, the other serfs performed similar sinister rituals on the remaining group of captured women. They were each restrained on the dirt beside their respective crucifixes, but were not yet attached. Each victim was forced through her own private hell, but the countess paid little attention to them at this time. Her primary focus was Magenalene this month, and the insignificant others would serve mostly as side dishes.

"This is my feeder!" yelled the noblewoman as she faced the black-haired vassal directly. Magenalene's eyes widened quickly, and her disbelief and horror crunched her brow very low over her eye sockets. A trickle of urine slid down her inner thigh.

As the liquid made its tiny yellow splash on the dirt beside the girl's foot, Lisbath had a myoclonic jerk. This shook her out of her hellish sleep, thrusting her into another day of encroaching bewilderment and fear.

Lying on her side and perspiring heavily, she opened her eyes. Lisbath was immediately shocked by the startling, steady stare of Lad. His head was pointed directly at Lisbath's, his front claws insinuated onto the bed. Had this animal simply heard groans in his mistress' sleep, or did he have some connection with the cruel visions crowding Lisbath's uncommanded, unconscious terrors?

The animal's thick tail was straight and stiff, and his breathing was deliberate.

Twenty-three

Monday morning the Bridgeport Police Station was as bustling as ever.

"So, what'd you get?" asked Sergeant Stevenson as Haberdeen headed toward his office. "Is the bitch midwife clean?"

"I don't know," he said, heaving off his coat. "Can't really tell yet. She got defensive toward the end, but I see that all the time."

Haberdeen had come down pretty hard on Nurse Milliken the night before, but it was more technique than anger. You've got to put some heavy pressure on the boat before it'll leak.

"But I know *something's* up, Judd. I just need something more solid to go on. It won't be easy to make her crack unless we can get her down here for more interrogation."

"So all you got was one mad nurse?"

"Well, I got a little. She lives in a basic apartment. She's overweight. Dog named Lad with really strange markings."

Stevenson's eyes aimed upward as he visualized a dog with uneven, multicolored spots.

Haberdeen continued. "Some strange smells in the place, but maybe nurse's places smell weird from disinfectant or something."

Stevenson shrugged as he thought over what he'd just heard. Haberdeen abandoned his plan to go into his own office. Instead he sat down on the desk next to the sergeant.

Something began to tickle Stevenson's thinking a bit.

"George, did you say this bitch calls her dog 'Vlad'?"

"No, *Lad*. Nobody'd name their dog 'Vlad.' No American, anyway. Sounds like some creepy foreign name. How'd you come up with that?" asked Haberdeen. "Your hearing going down the tubes?"

Stevenson admitted, "Maybe because of the movie I saw last night on cable. Some vampire movie. It had a 'Vlad' in it. No, no. It was about a Vlad, or something. I've been thinking about the flick all day today. It was pretty good."

"You some kind of sicko, watching vampire movies all the time?" taunted Haberdeen.

"No, not really. But this thing was supposed to be based on real history."

"Don't tell me they're claiming vampires are part of history. Come on!"

"Hey, G-Man! Don't you ever watch AMC on cable? You know. They give the background on the movies before showing 'em."

"That doesn't make vampires part of history," said Haberdeen.

"Of course not. But they said something about a real Vlad in history and that the movie was based on him or something. I don't know—I wasn't really paying attention to that part. Just that the name 'Vlad' struck me. That's all. Like I said. Creepy." Stevenson folded his arms across his chest.

Haberdeen smiled. "Okay, Dracula. See you later." He got up and went into his office. Stevenson just shook his head.

🜸 🜸 🜸

Lisbath had been jarred out of her night terror. Lad had held her on her bed with his motionless stare for more than a minute, but he had finally backed off and moved into the kitchen. Lisbath finally got the strength to get out of bed. She was unsteady as she made her way to the couch. She sat down, unsure of herself. Lad approached her with an intent stare that, this time, had the calculated effect of calming her. His tail still did not wag. He climbed onto Lisbath's lap. His body heat warmed Lisbath, mixing with her own in a thin veil of sweat mingling between the dog and her skirt. Almost an hour had passed since she had risen. She was far from over that mean detective's "visit" last night. She had been traumatized upon waking. During that entire hour on the couch, Lisbath had moved nary an inch.

Her fearful mind roved haltingly over her predicament. It was excruciating for her. Clearly, the police had somehow gotten information about her private world. For the first time in over a decade, Lisbath felt some semblance of public embarrassment.

This was a severely foreign experience for her. The last time Nurse Milliken had felt embarrassed, she had been with a student nurse named Francine Forman. Ms. Forman was a friend of Sharona's family; in fact, it was Sharona who'd convinced the girl to apply to nursing school.

From time to time Lisbath would bring a young student along, and of course during those sessions she would refrain from any collection "duties."

Once, Milliken had been showing tag-along Forman how to tie the umbilicus. The human tube had slipped out of Lisbath's hand and spewed liquid all over the floor and on their shoes. It was a stupid mistake that made the nurse-midwife look unprofessional. She felt exceedingly self-conscious as she and her young protégé mopped up the mess.

But this time the feeling was different. It wasn't the embarrassment of a slip-up in technique; it felt instead something like being caught "red-handed." This rather base emotion didn't suit Nurse Lisbath Milliken at all, and she began to squirm in a helpless couch-dance of avoidance. She could not reconcile this feeling.

For the first time in her life, Lisbath wished that she were a smoker so she could soothe herself with that nicotine poison.

As she continued to mull over her plight, Lisbath began an involuntary trek down an extraordinary emotional road she had avoided in the past. She began to think—maybe to admit—to herself: *Is it possible that I'm actually doing something wrong?*

She knew that many people would lack tolerance for her natural acts. After all, she deliberately hid her work. Sneaking beside the bed and spiriting the luscious redness away in a Thermos nestled in her carpetbag were incontrovertible acknowledgments. Milliken knew that other people would think ill of these bloody procedures.

For the first time in her life, Lisbath Milliken was in an enveloping, unique quandary. She felt like she might be unclean. Somehow unworthy.

She felt like a little girl about to be punished.

She felt like hell.

Her rough sleep last night had left her completely unrested, and as this burden of uncertain guilt and pressure waxed, Lisbath's head began to fill with images of her bloody manna. She imagined being swathed in the red liquid. She visualized her navel a small, red pool and the rolls of fat on her abdomen bifurcated by precious horizontal streams of the stuff. Her mind's eye saw red fragrance creeping out of her labia.

On the couch, Lisbath's mind was attempting to recuperate. At this same time, George Haberdeen was already energized at the police station. He walked briskly through the doorway of the detective office and saw Moraga doing a crossword puzzle. Moraga's feet were up on his desk and the newspaper crinkled and wiggled on his thighs. His blunt pencil printed vertical words.

"Do it on a desk, man," said Haberdeen. "You'll poke yourself in the leg."

"Since when are you worried about my legs?"

"Hey, man. I worry about our Men in Blue. Never heard of *esprit de corps*?"

"On my beat it's *esprit de* corpse."

"Ha-Ha," Haberdeen mocked. He threw the Milliken file on his own desk and sat down.

"Hey, G-Man. What's this about you and the Sarge and vampires?" asked Humberto.

"Oh, Christ. Nothing. Stevenson's got some *thing* up his butt about the name *Vlad*. He thinks the American Movie Classics channel is The History Channel. Cops aren't too smart, you know?"

"What movie were you guys talking about? I get AMC on cable."

"I got no idea. Ask Judd. Some stupid vampire movie, that's all."

"Oooooooo! *Blood*suckers!" exclaimed Haberdeen's girlfriend Lisa. She had been standing silently in the doorway for a few seconds.

Haberdeen turned in his chair. "Hey! Hi, Lisa! I didn't know you were coming by," said the G-Man. He was always pleasantly surprised to see his girlfriend show up at the station, especially this early on a Monday.

"George, can we talk?"

Oh-oh; here it comes. George and Lisa had never really made up about her Milliken assignment. They had had a few phone conversations since Lisa's stressful reportage a few days ago, but both of them had been skirting the issue. George felt like he was walking on eggshells every time they spoke on the phone, and Lisa kept listening for some form of apology and gentility that Police Detective Haberdeen's machismo just couldn't secrete.

"Sure we can talk, babe. Wanna go out for lunch somewhere?"

"No. It's too cold outside. I just want to talk."

Moraga looked toward George, who gestured toward the door. Right now, three was definitely a crowd.

"You two hold down the fort," said Moraga. "I need food." He left.

"Honey, I don't feel good about the nurse thing," said Lisa. Her voice was soft and she sounded vulnerable.

"What do you mean? Did she do something to you that you that you didn't tell me about? Did that bitch . . ."

"No, nothing like that. I'm getting over that part of my experience. It's *you*, George. The way you treated me. It's like you don't care. Like you were angry that I didn't 'get the goods' on the woman."

Shit. Here comes more girl stuff. His diaphragm leapt.

"I care lots, Lisa. C'mon."

"Well, what did you expect me to do? She didn't ask for any of my blood or anything and she didn't say anything wrong or mean, and she just talked to me for a while and . . ."

"Okay, Lisa," George interrupted. "I get it. Listen: I appreciate what you did. Really. Nobody scores every time, baby."

"Nobody *scores*?" Lisa voice rose as she began to turn red. George knew he'd just about blown it. He figured Lisa was on the rag, pregnant or not.

"Lisa, Lisa," said George. She waited as patiently as she could.

George continued. "That's just cop talk. Calm down. Please. It's okay. Let's forget about this, okay? I won't ask you to see her again."

"No shit, Sherlock."

"Just put her out of your mind, okay? *Please?*"

George had that cute little whine in his voice when he said "Please," and Lisa just couldn't stay mad or hurt. He brought that voice out whenever he needed to, and it always worked with Lisa. George smiled and held his arms open. The big man tilted his head the way Lisa always loved. *Big, dumb grin*, she thought.

Lisa fell right into his arms. It felt to her like all this was a little too quick—maybe she felt manipulated, or that George hadn't done enough penance yet. But what mattered now was that the two of them were together, and the stresses that had been eating away at them were dissipating like steam over simmering spaghetti.

George and Lisa realized that they were both standing and embracing, so they headed slowly to sit down at George's desk. In a deliberate signal of capitulation and respect, George sat down in the interrogatee's chair, leaving the better, larger, reclining, squeaking wooden chair for his lady.

"So did you guys catch a vampire?"

"Oh, we were talking about my interview with the Milliken woman. I got about as much out of her as you did." Realizing that he might have just made another faux-pas, George's head shrunk into his shoulders and he looked straight at Lisa to see whether he was about to get hugged or hanged.

Lisa had mellowed. "It figures," she said. "That nurse is pretty much on the ball. I don't think she'd get tripped up very easy if she wanted to hide something." Sirens screamed in the distance.

"So what's the vampire stuff?" asked Lisa.

"Oh, nothing. I told Judd about Milliken's dog, Lad, and he thought I said 'Vlad,' and started telling me about some stupid horror movie he saw last night. That's all. Waste of time."

"Vlad? Like Vlad the Impaler?"

"What the hell's that?"

"Gosh, I don't know where that came from. It must be something I picked up in my Anthro 121 class. I think he was some freak from a few hundred years ago or something."

A fuzzy ball began to roll around in the G-Man's preconscious thinking. *Nurse-midwife. Medicines. Births. Blood. Vampires. Impaler. Licking her red fingers. Lad/Vlad. What was all this?*

"I thought anthropology was about skeletons and tombs and stuff like that. Indiana Jones stuff, right?"

"Depends. It was a Magic, Witchcraft and Religion class at Minion. They talked about all kinds of stuff like Voodoo and vampires and Wicca."

"Wicca?"

"Forget it, George. Your opinion of women is bad enough!"

George's fuzzy ball was gathering moss. It was growing.

"What else can you tell me about this Lad? I mean Vlad?"

Lisa was leaning back in the G-Man's chair. It squeaked rhythmically as she watched him.

"I don't remember much detail. Mostly the name and that he was scary. But listen, George. I have tomorrow off and the college is just a few miles from my apartment. Maybe I'll go by and see if I can catch Professor Cane. He taught the class. He can remind me."

"Don't go out of your way, Lisa. I was just making conversation, you know? This has got to be bullshit anyway."

"No, I want to go. He was cool. Lots of neat stuff in his office, like a real old skull that's all warped. Anyways, sometimes I go the campus just to walk around; it's nice and green; makes things feel less urban. I'll go when the weather's a little better. Maybe tomorrow. You know, it makes me feel young to be there."

"Baby, you *are* young."

"You're sweet, George."

"You finally noticed?"

Lisa smiled, stood up, gave George a peck on the top of his head, and swished out the door looking as little-girlishly pert as a pregnant late-twenty-something woman could look.

And George noticed.

Twenty-four

Lad lay limp in Lisbath's large lap. This was a bad moment for both of them. The dog's breathing was unusually shallow, and the color of his lips appeared to be washed out. His stomach was growling and his yellow left rear leg was vibrating. It looked like it could be malnutrition, but he had been eating his meals regularly and had been having normal, predictable, firm bowel movements.

Lisbath knew what was wrong. It was wrong with her, too. Neither she nor her familiar had had a full, satisfying blood meal for much too long.

In past years, Lisbath had had plentiful nurse-midwife calls—often four or five a week. Each one afforded an opportunity for collection, and each yielded at least a Thermos full. Sometimes even more.

But a couple of years ago, a very damning *60 Minutes* report on home births had aired on national TV. Big T, that Bridgeport newspaper reporter with the cutesy nickname, jumped on the bandwagon. She decided to run a series of sensationalist follow-up articles. Big T's yellow journalism linked midwifery to everything from low birth weight to intensified postpartum depression.

These terrible articles had frightened women away from the naturalness of home birthing and eaten conspicuously into Lisbath's employment picture. Public opinion about what was now seen as a "risky" birth procedure plummeted; therefore, so did Lisbath's nurse-midwifery call volume.

To survive this dry season, the proud nurse often had to lower herself to bathing geriatric patients and suctioning the smoke-gummed chests of lung cancer patients. To Lisbath, this was no better than scraping out bedpans.

Prior to the *60 Minutes* fiasco, she and Lad could enjoy at least a quart of the precious, purplish liquid every couple of weeks or so. But these days they were lucky to share even a pint a month between them.

During this anxious, stressful period Lisbath thought of as "the drought," she had tried other blood sources. She had gone to butchers, choosing the bloodiest cuts of meat. She tasted the blood alone and found it not only unpalatable, but disgusting. Lad wouldn't touch it, either. She tried liver. It, too, was unacceptable. There was something about human blood that made it significantly different in flavor and, more important, in its revitalizing effect. Nothing could replace it.

The germ of desperation was now intensifying fiercely in Lisbath Milliken.

Lad peered up at her. It was a remarkable stare with the focus of a diamond cutter and the intensity of a surgeon. Lisbath was captured by his glaring countenance; she was pinned like a butterfly specimen. The pair of them seemed to be locked in a strange, symbiotic and inviolable communication that surpassed simple body language.

"I know, I know, Laddie," said Lisbath. "I've got to get us some. I'll think of something. I promise."

Lad's left leg stopped vibrating, and he began to move his tail back and forth very slowly. The tail made a faint swishing sound as it swept over Lisbath's thigh. This wasn't a joyous, whipping tail wag. The motion was instead like the eerie preparatory undulations of a snake deciding where to strike. Lad was thinking—evaluating. More than that, he was dreaming. Perhaps commanding.

The dog jumped off Milliken's lap before she could move a muscle. He went into the bedroom.

Lisbath felt strange. Her eyes squinted, and her gaze began to move over the room, paying attention to nothing. She rose and began to make her way toward the kitchen, and she began to fight the urge to walk. She wanted to stand still, to understand what was happening, but there seemed to be something urging her to go, something invisible and powerful and not within her control.

Lisbath glanced at her reflection in the glass over a photo of Lad by the couch. She looked old ... much older than she should. She knew the paucity of blood was to blame.

She found herself at the kitchen phone. Her hand extended from her body toward it, and as soon as the hand touched the phone, everything clarified. Whatever it was that had affected her had ceased, and she was Lisbath Milliken again. Fully in control, but a little rattled nonetheless.

Lisbath paused. She moved her thinking quickly away from whatever had just happened. She needed to feel comfortable—stable. She figured that this episode had happened because she was running low on blood. She needed much more—to take in the precious fluid on a daily basis, like she used to before "the drought." She decided to take a strong, proactive role in her pursuit of the blood she so urgently needed. She dialed the phone.

"Dickinson's Registry. May I help you?" answered Sharona.

"Sharona, this is Lisbath."

"Hi, Lisbath. How come you're calling? Monday's your day off."

"Yes, dear. I know. I have some extra time this week. I'd kind of like to work today. Have anything for me?"

"Well, no, Lisbath. You know I'd call you if we had any tough midwife calls. But today's slow for us anyway. Although ..." Sharona's voice trailed off and Lisbath caught it immediately.

"What is it, Sharona?" implored Lisbath. "Come on, dear. *What is it?*"

Lisbath was becoming more and more insistent. Her blood hunger gnawed away at her insides. Sharona heard the desperation in Lisbath's voice.

"Well, we did get a call this morning for a midwife. It's for Doris Wallace way over in Shelton. You know that's out of our normal service area. Still, you did her intro exam about six months ago."

Lisbath considered this situation. *So hadn't Sharona thought about follow-through? Continuity? Come on, Gomez! I should be over there!* She stomped her feet on the kitchen floor. Sharona heard it on the other end of the line but had no idea what the noise was.

Sharona continued. "It's a very straightforward case, Lisbath. Negligible potential for complications. And the mom has already borne two children at home."

Sharona took a long sip of her coffee while Lisbath continued to simmer.

"So why didn't you call?" The nurse-midwife's tone became increasingly angry. "I've been home the whole morning. Available."

Sharona thought to herself, *It's her day off and she's complaining that I didn't call her in for a job. Days off are days off except in a case of a real emergency. And this certainly wasn't an emergency!*

But Sharona Gomez also began to think to herself, *Maybe I am a little worried about Lisbath since the police started bugging me about her. I always respect and protect my people, but this is a little scary. Never mind that man Haberdeen being such an ass.*

"So where is the job?" Lisbath continued. "She must be pretty far along by now. How long ago did you get my call?"

"Lisbath, it's not really *your* call."

"What do you mean? I'm your midwifery specialist, right?"

"Yes, Lisbath. Surely."

"So?" Milliken was strong and demanding. Dickinson's owner had never heard Lisbath sound that way.

Sharona finally got up the gumption to lay it out for Milliken.

"Lisbath, do you remember Francine Forman? The young nursing student you trained—who did a clerkship under you—a few years ago?"

"Of course." This was the girl Lisbath had been with when she'd let the umbilical cord slip out of her fingers. One of the few people who had ever seen Lisbath make a mistake. Someone who had seen her embarrassed. It was not a happy memory.

Lisbath's thoughts returned fast to what was going down here. She smelled a rat. She was beginning to suspect disenfranchisement.

"I assigned Fran to the call," Sharona said. "She needs the experience, and this really is a simple job. And it is your day off."

"How could you?" implored Lisbath. She was almost in tears—tears that would have boiled off a face that was burning up with anger.

Sharona was getting a little fed up herself. Lisbath was, after all, a subcontractor like all her nurses. Under suspicion of the police at that. And Fran was a friend of the family. Also, Nurse Forman was now legal to perform midwifery.

"I felt she was ready, and that's just how it is. You're going to need to accept that, Lisbath."

"I don't have to accept anything!" Lisbath lashed back. "You're going too far, Sharona." Lisbath was shaking harder and harder. "You've got to respect your sustainers, Sharona. Otherwise you can get hurt."

Hurt? Sharona thought to herself. Was Milliken actually threatening her? She had never encountered anything like this in all her working years, and the last person she would have expected to say anything like a threat was Lisbath anyway.

"Lisbath, I don't know what's been going on with you the past few days. Something seems to be really wrong." Sharona was cooling off—regaining her professional demeanor. "Lisbath, why don't you come in and we can talk? I'll brew some fresh coffee. Okay, dear?"

Damn you is what Lisbath reflexively wanted to say, but she had just enough of a shred of self-control left to refrain. Instead, she thought for a second, then said, "Sharona Gomez, you can't treat me this way. I'll be in touch."

Lisbath hung up the phone hard. She was shaking so much that the receiver didn't come down straight; it hit the protruding cradle, making a hollow, plastic crashing sound that must have hurt Sharona's ear. Lisbath grinned through her gnashing teeth.

The slam startled Lad out of his dog nap, and he burst into the room and jumped up on the table on which Lisbath's elbows rested. He moved deliberately into position where his snout was just millimeters from Lisbath's own.

Lisbath was still shaking, and the two of them stared into each other's eyes not so much like lovers, but rather like Sumo wrestlers about to have at it. This engagement reached far behind their eyes; it involved their brains and their souls. And, in a queer way, their stomachs as well.

There was an immediate understanding between dog and human. No matter what it took, Lisbath needed to obtain their special feed. And the opportunity had just presented itself to do so, albeit by violating Lisbath's former ethical limits.

Lisbath thought, *Fuck it*. Need outweighs self-respect any day of the week and twice on Sundays. She got her bag and headed out.

The fifteen mile drive to Shelton had little traffic. Lisbath steamed as she pounded the accelerator pedal on the old Ford.

When she arrived at the Wallace residence at 118 Front Street, Lisbath saw Francine's car parked in front. She could tell it was Fran Forman's car by the nursing textbooks strewn all over the rear window shelf. Lisbath responded to this vehicle as her enemy's transport: the Trojan Horse placed so apparently innocently in the city's midst.

Running on the fuel of adrenaline and with virtually no planning to back her up, Lisbath stormed up to the front door and pounded four times. She hoped the knock's violence would startle everyone inside—the traitors who had accepted her substitute as well as Forman herself. Lisbath conceived of Fran Forman as an incompetent and an enemy all rolled up into one stinking package. She wanted to dispatch this horrid parcel as fast as she could—to clear the way for the proper nurse-midwife to collect her nurturing due.

SPECIAL DELIVERY

Kevin Wallace, the father-to-be, came to the door quite quickly. He was a pudgy man with only a few strands of hair combed in an arch over his scalp. His eyebrows were strangely thick and black, giving his head an unusual, unbalanced look. He looked extremely tired. The impending birth of his new child clearly had already taken a lot out of him.

"Why, Nurse Milliken! It's quite a surprise to see you!" remarked Mr. Wallace. He raised his bushy eyebrows. He was looking at a very red-faced nurse in a starched-white uniform. Beside her sat her carpetbag. In her hands was a black plastic trash bag wrapped around some kind of cylinder and what looked to him like a plastic stew pot. None of this made any visual sense to him. Why would a second nurse appear? Nurse-midwife Forman had already been on the job for over an hour.

Wallace said to Milliken, "We already have a nurse here, you know." He sounded like a child trying to keep a rival out of his special clubhouse.

"You bet I know someone's here, Mr. Wallace," said Lisbath as some of her chins wiggled. "She was sent by mistake. This is my job."

"But Miss Gomez said this was your day off and that this Miss Forman was available instead."

Lisbath Milliken was fuming. She didn't give a shit whether Forman had been sent or not. "Mr. Wallace, this is my job. Please allow me to pass and I'll straighten everything out."

The man was stunned at hearing the forcefulness of Milliken's claim. Especially since he was under the unusual mix of stresses associated with a home birth in his own house today, Wallace became a frightened, emotional adolescent.

"Okay," he said, pointing to the bedroom door. "She's in there. Please make this fast; I don't want Doris upset."

Lisbath fired "Step aside!" at the useless man as she barreled toward the bedroom.

Milliken grabbed the brass door lever, shoved it down, and

threw the door open with such force that it banged against the wall and rebounded far enough to hit her in the elbow. She felt no pain.

Through the doorway, Lisbath saw Nurse Forman leaning over Doris Wallace's abdomen. Forman had her stethoscope seated in her ears and held the business end of the instrument midway between Mrs. Wallace's navel and perineum. Both women started at the door's swoosh. They stared uncomprehendingly at Lisbath's imposing bulk: a bright white shaking balloon of anger and forcefulness.

"Step away!" ordered Lisbath to a confused and frightened Fran. Lisbath lowered her head slightly, and to Doris and Fran it looked like a bull preparing to charge.

"What? What are you doing here, Miss Milliken?" asked Nurse Forman. She removed the stethoscope from her ears and straightened. Her subconscious brain hadn't told her how to react yet.

"Step aside *stat*, I said," yelled an angry Lisbath.

Nurse Forman moved reflexively back toward the bedroom wall, clearing the way for whatever Nurse-midwife Milliken needed to do. But Lisbath didn't stop at that. She wanted no competition—no complications.

Milliken continued to direct commands toward Forman. "Nurse Forman, you need to go now. Leave your equipment here; I will return it tomorrow. Get out now." Lisbath offered no explanation, and Forman was too bewildered to demand one. She left sheepishly and only began to sort out what had happened as she walked to her car.

Milliken followed her. "Get in and unlock the passenger door. I need to talk to you."

Forman didn't feel like having anything else to do with this woman, but Milliken was clearly her superior (and had more seniority at Dickinson's anyway), so she did as she was told.

Lisbath opened the passenger-side door, swished in and sat down. The small import car sagged noticeably under Milliken's substantial weight. She shut the door and reached into her pocket.

"Fran, you know that you're trying to muddle in my territory, don't you?"

"Well, no, Miss Milliken. Sharona assigned me this job, and I'm qualified, and that's all there is to it. I really don't understand you. Why are you so angry? It's not like I'm trying to usurp your work, you know."

"You have no right to do any midwifery through Dickinson's. Especially not with my patient! What the hell were you doing?"

Back at the house, Doris was just lying in a stunned reverie, waiting for a nurse—any nurse—to come back and finish the birth. She was in no mood to argue and in no mental place to analyze anything that might have been going on. Fortunately, she was between contractions.

Outside in Forman's car, Fran felt outclassed. "Miss Milliken, I'm sorry. I truly didn't know she was your patient. And yes, I know, you are much more experienced than I. It won't happen again."

"You bet it won't," spat Lisbath. She withdrew a pre-filled syringe saved for birth emergencies from her pocket, uncapped the needle, and shoved the *entire triple dose* into Fran Forman's side in one fast, practiced move. Forman snapped her head up in horror and disbelief.

"What is this? What are you giving me? Are you nuts?"

"Nuts it is, dearie. See if you can sleep this off until I figure out what to do with you. Traitors have no place in our profession," admonished Lisbath as she capped the sharp and pocketed the now-empty syringe.

"Lisbath, you're crazy. Did you drug me? What did you . . ." Fran's voice trailed off as her consciousness fled her body. She slumped over onto the steering wheel.

Lisbath opened her own door, got out, and dragged her fellow nurse over to the passenger side. She spied a blanket and pillow on the back seat. What luck! Lisbath placed the blanket carefully over Fran from her chest to her feet and propped the nurse's head up with the pillow. Any passers-by would simply think she was taking a nap.

So far, so good. She'd deal with this traitor later. The dose Lisbath had given Fran would keep her out for hours—more than enough time to complete Doris Wallace's birth, clean up, get the precious blood prize that occupied so much of her thinking, and return to Fran's car.

Twenty-five

Milliken went back into to the house and turned to Mr. Wallace. She was firm and clear and knew that every word she would shoot at this worm of a man would be taken as a military command.

"Stay out here. I will take care of your wife. Don't worry about anything you may hear. Do not open the door. I will call you in when we are ready. Do you understand?" she commanded.

"Uh... yes," said Mr. Wallace sheepishly.

That's what Milliken needed to hear. Now the way was clear for her to do the dirty—to obtain feed for herself and her Lad and to allow their lives to go on as they must.

Doris Wallace was in a growing muddle of bewilderment. When Lisbath re-entered the bedroom, the dumbfounded mother just stared at her blankly. Lisbath took over immediately.

"Doris, dear, I'll take care of you now. You know, *woman-to-woman*, you deserve the best care, and I'm the very best. We won't be bothered by that Forman woman anymore. Okay, dear?"

Doris just nodded her head as a contraction began. The nod ended with a jerk.

Lisbath had seen the contraction coming, of course. Years of training.

She helped Doris relax and began to take a mental inventory of the equipment Forman had left behind. *Well, at least she brought the right arsenal*, Lisbath thought to herself. *I trained her well.*

Mrs. Wallace's birthing went easily for her, and Lisbath found it so routine that she could have done it with her eyes closed and one fat arm tied behind her back. As Milliken worked on Wallace, she actively enjoyed the woman's rich aromas. Lisbath began musing about how she would collect her prize this time. She thought back to her immediately previous experience with a "donor"—the latest mom given the transparent privilege of contributing to Lisbath's special collection. That was so long ago—with La-TaKeisha Jeffers. Lisbath had needed no stealth with Jeffers, whose bulk and repulsive manner protected her from the mom's gaze and any neighbor's oversight. No family around to worry about, either.

The Wallace child slid out easily. This was Mrs. Wallace's third pregnancy. The nurse-midwife cleaned the infant, put the eye drops in, and made it into a neat little package with a pink receiving blanket. As Milliken handed Doris Wallace her new baby girl, the new mother was completely agrin. Her ecstasy was topped off by Lisbath's telling her that the baby was perfect. "*Woman-to-woman*, dear, you did a wonderful job. Just hold your little girl for a while. I'll be taking care of some clean-up before we let anybody in. This is your first private time with your fine daughter, Doris. Enjoy it fully, okay?"

"Oh, yes. Thank you. She's beautiful!" said Doris through sweaty lips. She nestled her little girl to her bosom and rocked slowly. Doris ignored Lisbath's machinations. It would turn out to have been a mistake to have done so.

Lisbath went directly to her carpetbag and removed the Thermos bottle. She unscrewed the top, aimed the placenta's cut end of the umbilical cord down the throat of the bottle, and released the pressure from the hemostat. Blood gushed into the Thermos, almost splashing out as it rushed into its special metallic cache.

This time Lisbath had brought a second piece of equipment. She knew that she needed to stock up. So as soon as the Thermos was full, she re-clamped the hemostat on the cord, put the metal tube into the waiting plastic bag under the bed, and brought out her Coleman camping container. This was a wide-mouth job with a green bottom, white top half, and three-inch, plastic screw-on lid. Lisbath removed the lid and slid the container up next to the mattress. She then brought the umbilical end toward its gaping mouth.

Doris' placenta was beginning to disengage from its uterine mooring, and this caused pressure waves to move throughout the placenta. Lisbath had a little difficulty holding onto the umbilicus correctly to ensure that the stream of blood made it into the Coleman—despite its having a big mouth.

With some unavoidable spillage, the blood flowed nicely. But it didn't fill the Coleman completely; there were at least three inches of clearance that yearned to be filled with precious blood. This was the first time Lisbath had tried to secure such a large load, and she was stymied and irritated and challenged.

Then it struck her.

"Here, dear. I'm going to give you a little injection. It will relieve any residual pain and make my next procedure more comfortable for you."

"What next procedure?" asked Doris. She had had the baby and, as far as she could remember from her two prior childbirths, there was really nothing else for the nurse to do other than helping the uterus return to its normal shape and cleaning up.

"Do you mean the uterine massage? Don't worry," said Doris. "As you say, *'woman-to-woman,'* that doesn't hurt a bit. My last midwifed births were pretty much painless after the baby had been born and the placenta came out."

"Mrs. Wallace, there are now some new procedures. They help ensure your rapid recovery. You do want to be at your best for your new, beautiful baby and for yourself, don't you? *Woman-to-woman,* it's the only thing to do."

"Oh, I guess so. Sure, Miss Milliken. Do what you need to. As long as it can't hurt little Linette."

"Linette! Such a pretty name," mouthed the nurse-midwife.

Lightning illuminated the room briefly. Doris started, then lay back down and extended her arm.

Milliken mixed a blend of the anesthetic Percodan and the antianxiety drug called Lorazepam. She gave Doris Wallace a hefty shot of this mix and waited a while for it to work.

As soon as Doris let go of the baby, Lisbath knew her concoction had had its desired effect. She carefully put little Linette on a clean blanket on the floor and padded her with thick stacks of towels on either side. Milliken then placed blanketing over the child and, after regular layers of blankets reaching from below Linette's feet to her chest, Lisbath added another few layers, covering her completely. Something like constructing a gun silencer where the baby played the barrel. But without suffocating the poor dear, of course.

That done, it was time to milk mama. So to speak.

Lisbath first grabbed the umbilicus and literally ripped the placenta out of the woman. She knew this would rupture numerous blood vessels in Doris's uterus, and that plentiful internal bleeding would leak out the vaginal os in just seconds. And Milliken was ready.

She cupped her hands below Doris' vagina. As the syrupy contents exited, Lisbath bailed it into the Coleman. It didn't matter that much of it slopped over the sides; the flow was good at the moment. And Lisbath had further plans when this source dried up.

Thunder outside helped muffle the baby's cries. The nurse was one inch short of crazed. Doris was virtually comatose.

Outside the bedroom, Kevin Wallace was vacantly watching *What's My Line?* on the Game Show Channel and eating peanuts. He thought of his two older kids staying with Doris' sister. Dorothy Kilgallen's jeweled blindfold wiggled as the society girl congratulated herself unabashedly on her own insightful questions directed at Mystery Guest Satchmo. He was trying to make a little kid's voice as he answered inane questions about whether or not he was appearing on Broadway this week, but his breathy sounds fooled no one.

As she stood over her victim, Lisbath began to visualize poor Lad, starving of blood. He was so loyal—so kind—so supportive.

The little dog needed his meal just as much as she needed her own. This easily justified what was happening. And anything else that was about to happen.

Lisbath was more primally hungry than she had ever been before. The nurse-midwife reached into her carpetbag and located a scalpel. It was one of the disposable variety, sealed in a blue, crackling plastic enclosure like a sterile candy bar. She tore the bag open, revealing a green-handled masterpiece of engineering. It had a curved blade half an inch long, and there were gripping ribs all along the handle's length. The metal blade was covered with a thick, clear plastic protector which was ready to be slid off. The whole thing was clean and lethal all at the same time. *The better to cut you with, my dear.*

Milliken stood there for a moment, deciding where to slice. The jugular veins were most accessible, but those cuts might be too obvious. She decided instead to perform a postpartum episiotomy. She wanted the freshest blood she could get. An episiotomy—a deep cut along the side of the vagina—was often used in situations where the baby's head would otherwise rip the vagina open irregularly. Never mind that she was doing the cut after the birth—which was medically useless—rather than before it. This was the best bet to get more blood without suspicion. So in she sliced. Deeply. More deeply than she should have.

Doris was already unconscious, so there was no scream of pain. Lisbath was greeted with exactly what she wanted: bunches of gushing, ruby-red blood, shooting toward her in multiple streams of refreshing, warm sustenance. She realized there was more volume issuing from Doris' gaping hole than her Coleman container could accommodate. The idea that so much precious fluid might go to waste threw her into a panic. Lisbath needed some additional way to capture and transport the blood, and she needed it *now.*

She scanned the room. The first actual containers the midwife saw were a collection of multicolored perfume bottles sitting on a mirrored, filigreed tray. Lisbath flung herself toward the dressing table on which the tray sat. She quickly opened and shook out each bottle onto the mirror, creating a mixture of fragrances that no doubt outshone even the basest French whorehouse.

She realized immediately how fruitless this approach would be. The bottle necks were tiny, and on top of that, each had a pitifully small carrying capacity. Lisbath threw the cache of opened, stinking bottles into the burgeoning pool of spilled blood between Doris' spread legs. She needed to find something better.

Initially, she saw nothing useful. Lisbath began opening drawers willy-nilly. She threw their contents onto the floor, scanning for anything potentially useful. Underpants, bras, scarves. Nothing, nothing, and more nothing.

She moved next to the closet. Lisbath went first to the top shelf and chucked everything onto the floor, sifting as she worked. There was nothing usable.

Lisbath's panic intensified. She looked over at her blood source and noticed that the flow was decreasing. Violent desperation enveloped her like an armada of bees defending their hive. She had wanted everything to be secret, but the risk of discovery paled in comparison to the potential of wasting all that great blood.

She rushed from the bedroom, startling Mr. Wallace out of his couch-potato reverie. Kevin looked at the speeding, blood-soaked nurse with wide, uncomprehending eyes. He dropped his coffee cup, the contents spilling all over his lap.

"What's going on? Is Doris okay? What are you . . ."

"*Shut up!*" yelled Lisbath as she made her way toward what she deduced would be the kitchen.

"What are you saying?" Kevin asked as he started to get up.

When Lisbath saw him rise off the easy chair, she changed direction and barreled into him with all her heft. She knocked Wallace back so hard with her charging, heavy mass that his chair tipped over backward. In other circumstances the scene could have been funny, but in the present situation it was pathetic.

Kevin's backward fall rammed his head solidly against the

brick fireplace's raised ground-hearth. The force knocked him unconscious. Blood began to seep from his thinned hair onto the bricks and then on to the carpet, but Lisbath didn't see it. She was heading for the kitchen.

Immediately, the nurse-midwife threw open every cabinet she could reach. She came upon one filled with glass canning jars, lids loosely placed atop each one. *Perfecto*. She grabbed as many as she could carry in her flabby arms and moved quickly toward the kitchen door. As she ran, one of the jars slipped from her grasp and shattered on the linoleum. It gave her no pause.

Lisbath slammed the bedroom door behind her with her foot as she re-entered. The nurse genuflected, bending quickly over the bed, padding the jars as she released them all over the mattress.

She grabbed one, twisted the top off, and shoved it vigorously against Doris' buttocks. Blood splattered a few feet in all directions, but it was no matter. Lisbath held the jar fast and placed her free hand over Doris' uterus. She began to pump fast and deeply, tilting the jar's mouth as she did so to catch every cherished drop.

As each jar filled, Lisbath replaced it with another. And each time, she would drink a slug of the red manna. She was *thrilled* to madness.

The flow rate was decreasing despite Lisbath's pumping harder and harder with each thrust of her forearm. She had filled two and a half jars when the blood flow essentially stopped.

Lisbath was angry. "*Bleed, you bitch!*" she screamed. She let go of the partly-filled jar and placed both hands on Doris' reddened abdomen. Milliken began to pump with all her might; a mockery of CPR. It looked like an oil derrick's nodding head sucking every morsel of rich oil from the fallowing ground. Doris Wallace's head lolled from side to side as her body was literally beaten like an exhausted sponge.

Then a new idea struck Lisbath. Why limit the collection from the vaginal area? There's lots more blood hidden in rubbery nooks and crannies all over the body, and all it would take to find it would be incision after incision. Lisbath felt like she was sitting in front of a fleshy gold mine, but the gold was red and infinitely consumable.

As she capped her fourth jar, it struck Lisbath that her patient wasn't moving. No thoracic respirational motions. No twitches that sometimes happened under anesthesia. Beyond that, Doris was quite pallid.

Oh, no! thought Milliken. *Could I have killed her? Could this woman actually have perished under my hand?*

Quickly the nurse grabbed her stethoscope and checked Doris's heartbeat. There was none. Lisbath put her face beside Doris's mouth and felt for breath as she watched the woman's chest. Again, no evidence of life.

Milliken began to shake. She began to realize what she had done. In her feeding and collection frenzy, she'd had no thought of Doris's continued health—hell, no thought of her continued existence. She had forgotten completely about the little baby on the floor, about the husband lying in his own blood on the living room floor. She had had something akin to an alcoholic blackout.

But now she was coming back, and the trip was one of true, bone-rattling terror. Lisbath began to realize she had murdered her own patient. She had left a baby motherless. She remembered nothing about the disposition of the father, but she was sure that somehow she had hurt him as well.

In an uncharacteristic panic, she gathered her belongings—including her most precious liquid cargo—and went straight out to her car. She opened the trunk and, while piling everything she had in, Lisbath saw Nurse Forman's car parked a couple of spaces in front of her own.

She reached into her carpetbag and withdrew another syringe. This one was fuller than the last and held a darker, more potent liquid.

She went to the car with the drugged nurse lying over the steering wheel. She must have partially awakened and made some futile attempt to escape.

The nurse-midwife reached her hand through the open window and inserted the needle directly into Francine Forman's neck. She pushed on the plunger with great pressure, knowing that she did not have to protect the neck tissues from damage from too fast an infusion of drug.

Lisbath's drive back to Yankee Pines felt to her like she was on a macabre circus ride. She couldn't focus on the road and, when she got to traffic signals, sometimes couldn't tell whether they were red or green. She was actually stoned, under the influence of the very drugs she had shot into Doris. Drinking so much of the mother's drugged blood and driving just didn't mix.

The nurse's physical and sensory distortions were no match for the horror of her own thoughts and emotions. Through her partial drugged stupor, Lisbath realized she had killed and maimed and, worse yet, had left a trail that could ultimately be easy to follow.

She was falling apart in every way a person could. But at least tonight she and Lad would drink of that precious fluid again.

Perhaps, all in all, it would be worth it.

Twenty-six

Minion Valley Community College isn't really in a valley. It was named for the beloved Minion Valley community of eastern Canada that was home to the college's founders. Despite its being a private school, it still took the name of "Community College" because the creators of the school wanted as homey and parochial an image as possible.

In the service of this image, the college is almost overgrown with greenery taken from all over the North American continent. Since many of the tree species came from significantly cooler climates, they take great botanical attention. It stands to reason, then, that the biology department is well-known in the region.

As Lisa moved through the ivy-covered front gate of the school on a Tuesday morning, she felt like she had shed at least ten years. Walking on the cobblestones and smelling the fragrances glinting off the greenery brought her back to her earlier, simpler days. She remembered her naïve view of Bridgeport as an idyllic town with no crime and just good, honest people doing their daily work. Lisa smiled to herself partly out of relaxed joy and partly because she saw how truly ignorant she had been those many years back.

She made her way to the brick social sciences building, ascended to the second floor, passed by miniature lecture halls and small, smelly labs, and eventually arrived at the office suite at the end of the hall.

Dr. Robert Cane's office door was awash with newspaper cartoons. Over the years he had cut out most anything that had an anthropological bent and had taped it there. His favorite was a faded color one-pane cartoon, maybe by Gary Larson, of a dinosaur and a caveman. Of course, *Homo sapiens* and his ancestors had appeared millions of years after the dinosaurs became extinct, but what the hell? The cartoon showed the lizard riding atop a bearded caveman with the caption, "Cowboy training gone bad." It made little sense, but anthropologists just love stuff like that.

Lisa began to knock on the door, but it wasn't latched so it opened a crack when her knuckles hit. Dr. Cane had been hunched over his desk. It looked like he had been studying some kind of specimen, but he was just reading a book. His vision was deteriorating rapidly, he hadn't made time to go to the optometrist for almost five years, and he couldn't read worth a damn with his old glasses. But his distant vision was okay, and he recognized Lisa immediately.

"Miss Ipple! How are you? Gee—it looks like I should be asking how *both* of you are!"

"Hi, Doc! Nice to see you. I'm—we're—doing just fine, thanks. How are you?"

"Oh, just the same. Anthropologists don't seem to change much from year to year, you know. It's part of the package."

Old-man humor never really hit Lisa's funny bone, but she smiled for him anyway.

"So what are you doing here, young lady? Are you going to take some more classes? I surely haven't seen you around for a long time." Dr. Cane sat back in his chair and rubbed his lumbar region as he spoke. "Not too many people come around unless they're doing some kind of class project."

"Well, Dr. Cane, the fact is I am doing a kind of project, but it's not for a class." She sat down in the chair across from the professor's desk and put her purse down on the floor. "Actually, it's for my boyfriend."

"And who is that?"

"George Haberdeen."

"Haberdeen? I think I've heard of that name. Or maybe read it. Did he attend class with you?"

"Oh, no, Doc. He's a PD detective."

"A policeman!"

"Yes. I like him a lot."

"So tell me about him."

Lisa blushed. She had primed herself to launch into her Vlad the Impaler inquiry, and now the professor was asking her about her personal life. Still, it felt good that a man of this stature would be interested, and she liked talking about George.

"Well, okay." She shifted in her seat and crossed her legs. "George is actually a nice guy to me even though he's a cop. He comes from a small town in North Dakota—I think it's called Wing, North Dakota. He told me that everyone there is so peaceful that it felt weird for him to become a cop. Personally, I think a small-town upbringing makes a person more interesting."

Dr. Cane replied, "Anthropologically, smaller groups of people tend to be necessarily interdependent, so an increased sense of teamwork and mutuality naturally arises." He took off his glasses and leaned back. "Maybe that's why he can be a nice guy and a cop at the same time."

"I guess so," said Lisa. "Still, he can be a real son-of-a-bitch at work. Sometimes when I come into the station to visit him, I see him interrogating someone, and he's really scary."

"I bet," agreed Cane.

"But he tells me that it's just his job. He can't be an effective interrogator without playing bad-cop some of the time," explained Lisa. "Lots of cops seem real cold, but I think George is soft at the core."

"Is he about your age?" asked the professor.

"He's quite a bit older. He's got a little pot belly, too, but I love to lie on it!" Lisa's face turned beet-red right after her revelation, but it didn't matter.

Dr. Cane visualized the girl's head resting on a pot belly, and he smiled.

Lisa was in a good mood—having fun—but decided it was time to get down to business. "Doc, George wants me to check something for him."

Dr. Cane was intrigued. With the tiniest of vocal tremors, the professor asked, "Miss Ipple, is this a police investigation? Did George send you officially?"

"No, nothing like that! I just want some academic information."

"Well, Miss Ipple, I'm full of it." Cane enjoyed his pun and his tension level dropped. "So ask away."

"I want to ask you about something we talked about in class a few years ago. And why don't you call me Lisa now? I graduated, you know."

"Good to know you remember your lessons, Miss Ipple. I mean, Lisa."

"Oh, I only remember some things."

"So what's on your mind?"

"You remember we talked about vampires in the Anthro 121 class?"

"Yes. I always include that. Gets people's interest up even though it's all just a folk tale."

"But didn't you say something about a Vlad? Wasn't that someone real? Who really existed?"

"I'm impressed that you remember such detail. Well, yes. Vlad the Impaler was a real nobleman in the fifteenth century."

"And he had something to do with vampires, right?"

"Sort of, Lisa. But listen. Do you know Dr. Bodnir? The head of the Anthro department?" He gestured to the hallway, toward Dr. Bodnir's office.

"No. I mean, I heard the name when I was a student here, but I never had a class with him or anything."

"Well, Andre Bodnir is really the specialist here. Fact is, I learned most of what I teach about that time period from him. His hobby is ancient aristocracy. He's the one who introduced me to Vlad the Impaler. Would you like me to take you over to his office?"

"Well, I don't know. I never met him. I feel more comfortable talking to you." Lisa squished around on her chair, sending an involuntary message of mild discomfort.

"Lisa, I can tell you very little more—just what I said in class. I really think you should talk to Dr. Bodnir. He's a very nice man and I think he'd get a kick out of telling someone genuinely interested about Vlad. That kind of thing is his hobby."

"Well, okay. Do you think he's here now?"

"I just spoke with him not half an hour ago. Let's see."

Dr. Cane got up slowly and Lisa followed him. As they spoke, their voices echoed in the empty hall.

"Lisa, why do you want to know about Vlad the Impaler?" Rumbles of distant thunder made the humid, heated winter air feel cloying. "Doesn't seem like a typical kind of thing for people to be talking about. Especially police."

"My boyfriend asked me to check him out."

"Yes, but why?"

Dr. Cane could hear the anthropology chairman's voice through his open door. He was concluding a phone conversation.

"Wait a second, Lisa. We're almost there. Tell both of us."

Lisa nodded.

Robert Cane rapped a couple of times on Dr. Bodnir's door and then just opened it without waiting for an invitation. Things were pretty relaxed in the Anthro Department.

Bodnir's office had the stale odor of ancient books and wet papers. There was a set of wooden shelves with books on the two bottom levels and more interesting things above them. The top shelf had a few bones and assorted, dark artifacts like small boxes and hand weapons strewn about. The shelf below that, at Dr. Bodnir's shoulder level when he was seated, had a box of Kleenex, a hat, and several stacks of papers in irregularly-placed brown expandable file folders.

Dr. Andre Bodnir was an immense man—perhaps 265 pounds and over six feet tall—and had tremendous hands with fingers the size of hot dogs. He was tapping on his desk as he spoke to the textbook buyer at the student store. When he saw Dr. Cane and Lisa come in, he decided to end his conversation right away, asking the buyer to call him back tomorrow morning.

"The books still aren't in! Can you believe it? I asked for them over two months ago," Bodnir complained to Dr. Cane.

Cane shook his head in shared disgust while he brought Lisa forward. "Dr. Bodnir, this is Miss Lisa Ipple, a former student of mine. She took 121 with me a few years ago."

"Hello, Miss Ipple. Pleased to meet you."

He extended his hand and Lisa shook it, temporarily shocked at the sheer volume of meat attached to his wrist. She could barely wrap her fingers even part way around his palm.

"What can I do for you, Robert?"

"Miss Ipple asked me about Vlad the Impaler, and I decided to bring her to the expert."

"Vlad! *Vlad!* Oh yes, what a masterful fiend!"

"I know," agreed Lisa. "One of the first *official* vampires." She had in fact benefited from her education despite not remembering all the details.

Bodnir settled back in his chair and motioned for both of his visitors to sit on the wooden bench on his far wall. They had to move a few books out of the way to avoid an inappropriate butt-to-butt arrangement.

Bodnir continued. "Vlad Tepes lived in the fifteenth century. He was the son of Vlad Dracul, another vicious potentate. Eventually, Vlad Tepes became the Prince of Wallachia in my country—Hungary.

"The boy Vlad Tepes was born in Transylvania in 1431. Town of Schaassbourg. On his father's death he was due to take over rule of Wallachia—to become what they called the 'voivode.' But politics and other problems, mostly with the Turks, kept him from assuming the throne until he was twenty-five. He was only seventeen years old when his father Vlad, shall we say, 'passed away.'"

Lisa was totally engaged in this wonderful diatribe by Dr. Bodnir, and Dr. Cane was pretty attentive himself. Rain began to fall outside the multi-paned windows of Dr. Bodnir's office.

"Once Vlad Tepes took on his father's throne, he had Castle Dracula built in honor of the man who spawned him. Of course, he used slave labor to put the castle up.

"Vlad Tepes' father was at war with the Turks for a long time, and Vlad the younger blamed them—rightfully so—for his father's demise. So he took his revenge on the battlefield. Vlad had his men impale 20,000 of the captured Turkish soldiers on wooden stakes. Can you imagine the horrible spectacle? It came to be called the 'valley of corpses.' Vlad's soldiers impaled the Turks while they were still alive.

"The extreme bloodiness of the battlefield scenes—you know, he could have just piled the bodies in a heap but instead he felt he needed to make this bloody spectacle of his 20,000 victims— began his reputation as a relentless, frightening villain. But this was just the beginning of the story.

"Our Vlad was eventually inducted into the Order of the Dragon —a group of knights sworn to defend Christian Europe against the Ottoman empire. By popular decree, he came to be called 'Dracula,' which translates from Romanian into 'son of the dragon' or, equally well, 'son of the devil.'"

Lisa drew her knees up to her chest, completely focused.

"Vlad had a foul core. He had villagers tortured and burned and impaled seemingly at random. And he was known to give some of the locals a good meal only to be followed by incinerating them if they couldn't pay for the food. The thing is, he knew ahead of time that they couldn't pay."

Lisa's eyes widened and Dr. Cane pursed his lips. Both were deaf to the rain outside.

"And, most interesting, Miss Ipple: Most of this information comes from a pamphlet printed in Nuremberg in 1488. We believe it to be historically accurate."

"God!" said Lisa. Dr. Cane just shook his head. Rain spattered the windows of the good professor's office and it began to get darker outside.

"Nobody was immune. To show his power in 1457, Vlad the Impaler had the wives and children of a group of religious celebrants impaled around the feast tables before having the men carted away to become his slaves.

"Yes, this was a seriously mean man," concluded Bodnir.

"No kidding," Cane said, breaking his demeanor. All three began to laugh, and it broke the tension quite nicely.

"There was no end to his meanness. Let me read something to you."

Dr. Bodnir went to a shelf behind his desk and brought out a small volume with a red cover. He rubbed his back for a moment. "This is from *Visum Et Repertum*, by H. David Blalock. This is from a section called 'The Vampire in History':

> " 'He is accused of the deaths of 40,000 to 100,000 people, and not just by impalement. He employed strangling, hanging, burning, boiling, skinning, roasting, and burying them alive. He is known to have ordered cannibalism on prisoners.' "

Dr. Bodnir closed the book slowly and put it back in its niche. He had a mildly satisfied look on his face, and he rubbed his tremendous fingers together as he faced Lisa.

"So what do you think, Miss Ipple? Not exactly the kind of man you'd want to marry?"

Lisa appeared to shrivel, but then she got up her nerve and said to Dr. Bodnir, "Vlad the Impaler must have been a horrible human being. But there's nothing supernatural about him, right? I mean, there's no such thing as vampires, right?"

Dr. Bodnir loved dealing with questions like this. They opened the door for the old science vs. magic debate, which he always relished. He glanced at Dr. Cane, smiled, then faced Lisa directly.

"Young lady, there is a significant body of lore about vampires, much of it based on our Vlad and his exploits. And some of it *may* just be true." He grinned, then continued.

"Some of the stories have a pretty logical line to them. Satan attempts to infuse evil into those unfortunates too weak to resist. The blood drinkers, drawn primarily to human blood because of its rich cobalt content, are themselves able to impart their spirit into others, or so the lore goes.

"Vlad disappeared in late December of 1476. Our best information is that disgusted troops left him alone and mortally wounded on a battlefield north of Bucharest."

Lisa visualized the injured, vicious nobleman lying on a dirt mound surrounded by bloody bodies. She asked, "'Mortally wounded' means he was going to die, right? So he wasn't supernatural after all?"

"Not so fast," answered Dr. Bodnir. "The body can die, but, remember, the spirit may go on if it can be transferred."

"But you said he was left 'alone.' So there was nobody else there to receive the spirit, right?" said Lisa.

"The ancient stories say that the transfer can be into a lower being, like a sheep or a cat."

Dr. Cane broke in: "But how could a sheep get enough blood to satisfy the spirit? Can you imagine a sheep trying to attack? It might be scary in real life, but it'd be pretty easy to get away, don't you think?"

They all laughed.

Dr. Bodnir continued, "The stories also tell us that animals infused with evil can create 'familiars.' These are often humans under their control but who lack the spirit's full powers. They're kind of like evil assistants."

"This is just too creepy," said Lisa. "Are the familiars zombies?"

"Well, no," answered Dr. Bodnir. "Zombies aren't doing the

bidding of a 'master,' but familiars are servants of some malevolent creature.

"Beyond that, the animal spirit carriers, according to legend, may be able to carry more than one monstrous entity within them. They become what I call 'spirit magnets.'"

Lisa asked, "Are you saying that one animal could be two or three vampires? God, that's unbelievable! I mean, over the top!"

"Well, it is just folklore. Maybe." Dr. Bodnir grinned, pushing his pudgy cheeks up so high his eyes almost winked out. "There are stories that wolves, dogs, cats, and even rats can be spirit magnets. One legend even claims that the spirit magnets can be full-blown vampires who either prefer or are trapped in the 'familiar' form."

"How many of these spirit magnets are there supposed to be?" asked Lisa. "Are they everywhere?"

"We don't really know. The lore says that they tend to travel all over the world at will. They induce their familiars to do whatever they want. Like stealing money that their masters could use to pay for long-distance travel, obtaining sustenance, bringing them victims for their rituals. That kind of thing."

"Amazing," said Lisa.

"So, young lady. Why have you come? I told you all about Vlad and vampires and spirit magnets and familiars, but I don't really know why you're asking about all this."

"Oh, Professor. I'm sorry. I should've told you. My boyfriend is a cop—actually, a detective with Bridgeport PD—and he's investigating a nurse-midwife."

"A nurse? What has that to do with our friend Vlad?"

"It's something about her handling of blood," answered Lisa.

"Go on," said Dr. Bodnir.

"Well, she has a dog named 'Lad' and that kind of sounds like 'Vlad.' It just rang a bell, that's all."

Both professors crinkled their brows. Their body languages said *That's a far stretch, young lady.*

"Yeah, I know. It sounds kind of stupid. But I remembered

about Vlad the Impaler, and all the stuff I've been hearing from George—that's my boyfriend—has been pretty strange. And somehow blood figures into all of this. So I figured, why not? I'll visit Dr. Cane here and ask about it." She gestured toward Robert Cane, who bowed slightly to add to the mild humor of the moment.

"So has any of this helped you?" asked Dr. Bodnir.

"I really don't know. I'm going to write some of it down and take it to George. And if nothing comes of it, at least I had a good time! It's been like going to a horror movie. Oh, sorry, I didn't mean to offend."

"Well, we had a good time too," countered Andre Bodnir, smiling. "No offense taken." Both men felt somewhat refreshed to have a youthful woman interested in their field, and Dr. Cane had learned some things that he could use in future classes.

"Okay. I've got to go to work now," said Lisa. She had actually stayed longer than she'd expected, but she felt that it was worth it.

"Good-bye, Lisa," said Dr. Cane. "Nice seeing you again."

"Good-bye, Miss Ipple," said Dr. Bodnir. "I hope this was helpful."

"Thank you both. This was great."

Lisa put her feet down from the bench and nodded deferentially to the professors. She picked up her purse, withdrew a small notebook and pencil she had brought, and walked out in a swish of fresh air.

They watched her with slightly twisted grins.

Twenty-seven

Beardsley Park is a verdant area of Bridgeport made for relaxing and relating. It provides a beautiful environment; just the thing for a wine-and-cheese picnic. Though the temperatures were staying in the low 40's, this Tuesday morning was mostly sunny. There were just a few puffy clouds and no wind to speak of. The skies were darker to the east, but they didn't seem threatening.

Sharona and her college friend Barbara had decided to meet at the well-known wooden bridge by the pond. As Sharona walked toward the bridge, she saw Barbara leaning over the rail at its apex, staring contentedly into the slowly-moving stream flowing beneath it. Barbara had on a pair of faded jeans, knee boots, a brown turtleneck sweater, and a leather jacket. Her long, dark brown hair had slipped over her shoulders and was swinging over the water. From a distance, at least, she looked as young and perky as she had almost fifteen years ago as a student at the university.

Sharona began to walk faster as her girlish excitement grew. It was such a pleasure to see her old friend, and they finally had time to talk and leave the rest of the world behind.

Both women embraced each other, tears threatening. Neither could speak. They needed this respite so very urgently, yet until Barbara's phone call to Sharona a few days ago, neither of them had known how much.

Finally, they loosened their grips on each other. Sharona put down her bag and just smiled. Barbara spoke first.

"Hey, Tweedles! It's great to see you! You look wonderful! How do you keep that incredible face and figure? No wrinkles! Don't you age?"

"Oh, Barb. This is so nice. I'm glad you talked me into it."

"So how did you get away? Your place is open every day, right?"

"Yes, yes. I got one of my ladies—a nurse named Wanda who's really on the ball—to handle things today. I almost never do anything like that, but I think it's going to be worth it."

"I know it is. Let's go sit down. I brought a blanket and some goodies."

The women went to sit beside a tree, choosing to be in the sun for a little more warmth. They worked together laying out the blanket, the plates, the wine and the cheese. Sharona opened her large bag and brought out some reduced-calorie Wheat Thins and a large, triangular Toblerone chocolate bar. The girls had always eaten Toblerone together when they studied.

"Lo-cal crackers and high-cal chocolate? Don't tell me you're still a Tweedle-dummy!" exclaimed Barbara. She pointed a finger at her own head and rotated it around her ear a couple of times. Both women laughed.

Barbara poured the Chardonnay, chilled perfectly by the ambient air. It was as smooth and tasty as she had promised, and the bottle was all but gone within ten minutes.

"So whatcha doin' for fun these days, Tweedles?" asked Barbara.

"I really don't have much time for anything," answered Sharona. "About the only thing I really can squeeze in is my once-a-month thing at the Bridgeport Home for Girls. You remember? That place for pregnant girls? And sometimes I can only give them an hour or so. I feel bad about that."

"What do you do there again? You're teaching them to sew or something?" asked Barbara.

"No. Nothing like that. I teach them money management. Like how to balance a checkbook. Why it's so important to save a little each month. Stuff like that."

"That must make you feel real nice."

"Yes. It recharges me. I go again tomorrow, actually. It's been a long time. They're so *needy*, you know?"

Sharona and Barbara went on to speak of the weather, the recent work on the park's dam, their all-nighter study sessions when they were roomies back in college. They talked about recent movies (none of which either had had time to see), about the news, about people with whom they had gone to school. It was almost as if they were avoiding talking about their real-here-and-now lives.

Then Sharona broke that bubble.

"Barb? You ever have anything to do with the police?"

"What?" asked Sharona's surprised friend.

"I don't mean being arrested or anything. Just—did you ever talk with them? Or have them call you?"

"I have no idea what you're talking about, Sharona. We don't get many criminals at the hospital, you know. Except maybe because of that slimy janitor who got caught lifting the sheets off some sleeping patients."

Sharona's eyebrows rose.

Barbara continued. "I did get a ticket once. But it was just for parking. A breakfast meeting at a local coffee shop went late, and that was that. Thirty-five dollars' worth of street parking."

"No, Barb. That's not what I'm talking about."

Sharona sighed. Then she went on. "Barbara, there's something going on at work, and I have nobody to talk to."

"You have me. You *always* have me." Barbara nodded her head and pursed her lips like Shirley Temple, showing her conviction to help. Barb's hair slid over her shoulders. "Out with it," she said.

"You sure? This is pretty bad."

Sharona's college buddy sat back against the tree, folded her hands in her lap, and just waited. Thirty yards away, first-graders brought to the dam on a field trip were marching over the bridge. They formed a curvy line led by a teacher wearing a day-glow orange cap and a whistle. The kids' talking and giggling lightened the tension a little.

Sharona straightened and began. "Well, I've got this nurse-midwife named Lisbath. She's worked with me for years and I've always had good feedback about her."

"Uh-huh," said Barbara.

"She's really old-school. Always wears her cap. Starched uniform. You know, Barbara, these days, most nurses working registry don't even *wear* a uniform. Casual is the rule. Lisbath Milliken is *not* casual."

"Go on," said Barbara. So far, she'd heard nothing unusual, but she knew it was coming.

"Well, there might be something going on with her."

"That's pretty vague," observed Barb.

"Just hold on a second, okay? I haven't really put all this together myself before. Talking to you is forcing me to make some kind of sense out of it. This is hard, Barb."

"I know it is. And I'm here for you, Tweedles." Barbara reached out and placed her hand on Sharona's forearm. She squeezed it slightly as the bond between the girlfriends continued curing.

"Barb, this woman Lisbath might be doing something wrong. I've had the police contact me twice—*twice*—about her, and they're not giving up."

"That must be scary," said Barbara. She paused for a moment, then said, "But I thought you just ran the registry. So technically, you're not responsible, right? They're subcontractors?"

"Yes. I don't have any liability for my nurses' actions. At least I don't think I do. Oh, God. Maybe I have to call my lawyer. I hadn't even thought of that before. But I still feel responsible. They're like my own kids, even if half of them are older than I am."

"So what do the police want with you?"

"They want me to stop Lisbath from doing her nursing. Can you imagine?"

The heavy burdens Sharona had been carrying were beginning to coalesce as she tried to describe for the first time everything happening to her. The Chardonnay was easing the communication a little, too.

"Stop her? How could you do that, even if you wanted to?"

"Barbara, that's not the point. The point is that my whole business might be threatened and that I might be somehow contributing to hurting all the women Lisbath has been working with, and Lisbath and I have been really good friends for a long time and that mean detective actually *threatened* me and..."

Sharona's voice began to crack as her eyes became swollen with tears. She stopped in mid-sentence and began to cry.

Barbara immediately cradled Sharona's head in her arms. She stroked Sharona's side and rocked quietly. A light wind mingled their hair as Barbara's empathy warmed the area around them.

"It'll be okay, Tweedles. It'll be all right," comforted Barbara. Then she asked, "What do your parents say about all this?"

"God, Barb. I don't know what happens when people get old. Neither of them wants to talk about it. It's like their stress tolerance has gone to zero. I love them dearly, but they're no help at all."

Barbara shook her head slowly.

"I'm sure glad I have you, Barb. I mean, maybe it sounds almost maudlin, but I really don't have anybody else."

Barbara tightened her grip on Sharona, and Sharona began to regain her composure. It felt good to have someone to talk to. Someone who could understand.

Sharona went on to describe what felt to her like Haberdeen's ongoing harassment. She also told Barbara about the argument she and Lisbath had had about Nurse Forman's taking on a midwifery assignment on Lisbath's day off.

A light wind began, and it became quite cold at the park. It looked like it might actually begin to snow. The two decided to go to Sharona's place. There they talked for a while more, had a pizza delivered for an easy dinner, and came to value their friendship increasingly over every passing hour.

Twenty-eight

"Oh, Mama! *Oh, Mama!*" La-TaKeisha Jeffers was screaming at the top of her lungs. Her body vibrated like a tremendous, live jellyfish thrown violently against a wall. "I be *sick*. Oh Mama, oh, Mama, *oh Mama*!"

Down the hall at the ER admitting desk, Deputy Dr. Robert Peters of the State of Connecticut Department of Health was interviewing the admitting nurse. He had received the Infocard that Dr. El-Kareem had sent in when Jeffers' vaginal *Strep* infection became evident. He showed his badge to the admitting nurse and began his questioning.

"Miss, do you have one La-TaKeisha Jeffers here?"

"Yes, sir. That's her you hear down the hall."

Peters, an old hand at hospital operations, thought something was amiss. "Why hasn't she been moved to a regular patient room?"

"*Sheeeeeiiittt!*" screamed Jeffers. Liquids gurgled in her throat as the profanity squeezed its way out.

"Believe me, we don't *want* her here. Do you hear that? She doesn't stop. She does not stop! I don't think the woman even sleeps!"

"Nurse, she definitely sounds irritating, but you are not answering my question. Why hasn't she been moved?"

"Take a peek in her room." The admitting nurse gestured in the direction of Ms. Jeffers' room by tilting her head.

"What?"

"Just go have a look. A picture's worth a thousand words."

Intrigued, Peters headed down the hall. When he was within fifteen feet of the door, the repulsive smells of Jeffers' room hit him like a cattle ranch on a hot day. Although he was an experienced health department deputy, he couldn't quite make out the source of the foul odors.

Peters stood by the door just past the curtain and leaned forward to have a look. What he saw immediately answered his question. There she was, lying in a pool of sweat like one of those beached whales that commit suicide for no discernable reason. But this whale was alive and very, very sick. Peters could tell from her deep red-toned fleshy palm that was hanging over the mattress that she had a high fever. There was vomitus lying in several rough pools on the floor and on the bed sheets. A makeshift diaper comprised of several pinned-together pillowcases was miserably stained, and the weighted contraption was pulling at her waist.

"*Oooh whoa!*" shouted La-TaKeisha.

Peters had his answer and shrank back a few feet before turning to walk back to the admitting desk.

"I got it. She probably shouldn't be moved."

He continued: "Does she communicate intelligibly?"

"I haven't seen it," the nurse said dryly.

The hospital air conditioning kicked in and the Jeffers stench began to be pushed down the hallway. Peters decided to expedite his interview.

"Nurse, I need to speak to Dr. . . ." Deputy Peters had to check his file since Arabic names were strange to him ". . . to Dr. El-Kareem. Is he on staff here, or is he transient?"

"He's been here forever. Nice doc. He came through less than a half-hour ago; he's probably still on the floors."

"Thanks." Peters made his way out of the ER and into the main hospital.

Two minutes after his paging call, the white hospital phone next to the doctors' cafeteria rang and Peters picked it up.

He heard, "This is Dr. El-Kareem. Is that Deputy Peters?"

"Yes, Doctor. Bob Peters from Connecticut Health. Can we meet for a couple of minutes before you leave tonight?"

"Surely, sir. I have only one more patient to visit. Do you want to come by my on-site office?"

"I'm by the doctors' cafeteria now."

"Oh, that's fine. I could use a cup of coffee. Let's meet there. How will I recognize you, Dr. Peters?"

"I'm wearing a light blue suit and have a steel clipboard. No lab coat."

"See you in a few minutes."

Dr. Peters went into the cafeteria and put a cup of coffee on his tray.

Fifteen minutes later, Dr. El-Kareem entered. Peters knew him immediately by his dark-olive skin and neatly-trimmed beard. The doctor's white coat was immaculate, and he had a tiny rose pinned carefully to his lapel. The top of a rose-red pen peeked out of his coat's breast pocket. His shoes gleamed.

Peters got up and walked over to Dr. El-Kareem while he was paying at the cash register.

"Hello, Dr. El-Kareem. I'm Dr. Bob Peters, County Health. Pleasure to meet you."

Dr. El-Kareem smiled. He picked up four packs of sugar. "Where are we sitting?"

Both men walked over to the table and settled in.

Peters got right to the point. "Doctor, this is about the Infocard you sent in on patient La-TaKeisha Jeffers. You remember?"

"Who could forget?"

"A new mother with *Strep*, 100.9 temp, typical high-temp tachycardia, tenderness on lower abdominal palpation, parametrial tenderness with bimanual examination, low urine output, fever, nausea, WBC around 34,000. Sound to you like puerperal fever?"

Dr. El-Kareem answered, "I think so. Very unusual, especially these days. Especially in this environment."

" 'Childbed fever,' right?"

Dr. El-Kareem said, "If it's *Streptococcus pyogenes* or one of its variants. And in this case it is. Yes. That is the common term." His accent was pleasant to the deputy's ear.

Dr. El-Kareem felt his coffee cup for temperature, then continued: "This disease was rampant before the 20th century, but as childbirth support technique and general medical hygiene improved, childbed fever seceded almost completely."

The staccato, muted explosions of microwave popcorn and the clanking of institutional dishes sounded curiously distant.

Dr. Peters asked, "Do you remember the history—why it's called 'childbed fever'?"

"Well, it showed up in women shortly after childbirth. Sometimes it would spread from one to another because the doctor or midwife would passively act as a disease vector for the *Strep*. If you don't wash your hands and equipment well enough, the stuff can live for some time and enter the patient's body through virtually any compromise."

Dr. Peters added a little cream to his coffee, then stirred.

El-Kareem continued. "Like when the skin is compromised —cut or scratched—or when a vessel is bleeding during a birth sequence. It's an open door to the body through which bacteria and viruses enter freely."

"Right."

"The same bacterium is responsible for scarlet fever," added the good doctor.

"Yes, scarlet fever," said Dr. Peters. "Do you think we could be facing an outbreak?" He was getting excited. He envisioned people lying dead all over the streets, more major newspaper headlines, and untold overtime at his job. The latter bothered him the most.

Dr. El-Kareem straightened all four packs of sugar like a deck of cards, tore off all four tops at once, and poured the sweet granules into his coffee. "This is what keeps me going all day," he said to Dr. Peters as he smiled and stirred. "Healthy? No. Energy? Yes," he added. He paused, pensive.

"Well, I don't think we're facing a scarlet fever outbreak here," said Dr. El-Kareem. His manner was soothing and reassuring. "This is certainly the only case I know of. Still, did you see the article in the paper a couple of days ago? That woman found in the gutter with *S. Pyogenes?*"

"I heard about it," said Peters. "I'm slated to meet with Coroner Pelt to discuss it tomorrow."

"Doctor El-Kareem, in the last three weeks, I've received no fewer than three Infocards that are almost carbon copies of each other. Symptoms are analogous, all present in recent mothers, and all within a ten-mile radius." Dr. Peters sat back and took a sip of his coffee.

El-Kareem's brow furrowed. It was clear that this could be more than mere coincidence. And it could mean danger for Bridgeport and the surrounding area. "No wonder you're here," Salah El-Kareem voiced. "Do you have any reports of *S. pyogenes* showing up in anyone other than recent mothers?"

"Well, other than the woman in the paper, no. That is strange. That's why puerperal fever may be the most rational diagnosis."

"So there must be some common link," said Dr. El-Kareem. "Are all the victims here in the same hospital? "

Dr. Peters said, "No. When I said a ten-mile radius, I meant hospitals all within ten miles of each other."

"So what's acting as the vector?" asked Dr. El-Kareem.

"You mean *who*," responded Peters.

"What are you talking about? You certainly can't be suggesting that someone is traveling from woman to woman infusing them with the bacterium. That's sinister."

Dr. Peters said, "We're on the trail of the probable vector. She is the nurse-midwife who handled your patient Jeffers. And maybe others."

Dr. El-Kareem thought for a moment, then said, "That would be Lisbath Milliken. I've handled many of her mothers. She knows what she's doing—Milliken has been actively practicing midwifery for many years," El-Kareem said. "And I've observed her often on the GYN floor. Her techniques are just fine. Medical standard."

"Well, we suspect her," said Dr. Peters. "After all, all three women had their children with her."

"Highly suggestive, to be sure," remarked Dr. El-Kareem. "So did you come here just to talk to me? Surely we could have spoken on the phone."

"Doctor, I came to speak with Miss Jeffers, but she doesn't seem to be communicative at this time."

"No, she is not. Her fever-induced delirium hasn't abated. I'm afraid she won't be able to give you any meaningful information for perhaps an additional day or two at least."

Dr. Peters asked, "Did Ms. Jeffers say anything about the midwife when you admitted her?"

"She was barely cognizant of her situation even then. And I had no reason to suspect anything, nor did I know on admission that she had had the baby with a midwife."

"I see," said Peters. "Well, maybe I'll check back with you and the patient in a couple of days. Would that be all right?"

"My pleasure, sir," said Dr. Salah El-Kareem with a slight bow.

"Thanks. Enjoy the coffee."

"*Mah saalem,*" said the good doctor.

🜂 🜂 🜂

G-Man Haberdeen was working in a partial information vacuum. Because Lisbath Milliken's recent double murder of Doris Wallace and Francine Forman had taken place in the Shelton police jurisdiction, the inter-agency notices had not yet been circulated outside of Shelton. The press had not picked up on the horrible killings, either, and the police were doing everything they could to keep the murders quiet.

Despite his not yet knowing about the Wallace-Forman tragedy, the information Haberdeen did have at hand made it increasingly obvious to him that his prey Milliken was dirty. The G-Man realized that Mandy Shapiro's claims about seeing the woman ingest blood were probably reality-based. Haberdeen knew that he needed to find a way to arrest the nurse-midwife or otherwise stop her. Fast.

He thought long and hard. What could he get her on? The three alleged problems with her were that she might be drinking blood, she might be taking the substance from women for her own use, and she might be spreading disease. He decided to tackle the first question first.

There is no law against drinking blood, he realized. If there were, people couldn't order steak rare. For that matter, cunnilingus between consenting adults in some cases would be outlawed if any blood were present. *Nope*, he thought. *Can't get her on that. It doesn't matter how weird it is. Too bad*, the G-Man mused.

Taking blood for her own use? He'd either need a witness past the age of majority, or he'd have to get a judge to approve a search warrant for her premises. The detective decided to hold that warrant idea in reserve for a while. He wanted a super-solid case.

Haberdeen then turned his thoughts to the spread of disease. Yes. Deliberately spreading disease is an abrogation of a person's biological sovereignty. It's illegal to fail to inform someone you have AIDS before a sexual encounter. *This is my trump card*, thought the detective.

The G-Man left a message for Dr. Peters at the health department. Haberdeen needed confirmation that Milliken could be fingered for sure as the transmitter of this childbed fever.

Deputy Peters called Detective Haberdeen as soon as he returned to his office. Peters' phone call interrupted the G-Man's report-writing time. This irritated Haberdeen a little, but when he heard it was Peters, he was much less annoyed and very interested indeed. He wanted to finally get this case off his desk, and the more information he got, the closer he got to closing the case. Or so he thought.

"Dr. Peters, what do you have for me?" asked Haberdeen.

"Well, Detective, what I have amounts to coincidence. Lots of it, but coincidence nonetheless."

Haberdeen sat back in his squeaking wooden chair and propped the phone between his left shoulder and his ear. He absentmindedly picked his teeth with a paper clip while he listened.

Peters continued. "It looks like a strain of bacteria is being transmitted to several women, and it's likely that our Nurse Milliken is the one transmitting it. We're talking about a type of *Strep*."

"Strep throat? That's all this is about? You've got to be kidding. This is bullshit." Haberdeen was about as indignant as a cop can be.

"There are lots of strains of *Strep*, Mr. Haberdeen. This one is *Streptococcus pyogenes*. Very special."

"Why?"

"For one thing, it's the basis of scarlet fever." Peters believed that he really wasn't talking about that dreaded and well-known ancient disease, but Haberdeen's offhandedness deserved at least a small zinger in retaliation.

"Shit! You've got to be kidding. You buy into this?"

Peters decided to remain silent for a few seconds to relish his minor if sophomoric triumph.

"Talk to me, Peters." Haberdeen was pretty demanding, and the health department deputy decided it was time to be slightly more straightforward. Just slightly.

"Detective, we may be facing a scarlet fever epidemic; a childbed fever epidemic."

"Children getting sick in bed? Tell me what you can about it," asked the G-Man.

"No. Childbed fever is a very old disease too, but it's the mothers who caught it. Who *catch* it. It happens when a bacterium—usually the *Strep* strain we're talking about—is transmitted during childbirth."

"Oh, *yeah*," said Haberdeen. These were golden words for the G-Man's ears.

"George, it appears that all the current cases of childbed fever are local and, more significantly, that all of them are from women whose births were at home and—you guessed it—were handled by Nurse Milliken."

"Jesus Christ!" said Haberdeen. "That's *exactly* what I thought!" He didn't care that this outsider had called him "George." Things were beginning to come together. Haberdeen's simple cop's hypothesis had now been validated by the health department. There seemed to be much more to this case than had originally met the G-Man's eye.

"What else can you tell me?" asked the detective. He was genuinely interested now. He even dropped the paper clip toothpick.

"Well, not much more, unfortunately. Puerperal fever is rare these days. Yet the maternal death rate from all infection tends to be well over five percent, so it's pretty bad."

"Purple fever. Yeah. Dr. Gold told me that, too. So what else do you have for me?" Haberdeen picked up his discarded paper clip toothpick and began tapping it on the desk. He wrote notes on his yellow pad.

"I couldn't talk to the patient I had gone to see. She was too sick. But we've got to stop this Milliken woman, at least temporarily." Peters cleared his throat as he thought for a moment. "Whatever's happening is probably inadvertent, but it's dangerous anyway."

"You think that she's making them sick by accident?"

"Just a hunch," hazarded Peters. "Can you do something to keep her from handling any other women until we know more?"

"Nothing unless we charge her with some crime. Don't you have any power to stop her? You're the fucking *health department*, for Christ's sake."

"I don't think so. I'll have to check. Maybe we can stop her as an active disease vector. For now, though, I guess we'll just have to cross our fingers."

"How about my just asking the bitch to stop for a while?"

"Now, why didn't I think of that?" asked Peters.

"I'll call her supervisor. Keep at it," said Haberdeen.

"Keep in touch. Good-bye, Detective."

Haberdeen hung up. Cops never give the final greeting on the phone. It makes them seem too accommodating.

◆ ◆ ◆

Everything was quiescent at the nurse registry. Then the phone rang.

"Dickinson's. May I help you?"

"Is this Miss Gomez, the owner?"

"Yes. Who is calling, please? What can I do for you?"

"This is Detective George Haberdeen. You remember?"

Sharona remembered, all right. This was one of the few men she had ever met who made her instantly uncomfortable. Even his calling her "Miss" instead of "Ms." got her goat.

"Yes." Sharona's voice was dry and her hackles were lifting.

G-Man got right to the point. "Miss Gomez, I need you to stop Milliken."

Sharon truly had no idea what Haberdeen was talking about. The detective's statement just did not compute. She knew that Lisbath had headed over to the Wallace birth to replace Fran Forman, but she had not gotten her follow-up reports yet. Sharona assumed everything had gone well even though Milliken had left angry.

"Are you *there*, lady?"

"Yes. What do you mean, 'stop her'? What the hell are you talking about?" All heads at Dickinson's turned toward Sharona as tears began to well up in her eyes. She rarely raised her voice and she never swore. Sharona's worries of some cop shutting down Dickinson's began their trek through her thinking. Something was definitely going down hard here and now.

"Miss Gomez, you need to keep your Milliken from doing any more work until you hear from me. We have a problem and she seems to be in the middle of it."

Sharona was stunned. Her prize possession, so to speak—her

primary nurse-midwife and her old friend—was somehow under the scrutiny and accusative eye of the police. Not just the police, but this Haberdeen character. This did not feel good.

Besides that, there wasn't anything she could do to comply.

"Detective?"

"Yeah?"

"Do you remember what I told you about my people?"

Haberdeen was at a loss. "No," he said. He meant to say *What the fuck are you talking about*, but he held his tongue.

"I already told you. My nurses are independent contractors. I have no power over them. I broker their services, and they decide what jobs to take and when and where to do them. I do not have the power to do anything except maybe to hold back on additional assignments for her. *Temporarily*."

"Do it!"

"What?" Sharona's normally-pretty face was contorted in anger. Her eyes were squinting. She pretty much knew what the man wanted, but she *needed* to give him a hard time.

"Stop giving her assignments. If you don't, you could be considered an accessory."

"An *accessory*? What the hell are you talking about? What right do you have to accuse me or threaten me?" Sharona was standing up, holding the phone. Her knuckles were white and she was absolutely blind with rage.

All of Dickinson's was stone-silent. Even the traffic outside the window seemed to stop dead.

"Yes. An accessory. Now are you going to stop her or not?" Haberdeen was insistent, but knew he had virtually no power at this point. He didn't care.

Sharona just stood there, phone to her ear. She didn't know what to say. She had gone from a complacent businesswoman surrounded by competent, caring nurses and the warm fragrance of coffee on a drizzly day to a woman about to be taken to jail for no reason. She was stunned and speechless and confused.

The G-Man pretty much knew what was happening on the other end of the phone. He had deliberately placed this woman in a completely untenable position. Right now he was getting nowhere. He decided on a new tack.

"Miss Gomez, is your nurse Susie Rime there?"

"What? I thought we were talking about Lisbath."

Haberdeen had had his fill of Gomez's resistance. "Put Rime on the phone."

Sharona's eyes glared directly at Susie's. Like everyone else in the place, Susie was watching Sharona and wondering what was going on. When Sharona's eyes fell on her, Susie felt like someone had just infused her with a surprise ice enema.

"Why are you looking at me?"

Haberdeen was hollering into the phone, and Sharona squinted and moved it away from her ear. Everyone in the room heard his voice emanating from the receiver, but it was so distorted nobody could make out any details. But Haberdeen's emotional state was obvious.

"That Detective Haberdeen is on the phone. He wants to talk to you." She aimed the receiver at Ms. Rime.

Immediately, Susie felt like a rat caught in a trap. She turned red as a beet. Nobody had known anything about the forced collusion between Haberdeen and the young, sweet thing. Susie had been careful to say absolutely nothing about her arrangement with the G-Man. Her silence was motivated partly out of a sense of fear and partly from the titillating hint of devilishness working undercover for the police created.

All the other nurses were snickering as soon as they heard that the detective was asking for Susie. Every magazine at Dickinson's was put down simultaneously. *What's this all about?* they wondered. *This must be juicy!*

"Let me take it in your back room, okay?" asked Susie.

"Okay. But you'd damn well better tell me what's going on when you get off."

It looked like lightning bolts alternated between Sharona's and Susie's eyes.

Sharona put the call on hold without warning Haberdeen that she was going to do it. He had overheard some of the conversation and knew what was happening anyway.

Susie first went to her chair and got her purse, then walked to the conference room door without turning her head at all. She closed the door behind her and sat down at the table. She cleared her voice, got a pencil and some scratch paper, and continued finding ways to stave off actually picking up the receiver and taking the call off hold. She fidgeted like Art Carney in an old *Honeymooners* episode preparing to write a shopping list.

But ultimately she had to face the music even if it was going to be a dirge. She picked up the phone and hit the flashing button.

Even before she could speak, the G-Man was bellowing through the phone.

"Is this Rime? What took you so long? Do you think this is some kind of a game or something?"

"Sorry, Detective. It took me a minute to get myself together."

Understatement, thought Haberdeen.

"What do you want?"

"I need those Milliken patient names and information. Now."

Fearful of what Haberdeen might do to her, Susie had gone through the file cabinets the night before. She had the information written down on small slips of paper in her purse.

"Well?" pressed Haberdeen. "Are you going to keep the law waiting, Miss Rime?"

"Okay, okay," said Susie. She began to shake while she read him the patient information.

"And Milliken's address."

She gave it to Haberdeen reluctantly. Susie suspected he already had the information, but she felt completely helpless against this horrible, powerful man.

Susie's emotions were in an uproar. It seemed like so long ago, on Dickinson's porch, that she had told the detective that Milliken hurt her own patients. Susie had wanted to get revenge on Lisbath Milliken for taking all the good jobs away, and for doing her sickening "victory dance" every time she got an assignment. But now things were going way overboard. She almost felt like protecting Lisbath against this mean detective who seemed to threaten everybody. At the same time, she still felt wronged by the bitch.

Haberdeen belted out a new command. "I need you to stop Milliken."

"*What?*" asked a stunned Susie Rime.

"Stop Milliken. Keep the woman from doing any more work."

"No! I can't do that! What are you talking about? This is awfully strange, you know."

"I don't care how strange it is. I need her stopped and you need to help me!" There was absolutely no flexibility in Haberdeen's voice. Police call this the *command voice*, and it is well-practiced and usually very effective.

Susie was being thrust into a quandary even more difficult and untenable than it was the last time this creep had ordered her around. It reminded her of when her father used to start screaming at her for no reason. His drunken rages were frightening. He would beat her if she didn't do this or that, so Susie learned to be helpless on command.

But this time was different. She was a nurse—a professional—not some little girl trapped beneath her threatening father's shadow. And this bastard detective was ordering her to do something completely beyond her power. More importantly, it was outside of her sense of right and wrong. It was simply unacceptable.

"Mr. Haberdeen," Susie's unsteady voice said, "you are asking me to do something that I cannot do. Even if I wanted to stop her, I couldn't. And I don't want to. You're going to have to find someone else to do your dirty work!" Her jaw muscles twitched and she played compulsively with her watch strap.

Susie felt great and relieved and at the same time frightened.

She had just turned down the police. She was shaking like a leaf and her blouse was wet with perspiration. Susie did not know what her future would hold. But she had needed to express some inner strength, and it felt liberating to have done so.

The phone was silent for upwards of ten seconds, except for the sounds of heavy, unsynchronized breathing on both sides of the line. Two minds, in angry contest in a confused fog, tried to work out their independent strategies. Haberdeen was the first to break the tense silence.

"Young lady, you're risking big trouble," the G-Man said, knowing it sounded weak.

"What trouble? I haven't done anything wrong and you know it."

"Wanna bet? Remember those records you just gave me?"

"Yes. So what? I was directed by the police to do so." Susie felt mildly triumphant.

Haberdeen began to turn the tables. "Who's going to believe that? A cop can't order you to break the law." Haberdeen was fumbling for some way—any way—to prevail in this little battle of wills. "You stole proprietary records."

My God, thought Susie. *That bastard set me up!*

"You go ahead and arrest me, then. I'll just tell the truth."

George Haberdeen was feeling more comfortable now. The girl's naïveté would be her undoing, he thought.

"I've got my eye on you, young lady," Haberdeen admonished. "You'll call me when you see the light. You have my number. Better hope I'm not the one to make the first call or you might find yourself behind bars."

Shit, thought Susie. *Maybe he means it.*

Susie Rime was a young lady growing older and perhaps wiser much faster than she ever expected. An hour ago she was thinking happily about shopping for some CDs after work and wiggling her derriere as she heard the pop music in her head. Now she was figuring out how to stay out of prison. Growing up's so very hard to do.

Twenty-nine

The Bridgeport Home for Girls was in a cinderblock building situated in one of the many poor areas of the city. It was in the middle of the downtown block, sandwiched between two small-potatoes factories. Both businesses were closed on this cold, wet Wednesday. The bleak winter weather had laid a foreboding cast over the whole town. Sharona had to negotiate freezing puddles to get to the Home's black-painted metal front door. She was looking forward to this special time. It would take the bad taste of that Haberdeen phone fiasco right out of her head.

She pushed the buzzer under the security speaker and waited.

After a second push of the buzzer, a tinny voice came through the speaker. "Yes?"

"Hello. This is Sharona Gomez. I'm here to give my money workshop?"

"Oh, yes! Miss Gomez. I'll be right there."

Sharona heard no fewer than three locks being worked. Finally, the door swung inward. An extremely thin, severe-looking woman with close-cropped hair and a white blouse buttoned all the way to the neck beckoned Sharona's entrance.

This was the live-in director, Miss Penelope. She showed her pleasure in Sharona's presence by bowing slightly. Sharona just smiled and said hello, then headed for the classroom off to her right.

The girls were already in the room. A few were at their desks, and the rest were huddled by a corner of the blackboard drawing and talking about something that looked vaguely like a bassinet. When they saw Miss Sharona come in, they all smiled and took their seats. It was pretty rare for an outsider to come into the Home, and all of them liked Sharona's patience and demeanor.

"Hi, girls!" said Sharona.

"Hello, Miss Sharona," they all said more or less in unison. The sound was remarkable in part because the words were spoken in a sonorous vocal melting pot of Hispanic, Asian, and American accents.

Miss Penelope was standing at the door looking in, and she smiled at the scene. Many of these girls had been in gangs or in other trouble before being remanded to her custody. It was unusual for a large number of them to behave like a flock of veritable angels. Penelope was taking all of it in like a dry sponge sucking up the water it craved.

"Today we'll talk about credit cards," said Sharona. "What they are and why they're good and why they're bad."

The girls settled in as their pecuniary sophistication levels began to rise.

As Sharona spoke, she experienced something deeply unsettling. She was advising the girls about what credit was and how to protect it, and as she did so, Sharona began to think in parallel about her own situation. How terrible it would be if she were to lose her Dickinson's business. Especially over the actions of one of her prized nurses!

In some remarkable and instinctive way, a few of the more empathic girls picked up on Sharona's internal conflict. Their teacher seemed to be talking about one thing, but her eyes showed concern and maybe sorrow about something else.

Some of the older girls began to chatter as Sharona continued her lecture, and of course she noticed. "Girls? What's up? Don't you care about taking care of yourself and your baby?"

A fifteen-year-old pregnant Hispanic girl spoke up. "Miss Sharona, this credit stuff is kind of interesting, but is something wrong?"

Sharona was thrown off guard. How could any of these kids know? She was experiencing an internal, private dialogue. Could these kids be that perceptive?

She had to take a moment to decide how to handle this. After an awkward pause, Sharona responded. "I really want to thank you for thinking about me. For caring about me. And I care about all of you, too. That's why it's so important that you learn about this credit stuff."

The girls were spellbound. None heard the rain starting outside the window.

Sharona continued. "As I talk to you in our classes, I have to think real hard about the real world. That's where you'll be going eventually. I'm out in the real world every day, and sometimes it's just a little scary."

She caught her breath, deciding how to go on—how much to reveal. Sharona wanted to be able to teach an object lesson without frightening the girls. She was warmed by their attention and concern and wanted very much to give something positive back.

"Girls, right now my business is going very well. You remember? I own a nursing registry.

"But businesses, just like regular people, have good times and bad. Sometimes I have to think about what would happen if things were bad. If they go bad, then credit is hard to get. That can be a problem. It can make it so the business might have to stop."

Sharona felt herself shudder and figured she had said enough. She didn't want to share details of how the police were hassling her, how her prized nurse was in trouble with the law, how she was feeling daily stress that threatened to become overwhelming.

As she thought about these things, a tear crept out of the corner of her eye. Four of the girls saw this and got up from their seats. The went up to Sharona and encircled her with their arms. They laid their heads around her, and their pregnant bellies pressed up against Sharona's legs. They gave off a wonderful warmth.

Sharona had not felt this good and this bad in a long time. She placed her hands over the girls' and smiled through her tears.

She was able to resume her lecture after a couple of minutes. She felt infinitely closer to the girls from that point on. She felt a little stronger, too.

This moment would reverberate in Sharona's memory for the rest of her life.

◆ ◆ ◆

Nurse Susie Rime couldn't sleep the night of her phone conversation with Detective Haberdeen. She was scared that Haberdeen was somehow going to arrest her or otherwise harass her because she had refused to "stop" Lisbath Milliken. And she was angrier than she had been for a long time. How dare this man threaten her when all she was trying to do was to help the police in the first place?

She got up in the middle of the night and got a bag of sour cream-flavored potato chips from the kitchen. She got a towel from the closet, propped herself up in bed, laid the towel down over her chest and lap, and opened the bag. Potato chips were Susie's warmth food. Other people had their chocolate, and Susie had her chips. She tore into the bag, anxious for solace.

While crunching away, Susie realized that her "sister" nurse Lisbath was probably in lots of trouble. She also saw that, while she had refused to help Haberdeen, she had done nothing to help Lisbath either. She was just angry enough to want some kind of revenge against the man who had treated her so badly, and what better way than to tip Lisbath off about what was happening?

Susie knew nothing of Haberdeen's interview with Lisbath earlier in the week. She resolved to spill the beans to her fellow nurse in the morning.

As soon as she arrived at Dickinson's, Susie walked in and asked if Lisbath was there. Of course, the entire place was buzzing with yesterday's phone call, and Susie's entrance and immediate question fueled the fire nicely. Everyone oriented to Susie Rime like snipers on a target.

"No, it's her day off," said Wanda. "She's off Mondays and Thursdays." She was sitting in Lisbath's usual spot and was smugly aware of the matriarch's absence.

"Oh, yeah. That's right," Susie remembered. "Sharona, mark me off for this morning, okay? I've got to take care of something."

"What?" asked Sharona and every other silent nurse in the place.

"Just something I've got to do. I'll be in by twelve."

"Okay. See you later." Sharona's voice rose at the end of her greeting. It was clear that Susie's entrance and exit held a certain fascination for Boss Gomez and everyone else too. But the details would have to wait.

🜢 🜢 🜢

Lisbath was startled by the knock at her door. The moment the sound registered, she imagined it could be that terrible man whose horrible visit had given her such trouble. *Oh, God, I hope he's not back again*, she thought.

Lisbath remained silent. So did Lad, who noticed his mommy's stress and held perfectly still except for the twitching of his ears.

Susie knocked again, this time saying, "Lisbath! It's Susie from Dickinson's. Are you there?"

The moment Lisbath heard that friendly voice, her entire demeanor softened. She pushed off the couch, Lad started wagging his tail, and both of them trotted to the door with great senses of relief.

But as Lisbath reached toward the door chain to unhook it, she stopped abruptly. Her thoughts began to race. *What would this young girl be doing here? She has never been here before. How did she find out where I live? Is this some trick of that terrible man's? Wouldn't it be wonderful for this door to have one of those viewing devices in it? It would be so much easier! Oh, what do I do?*

She removed the chain and opened the door.

"Hi, Lisbath! Nice to see you!" said Susie, perky with confidence.

"Hello, young lady. I'm very surprised to see you here. I didn't know you knew where I lived." Milliken covered her mouth and coughed lightly.

"Oh, everyone knows, Lisbath. You're such a fixture at Dickinson's, you know."

This made no sense to Lisbath at all, but she accepted it. After all, this young thing seemed so innocent. What could be wrong?

"So why did you come, Susie? I can't for the life of me figure it out," admitted Lisbath.

"Can I sit down?" asked Susie. Despite Ms. Rime's jealousy of Lisbath, she felt Lisbath could help her get back at that harassing Detective Haberdeen. Of course, she wouldn't admit that to Lisbath Milliken.

"Oh, I'm sorry. Of course you can sit down. Please—come in and have a seat right here." She pointed to the stuffed chair. "This is Lad," said Lisbath as she turned her head toward the jumping-bean dog. Lad was very, very happy to see someone non-threatening. And, unbeknownst to his mommy, he loved the rich smells coming from the girl's nether regions.

"So what brings you here, dear?"

"Lisbath, are you okay? You look a little pallid."

Milliken coughed again, this time bringing up some phlegm. She caught it in her pure white hankie.

"Yes, Susie. Sure. I'm fine." Milliken was perspiring, yet the room felt to Susie like it was about 65 degrees. "So were you at Dickinson's today?"

"Yeah. But I wanted to see you, so I took the morning off. I *needed* to see you. Okay?"

"Okay. . ." Lisbath was tentative. Her mind raced. Sharp, painful memories of Haberdeen's onslaught at her apartment flooded into her. Joining the flood were the blood of Doris Wallace, the neck of Francine Forman, images of bleeding vaginas, and images of blood in beakers.

What could this young girl have to say, coming here out of the blue?

Lisbath was confused and frightened. Perspiration ran down her back. Thunder sounded in the distance, and the limited natural light that had been making its way through Lisbath's window began to disappear.

"What did you need to see me about, dear?" The midwife's sphincters had already begun to tighten. She coughed again.

"Well . . ." Susie hadn't considered how hard it might be to express all that she had to say to Lisbath. She had basically blundered into this situation, driven more by emotion than by strategy. For this young girl, all of a sudden, everything was immediate and real. She was on the spot. But she had put herself on this spot, and she needed to be okay with having done so.

"Lisbath, is there anything really unusual going on?"

"That's a pretty strange question," said Lisbath. Yet she had a strong and immediate internal reaction to the question. Lisbath put on the best poker face she had ever created.

The young girl asked, "Have you ever heard of a man named Haverteen?"

"You mean Haberdeen," Lisbath said without even thinking. As soon as she said it, the nurse-midwife felt like she had betrayed herself prematurely.

"Okay. Haberdeen. So what do you know about him?"

"What do *you* know about him, young lady?" asked Milliken. She was trying to turn the tables, but the tables were feeling pretty heavy just now. Lisbath simply could not believe that Sharona had told all of her troops about that police bastard, so Susie must have learned about him in some other way.

Susie got up her strength. "Lisbath, this policeman has been talking to me about you." Susie shifted in the soft chair.

Lisbath nodded slowly and pursed her lips. "Tall with a big belly and scraggly hair?" She stifled a cough. Her eyes were getting redder around the rims.

"That's him. But his hair was combed," Susie said.

Neither chuckled. Both women stared at each other for a moment, sharing a common hatred of Detective George Haberdeen.

"So what did he say?" risked Milliken.

"Well, a few days ago he made me give him information on your patients."

"*What?*" Lisbath was indignant. This was a breach of confidentiality but, more important, it was a violation of her privacy.

"He made me do it."

"How did he make you? Did he hold a gun to your head?"

"No, of course not. He threatened me, Lisbath. There was nothing I could do."

Susie Rime was lying. She conveniently left out the fact that the day she and the G-Man had met—on the porch at Dickinson's—she had volunteered to help because she was so jealous of Lisbath. That the nurse-midwife got all the good jobs. That even new nurses should get lots of jobs, too. And that Lisbath's victory dance was sickening.

Yes, Haberdeen had tried to force her to stop Lisbath, but that was only after the young nurse hesitated to help. Now Susie Rime felt that she was compensating for her actions.

Lisbath had a strained mixture of emotions. This girl had hurt both her and her beloved patients. But at the same time, Susie was in the Milliken Confessional now. She seemed to have come of her own free will, and she could probably be helpful. Lisbath flushed red, then blanched white. Lad stayed close.

Susie rubbed her temples as she continued. "Lisbath, there's something else. Yesterday I got a phone call from him."

Lisbath wiped her perspiring forehead with her hankie. "A phone call? Does he call you at home now?"

"No. He had actually called Sharona. Whatever they talked about, she didn't satisfy him, so he asked for me."

"Because he had already put you under this thumb."

"That's how he sees it. Or at least I assume so."

"So what did he want?" asked Milliken.

"He told me to stop you."

"To *stop* me? From what? That makes no sense." Lisbath's eyebrows rose.

"To stop you from nursing. I think that's what he had wanted Sharona to do, too."

Lisbath was devastated. She believed every word Susie was saying. Every syllable was newly painful.

Now this horrible policeman wanted to take away her career —her identity. And her source of blood. This was unacceptable, plain and simple. Something had to be done about him. *He* had to be stopped.

"Tell me more," said Lisbath. Her voice was shaky yet determined. She coughed.

"Well, Lisbath, that's about it. I decided last night that I was going to tell you what was going on right away. This feels terrible to me. I really *hate* this. All of this. I'm sorry I got mixed up with it in the first place."

There was a silence as each woman considered what was happening. Then Susie spoke up, but very quietly.

"Lisbath? Why do you think he wants you stopped? He didn't give me any reason—he just demanded that I help him. What's going on? Are you in trouble?"

"Well, obviously I'm in some kind of trouble, but darned if I know why. This man apparently has it in for me." She coughed a brief spurt. "I wish I knew why; then maybe I could do something about it."

Now it was Lisbath lying—lying through her teeth. But she needed to protect herself, particularly when talking to another Dickinsonian.

"Can I go the bathroom?" asked Susie.

Lisbath was glad for the respite—to be able to spend a few moments to begin to sort things out. "Sure, dear. It's right over there."

Lad had climbed up onto the couch during the conversation. He had lifted his head from Lisbath's lap when Susie stood up, but immediately returned it when he sensed no threat.

Lisbath began to revisit her own self-doubts. Was there really anything wrong with what she did? She and Lad needed blood to survive. Period.

And she had such a craving for more blood. It's not like chocolate, where it's wonderful when you have it but you can live without it for months at a time. No, blood was sustenance. Blood was a need as real and inviolable as the needs for water and warmth and shelter.

Lisbath began to get very down-to-earth in her thinking. *What would happen if I were somehow taken to jail? I would have to do something to get blood. Maybe go through trash cans for discarded sanitary napkins? What's my last resort? To see if rats' blood would be acceptable? To cut myself regularly and lick up my own red drippings? Could that satisfy me, or would it just be some horrendously macabre and useless recycling effort? Oh, God! Oh, God!*

And what of Lad? Poor Laddie! He'd die without the precious stuff. Wouldn't he? How would he get his blood? Attack other dogs? Or would he just shrivel up and die without Mommy's provisions?

This was becoming overwhelming. Lisbath was shaking. She was twisting her hankie so hard that its coughed-up mucus load was seeping through the material. Tears were coming to her eyes, and she didn't even realize it.

Susie came back from the bathroom as the toilet tank completed its replenishment.

"Lisbath! You look awful!"

Milliken was barely aware of Susie's presence. Her sour reverie was deeply consuming, with little room for anyone else's thoughts.

Lisbath's voice shook. "So why are you here? Really? Are you a friend of mine, or are you some kind of police moll?"

Lad mumbled a growl.

"Shit, Lisbath! What do you *think* I'm doing here? I'm not here for my health, you know! I'm trying to help you. To let you know what's going on! With that asshole detective. Shit, Lisbath!"

Milliken realized that the girl's vehemence was real. She thought that Susie had her best interests at heart. And that this must be very, very hard for the novice. She softened.

"I'm sorry, Susie. I've just been under a lot of stress lately."

"I bet," leaked out of Nurse Rime.

Milliken became silent for several seconds. Then she began to stir. To digest what was happening.

"Oh, no! *No!*" Lisbath began to wail like a mother at her child's funeral. Her stomach began to churn and she suffered a coughing fit that almost brought up solids.

Susie went to her side and sat down. She reached over to the Kleenex box on the table, withdrew a handful, and pressed them into Lisbath's shaking hand. But while she did this, she turned away to hide a sinister grin.

That bastard Haberdeen was now going to be on Lisbath's shit list. Little Miss Rime was orchestrating her revenge on him, feeling more powerful. She was much stronger in her resolve to resist his pressures.

"It'll be okay, Lisbath. I'm not going to help them out. We've got to stick together, right?"

Lisbath just continued to bawl.

Both of them sat there in sad communion for several minutes. Lisbath went over her predicament silently while Susie ruminated on her revenge.

"Lisbath, I have to go now," said Susie. "I hope you feel better soon. I *promise* I won't tell the police anything else. I won't help them. Cross my heart and hope to die." Her fingers crossed over her chest in a childish gesture that warmed Lisbath a little. And now she meant her promise.

Susie rose, got her purse and headed out. She closed the door behind her as softly as she could. "Yes!" she said as she strutted toward her car.

Lisbath felt that whatever vestige of self-control she had been maintaining was no longer necessary. Alone except for her canine companion, the older woman collapsed onto the couch, shaking her head from side to side, crying, beating the cushions weakly.

Lad watched Lisbath in a silent blend of horror and wonderment. He knew things were bad and that he couldn't help ameliorate his mistress' tortures.

Or wouldn't.

Hearing his mommy's bawling made Lad uncomfortable. He moved off the couch and went to the apartment door, making a slight tear in the cushion as his claws achieved purchase. He began to whine and scratch at the door, removing minutely thin strips of paint as he had never done before. Lad needed his mistress to pay attention to him, to let him out, to let him distance himself from this stressful environment.

During a pause in her cries, Lisbath did hear the unusual sounds of Lad's scratchings. They reverberated in the cheap, hollow apartment door and were intrusive enough to motivate her to move. She got off the couch and stumbled for a moment, quite weakened by this ordeal. Still, Lad was relentless in his door scratching, and Lisbath opened the door for him.

Lisbath held her abdomen with both arms as she returned to collapse into a self-pitying, weeping heap on the couch. Ten minutes later, she had entered a deep sleep, drooling onto the couch's pillow.

Thirty

It was two hours after Lisbath had been shaken to her very soul by Susie Rime's stressful visit. Sharona received a request specifically for Nurse Lisbath Milliken to handle the imminent home birth of Mrs. Jackie Turnbull. Gerald Turnbull, the husband, had placed the call.

This put Sharona in a strange predicament. She had recently spoken with that horrible Mr. Haberdeen, and the man tried to force her to stop giving Lisbath work. While Sharona would not learn of the Wallace-Forman murders for a couple of hours, it was still problematic to assign Milliken to a birth. Yet Sharona felt she had to believe in her troops, this man had requested Milliken directly, and damn the cops.

Lisbath had examined Jackie just a couple of months after she'd conceived—seven months ago—and the pregnant woman hadn't contacted anyone at Dickinson's since. But in the interim Mrs. Turnbull had read lots of women's magazines, and finally decided that a home birth was the "natural" way to do things. She had her husband place the call.

Lisbath's loud phone ring jarred her awake in a pool of sweat. There were soiled tissues strewn over her pillow and around her torso. She didn't remember using the tissues, and that bothered her initially. She began to cough and sputter. She felt ill. As Milliken woke up more, she remembered Susie's visit.

She reached over and yanked the receiver off its hook.

"Milliken." She sounded like a smoker with lung cancer. Like shit.

"Lisbath? Is that you?"

"Who's this?" Milliken's ears were stuffy, just like her nose and her thinking.

"Lisbath! It's Sharona. What's wrong? You always recognize my voice."

Mixed thoughts sped through Lisbath's mind. *Sharona's call could represent a chance to replenish my blood supply, and that's vital. But if I let on that I feel sick, that could blow the whole thing.* Lisbath did the equivalent of straightening her tie before responding to her "boss."

"Oh, Sharona! Sorry. I just woke up." She sounded pretty convincing.

"Got it. Lisbath, I have a job for you."

"Uh-huh?"

"But I wonder if you're up to it," Sharona mused, both to Lisbath and to herself. This could give Sharona an out—a chance to assign someone else if there was any doubt whatsoever about Lisbath's readiness.

"No prob," said Lisbath, trying perhaps a little too hard to sound "up" and "cool" and of course healthy.

"Well, dear, do you remember Jackie Turnbull?"

Lisbath had to take a moment. Her thinking was impeded by stress and impending illness, but she needed to clear her head so Sharona wouldn't suspect anything. Initially she lied. Fortunately, the lie would turn into the truth in less than thirty seconds.

"Sure. I remember her."

"Her husband called."

"Oh?" Thirty seconds had not yet elapsed.

"They want you. Now."

"Now?" She stifled a cough with her blanket, and tiny chunks of warm mucus shot out of her nostrils.

"Now. Her contractions are only a few minutes apart."

"Nothing like waiting until the last minute. Has she had a work-up by someone?"

"Yes. Her regular OB-GYN. She's ready to go. Lisbath, I'll ask you again. Are you up to this? I can call someone else."

"Sharona, like I said, I'm ready. Can you remind me of the address?"

Sharona gave her the address. Milliken wrote it on the notepad on her bedside table. She thanked Sharona, then got up, went to the bathroom, and did all of her pre-job preparations, normally an almost-sacred ritual, this time rushed.

No matter. It was still a safe cache, and it would have a new glass denizen before the day was out. And more to join the six remaining Doris Wallace beakers from a few days ago.

♦ ♦ ♦

In their attempt to keep public outcry from muddying their investigation, the Shelton Police Department had been keeping the double murder of Doris Wallace and Nurse-midwife Francine Forman out of the eye of the press for as long as they could. The Shelton detectives were impeded by the fact that the Wallaces were very private people. Doris and Kevin had never told their neighbors anything about their birth plans—not even that a nurse-midwife would be involved, let alone the name of the registry where she worked.

Shelton Police finally decided that what information they had should be distributed to nearby police departments. In mid-morning on Thursday, they sent out an interagency release. The cat had finally exited the bag.

Every detective's desk got a copy of the information release within five minutes, and it was moments before the press got wind of it through their department informants. News hound Constance Teitelmeier was on the radio with a special announcement before noon.

"This is Constance Teitelmeier with a Special Report. We have just learned that three days ago two women were murdered in Shelton, fifteen miles north of Bridgeport. One was Doris Wallace, who was giving birth at the time. The other was Francine Forman, a nurse, who was murdered in her car in front of the Wallace residence. Kevin Wallace, Doris' husband, is in a coma with undisclosed injuries.

These grisly killings are being investigated this very minute, and we will bring you details as they become available.

This is Constance Teitelmeier, Real News Right Now."

Two minutes after the news story hit, Sharona's phone started to ring. It was unnecessary. Her radio had been on.

Sharona felt she needed to take immediate action. She first called the Bridgeport detectives, asking for Haberdeen. All the police lines were busy; she would have to try in a few minutes.

Sharona then looked for the Turnbull phone number, found it, and dialed. She wanted to get Lisbath out of there. But there was no answer at the Turnbull residence. That often happened during a home birth—the family was too involved in the proceedings to care about phone calls.

She finally got through to the Bridgeport PD, but Haberdeen was not available. She told the officer who answered the phone about who Lisbath was, about Lisbath's former assignment at the Wallace birth, and that she was currently assigned to the Turnbull job. The wheels of justice sped up.

♦ ♦ ♦

Halfway through the Turnbull birth, Lisbath felt that her own strength and capability were fading. Whatever bug had caught her, it was mean and nasty and interfering with her concentration and her competence. This increasing sense of illness and lack of professional control made Milliken angry, and the energy that went into her anger further depleted her personal resources.

As she worked on Mrs. Turnbull, ignoring the screams of pain and the splashing fluids, Lisbath began to visualize how she would take her spoils this time. She saw herself with the Thermos, aiming the umbilicus, taking the blood.

Stealing the blood.

The guilt that had surfaced several days ago reappeared. *What am I doing?* she thought to herself. How can I do this? *What... what will God say when I meet him?*

Milliken's conflicted thinking made her hands spastic, and she accidentally poked Jackie's arm diagonally with a needle.

"Ouch!" said the surprised mother-to-be. Jackie began to rub the area where she had been stuck, and a trickle of blood emerged. Lisbath caught herself going for it. *My God,* she thought. *It's like some foreign thing inside me is making me do these things.*

The nurse became very frightened. Her head was pounding and her eyes had begun to tear. She actually felt like fleeing the house: running outside to her car and getting as far as she could from this scene. She began to gather her things, with no thought about what would happen when she left this mother in labor with no birth assistance. Lisbath was in true, shaking panic, and her fears and confusion had become the only factors driving her actions.

All of a sudden, something stopped Milliken cold. Something in her brain or perhaps in her soul. She was thrust into a mental cold shower. Her thoughts stopped rushing toward escape and reinstated her to Professional Nurse With A Job To Do. And with a subsurface blood lust that cried out for satisfaction.

Jackie Turnbull had been staring at Lisbath during this episode and sensed that something was wrong. But as Milliken regained her composure, she returned her smooth attention to the matters at hand.

"I'm sorry, Mrs. Turnbull. My hand slipped, that's all. You know, *woman-to-woman*, these things happen sometimes. But they're harmless."

Turnbull still couldn't figure out why the woman had been

virtually catatonic for fifteen or twenty seconds, but her next labor contraction was so vicious that she ceased caring.

As the birth progressed, in some kind of cosmic amelioration, Mrs. Turnbull turned out to be a model birth-mother. She actually screamed very little. She came to trust Lisbath implicitly. She had ordered everyone out of the birth room even before Lisbath thought to do so. And she had positioned herself on her adjustable bed so she had absolutely no view of anything lower on her contorting body than her recently-amplified breasts.

It was a boy! The child earned a five-minute APGAR of 10, which is the best rating a newborn can get.

Milliken severed the umbilicus between the clamps slowly with a fresh, new scalpel. She used a sawing action rather than the slice that was taught in nursing school. As she did so, beginning with the most superior aspect of the umbilicus, she watched for the slight arching spurt resulting from the residual pressure in the centrally-isolated part of the double-clamped cord. About two teaspoons of blood shot gracefully into the air. They produced a rain of ecstasy for Milliken, and she smiled unconsciously as the tiny airborne droplets fell in a cute spray pattern onto the starched, clean sheets.

Lisbath placed the crying newborn boy on Mother Turnbull's chest and left the two of them alone. She knew from experience that the mothers, despite being exhausted and in a special stunned state, enjoy deeply holding and cuddling and loving and talking to their newborns.

Jackie was in heaven. "Come here, little Henry," she cooed. Mrs. Turnbull began to commune with her baby—to give him all her maternal attention. This cleared the way for Milliken to get on with her work.

As the nurse-midwife continued her duties, she let her mind wander on autopilot. She began to consider her situation. Lisbath began to realize that if that policeman had his way, this could be her very last birth: the termination of her deeply-loved career. And the end of her fresh, incomparable placental blood supply.

She began to panic, with anxiety, dread, and a web of sad and angry feelings welling up in her like a fountain on overload. She coughed several times, stifling them as best she could.

Milliken felt like she needed to get the very most out of this moment regardless of the cost. This could be the parting shot—the last hurrah.

The end of life as she knew it.

She began to think quickly in fractured logic. *What can I do? How can I make this special enough? What am I doing? Is this right? I must set this time apart from all other experiences. There must be something I can do—some way to approach this moment that will live in my memory forever!*

And then it struck her. The perfect if lasciviously crude solution. The marriage of lusts that she had gone without for so many years. The crowning action that would confront all her melded frustrations.

Yes, she would do it.

Milliken quickly checked Mrs. Turnbull. The new mother was fully engaged in enjoying her soft newborn; the woman probably wouldn't have cared if the sky were falling.

The nurse-midwife then went to the bedroom door and listened. She heard muffled social conversation: nobody trying to get in; everyone trusting in her to call them in at the proper time. Good.

She turned on just one lamp by the head of the bed and then drew the curtains. Mrs. Turnbull looked her way when the room became darkened. Lisbath said in as sweet a voice as she could muster, "Just to soften the mood. Enjoy your fine baby, Jackie. I have more work to do."

Jackie shook her head slightly and turned her exhausted yet loving gaze to her baby.

After she was satisfied that she had adequate privacy, Lisbath had Jackie spread her legs further apart and raise her knees into a birth position. She then laid a trash bag down before Mrs. Turnbull's vaginal os. Lifting the protruding, cut umbilicus, the nurse tucked one side of the bag under the woman's buttocks.

Lisbath splayed the remainder of the trash bag out in a fan, spreading the edges under each leg and extending the distal edge as far as possible.

She had set the stage for the arrival of the Turnbull afterbirth. While most saw this messy, joint organ simply as the source of a sloppy clean-up task, Lisbath's take on it was decidedly different. Jackie's afterbirth—the placenta, umbilicus, and associated fleshy protuberances—was a human bag o' treats. It was to Lisbath a soft, warm, squishy sack of bloods and other mannae. A human bota bag, ready to squeeze and squirt that specially delicious wine on which Lisbath thrived so. And maybe it could be even more this time. This desperate time.

The nurse-midwife then placed her thick, flattened hand on Mrs. Turnbull's distended lower abdomen and pressed down slightly. This served two purposes: to help the uterus in its slow return to a more normal, postpartum shape, and to help express the afterbirth Lisbath anticipated so joyfully.

Jackie was a little surprised at the sudden abdominal pressure since Lisbath, in her impending ecstasy, had neglected to warn her about what was going to happen.

"What are you doing?" she asked. She held her baby just a little tighter, her protective maternal instincts already in operation.

"Oh, just helping with your uterine tonus and easing your afterbirth."

"Oh." Jackie was exhausted enough, and this explanation was just fine with her. Back to baby.

Lisbath wanted—needed—her pleasures sooner rather than later. As she continued to press rhythmically on Mrs. Turnbull's abdomen, she grasped the umbilicus as close to Jackie's vaginal opening as she could. Then she pulled with a steady, practiced hand. She continued pressing with her left hand and tugging with her right until the entire relatively massive organ began to emerge easily.

The jelly-like mass had detached from its rubbery anchor in Jackie's uterus and was now slipping out onto the plastic bag easily.

SPECIAL DELIVERY

It made a soft squaddling sound like a limp water balloon slipping unevenly out of a greased jar. It was wet music to Lisbath's ears.

Once the oily human unit was fully expressed onto the black trash bag, Lisbath let the last few drops of following fluid leak onto the plastic. Then she picked the folded bag up by its corners, lifted her prize up and brought it down with her as she knelt down to the carpeted floor. Milliken glanced again up toward the bed and also at the bedroom door, and this final environmental scan left her feeling safe enough to begin her vile, personal indulgences.

First Lisbath reached under the bed for the Thermos. No matter what she was about to do, she needed to spirit some of the fine liquid away for Lad. Some blood and some other special liquid surprises. She unscrewed the top quickly, thrust the umbilical tip a short way into the jar, and released the clamp. She heard no trickle and realized that in this unusual position on the floor, the umbilicus was actually slightly above the placenta. She slowly brought her elbow down on the afterbirth, much like a bagpipe player squeezes his plaid instrument.

The liquids began to fill the Thermos. The sanguine fragrance, now so warm and pungent, was a magical drug to Lisbath. It was a perfume that made her drunk with pleasure.

Lisbath talked silently to her absent Lad. "Here you are, baby. What you like and what you need. *Treats a-comin'*, little Laddie."

Once the Thermos was almost full, Lisbath re-clamped the flopping umbilicus and closed off the metal cylinder. She wrapped it quickly in a towel and placed it carefully into the carpetbag she had brought.

That done, the nurse-midwife turned her attentions to her own needs and pleasures. The wonderful blood smells became denser, swirling about Lisbath in luxurious, heated zephyrs. The fragrance took over, an airborne heroin that brought the nurse-midwife into an uncontrolled, drugged reverie.

She shuffled her legs down toward the foot of the bed, then laid down next to her prize. Lisbath fingered the umbilical end briefly like a man caressing the opening to a wet vagina.

Then she brought the umbilical tip to her mouth and touched it to her lower lip. She withdrew the tube and pressed her lips together as if applying lipstick. She slowly extended her tongue between her lips, allowing whatever liquid had transferred from the umbilicus to apply itself to both the top and the bottom of her tongue simultaneously. She withdrew her tongue into her mouth and savored the light, titillating flavor as a wine connoisseur determines the quality of a vintage.

This was about as much restraint as she could show. Milliken thrust the end of the umbilical cord into her mouth and opened the clamp fully. She began to suck, her eyes rolling up into her head. She sucked and sucked, and when the flow began to decrease, Lisbath rolled her entire hulk slowly onto the afterbirth.

Her clothes were becoming filthy with body parts and fluids, but she didn't care. The increased pressure on the human bag created a new, wonderful flow of blood into her gullet. She shoved the umbilicus further into her mouth.

Then she began to withdraw it partially and move it back and forth, back and forth. She was sucking and fellating the three-vessel tube. And as she did so, her own feminine fluids began to flow in her vagina. Virtually dry for so many years, she was now getting sexually excited as she continued to molest Jackie's afterbirth.

More and more she sucked. She was losing her control. She began to bite tiny bits of tissue off the very end of the tube. She had drunk blood before but had never tasted bitten solids. Somehow they reminded her of times too far back in her genetic memory to seem real, but they were redolent nonetheless.

She rubbed the now-irregular tube end onto her front teeth, sucking from time to time, snipping off a piece here and there. She was in a blind ecstasy surely better than heroin and LSD and whatever else may swirl the brain to new heights.

As she continued writhing, a most lascivious idea occurred to her. Virtually without thinking, she gave in to her immediate fantasy. Lisbath shoved the umbilicus further into her mouth—almost to the opening of her throat, and bit down just enough to ensure it would not slip out of her mouth. Parking it.

Sirens in the distance did not pierce Lisbath's physical reverie.

Now with both hands free, the nurse-midwife began lifting her own stained white skirt to reveal her underpants. She arched her back and pressed on her heels to allow the skirt to slip up to her waist, then with amazing strength held that posture as she slipped her white underwear crotch down to her knees.

It began to thunder outside, but nobody noticed, least of all Lisbath. Her thunder was inside.

Lisbath Milliken let herself back down to the floor. Still holding the precious human tube in her mouth, she allowed her hands to move between her legs. Her bestially-thick thighs were in the way, so she brought her two feet together, bottom-to-bottom, her heels coming up toward her crotch, spreading her thighs apart as her legs scissored upward and outward. Her underpants slid down toward her ankles.

Given room to work now, both hands made their way toward her own vaginal lips. Her hands quickly spread her untamed bed of pubic hair out of the way and felt for her forbidden vulva. Fragrant liquids were already leaking out, and Lisbath slipped her right forefinger in so easily that it surprised her. The pathway was ready.

She began breathing even harder as she removed the umbilicus from her mouth and began to work it down toward her vagina. Lisbath's eyes were vibrating wildly and she was breathing irregularly. Liquids dripped from the corner of her mouth. Her heart was going a hundred miles an hour, and she was oblivious to everything around her.

As she slipped the organ into her cunt, Lisbath gasped almost loud enough for Jackie to hear. But the new mother on the bed was too wrapped up in her own maternal ecstasy to pay any attention to sounds coming from the floor beside her.

Lisbath shoved the tube in. She moved the placenta closer to her buttocks and shoved further. Further.

Then she partially withdrew the tube, then shoved it in again. She began pumping it, over and over, sometimes hard, sometimes soft. She moved it deeply in, reaching her cervix, then only slightly as if toying with her own vagina. Sometimes her lubrication would reduce a bit, and the fucking tube would bend her lips inward on one stroke and outward on the out stroke. She felt and enjoyed every nuance of this ethereal sex.

During all of this, her left hand sometimes worked its way into her mouth, and she sucked on her own fingers. After a few moments, she would move her hand down to her crotch, to her clitoris. She rubbed so vigorously and unconsciously that her nails, while short, made small slits in the umbilical cord being drawn back and forth under her rubbing fingers.

As she pumped, her intensity increased. She began yanking the cord into and out of herself. So hard were her tugs that the cord ripped off its mooring on the afterbirth. The immediate easing of the effort it took her to pump the thing into her cunt made her thrust all the faster.

Lisbath groaned ceaselessly. Her hips were undulating, flab moving almost randomly as its underlying skeleton writhed. Her head lolled from side to side as she came closer and closer to full orgasm. She was approaching the true pinnacle of her feelings—of her emotions. She had never felt this way, and nothing could stand in her way. Pumping, feeling, sexing, sucking. Blood, juices. Hands, tubes, wetness. Her body shivered uncontrollably, every morsel of her being moving toward the ultimate pleasure.

BANG! BANG BANG! Someone was pounding on the door with such power and ferocity than it almost flew off its hinges.

"Open the door, Milliken! *This is the police!* Open up NOW!"

Haberdeen and two officers, one of whom was female, were at the bedroom door, beginning to force entrance.

Lisbath almost hadn't heard the pounding, but Haberdeen's overpowering command voice penetrated her consciousness. All of a sudden, she realized what she had been doing. Almost as if coming out of a fugue state, the nurse-midwife found herself on the floor of a birth room, fucking herself with the newborn's umbilical cord, the placenta lying off to the side, her underwear around her ankles, and her nurse's skirt hiked up over her hips. And someone was crashing against the door, trying to break in!

It took Milliken a moment to clear her thinking enough to begin to comprehend her situation fully. Reflexively, she began to pull her underwear on.

As she was pulling them up, part caught on her knee. She began to pull harder and harder and to cough uncontrollably. She was still strewn on the floor, five seconds to orgasm and more frightened than a criminal being strapped to the electric chair.

As she tore the underwear almost in half, Haberdeen and the two uniformed officers broke through the door. Chunks of the door's wood splintered into the room as the three of them tumbled in.

"Good Christ!" yelled Officer Jane Gray. "What the hell is all this?"

The officers surrounded Lisbath, who lay helpless on the carpet. She was tugging fruitlessly at her torn underwear. The dead, deflated umbilical cord was sticking out of her vagina like a blanched trunk on a baby elephant. Everything around her was wet. The placenta had released most of its remaining liquids into a chunky puddle beside the pitiful nurse.

From her sheltered vantage point, holding her newborn, Jackie Turnbull was nonplussed. Reflexively, she held him close to her breast. She became virtually catatonic, unable to move save to hyperventilate, shake her head, and stare down over the side of the bed. Her head was moving so fast from side to side that it looked like it was vibrating. Her straggly, wet hair made regular flapping noises as it was thrown across her widely-open eyes.

Although the rest of the Turnbull family had been told to leave the premises when the officers came to the residence's front door, Mr. Turnbull of course remained in the house. A few seconds after the officers stormed into the bedroom, the new father followed.

"Jackie! Are you all right?" he asked.

She hesitated for a moment, not so much to gather her thoughts but rather to register that she had been asked a question.

"Well... I suppose... Gerald, what's happening? What's going on? What is all this?"

"Don't worry, honey," said Gerald. "It'll be all right."

"Is the baby okay?" She was asking about the infant who was already clasped by her own arms into her breast.

"Yes. He's fine."

The father could see the infant's penis. "A boy? That's great!" Mr. Turnbull was of course more concerned with his wife and new baby than with police business.

The officers had other things on their minds.

Haberdeen stared down at the midwife. "Lisbath Milliken: You're under arrest."

"Arrest?" Lisbath was as stunned and incapable as a two-year-old faced with a calculus exam.

Officer Gray reached down to help Lisbath bring her skirt down over her genitals. As she did so, she noticed that Milliken appeared to have fainted.

Thirty-one

He shelled peanuts while holding the receiver to his ear with his shoulder. "Yes, she's in custody," Haberdeen said to Deputy Peters. "Do you need to talk to her?"

"Not at this time. Just keep her as long as you can." Peters was surprised at the high level of support he was getting from the police. Usually the cops and the health department people were engaged in turf wars, but this time Haberdeen seemed actually to be grateful for their working together.

"I can hold her at least 48 hours. Maybe more. Call if you come up with anything else," Haberdeen said as he hung up. He finally had the bitch where he wanted her. Now maybe the spread of disease would stop. He began to appreciate the vile, perverted panorama. Haberdeen was going to sink his teeth into this woman-creature.

The detective began an S.O.P. background check on the woman. Immediately, there were problems, some of which were unforeseen.

Milliken had no prior criminal record. Tough luck. A record would have made things much easier.

In addition, her fingerprints weren't on file. The absence of prints wasn't terribly unusual since Connecticut hadn't started fingerprinting new nurses routinely until many years after Milliken registered herself with the State Board of Nursing. Her driver's license was almost coming up for renewal, but it was just recently that Connecticut had considered asking not only for pictures but also for fingerprints of renewing drivers.

Milliken had been put in a holding cell pending her return to consciousness. Word spread rapidly to the jail staff that this was the suspect in the Shelton double-murder case. A tiny circus assembled just outside the holding cell, and sounds of "Monster!" and "Bitch!" and "Look at the blood all over her! What's that about?" and "How the hell could she be a nurse?" reverberated against the unpainted concrete walls.

When Milliken finally returned to consciousness, she began screaming, "Where am I? Give me my sunglasses! What are you doing to me? Turn off the lights! *Where in God's name am I?*"

Hoping to calm the woman down, the attendants reduced the lighting. It helped. Lisbath stopped screaming but continued to look around, blinking in bewilderment.

The jail attendants donned gloves, cleaned her up, swabbed her with disinfectant, and began the standard barrage of questions: Name, address, marital status, date and place of birth, driver's license, social security number, employment. Lisbath was disoriented in the jail environment, but finally got herself together enough to answer some of the questions. She was thoroughly frightened.

Next came Lisbath's body cavity search, and as horrible as it was for Lisbath, it was a big hit with the jailers. A small crowd of uniforms stood nearby and cheered grotesquely when they heard Lisbath grunt through the door. A sergeant nearby heard the commo- tion and broke up the group, then stayed a minute himself to listen.

When Milliken's intake procedures were completed, she was transferred to a four-woman cell. It was occupied by only two others: one Black and one Hispanic. Both looked like old hands at the jail game, and Milliken looked like a beached whale out of water. She was deadly silent. Her roommates eyed her with contempt, and Lisbath, smelling like her own private closet of blood and chemicals, shrank back in bewilderment.

Among the background information the intake interview had revealed about Milliken was that she had been born in Avondale Lake, Ohio. Once Haberdeen got the report, he contacted the Avondale Lake Police Department and asked for a search for any Millikens born since 1930. Anyone coming up could conceivably be in the Milliken woman's age range. Constable Oddwad's limited records showed just two Millikens born in that town anytime after 1930: a Claire J. and a Deborah no-middle-initial, both to parents Andrew and Charisse Milliken. Andrew had worked at the power plant on Lake Erie until his death in 1967, and Charisse had disappeared without a trace the following year.

Problematically, however, there was no birth record for any Lisbath Milliken in Avondale Lake. FBI files also had no birth record for any Lisbath Milliken of Lisbath's general age range existing anywhere else in the country.

The woman was clearly American and wasn't old enough to predate public record-keeping. This was one mystery Haberdeen was intensely motivated to solve.

City Animal Control had been dispatched to Lisbath's Yankee Pines Apartments on Friday morning. Milliken's neighbors had complained of incessant, violent barking coming from her apartment. Normally the police wouldn't know anything of Animal Control's operations, but the piles of dog droppings, the overarching stench of urea, other animal-like smells they could not identify, and the apparent malnutrition of the animal they found suggested criminal neglect, so a formal report was made to Bridgeport PD.

The women assigned as animal control officers inadvertently—or because they considered it irrelevant—failed to include a few items in their report to BPD. For one thing, they didn't mention that when they first entered the apartment there were no barking sounds. But when they went into the bedroom, a dog pounced from the top of a high, free-standing bookshelf. It was a location a dog of Lad's size could not climb or jump to without the claws of a cat. And surely no one had put him up there.

Lad had changed in the brief time since he had effectively been abandoned by Milliken. The formerly content hound so thankful for his blood meals now had gone without blood for too long, and he could no longer play the dependent little doggie humans so loved to see. He needed to take a more pervasive and proactive role in the service of his survival, and that more intense, deliberate role emerged the day the officers came to the apartment. The dog attacked and successfully bit through their boots and gloves as if rabid, but there were no signs of foaming saliva or other hydrophobic indices. The animal's ability to pierce their protective gear was something they mentioned only as an afterthought. They get attacked and bitten often, but this time, the dog had fought both of them violently as he worked at licking virtually every drop of the blood on their clothing and boots. He was finally captured with a combination rope-pole and dog net. The animal control officers had not paid attention to his glowing eyes; when attacked, experienced animal people focus on jaws, teeth, and feet.

Haberdeen read their report with some mild interest, but had nowhere to place that in his thinking. Yet.

In custody, Lisbath herself was becoming increasingly ill. She looked old. She was coughing incessantly, appeared quite greenish, and was unconscious most of the time. Both of her roommates had been campaigning to get her the hell out of their cell.

Women's Jail supervising officer Maxine "Max" Willis removed Milliken from four-woman incarceration and had her placed in a private cell. Then she called a doctor to examine the nurse-midwife.

Dr. Mark Howard's routine blood tests came up with *Streptococcus pyogenes*. Her optical exam revealed that she had red-tinted cataracts, something that Dr. Howard had never seen before. Milliken was moved immediately by special ambulance to a jail cell at Park City Hospital (all the cops called the jail ward "The Park"). She was placed in medical isolation. Max called arresting officer Haberdeen. She caught him in the middle of coffee and his favorite glazed donuts.

"Haberdeen, detectives." Willis could hear the saliva sloshing.

"Detective Haberdeen, this is Officer Willis of Women's Jail."

"Okay," he said through his donut. He reached for a napkin. The G-Man knew this would be about Milliken.

"Your prisoner Milliken is sick. I thought you'd want to know that she has a pretty rare condition, according to the doctor."

"Don't tell me. A *Strep* infection in her vagina, right?" The G-Man tried to suck a couple of his sticky fingers clean.

Max Willis was surprised. How the hell would he know it would be *Strep*? But that didn't matter.

"Well, I don't know if it's in her vagina or someplace else, but, yes, it's *Strep* something. And it's not just a sore throat." Even Max realized the humor of her throat reference, but her demeanor was too dry to pursue it.

Max continued, "And she's got a cataract. Weird color, Doc Howard says."

"Who gives a shit?" remarked Haberdeen.

"Listen, Detective, I'm just trying to do my job. I give complete reports." Willis was hard, but she was good.

"Okay, Willis. What was that doctor's name again?"

"It's Dr. Mark Howard. He's an internist. Nice guy. And we've moved the suspect to The Park."

"Got it. Ask that doctor to call me, okay?"

"Yeah," said Max. It sounded like sludge coming out of her.

"Okay. Keep me informed." Haberdeen hung up and immediately transmitted the news to Peters at the health department. Both of them found it confirming. One more piece of the puzzle falling into place.

The G-Man now decided to pursue further Milliken's background investigation for several reasons. First, if she eventually came to trial for endangering her patients or the general public, then her history would be important for the prosecution. The DA and the police needed to know as much as they could about persons they were prosecuting if for no other reason than to be ready for the defense attorney's tactics.

Also, he wanted to know what kind of person would be so unthinkably involved in drinking blood. This was truly the weirdest case he'd ever come across, and its more macabre aspects intrigued him.

Finally, he wanted to "repay" Deputy Peters for his help and support. Haberdeen thought he might uncover something useful to the health department in the course of his further investigation.

Since he had learned from Oddwad at the Avondale Lake PD that there were two Millikens born there within the possible timeframe for Lisbath's birth (neither of whom was named Lisbath), Haberdeen decided to check further into the woman's birth and childhood.

He grabbed another glazed donut and called the Avondale Lake Public Records Office. It was just a tiny room stuck in the rear of the public library on Electricity Street. The part-time records clerk was old-timer Karlon Mire.

Mire restored Karmann-Ghias for AutoWorld Classic Cars in Rocky River for the other half of his gainful employment. His callused hands were flipping through *Hot VWs* magazine when his black rotary-dial phone rang. The bespectacled clerk shoved piles of papers out of the way to answer it.

"Public Records. Can I help you?" Haberdeen was lucky to find someone in the office.

"Yes. This is Detective George Haberdeen from the Bridgeport, Connecticut Police Department." Haberdeen sounded at once officious and bored.

Big deal, thought Mire.

"I need information on a birth."

"Bet you're calling about the Millikens. Some other guy from Connecticut called about them just the other day. Health department, I think."

"Yes. I need more information."

"Well?" Mire's knee hurt from recent replacement surgery, and he wanted to get the call over with so he could get up and walk around a little.

"What were the Milliken names?" Haberdeen knew full well what they were, but this method ensured the accuracy of his second-hand information and got his interrogatee—Mire—thinking in the direction he needed him to think.

"Hold on. It's gonna take me a couple of minutes. Got a bad knee." Mire already knew too, but he wanted to get the books down from the shelf before answering more questions. Besides, this gave him an excuse to exercise that damn knee.

"Deborah is one. She was born on January 9, 1942. War baby."

"Okay."

"Like I told the other guy, parents were Andrew and Charisse Milliken."

"What about the other kid?" asked Haberdeen.

"Hold your horses. I need to look in another book."

Haberdeen tapped his pencil on the desk. So far this was pretty unexciting.

"That'd be Claire Milliken, Detective. Born September 29, 1943."

"Can you tell me anything else about these girls?"

"Ain't girls now, are they?" mocked Mire.

"Just tell me what you've got."

"Like I told the other guy. Deborah works at the A & P. Woman ought to retire real soon. Always sick as a dog."

"Okay, good. Peters didn't mention that to me. What about Claire?"

"Claire left Avondale Lake some time around 1961 or 1962. Right after she changed her name. She's not 'Claire' anymore."

Bingo. *A name change.*

"Did you tell Peters about that?"

"Peters? Is that the guy who called a couplea days ago?"

"Of course."

"Don't think so. Nope. He didn't ask."

What a dope this Mire guy is, Haberdeen thought. Come to think of it, Peters should have asked about name changes. So Peters was a dope, too.

"When did she change her name?"

"Like I told you, *Detective*, 1961."

"Well, what did she change her name *to*?"

"Don't rightly remember. I didn't really know the woman."

"Can you find out?"

"Sure. It's in the 1961 book."

Well, get it, you prick, thought Haberdeen. But instead he intoned, "Please check."

It took Mire almost three minutes to find the book. The ancient phone had no hold button, so Haberdeen was forced to listen to the old man move about the tiny office belching, farting, and singing to himself. Finally, success.

"Mr. . . . what did you say your name was?"

"Haberdeen."

"Yeah. Mr. Haberdeen. I found the book." The G-Man heard large, heavy archive pages turning.

"Claire Juditha Milliken changed her name to. . . Lisbath Juditha Milliken on December 22, 1961."

It sounded like this guy Mire was an old local. Maybe he'd know something more than dates and times and how to hum "Dead Man's Curve."

Haberdeen was having trouble phrasing his question in a way that wouldn't sound ludicrous. He wanted an intelligible answer rather than an incredulous one, so he worked carefully on his phraseology. How could one ask someone—particularly a crusty old-timer—about any connection between Lisbath-maybe-AKA-Claire Milliken and blood lust? Detective or not, it was hard to come up with a reasonable approach.

Finally, something suggested itself .

"Mr. Mire. I need to ask you something else."

"Yeah?"

"Is there anything unusual in Lisbath Milliken's—Claire Milliken's—history or background?"

"Whaddya mean?"

"Anything you might remember. Although she doesn't have a police record, maybe there's something."

Haberdeen continued. "Maybe a strange accident, or something having to do with blood—she's a nurse now, you know—or maybe something having to do with having babies?" There it was. The G-Man had nested "blood" with finesse.

"Sounds *weird* to me. I've got no idea . . ."

Mire's voice trailed off like something may have been crawling around on the tip of his tongue. It was pretty clear that he was remembering something. But he decided against saying anything that would make him sound like an idiot.

"Nope. Nothing," said the old man.

"Mr. Mire, this is an official police investigation. You need to tell me anything and everything you can remember, no matter how stupid or weird it might sound. Anything at all. Withholding information could get you in trouble."

"Well, Mr. Haberdeen," Mire said, "I do remember something, but it was just some kid reporter's article in the *Avondale Register*. Local paper. Not very believable. Editorials are the only articles worth shit in that rag."

"Tell me."

"*Well*, Mr. Haberdeen," droned Mire, "it was about a fight or something like that. Between Claire and a stray dog. Right before she changed her name, too. Real weird stuff. Stupid stuff, if you ask me. It's only the weird stuff that I remember, though. Strange, isn't it? Maybe it's just old age."

A dog? thought Haberdeen. *Couldn't be.*

"Where can I get a copy of that article?"

"In the next office. I'm in the Avondale Public Library building. The periodical room has all the papers way back to when the library was first built."

"Can you do me a favor?"

"I can just guess. You want me to get the article, right?"

You're such a bright son of a bitch. "I'd be grateful, sir."

Mire just put the phone down without acknowledging that he was going next door. But he was.

More typically, to look something like that up, Mire would have to get the cop to call back. But he thought that the fight between the woman and the dog took place a day or two before Milliken changed her name from Claire to Lisbath. Name changes in a small town are rare. And since he had the date for the name change, he could get to the right newspaper quickly.

Through the earpiece Haberdeen heard Mire open and close the door to the records office, so he decided just to sit tight and chomp on his donut.

Mire came back to the phone in just under five minutes. He was out of breath, and Haberdeen figured correctly that it was because the old man had a bad knee, so getting around took lots of effort.

"Mr. Haberdeen, I have the article," he puffed.

"Can you fax it to me?" he asked. "Now?"

"Yeah. You didn't expect me to read it to you, did you?"

The G-Man gave Mire the police department's fax number, hung up, and settled into his seat to wait for the Police Explorer cadet to bring him a fresh fax.

Haberdeen got it within ten minutes. The fax was less than a full column and appeared at a slight angle on the glossy, brownish fax paper.

Local Resident's Bloody Confrontation with Stray Dog Required Medical Help

Avondale Lake. Wednesday, December 13, 1961.

By Larry Pink

Yesterday native resident Claire Milliken was on her way to the Super Five And Drugstore on the 300 block of Jaycox St. around 4:00 p.m. when a stray dog appeared on the wet sidewalk.

According to witnesses Harry and Jeannie Pantuquee, the dog started to move back and forth on the sidewalk as Claire walked toward it. When she saw the dog, she acted frightened and backed against the Juniper Bike Shop's plate glass window.

The dog then charged toward her and knocked Claire down. Immediately the mutt went for her face and seemed to be biting her in the area of her cheeks. Jeannie Pantuquee says that the dog actually licked some of the blood.

Harry says that the dog then put his muzzle over Claire's face. "It looked like the animal was trying to eat out of her mouth, and there was a bunch of greenish brown stuff all around its lips. It was scary and disgusting," Mr. Pantuquee said.

Pantuquee then ran at the dog, yelling for it to get off Claire and banging his cane on the ground as he ran. The dog looked at him and went away slowly, according to Pantuquee.

Claire Milliken was taken to the Meshboig Clinic on Main Street and was released a few minutes later. When asked for comment, Milliken just stared at this reporter with tears in her eyes. She had a bandage covering most of her right cheek and her eyes were very red.

Be on the lookout for a spotted mostly black-and-white dog about a foot high. Dirty, floppy ears. Yellow left rear leg, black right rear leg. Bad news.

Christ, thought Haberdeen. *That sounds like her dog Lad, doesn't it?* The animal matched the description perfectly, all the way down to the legs. *But a dog year is equal to seven human years, right? The animal would have to be well over 280 human years old by now. Couldn't be.*

As he was imagining dogs turning gray and dying of old age, Haberdeen's phone rang. It was Milliken's Dr. Howard.

"Yes, this is Detective Haberdeen. Thank you for returning my call." He pulled out his notepad.

"My pleasure. So you're interested in my patient Lisbath Milliken?"

"Yes."

"And this is an official police inquiry? You know I need to ask just to determine how much I can say."

"Absolutely. This is about as balls-on heavy a police inquiry as you can get, Doc. I *do not* understand that woman." Haberdeen was usually loathe to admit any failing, especially to an outsider, but he needed to let Dr. Howard know just how critical his need for information was.

"Are you sitting down, Mr. Haberdeen?"

He placed his hand on his stomach. "Yeah. But you know in this line of work I've heard a lot of shit. Hit me."

"Fine. The woman is getting older. Fast. Like two to three years a day."

"*What?*" asked a flabbergasted Haberdeen. "What the hell do you mean?"

"Just what I said. Right in front of us. Like someone with Werner's syndrome, where all of a sudden a twenty-something-year-old adult starts aging real fast. You've probably seen something like it on TV. Sometimes premature aging occurs in kids in a disease called progeria. When they're maybe seven or eight and they look like they're eighty-five? Genetic problem for those poor kids. The adult variant is Werner's syndrome, but with Milliken, it's definitely *not* Werner's. We karyotyped her—checked out her chromosomes—and they're normal."

"So what is it? What's going on with that woman?"

"Don't know yet."

Crap, thought Haberdeen. Finally something tangible and still no answers.

"Will you let me know when you do?"

"Sure."

"Do you have anything else for me?" asked Haberdeen.

"Don't think so. We haven't been able to figure out what's going on yet," said the doctor.

"Okay. That's it for now. Bye."

"Good-bye, Detective."

Both men hung up in shared bewilderment.

The G-Man decided to call it a night. He had had it up to here with the aging blood woman, the biting dog, the sickie new mothers—everything. He wanted to watch some TV, down a couple of beers, and hit the sack. Maybe more than a couple of beers.

Thirty-two

The mind works all the time, whether we like it or not. Awake or sleeping, watching TV or peeing out that latest brace of beers, it cranks away. Even Haberdeen's.

While Haberdeen stabbed at his TV dinner's greenish-tinted peas in front of a *Columbo* episode on Channel 6, he couldn't get over all the weirdness he'd been bringing together with the Milliken case. He had a woman who drank blood. He had a dog that licked blood. He had about five sick new mothers all with the same rare, stupid fucking *Strep* infection.

And he had pressure. Yesterday the sergeant had left a note in Haberdeen's mailbox asking for an update. His desk spindle had a pink phone message from the rabbi; he had called again, and his kid was still having the shakes. Like almost every other message slip he'd ever gotten, the "Urgent" box was checked.

Worse yet, that damn Big T news reporter had apparently sifted through the recent public-record police reports and had asked him to call back, too.

Haberdeen tossed and turned all night. In his troubled sleep, he saw images of large, bloody fangs. These sights were interspersed with overhead, slowly rotating views of newborn infants all lined up in identical, tiny white cribs like eggs in a pristine crate. And in this vision he flashed on hospital rooms filled with women. All of them had sheets with great red wet splotches over their crotches.

Yesterday's late messages had included a fax Doc Howard had sent on Milliken's medical condition. In his dreams, Haberdeen saw snippets of the report. Things like "hyperfatigued" and "unanticipated appearance of new integumentary wrinkling" and "eye color shift" flew past his unconscious gaze.

Over the course of the night, Haberdeen drooled, his nose ran, he farted, and he cogitated unconsciously and relentlessly. When his alarm clock startled him awake at 6:15 a.m., the G-Man was exhausted. *Some fucking night*, he thought to himself. But he was enlightened, too; his dream work was beginning to pay off.

Synaptic connections had been made despite Haberdeen's years of beers. His brain assembled for the first time that, even though Milliken appeared to be the common factor in all the new mothers' illnesses, the nurse's own sickness was *different*.

How the hell could that be? Why wasn't Milliken subject to the same illness? Turned around: Why didn't the mothers get what Milliken had? The G-Man resolved to pursue this today.

He also realized that, strange as it might seem, that damn mutt Lad might have some role in all of this. Milliken had changed her name just after being attacked by a dog essentially meeting Lad's description. Could that nurse have looked for the thing right after it attacked her? And then adopted it? Or maybe a dog out of its litter? Why would she—anyone—do that?

Had this Mad Matron started feeding the dog human blood? Was that why he'd partaken of the animal control officers? Once again: Why would she do such a thing?

Haberdeen was getting overwhelmed with this array of questions and maybe-answers. He longed for those oh-so-simple cases. Like where the jealous boyfriend shoots the guy feeling up his girlfriend in the back seat of her car.

He needed help.

Then the issue Haberdeen had been avoiding all along crept into his consciousness like some unwanted, noisy animal scrabbling its way under the house.

Vampires. Blood suckers. Mythical humanoid monsters subsisting on the blood of unfortunates. The stuff "B" movies are made of.

It struck the detective that *whether these things were real or not*, he needed to know about them. Maybe—probably—Milliken fancied herself a Dame of the Night. This could give him clues to her thinking, her actions, or even how she related to her dog. Yes, he'd have to pursue this too. He was sure that he would have to suffer ridicule along the way.

As he was shaving in the bathroom, Haberdeen's phone rang. *Shit*, he thought. *Only when my face is wet, I'm in the shower, or on the pot.*

He toweled the shaving cream off most of his still-unshaven beard as he walked to the living room phone.

"Haberdeen." He answered his home phone almost like he did his office phone.

"Hi, George! It's Lisa. Up and at 'em yet?"

"Hi, baby. I'm just shaving. Let me call you back in a minute, okay?"

"Sure."

Both hung up and Haberdeen finished his morning rituals.

He called Lisa back. She had decided to catch Detective George Haberdeen before he left for work to "report" on what she had learned at the college. Over the next several minutes, Lisa filled Haberdeen in on the Vlad Tepes history and some of the vampire stuff she had gone over with Professor Bodnir. She told him not only about the power struggles of the 1400's and the tortures Vlad Tepes had inflicted, but also about the creation of 'familiars' and spirit magnets.

George took notes avidly as the fresh aftershave evaporated from his face. It felt weird to him to be grateful to learn about these creatures of the night. To a typical cop, vampire stuff would be ludicrous. But right about now, the G-Man was not in a typical spot. He needed to know how people thought about these things, whether they existed for real or not.

"Thanks, Lisa. I really appreciate the info. You did a great job. You're so good to me," he said.

They made a date for that evening.

♦ ♦ ♦

When Haberdeen arrived in the police parking lot off Henner Street, it had just begun to snow. The light flakes fell, random, soft, settling on pavement.

The G-Man poured himself a cup of office coffee and carried it to his desk. There were two more messages from the rabbi and one that had just come in from Milliken's Dr. Howard on Haberdeen's desk.

He needed to call Milliken's doctor back right away—that way he'd probably catch the physician before he left for the hospital or maybe while he was doing his morning rounds. He found Howard's number and dialed. Dr. Howard's office told the G-Man that the physician was on rounds at Q of A, so Haberdeen called the hospital. As soon as he identified himself as a cop and asked to speak to the doctor, he was put on hold.

"Hey, Doc," said Haberdeen as Dr. Howard's voice interrupted the hospital's bland music-on-hold.

"Hello, Detective." Then, with virtually no break, the physician continued. "Maybe it's time for me to start asking *you* questions. We've made essentially no progress in diagnosing Lisbath Milliken's condition. Her aging is relentless, and I do *not* want to lose a patient without putting up a fight. So, Mr. Haberdeen, what, if anything, can you tell me that might be helpful, even if marginally so?"

"Listen, Doc. This is damn near the weirdest thing I've ever seen. Milliken is a nurse-midwife—oh—you already know that stuff, right?"

"Don't assume I know anything about her background. Please continue."

"Okay. Well, she's a nurse-midwife. Something like five of her recent patients are all in the hospital right now with *Strep* infections."

"I see. What kind of *Strep*?"

"Hold on." Haberdeen riffled through his notes for a moment.

"*Streptococcus pyrogenes*," mispronounced Haberdeen.

"You must mean '*pyogenes*.' Odd. That's a rare form."

"I know," grumbled Haberdeen, finding a paper clip and unraveling it. "Peters of the health department is in on this because of that weird bug."

"Robert Peters? Connecticut Health?"

"I think it's Robert," said Haberdeen as he began to look through his business card file. "Yes. Robert. Connecticut Health Department."

"Good guy. I'll have to give him a call," said Dr. Howard. "And what else have you got, Mr. Haberdeen?"

"Here comes the creepy stuff. It seems Ms. Milliken drinks blood. *And*. . ." Haberdeen stretched out the moment for dramatic effect ". . . she may be feeding it to her dog."

"Disgusting."

"*Human* blood, Doc. Human."

"No kidding? You sure?"

Dr. Howard was sounding less and less medical as the information he was fed was getting more and more bizarre.

"Yeah. Sure. She may be stealing it from her clients while they're giving birth."

"Uh-huh."

Haberdeen fell silent. The paper clip wire grew warm in his hands.

Dr. Howard asked, "Is that all?"

"Isn't that enough?" said Haberdeen. Then he softened. "Well, doc, that's all we've got any evidence on."

"What do you mean? I do *not* like feeling like I'm at a loss. I need anything—everything you've got."

Haberdeen was somewhat embarrassed to say anything about his almost-subliminal vampire theory. But he figured at this point he had to.

"Well, there is something else," admitted the detective.

"Out with it."

"Let's start with this. Her dog? Its name is Lad."

"So?" asked Dr. Howard.

"Sounds like Vlad."

"*So?*" More vehemently this time. Irritated. The doctor was losing faith rapidly in his law enforcement contact.

Haberdeen's embarrassment was transmuting into annoyance. He didn't need to be made fun of, especially in this moment when he felt ludicrously vulnerable. "You need to hear me out, Doc, or our conversation is over."

"Sorry. I wasn't suggesting irrelevance. I just don't understand how some dog's name can play a role in Milliken's illness. I mean, *come on!*"

"Well, damnit, it probably doesn't. But listen: One of our detectives is kind of a movie nut, and when he heard the dog's name, he made the connection."

"What connection?"

"That 'Lad' sounds like 'Vlad,' and that Vlad is some historical vampire's name."

"You've just got to be kidding." The G-Man could just hear Dr. Howard's eyes rolling up in his head.

The doctor continued. "Detective, you are wasting my time."

Haberdeen felt like ramming the phone into its cradle right then and there. He wanted to do it hard enough for it to reach all along the phone wires and end up in the doc's rectum. But he maintained his composure just enough to respond. "One more of those and you're on your fucking own. No kidding, Doc. *Got it?*"

"All right. Yes. Just go on."

"Sit tight for a minute." Haberdeen was steaming. He bunched the paper clip up in his fist.

"Okay. I got someone to do an off-the-record interview with Milliken a few days ago. She also checked out the vampire story with a couple of anthropology professors at the local JC."

"And?" asked Howard.

"There was a Vlad the Impaler back in the 15th century. Vampire stories are supposedly based on this guy."

Dr. Howard spoke slowly. "Are you telling me you actually see some kind of connection between this guy and Lisbath Milliken's dog?"

"*God*, you make it sound stupid," said Haberdeen as his blood pressure rose. "Well, no, not exactly."

"So what the hell are you saying?" asked Howard.

"Maybe this bitch Milliken *believes* she's some kind of vampire. Why else would she be drinking blood and feeding it to her dog?"

The doctor paused for a moment. He was considering seriously this line of thought. He responded with measured words. "Mr. Haberdeen, my limited training in psychiatry suggests that you actually may be on to something."

Haberdeen felt some relief. His thinking was being respected, at least a little.

Dr. Howard continued. "But that still doesn't explain the premature aging, the eye color variations, or other medical indices."

Haberdeen was stunned. His apparently precognitive dreams had hit on some of these things. *Very weird shit*, he thought.

There was a long silence. Then the doctor had a new idea.

"Mr. Haberdeen, the woman we're dealing with is an experienced, educated nurse. I think we need to take that into consideration. If she is delusional about being some kind of vampire, then she may be exhibiting richer fantasy justification than would a lay person. Maybe she researched the myths; maybe she's well-read. This isn't just some produce clerk at a supermarket, after all."

The doctor's line of thought was eluding Haberdeen. But he listened intently.

"So I need to learn more about all of this, even if it's all bullshit. We need to know what Ms. Milliken may be thinking, and that may lead to understanding how to deal with her."

"But Doc, correct me if I'm wrong, but even if you find out how that woman's crazy head is working, how could that change her medical condition? Could knowing how she thinks somehow help you slow down her aging? Could it affect her eye color changes? This doesn't make any sense to me."

"Haberdeen, I don't understand either. But at least it's a line we can pursue. Nothing so far in medical science can explain what's happening to her. Maybe this will give us a clue."

"So where do we start? Were do *I* start?" Haberdeen's voice began to trail off as he realized that he was being drawn into the trap of being a helper to the suspect rather than her pursuer and jailer. The detective was getting annoyed. He dragged the lower drawer of his desk open, swept around the inside of the drawer with his hand, found an old bag of Fritos, grabbed them, and ripped the bag open so violently that the greasy crunchies splattered all over his desk.

Haberdeen shoved some into his mouth and then spoke through oily, masticated carbohydrates. "Doc, I really *don't* need or want to help that woman. I just want to know if she's dirty." He realized he was using jargon, so he continued. "In cop talk, Dr. Howard, that means whether or not she's done something illegal."

"Officer, I don't *care* what you want. My job is to get her healthy. I need to use everything at my disposal to do that. So I'm going to check this out further. Now, will you please help me?"

Haberdeen hesitated. He was being asked to look into vampirism, possibly to assist in his suspect's condition. It was antithetical for a cop to do anything to help a suspect out.

On the other hand, the doc was actually taking Haberdeen's vampire stuff seriously enough to be willing to research it. That meant that his own vague thoughts about this occult subject weren't being rejected out of hand. It meant that the detective was being paid some modicum of respect. That settled it.

"What do you want me to do?"

"Can you have that woman call me? The one who interviewed the people at the college?"

"Lisa? My girlfriend? I'm sure I can arrange it."

"Good."

"Anything else, doc?"

"Just make sure Milliken stays in custody until you hear from me."

"You're the one in control," said Haberdeen. "She's your patient. As long as you say she needs to stay put, she'll stay put."

"Okay. For now, she stays put."

"Done. Can I do anything else?" asked Haberdeen.

"Pray."

"Pray? What the fuck are you talking about? I thought you were a doctor. A scientist."

"A doctor's powers only extend so far."

Shit, thought Haberdeen.

The G-Man went for some more coffee. When he got back, there was a new file on his desk, on top of his Frito remnants.

He had asked Humberto to make a few phone calls for him (including one to Dickinson's), and the new file contained his report.

Haberdeen learned that one of Milliken's recent mothers, a Linda Boating on whom Lisbath had worked a few weeks ago and whose birth experience the child Mandy Shapiro had watched, had been very sick—high fever and all—when she had her baby. But now she was completely healthy. The Boating woman had been put on heavy antibiotics right after her postpartum check with a regular physician, and apparently the drugs had done the trick.

He continued reading in the file. Haberdeen learned from the results of an inquiry call to her home that another of the mothers —a Betty Perling—was very sick and had not gone in to get medical attention.

That's really getting fucking weird, thought Haberdeen.

He decided to play Mr. Nice Guy. He buzzed Moraga on the interoffice com line. "Amigo Humberto?"

"Yeah?"

"Call the Perling family back. Tell them to get her to the doctor Code 3. And have them tell the doctor to check for strains of *Strep*. Do it. Now, okay?"

"Bet there's no siren or light bar on their car," mused Humberto.

"Their loss," retorted the G-Man.

Thirty-three

Lisbath's physician, Dr. Mark Howard, finally got the phone call he had requested from Lisa Ipple. Lisa told him about what she had learned and that her main source was the Department Chairman Dr. Bodnir at the local college. Howard called the academician and obtained from him the name and contact information for the person Bodnir thought would be most likely to answer Howard's unusual questions. It was one Dr. Nicholas Edroiuan of Romania's Central University in Cluj-Napoca, Transylvania.

Dr. Howard called in the middle of the Connecticut night and caught Dr. Edroiuan in his office on a break between classes. The specialist in ancient Romanian history spoke little English but was still proficient enough to refer Dr. Howard to a knowledgeable medical doctor named Rade Fonescu at the university's adjoining hospital. Dr. Howard's front-office secretary tried that number the next day but had to leave a message. She got Dr. Fonescu's e-mail address and sent both Dr. Howard's office and home numbers to Dr. Fonescu's office.

At 6:10 a.m. the following day, Dr. Howard's home phone rang. It was the Romanian specialist.

"Dr. Fonescu, I am grateful that you have called me back."

"Yes. What can I do for you?" asked the physician in flawless, unaccented English. Dr. Fonescu had studied at the UCLA medical school in a special exchange program several years ago. His excellent facility with medicine was matched by his flair for languages.

Dr. Fonescu grinned to himself and started to chuckle. *Here we go again*, thought the Chairman of the Department of Surgery at the University of Babes Bolyai's adjunct hospital. *Another banal Dracul inquiry. These Americans always look for the extreme.*

"Doctor, I have a medical practice in Connecticut in the United States," explained Dr. Howard.

"Yes?" Physician or not, Fonescu was just waiting for the Dracul reference.

"I have a patient who is showing numerous atypical symptoms."

"Don't tell me she has closely-spaced suprajugular puncture wounds. Please don't."

Dr. Howard could hear Rade beginning to laugh through his nose. It confused him a little, but he persevered.

"Surely not. No. She has no such thing. Let me tell you first that my patient is dying. She is aging perhaps a year or more for every day she lives. She is experiencing some color changes in her pupils. The color changes seem to be associated with an unusual, colored cataract."

"This is interesting," said a more attuned Fonescu. He straightened in his chair. "Is there more?"

"Doctor, the woman drinks human blood. So for that matter does her dog. Now do you see why I am calling?"

"Perhaps." Fonescu's response sounded tentative, but his mind was silently racing.

Dr. Howard continued. "First, please, what can you tell me about deep red cataracts? And then about anything you have on non-genetic, premature aging?"

"Do you want the medical information, or do you want the real information?"

Howard's thinking performed an immediate, disorienting pirouette. This Romanian doctor was differentiating medicine from reality? Where was all this heading?

"Doctor? Are you there?" asked Dr. Fonescu.

"Yes, yes. Sorry. What do you mean 'medical or real'?"

"Precisely what I said."

"Okay." Dr. Howard still didn't understand what Dr. Fonescu was getting at, but he really had no choice but to go along. "Please," said Dr. Howard, "give me both."

"As you wish." Fonescu settled in, in some small way grateful that he finally had someone with a medical background with whom to discuss these issues intelligently. He ran little risk of ridicule by talking to this American physician.

The Romanian specialist began with an earnest voice, comforting in its depth and demeanor. "Doctor, how far along are you in your consideration of human hemophagia?"

"This is the first time I have ever dealt with deliberate, human blood ingestion, Dr. Fonescu."

"Then we will start at the beginning. You must suspend judgment while I tell you what I know. Is this acceptable to you?"

"This is exactly what I need. Please take your time. I will be taking notes."

"The history of human hemophagia predates even Romania's famous Vlad Tepes—you may know him as Vlad the Impaler. Or even as Dracula, which was his father's name. But most vampiric legends have grown up around Vlad himself and, to a lesser extent, his father.

"Vlad lived in the 15th century, and beginning at that time, many ideas were discussed related to supposed vampires. Few of them were correct or even believable, but there are a couple of things medical science—at least here in Romania—has discovered. Things that explain quite effectively the real trappings of the entities described as 'vampires.'"

"Fascinating. Please go on."

"All of the vampiric phenomena medical science has understood have their roots in protein synthesis. You know, of course, that DNA gives the body the code to make proteins."

"High school biology," replied Dr. Howard, trying not to sound trivial.

"People who refer to themselves as 'vampires' are usually genetically different from the rest of us. Or at least biochemically different."

"How?"

"Here in Romania we have found that vampires produce a protein structurally related to the p21 gene in humans. It is so similar that, when it is produced, it inhibits p21 synthesis. We call it p21-v. A little inside joke."

"Please slow down. I am not familiar with p21."

"Shame on you, doctor! You are not up on your own country's research."

"I try. Please fill me in."

"Very well. Late in the year 2000, at the University of Illinois in the United States, Professor Igor Robinson found that gene p21 produces a protein that plays a role in aging. When p21 is made, the body's cells begin to age rapidly. When p21 was turned off, the aging essentially stopped."

"Come to think of it, I think I read something about that. But the research is not fully integrated into the medical community yet."

"Nevertheless, this gene helped us understand many, many things about the vampire. And it is possible that certain viruses can create a genetic mutation that shifts p21 to the closely-related form, p21-v."

"Jesus," said Dr. Howard.

"So we have grave implications for vampires, or people who may have been virus-exposed and subsequently produced p21-v products. Once the gene is activated in the genetic vampire, p21-v inhibits his or her aging. But it must be *maintained*."

"Maintained?"

"Let's begin with the red cataract. Vampires are thought to be afraid of the daylight—or to be creatures of the night. Have you heard that story?"

"Only in vampire movies."

"Regardless of where, this is part of the vampire mystique. And now we know why. Have you figured it out?"

"No, I'm afraid not."

Fonescu paused and took a sip of his tea. He had a willing and intelligent audience for his findings, and he wanted to savor every moment.

"Dr. Howard, the red cataract you have found in your patient is genetically coded. Just as some families are more prone to normal cataracts, p21-v carriers—vampires—are significantly prone to these red cataracts."

"Go on. What did you say about 'activating' the gene?"

"Well, the cataract does not appear except in special circumstances. Blood ingestion provides for an unusual ratio of amino acids and their subsequent free radicals when the blood is digested. Further, we think the element cobalt is involved."

"Do you mean that once cobalt-rich blood is broken down by the body, the result is some kind of unique chemistry? That if the person ate—I mean drank—blood, then his internal biochemistry changes and the gene gets turned on?"

"Exactly so." Fonescu set his cup down gently. "As I said, it results in a special blend of amino acids. And a p21-v-positive person can only react to this blend if two conditions are met. First, the person needs to have drunk at least a full liter of *human* blood. Smaller volumes are ineffective."

"Why does the blood need to be human?"

Dr. Fonescu continued. "Other animal bloods have their own blends of amino acids and are much lower in cobalt. It's not the right 'recipe,' so to speak. So those blends don't operate on vampires."

"Okay. Go on. What's the second condition needed to turn on p-21v?"

"We don't know, but the phenomenon only happens in some of the genetic vampires. Perhaps with your patient, you will discover the second necessary condition. But there is more."

"More?"

"Once the gene is turned on, as I said, p21-v has to be '*maintained*.'"

"Got it." Dr. Howard wrote feverishly on his pad.

"You know that genes produce proteins. When p21-v manufactures its associated protein in large amounts, the cataract begins to form. The growth rate of the cataract varies with the individual. It can appear in the very young or it may take decades or more to appear. Its characteristic red color has nothing directly to do with blood; it is simply due to a large amount of iodine in the cataract."

Dr. Fonescu could hear Dr. Howard's pen scratching notes.

"The cataract, which is always subcapsular, grows on the very center of the rear of the eye's lens. That means two things."

"Yes?"

"First, that when light is shone into a vampire's eye, the pupil appears extremely red. Much more so than a normal person's eye might appear red because of a camera's flash."

"Oh?"

"Yes. When a very bright light shines into a normal person's eye, it passes through the clear lens and may reflect off the blood at the back of the eye. Photographers here call it 'red eye.' With the vampire, the light hits the red cataract in addition to reflecting the rear blood. It makes for a striking, deep redness not observable in the typical human eye."

"Fascinating," said Dr. Howard.

"More to the point, however, is the effect on day vision, which is different from the effect on the vampire's night vision."

Fonescu continued. "In the daytime, the pupil at the center of the eye is of very small diameter. The eye is trying to protect itself from letting too much light in. The small diameter narrows the pathway of light into the eye."

"Sure. So far, I'm following," said Dr. Howard. "Light has to go through a much smaller opening during the day."

"Yes. Now the red cataract is centered at the back of the lens, so when the light is funneled through the center because of the small pupil, the light cannot get around the cataract. The dense red tissue is in the way."

"Aha!" exclaimed Dr. Howard. "So they can't see in the daytime because the light is blocked by the red cataract. They're effectively day-blind. But at night, when the pupil is much larger, light can get around the cataract. So they prefer the night because they can see so much better when it's dark!"

"*Bravo*, doctor. That is precisely correct. The vampire is virtually blind in the relatively bright daylight, but he can see adequately in a darker environment."

"My patient has extremely limited day vision," said Dr. Howard, "so her cataract is apparently not fully mature. Yet. But this explains a lot."

The mutual respect between the two men was increasing measurably. This was the useful, wonderful communication Dr. Howard had been striving for. This was all paying off.

"There is more," said Dr. Fonescu. "We believe that p21-v may confer a certain immunity to some diseases, some viral, but mostly those bacterial in origin."

"No wonder supposed vampires can live so long. They don't get sick very easily."

"Correct," agreed Dr. Fonescu. "They rarely even get colds. P21-v carriers seem almost invincible—as long as they get their proper blood supply."

Dr. Howard felt comfortable in moving the conversation. "Speaking of living a long time, Dr. Fonescu, how might this relate to my patient's premature aging? She gets older visibly each day. Nobody at the hospital has any idea what to do. And we have already confirmed that it is not an instance of the child-aging disease progeria."

"Ah! I have already given you the keys to this puzzle, Dr. Howard. Think carefully. Gene p21 begins the aging process, remember? Do you remember also that vampiric gene p21-v inhibits p21? That when p21-v makes its proteins, p21 is halted?"

"Yes, but I haven't put it all together yet."

"Allow me," said Dr. Fonescu. "It is the ingestion of large amounts of cobalt-rich blood that, after digestion, turns on p21-v."

"Yes, I got that."

Dr. Fonescu continued. "Was your patient a young girl when you first admitted her?"

"No. A woman in her fifties," responded Dr. Howard.

"Then she may have been suffering from decreased human blood intake for a while. That could account for much of the aging she had experienced prior to admission to the hospital. Perhaps she was in her twenties or thirties when infected, then aged rapidly during periods of what we may call 'blood drought.'"

"Alternately," Dr. Fonescu continued, "The 'turn on' event may have taken place later in your patient's life. Either way, she could be a sorry victim, riding a roller coaster of fast and slow aging as her blood supply varies."

"Quite a concept, Dr. Fonescu. A roller coaster of aging. And right now it's heading downhill, toward death, much too fast."

"Yes. We want to stop your patient's aging immediately. So we need to stop p21 synthesis, right?"

"Okay, yes. *Wait a minute! I just understood!*" Dr. Howard became very excited as the pieces of this physiological puzzle began to fit together. "If we infuse the blend of digestive products that are made after large levels of human blood are ingested, my patient's body should make p21-v. And that will stop p21 production. And her aging will stop. Maybe even be reversed. Is that right?"

"Well, maybe not reversed. We don't know. But otherwise, yes. It should stop her aging. It is actually quite simple."

"*My God*," said Howard. "That means we need to feed her human blood or she'll age so fast she could be dead in a few days."

"Precisely," said Dr. Fonescu. He slowly rotated his cup in its saucer, lost in thought.

Dr. Howard was stunned. *The therapy for Lisbath Milliken would be to feed her human blood.* His basic humanity cried out for an alternative. Immediately he had a question. "Dr. Fonescu, how about animal blood? Cow blood? Even rat blood? Surely it doesn't have to be human!" Dr. Howard was speaking more from emotional horror than from scientific logic.

"Unfortunately it does have to be human. *As I already told you*, all animals produce unique bodily fluids, blood included. They are relatively low in cobalt, for example. That is in part why we are different from cats or monkeys. And we have found that only the precise ratio of blood elements in the *human* variety will turn on p21-v."

"And how about synthesizing something instead of using actual blood from people?"

"Do you have time to do that?" asked Dr. Fonescu. "We haven't succeeded at making a human blood substitute yet. If we had, we wouldn't need donors any more. You're looking at years of additional research, and your patient has perhaps days to live."

"You're right, Doctor," said Dr. Howard. "Synthesis is currently out of the question."

There it was, right in front of him. Dr. Howard had the only way to save his patient. By feeding her human blood. A million questions began to run through his mind. Where would he get it? *Should* he get it? The ethical questions alone were staggering.

Howard almost forgot he was on the phone. His reverie was interrupted by Dr. Fonescu's voice. "Dr. Howard, are you there?"

"Oh, yes, Doctor. Sorry. I was just considering everything you've told me."

"Fine. Well, I am glad to have helped. Maybe you will e-mail me with the results. The address is on the university web site. I must go now."

"Yes, Dr. Fonescu. Thank you so much for all of this fine information. I was truly helpless before talking with you."

"Be well, Doctor."

The phone double-clicked as Romania and the United States broke telephonic contact.

Thirty-four

For the first time since she had been remanded to the Park City Hospital's jail ward, Lisbath Milliken's brain toyed with regaining consciousness. She had been dreaming fitfully about blood, about Dickinson's, about ancient monsters, and about that most recent monster named Haberdeen.

But mostly she dreamt about Lad. She thought back to the first time he had had a blood treat. Just before her name change back in Ohio, on the day the dog had knocked her to the sidewalk, Lisbath had been admitted to the ER to be checked for damage. She was released the same day and found Lad waiting for her just outside the hospital exit. For some crazy reason she had taken an immediate liking to the animal.

In a mild daze, Lisbath had taken Lad home, had given him his name, and had gone to the refrigerator to find him something to eat. Lad had smelled blood in the trash can from Lisbath's most recent midwife job. He had run to it, had knocked it over, and had begun to indulge himself in the red, congealed stuff.

From that moment forward, Lisbath knew that her little Laddie loved the stuff, and at the same time, she developed an increasing, unimaginable urge to eat it herself. She loved giving blood to him; she loved sharing the wonderful liquid with her only true friend.

But then Lisbath's dreams turned back to Haberdeen. She saw his badge sweep past her at mouth level, its pin backing scraping across her face, drawing blood droplets in a faint moustache over her quivering lips.

The nurse awoke slowly and blearily into a sterile-looking room with no curtains, no side table, a closed door, and an IV running into her left arm. It felt like 200 degrees, but she was shivering.

Despite her nursing background, it took Lisbath a couple of minutes to begin to piece her situation together. She had no idea how long she had been unconscious, and the bare bulb stuck into the high ceiling robbed her temporarily of any semblance of day or night.

Milliken turned her head slowly to the side. Maybe there'd be a window there. Maybe a touch of nature to counter this hard, white chamber. Lisbath saw the late afternoon sun working its way through the denuded branches of winter.

It felt good to see something of the outside environment, but the pleasure was reduced seen through a window with bars on it.

Oh, yes, she recalled. Oh, God. *What is becoming of me?*

Lisbath was perspiring heavily, and as she raised her hand toward her forehead to wipe away the sweat, she was startled to see deep wrinkles in her arm. Normally her arms were plump and pink; now they were graying and aged. This only added to her confusion and was quite startling.

She lifted the sheet and saw a body apparently ten or fifteen years older than the one she had occupied before her arrest. The foreign thing lying in the bed was magnificently disgusting, particularly as rolls of her fat sagged limply to one side or the other. A few days ago, her corpulence was at least somewhat firm; it held some shape. Now her body was a gray bag of skin and fat, drooping and fetid.

A low gurgle-rumble began to surface in her aging lungs. As its intensity slowly increased, Lisbath's eyes became wider and wider. She gripped the sheets like a woman giving birth, pulling randomly in an uncoordinated expression of fear and loathing and loss of control.

Her voice became louder still, reaching almost a scream, and Lisbath began to flail. It was at that moment that the IV that had been shoved into her now-crinkling forearm skin cantilevered out, pivoting down to the bone as its attached rubber tube pulled backward. It left a deep gash that began to fill with blood.

At first Milliken didn't notice her arm. She was too crazed with fear and incomprehension to understand much of anything. But as her flailing continued and became wilder, her arm began to spray flying rivulets of blood all over the room.

Milliken was about to throw herself off the bed when a gob of her own blood splotched into her eye. She stopped dead. The blood began to run down into her mouth, and she tongued it gingerly. The nurse-midwife stopped screaming and shaking and flailing. Her eyebrows rose, flags of surprise traversing her forehead.

Like heavenly manna, the woman's own blood captured her attention so overwhelmingly that her only motions were her breathing, which was slowing down, and the stream of tears that continued to trickle from her wildly staring eyes.

But as the panache of blood began to overtake Lisbath's sensorium, her recurring primal imperative slithered again toward the surface. With less resistance than before, her staring eyes fluttered and eventually closed, shutting out this banal world and returning her to the 400-year-old past to which Lisbath was inextricably linked.

The girl Magenalene was standing defiantly before the countess. Derek the slavemaster went to the equipment bag and began to drag it toward Magenalene's station while the other serfs took their positions before the other crucified women. The tasks of these tenders were to emulate everything Derek did as closely as possible. Each serf had two or three victims in his charge, and each servant was expected to move and act swiftly so that the macabre dance of pain and body fluids would execute as choreographed.

"I will choose now," said the countess as she seated herself heavily on her stool. Holdar began to draw items from the equipment sack. He first placed yard-long tongs with burnt, encrusted tips to the countess' left. Their connecting point was a mere four inches from the flattened ends, so the leverage afforded the user (and the pressure that would operate on the object of the pinch or crush) was enormous.

Then came knives of varying lengths and shapes, triangular punches, and mallets. There were several sizes of what appeared to be thumbscrews. He also brought out many lengths of rope, some made of braided human hair. Metal clanked as Holdar brought out chains, chain mail with a spiked metallic rod running through it at the top, and a series of small, corked containers like thick cans containing various caustic liquids.

There were clippers, clamps, shackles for every diameter from finger to neck, flint and steel, nails, a primitive type of staple, rings, and lead weights with brass loops attached. These the slavemaster put in a pile near the center of the displayed equipment.

Across the top of this array Derek placed masks made of cloth, pounded metal, leather, bark, and chain mail. Some had feathers, but most were unadorned save the leather straps and crude buckles attached to them. There were also hoods: some with eye holes, some with mouth holes, and some with no holes at all.

Finally, the whips. These were placed from longest to shortest, from thickest to thinnest, along the bottom of the torture display. Cats o'nine, slappers, very long whips with sharpened metal shards and spikes toward the tips, whips with heavy metal weights at the tips, and more and more.

The countess was smiling and nodding, ready for the anticipation to end and for the festivities to begin in earnest.

"Erect them!" was the countess' newest directive. She extended her right arm and hand and made a grand sweep, left to right, over the crucifixion area. This was her signal to create the suffering array that would accompany her pleasures; her feast; her monthly unbridled joy.

    A pair of serfs was to work each crucifix. They took each screaming bitch, strapped her down, and then hammered her onto the wood. The serfs knew where to place the crude nails to minimize bleeding and maximize pain; this allowed the pitiful sufferer to remain displayed for many hours before giving in to the Devil's acumen.

    One serf would lift the top of the cross, working his way down the shaft toward the foot, thereby lifting the crossbar end. As he did this, the other servant sank the crucifix's foot into a well-worn hole. This cantilevering act required some coordination and from time to time one of the women would be dropped accidentally several feet to the ground, often landing face-down. To the countess, these unexpected surprises added spice to the proceedings. But it was only context: a chorus of screams and pain to surround her senses as the sovereign violated the chosen who excited her best.

    The noble then focused her attention on her special victim, the lithe Magenalene.

    "Derek, first the *garrote-neu*. Her breasts. I want them red; I want them full of my blood. I want them ready for me." The torturess gritted her teeth as she imagined the next few minutes; her jaw muscles worked evenly, from side to side. Her entire body began to tingle.

    Holdar selected the medium-length whip with three tails, each with a blunted spike at the end. The *garrote-neu*'s handle was crosshatched with leather straps. The user end was adorned with a crude carving of a falcon's head with an overly rounded beak so as not to slice the whipmaster's own arm during deployment.

    The countess stood and motioned for one of her servants to move her stool to a better vantage point. During these preparations, the other serfs brought out their own whips and tore open the blouses of those crucified women who had not yet been bared. As the women weakened, one by one, the screams gave way to groans of fatigued horror.

The slavemaster took his position before Magenalene, placed his right foot behind him for balance, and drew the whip back with his right hand and through the encircling fingers of his left. As she began to breathe much more heavily, Holdar swung the metal-tipped leather flails toward his victim's left breast. They struck with moderate force, but Magenalene's reaction was extreme. She shouted and twisted, throwing her head back and forth, experiencing the stinging of the new cuts and impacts to her formerly-beautiful breast.

"Aaahh, you monster! What are you doing? Why are you doing this? What is it?"

This spurred Holdar on. He began a merciless barrage of whip slaps and slices. He began to laugh hideously, stomping his foot in an irregular, animal rhythm completely out of step with the actual whip blows. The attacks moved from one bleeding breast to the other, hitting harder and harder each time until both breasts looked like stippled, wobbling pomegranates. With each heart-wrenching cry, Magenalene shook uncontrollably, pulling her hands inward and in so doing ripping the flesh on her individually nailed fingertips.

The countess was in her own heaven, was hungry for her next sip of life-giving blood.

"Derek! I will drink her now!"

Holdar put the whip aside and grabbed a short, viciously sharp knife. Its blade was curved like a miniature scimitar, and its wooden handle was red and green. He holstered the knife in a leather pocket tied to his belt. Then the slavemaster bent down to a small pile of metallic paraphernalia and selected a large, heavy clamp. Within a squared metal frame, the clamp had a flattened surface toward which a cylinder, which protruded through a hole in the frame, could be slid. The cylinder had closely-spaced holes through it, and a pin could be slipped through any of the holes, blocking the cylinder's retreat back out of the clamp's frame. In this way, the piston would be held down on whatever it was crushing. The clamping end of the cylinder had been scored and roughened to keep anything from slipping out from under it.

Holdar's back had been to Magenalene during his preparations. When he turned to face her crucified body, the poor woman saw a glint of metal and let out an unearthly sound like that of a cat being eaten alive. Derek's penis rose in response.

The countess, who had been seated while the slavemaster made ready, now rose and moved toward whimpering Magenalene. Derek Holdar put the square clamp over his right wrist like a bracelet and reached for Magenalene's left nipple. His filthy fingers pulled it out hard, squeezing deeply and forcing his thick, filthy thumbnail inward both to assure that, even though it was lubricated with blood, the nipple would not slip out of his grasp, and for the pure physical pleasure of it as well. Magenalene was horrified, and it pleased the lady to see the girl's incredulity.

Holdar's left hand slid the clamp over the extruded nipple and, with a practiced technique made perfect over the years of these horrors, pressed the cylinder over the nipple, smashing it down to the bracket's far side. As the heavy metal cylinder rammed down, Magenalene spewed out a deafening, monstrous "Aaaaaahhhh!" that frightened all the remaining crucified women and perhaps half of the countryside as well.

The slavemaster then ground the cylinder clockwise and counterclockwise, over and over, bruising and further flattening the painful breast-end. Magenalene's cries of terror and pain became pitifully more intense, but this only strengthened Holdar's resolve to crush any remaining connective tissue. It would add flavor to the countess' upcoming liquid treat. And still there was more.

Screams and the sounds of begging for mercy filled the air from every quarter as all of the crucified women experienced much the same torture. But Magenalene's treatment would be extra special.

When the wench's nipple was all but completely shredded, Holdar withdrew the small scimitar from the leather sheath. He then looked toward the countess to see if she was ready; she shook her head Yes and widened her stance a bit. Holdar flashed the blade before Magenalene's eyes and she recoiled as far as she could on her perch. She turned her head to the side in total disbelief or at least in denial of what was to come next.

The slavemaster brought the curved blade to a location just behind the stretched nipple. He tapped the areola with the blunt side of the blade, yet each tap pulled on the skin that was caught under the rough cylinder; each tap produced more pain and agony for the girl. Then he rotated the blade so the sharp side faced the deteriorating flesh of the areola and drew it down very slowly, making an incision about a quarter inch into the skin. Magenalene was blinded by the pain, and screamed over and over, asking for the mercy that would never come.

Holdar slapped the breast hard, tearing the nipple partially away from its areolar support. He then returned the scimitar blade to its former cut and sliced downward, this time quite quickly, all the way through. The remaining left breast tissue snapped back as the square clamp and its severed nipple thudded to the bloody dirt before Holdar and the crucified girl.

A smallish serf collected the prize and placed it on a tiny pewter pedestal. He brought it to the countess dutifully and on bended knee. She lowered her nose to the dripping body part, inhaled deeply, and smiled broadly. Yes, yes. Things were going well this day.

The lady immediately placed herself before the girl, and another obedient and knowledgeable serf brought her stool. The countess stepped up onto the stool, grabbed the flailing, decapitated breast with both hands, shoved the red, spurting tip into her mouth, and began to suck for all she was worth. She squeezed and pumped the breast like a baker's frosting tool, extruding not only luscious blood but globules of glistening tissues as well. Some were tubular; some looked like tiny clusters of grapes; some were yellow and shimmering; and all these pieces drenched in translucent blood made the countess' meal a warped delight. She gobbled with a gourmand's disregard for decency. She was totally self-involved and openly hungry for this incomparable blend of flavors and textures.

When the countess had her momentary fill, she stepped back, off of the stool, and moved haltingly to her table. She dropped her ample posterior onto her own plate and breathed hard, wiping her mouth, neck and chest with a filthy cloth.

"Derek, I want the other. Now!"

This time, the experienced slavemaster picked up the triangular blade—more a spike than a knife—and immediately speared Magenalene's remaining breast from underneath. She fainted helplessly from the pain as Holdar began to simultaneously rotate and twist the skewer counterclockwise. The maneuver almost ripped the breast from its mooring. As the now unconscious girl began to slump forward, a nearby slave took a long pole and shoved it into the captive's mouth hard enough to break most of her upper teeth. The brace was thrust far enough to get Magenalene's head back to the vertical jut of the crucifix, and the strong serf rammed the far end of the lance into the dirt. It held the captive's head almost erect in a macabre vision of vomiting a solid wooden rod.

Holdar reached for a small battle-axe with a bright, glistening edge as a few of the still-conscious crucified wenches several yards away began their shrieks anew.

The emotional pain this image caused Lisbath yanked her out of her vision and into a kind of netherland of unconsciousness. Her body, strewn across the hospital bed, relaxed a little as the corpulent nurse inched toward fuzzy awareness.

Milliken opened her eyes and reoriented to the blood upon her. It was both soothing and scary, but her overwhelming sensation was a kind of warped relief.

It was as if Lisbath had been crawling through a desert for many days and had just reached a water vending machine with free drinks. She became stimulus-bound, searching out the blood that would heal her.

Lisbath realized that her arm was bleeding fiercely. Immediately she used her undamaged arm to shove the needle's former nest up toward her mouth. Lisbath began to lick and suck as she never had before, each moment bringing her precious additional droplets of fluid.

Feeling that she was not getting enough blood fast enough, the woman began to bite and tear at her own forearm's skin, ripping what she could to increase the payout of rich blood. Oh, what a feast! She moved from the top area where the needle had been to the underneath. Juicier; much more flesh. More vessels. More and more and more!

Lisbath Milliken felt no pain and had no awareness of anything save the hearty flavor of her own sustenance swirling down her waiting throat. So she had no cognizance of the cadre of hospital guards and orderlies rushing into her room in response to the groans and screams she had emitted moments before.

"Jesus Christ!" yelled the first guard to unlock the door and enter. The well-built black woman behind the badge said, "What the fuck is this?"

A nurse and two orderlies came in next. One of the orderlies who had been on the job only a couple of months began immediately to vomit and moved to the corner of the room. The other orderly was a slight, blondish man whose pristine manner and impeccable grooming led all the guards to call him "Sweetie." At least Sweetie could hold his stomach, and he positioned himself at Lisbath's head, hands on hips, awaiting orders.

Another guard with four stripes on the arm of his uniform and a potbelly that preceded him entered and sized up the situation rapidly. "Get the restraints," he yelled to the next young guard through the door.

"Yessir," said the twenty-two-year-old sheriff cadet as he ran down the hall for the leather and buckles.

Then the second guard barked an order to the remaining orderly: "Grab her arms, Sweetie. *Fast*. Hold them at her sides."

The orderly had been trained to protect himself from patient blood at all costs. He was not wearing gloves, nor had he a face mask. He balked at the guard's order and began to shake his head slowly. Last thing he ever wanted was to get AIDS.

"Didn't you hear me, *asshole*? Hold her arms down!"

"But, sir, I don't have any protection!"

"You'll need to protect yourself from me for the rest of your fucking life if you don't get those arms of hers down *now*. Understand, asshole?"

"Okay, okay," said the orderly. He knew when he was out of his league. Besides, this was some crazy old woman; not someone likely to carry AIDS. He hoped.

Lisbath remained unaware of any of the festivities taking place around her until Sweetie finally grabbed her arms. Then she began to scream. To shriek. Like someone was dismembering her and forcing her to watch it all and pouring salt on her and roasting her with a blowtorch all at the same time.

The pitiful creature's screams echoed in The Park's small hospital ward, and the other two hospitalized inmates in separate, locked rooms down the hall became just a little more frightened.

♦ ♦ ♦

"G-Man, you're going to want know about this," said Detective-Sergeant Stevenson as he walked into the overheated general detectives' office.

"Ok, shoot," said Haberdeen, grateful for a break from looking over written reports.

"Do you remember hearing about the double homicide in Shelton recently?"

"Yeah. It was on the news. But I don't know any of the details. I don't trust reporters, so I try not to pay attention. And it was way out of our jurisdiction anyway. Sounded pretty severe, but that's all I got. So what happened?"

"One of the victims was a nurse, and the other victim was giving birth at home."

That caught Haberdeen's attention fast and hard. "No shit, Sarge? Give me more."

"Haven't got any more. I was just talking to Hawking in Shelton PD and he mentioned it. Thought you'd want to know."

"Yeah. I'm gonna call 'em."

"I thought you would."

Haberdeen reached for the phone immediately. He found the Shelton Police Department's internal detectives' number under the plastic cover on his desk pad and punched the buttons quickly. This was the kind of stuff the G-Man needed.

"Shelton PD."

"This is Detective George Haberdeen, Bridgeport PD. Let me talk to whoever's handling the double-murder case that included a nurse."

"That'll be Detective Hawking. Hold on."

While holding, Haberdeen turned to a fresh sheet of yellow paper on his note pad and rubbed and twisted his pencil tip at an angle to sharpen it a little. He didn't have to wait long.

"Detective Hawking."

"This is George Haberdeen, Connecticut PD. What can you tell me about the double homicide a few days ago?"

"Lots," answered Hawking. "What do you need?"

Haberdeen answered quickly. "They say there was a nurse and a woman giving birth. Is that right?"

"Yeah. Nurse was slumped over her steering wheel. The woman was a mess on her own bed. Third victim was the woman's husband, but he survived with head injuries."

"M.O.?"

"Nurse was drugged. Two drugs, according to the coroner. Second one did the trick."

"And the mother?"

"Drugged first. But then something really strange."

"What?"

"Half drained of blood."

No shit, thought Haberdeen. Things are beginning to click.

"What about the husband?" asked the G-Man.

"He's still in a coma."

"Suspects?"

"Well, the family kept to itself, according to the neighbors. The only thing we know for sure is something we got from the next-door neighbor. Says there were two nurses in that car."

"Was one of them real fat?"

"*Yeah*. How did you know?"

"Send me the file. We might have your perp in our jail hospital."

"Great!" said Hawking with more than a little surprise.

"So it was a birth, right? What happened to the baby?"

"Originally taken to Children's Services. Then some family members claimed it."

"Understood."

"So are you sure enough you've got the perp that we can stop looking?"

"Stop looking."

"Excellent."

Haberdeen hung up and sat back in his creaking chair. *Now we've got something*, he thought to himself. *We can get that bitch for murder one.* With great determination and a clarifying view of what lay ahead of him, he picked up the phone and dialed The Park.

"Park City Hospital, Prison Ward, Officer Spender."

"Detective Haberdeen, Bridgeport PD."

"Yeah! The G-Man! I've heard of you."

"Fine. What's the status of prisoner Milliken?"

"Detective, I don't get a lot of medical detail; I just make sure nobody leaves. But the word on the ward is that she's nuts and tried to eat herself."

Haberdeen was momentarily silent as he visualized the nurse working on her belly with a knife and fork. Through the phone he heard a metal door slamming shut and something like a gurney rolling by Spender.

"What the fuck do you mean, *eat herself?*" asked Haberdeen. "This is a bad time for jokes, officer."

"No, really, sir. I meant it. They had to put her in restraints. I wasn't there. She was biting her arm. And chewing, too, I was told. Very bloody."

Haberdeen wasn't overly surprised, and certainly not shocked. He ordered, "It's now a full felony hold, Spender. No visitors, no phone calls, door locked at all times, no sharp objects. You know the drill."

"Sure. She couldn't reach any sharp objects if she wanted to. But why make it a felony just because she's nuts?"

"There's more to it. Look, I'm rushed. Will you inform her med staff of her upgraded status?"

"Can do."

"Thanks."

Haberdeen hung up and started planning the rest of his strategy. Ultimately he'd need to put a case together for the DA. First, though, he needed to get back with Sergeant Stevenson with what they called a "package." Evidence, logic, and supporting documents and information enough to motivate the sergeant to OK the approach to the district attorney.

The one higher priority was a cup of the office's deadly coffee.

To assemble his package, the G-Man decided he needed to know if there was anything evidential at the woman's apartment. He dispatched Moraga to obtain a search warrant and then to take the woman's apartment apart piece by piece. In the meantime, Haberdeen would begin to organize the package.

Four and a half hours later, Moraga walked into Haberdeen's office.

"George, we hit pay dirt."

"Tell me."

"First of all, the apartment door was busted. Someone wanted in pretty bad. But the lock seemed to be intact. All we could find was some scratches about two feet above the ground. And no fingerprints except for Milliken's."

He continued. "There's a locked closet inside the apartment. When we got it open, it was full of medical equipment. Clamps and bowls and bandages and like that."

"So?" asked Haberdeen.

"Well, that's not all. On some of the shelves, there were these jars of stuff."

"Jars? Like medicines?" Haberdeen asked.

"No. Like organs or something."

"What do you mean?"

"There were thirteen glass jars. And almost every one of them had liquid and something solid floating in it. Each one held about a quart or two. Every one was labeled differently. A jumble of numbers and letters."

"So what was in 'em?"

"We sent the stuff to the lab. I don't have any fucking idea what was in those jars. Some of them were really dusty—like they were incredibly old."

"Okay. Did you bag all of the equipment and other stuff from the closet?"

"Of course."

"Find anything else?"

"Some drug canisters. We bagged them too."

"Good. Anything else?"

"Absolutely nothing. Unless you're interested in tent-sized underwear."

"Just take it home to your girlfriend."

"Fuck you, Haberdeen."

"Good work, guy."

"Thanks, man."

♦ ♦ ♦

Nurses Karen Stade and Wanda Pettridge were sitting on the Dickinson's sofa with their legs crossed. In this home-away-from-home, they were flipping through magazines and hoping for assignments for today. Both of them had already scanned every magazine in the place, but it was something to do while in their holding patterns. Nothing good on TV just now.

This morning, even the coffee was hardly enough to keep Wanda alert. It was dark and dreary. Wanda decided to drum up some conversation to keep herself sharp.

"Karen?"

"Yes?"

"What did you used to do before working here?"

"You don't know?" asked Karen. She thought everyone knew about her former job since it had ended so oddly.

"Well, no. Why else would I ask, girl? You know I only signed on about a year ago. You've been here a lot longer."

"Okay, sure. Well, I worked for a private doctor."

Wanda wondered why someone with a solid job in a doctor's office would end up at a registry. The office jobs had predictable hours and predictable pay. That wasn't so with registries. Of course, registries gave one more variety, and it was easy to take a day off.

"So why'd you quit?"

"Well, I didn't really quit." Karen became pensive. "Doc Stowage was killed."

"*Killed?*" It sounded so dramatic to Wanda. "Docs don't get killed!" she joked.

Wanda continued. "Car accident? Murdered? What?"

"Bowling."

"Oh, *come on*," said Wanda. "You've got to be kidding."

"No," Karen replied, "he really was killed in a bowling accident."

Wanda was smiling. This was working pretty well to help perk her up, and she thought Karen's sense of humor was nicely twisted.

"Tell me," Wanda said.

"Well, he was just at a bowling alley. He was sitting with his wife and some idiot accidentally threw a ball at poor Doc Stowage's head."

"How could someone accidentally throw a bowling ball?" Wanda still figured Karen was putting her on.

"Very, very poor bowler."

Both ladies started cracking up. It was so infectious that Sharona began chuckling too, even though she didn't know what the girls were laughing about.

The phone's electronic ring grabbed everyone's attention. Things were pretty slow, and Sharona picked up on the first ring.

"Dickinson's Registry. May I help you?" she asked.

"Is this Gomez?"

"This is *Sharona* Gomez. Yes." Sharona didn't like being called simply by her last name. It sounded so military. Business owner or not, Sharona had her pride.

Then her heart soured as Sharona began to recognize the voice on the line. It was that horrible Detective Haberdeen. Nothing good would be coming of this. She was sure of it.

"Gomez, we have arrested your Nurse Milliken."

Sharona was stunned. "Oh, my God! You're kidding? *Lisbath?* Sweet Lisbath?"

Both women on the couch sat forward. Sharona's phone had their undivided attention.

"Why?" implored Sharona.

"I need to have you come down to the station. I need to ask you a few questions."

"Me?"

"Yes, Gomez, you."

Sharona began to worry. "Am I in trouble?"

There had been bad blood between the G-Man and Sharona in past contacts, and he really wanted to scare her with something like *Deep shit, Sharona*. But he needed to be honest and professional.

"No. But I need some background on Milliken. Can you come now?"

"Well, no. I'm running the show here. How about after five?"

"Be here by 5:30?"

"Yes."

"Fine." Haberdeen hung up. No good-bye, of course.

Sharona put the receiver down slowly, then began to stare straight ahead. Her eyes were open but saw nothing. Tears began to fall on her blue silk blouse.

Sharona felt vulnerable, and that was pretty unusual for her. The last time she had actually cried at work was last year, when she learned that her dog had been hit by a car. As she spoke to the vet's nurse, she had fallen to pieces right there on the phone. That moment had really softened Sharona's image around the registry and brought a sorority-like solidarity to the place. That bonded feeling had never waned.

As Sharona began to whimper audibly, Karen and Wanda rose from the couch and went to her. Both of them embraced their good friend. After a moment, all three were weeping, and it helped a little.

Thirty-five

Sharona Gomez had never seen the inside of a police station before. Its stenches and the dirty benches in the foyer gave her the instant creeps.

With arms held close to her sides, she walked up to the desk sergeant. It was 5:25 p.m. "I'm here to see Detective Haberdeen," she said tentatively.

"Hold on." The desk cop picked up the phone, dialed, mumbled something, listened briefly, and hung up. "Have a seat right there," he said as he pointed to a wooden, cushionless bench. "Detective Haberdeen will be with you shortly." A fat Mexican woman and a slobbering child with a big smile occupied half the bench. Sharona chose to sit as far to the other side as possible.

After a fifteen-minute wait, Haberdeen walked up to see Sharona nervously tapping the tip of her high heels on the filthy floor.

"Gomez? Come with me."

He didn't wait to see her rise, but walked up to the swinging gate by the intake desk and held it open. Sharona picked up her briefcase and followed him into his office. She seated herself across from his desk.

"Miss Gomez, we now have your Nurse Milliken on a felony hold. Deep shit, in other words. And she's hospitalized."

Sharona gulped involuntarily. She waited to hear more or to see what she was going to be asked.

"What kind of trouble has she been in before?" asked Haberdeen.

"None that I know of," said Sharona. "What kind of trouble is she in now? What did she do? Or what do you *think* she did?"

"You'll answer my questions, lady. That's the way it works around here," said the G-Man. "When's the last time she made one of her patients sick?"

"What are you talking about? She doesn't make them sick, Mr. Haberdeen. She makes them *better*. We're nurses, you know."

"I don't need to hear your commercials. We know she's dirty. The more information you can give us, the better. Besides, it'll help protect your interests, won't it?"

"Well. . ." Sharona thought for a moment. "I guess if there really is something wrong about her, I need to know that too."

"Now you're talking, Gomez," said Haberdeen. "We need to be allies here."

That almost made Sharona vomit, but she didn't show it. She'd no more ally with this cop than she would feed her sister poison.

"I honestly don't know of any problems with her, Detective. Once in a while one of her patients gets sick, but that's common in our profession. When the body is compromised, such as during a birth, it opens the biological door for lots of things to attack. That's just how things work."

Sharona continued. "You said she was hospitalized. Why?" Sharona's composure was starting to erode as she became more nervous. "You bastards didn't beat her up, did you?"

"Of course not, lady. *Jesus Christ*. She is sick. And no, you can't see her."

"What's wrong with her?"

"A *Strep* infection. That's all I can tell you."

"You put her in the hospital for a simple *Strep* infection? You've got to be kidding!"

"Like I said, that's all I can tell you."

Haberdeen continued. "Listen, Miss Gomez. If you know or

SPECIAL DELIVERY

hear of anything unusual about this Milliken woman, you need to call me ASAP. We're moving fast on this investigation, and you're right in the middle of it."

"You're investigating me?"

"Not yet."

Asshole, thought Miss Sharona Gomez. She got up and left. Without permission.

◆ ◆ ◆

Apartment manager Joanie Perkins hadn't seen Lisbath for a few days. Still, with the nurse-midwife's unpredictable schedule, that wasn't unusual. But surely Ms. Milliken would have reported a broken door! That nurse was so fastidious. So this must have just happened.

A couple of third-floor residents had said they saw the Animal Control people take Lad away, so obviously the dog wasn't there anymore. The neighbors were too protective of Lisbath's privacy to ask the officers *why* they had been there, but the spinsters did spread the word throughout the building that Lad had in fact been removed. And that Lisbath's door had been broken.

Ms. Perkins took the elevator from her first-floor apartment to the third floor where Lisbath lived. As she exited the elevator, someone's radio blared the evening news:

"Scarlet fever still stalks the Bridgeport streets," the newscaster admonished. "Be careful where you let your children play! In this day and age of modern medicine, there's just no excuse for . . ."

Manager Perkins found the door ajar and thought that odd. It drew her attention away from the newscast. She held the door with her right hand so it wouldn't move and knocked with her left. She called out, "Lisbath! Lisbath! It's Joanie. Are you there?"

No answer.

As she was deciding what to do next, Joanie heard scratching in the stairwell just down the hall. She figured it was one of the apartment kids, so she went to the one-way safety door and opened it.

Quickly Lad bounded out, startling Ms. Perkins. He was filthy, with brown and reddish smears all over his fur. He stank as if he had begun to rot. Gummy paw prints marked his path.

After he was clear of the doorway, Lad pivoted around and held dead still for a moment. He took in the sight of a sixty-odd-year-old woman clasping her sweater to her breast, her eyes open, black saucers.

"Why, Laddie! What's happened to you? I—I thought you were at the pound!"

The dog's eyes narrowed. In a flash, Lad rushed toward the old woman, his white and supremely sharp canine teeth leading the charge. He growled quickly, then opened his mouth as wide as he could, thrusting himself toward the poor woman's right thigh and twisting his head just before the main bite to obtain maximum purchase. The fact that her skirt covered the leg was irrelevant to him; the dog knew there was a blood source behind the fabric.

Lad had broken out of the Animal Control holding area when a nice couple wanted to have a look at the dog's roommate, a perky black-and-white Yorkshire terrier. Lad had sped past the couple as soon as the chain-link door was pulled open and was long gone before anyone could catch him. Record-keeping and discipline at Animal Control were minimal, so the dog's escape went unnoticed.

Lad had feasted on passers-by on his way back to Yankee Pines. Mostly he chose children. Their blood was the freshest and uncontaminated with drugs or tobacco or alcohol. And the children were the easiest to approach as well. Most just loved petting cute dogs.

Also, Lad's sense of smell had made it easy to home in on Lisbath's apartment, a mere four miles from the dog pound. After he felt that he had fed sufficiently to go home, Lad found the apartment building in less than half an hour.

But now the vampiric dog-being continued his assault on the helpless apartment manager. He bit deeply into her thigh, and he began thrashing and yanking backward and sideways with his full body. As he threw himself about, the woman's old flesh parted easily. Lad worked his way in, contacting and then slicing open the large femoral artery.

This was the dog's Fountain of Youth. Perkins' blood washed over his head, and Lad lapped it up as if his life depended on it. He had an erection, the slimy, red, bone-stiffened penis wagging like a cylindrical flag, but it didn't get in his way.

The woman's screams tapered to soft groans, then to pathetic whimpers. Finally, Joanie Perkins fell silent as the bright red pool grew steadily around her.

Lad gorged himself on the fresh blood. Alternately he would lick the bright, cooling pool on the ground, then dip his tongue into the woman's hot slashed leg. He lamented the fact that he had no way to horde the stuff, but his hunting technique was now so refined that he could have fresh fodder almost any time he was hungry.

When the animal had had his fill, Lad/Vlad retired through the broken door into the apartment for a deep, wretched sleep.

Thirty-six

Instead of stopping at the Save-On drugstore to pick up some shampoo as she had planned, Sharona went straight home. The interview with that Detective Haberdeen had upset her far beyond what she had expected. Sharona continued to fear for her business as well as for her people. She feared heavily for her own peace of mind. Deeper still, her unspoken fear was for her ability to remain free.

Five minutes after she got home, Sharona dialed her good friend. Barbara could hear from the tightness in Sharona's voice that things hadn't been going well.

"God, I'm glad you were home, Barb. I just came from the police station."

"The police? What were you doing there?"

"That detective—his name's Haberdeen—is still messing with me. Barb, it's scary. Really."

"Hey, Tweedles. I'm really sorry to hear. Things really that bad, huh?"

"I just can't tell you. I feel so weak! And guess what? The bastard threatened me again."

"Oh, no."

"I just don't know what to do. It's like . . . I'm caught in this trap but I have nothing to do with it. How can I defend myself against something that's totally out of my control?"

"Gosh, Tweedles. It does sound bad. It must keep you up at night."

"Every night."

"Anything I can do?"

"Just continue to be there for me, Barb. I can't tell my parents—they'd go ballistic. You're it for me."

"Whatever you need, sweetie. What are friends for?"

There was a full thirty seconds of silence as both friends dealt with Sharona's predicament. Then Sharona could hear Barbara's doorbell ring.

"Tweedles, I think my neighbor's at the door. He said he'd come over and have a look at my TV set. It's been kind of on the blink."

"Okay, Barb. Listen: Can I call you if I need to?"

"Call me even if you don't."

♦ ♦ ♦

The following day, Haberdeen got back from his greasy lunch at the Ports O' Call and was a little surprised to see a red While You Were Out phone message from Erich Blücher. He remembered that the man's wife was one of Milliken's patients, and that she had been hospitalized. The G-Man decided to contact the man to get it over with; he figured correctly that the woman's husband would be relentless until he met with him.

On closer inspection, Haberdeen saw that Herr Blücher hadn't called, but instead was *waiting* in the PD's foyer. Or at least the husband had been there three hours earlier when the message had been placed on the spindle on Haberdeen's desk. The G-Man figured Blücher must have left by now, but called out front anyway.

"Front Desk."

"This is Haberdeen. Have you got a Mr. Blücher waiting for me?"

"Yeah. The guy's been here for hours. He just sits there, stiff. Doesn't even seem to be turning his head."

"All right. I'll be out in a few."

"Fine with me, Detective."

About five minutes later, Haberdeen entered the police department's foyer. Immediately he saw a blonde, six-foot-tall man dressed in a suit and sitting stiffly in a wooden chair. No doubt, this was Blücher.

"Mr. Blücher, I am Detective Haberdeen."

"Yes, sir. I must speak with you."

"Come back to my office."

Haberdeen led Herr Blücher through the turnstile, then through a small maze of hallways and doorways. Eventually, Haberdeen pointed to a chair in his office and Herr Blücher sat down gingerly.

"What can I do for you, sir?" asked Haberdeen.

"Detective, you have handled my wife's case, *ya*?"

"Well, not your wife's case. But, yes. I am handling the case of the woman who attended your wife's birth."

"*Ya*. Okay. Now: I do not like this Milliken woman. And it looks like maybe she made my wife sick. Correct?"

"Maybe. We're still checking into that."

"I am sure of it."

This piqued the G-Man's interest. "How do you know Milliken made your wife sick?"

"I simply know, that's all. She is a weak woman, that Milliken. She should not have done the birth. She is not doctor. It is clear to me. She hurt Ilse!"

"All right. Whatever you say." Haberdeen was not in a position to make accusations publicly yet. His package wasn't complete.

Taking advantage of the man's appearance at the station, Haberdeen spent some time asking Blücher some basic questions. The detective became satisfied that this man could add nothing to what the police already knew.

"Mr. Detective," asked Blücher, "where is this woman Milliken? In jail? Is she in this building?"

"She is in custody."

"What is 'custody'? My English is not yet perfect."

"It means that we have her under arrest."

"I want to see her. To talk to her."

Haberdeen's answer was fully automatic. "I'm afraid we can't do that, sir. She is our prisoner."

"Do not people visit prisoners?"

"Only their family members. And their lawyers."

"Who is her lawyer?"

"I don't think she has one yet."

"So how do I see her? In what room is she?"

"She's not in a room, mister. She happens to be very sick, so she's in the hospital."

"But I thought you said she was your prisoner! What means this? She is in hospital?"

"Yes. We have a jail ward."

"Where?"

"Well, it's in the Park City Hospital."

"The one near the water?"

"Yes. But it's a *jail* ward. It is secure. You cannot see her there."

"*Danke.* Good-bye, Detective."

Blücher walked out quickly, not waiting for a response. He followed exactly the path Haberdeen had taken when he brought the man in, and Blücher's officious demeanor gave nobody pause as he made his way through and out of the police department's offices.

💧 💧 💧

Fifty-five minutes later, Herr Blücher's VW pulled into the temporary parking lot at Park City Hospital. He was dressed impeccably in his pin-stripe suit and fedora, and he carried a leather briefcase. Blücher walked directly to the information desk.

"Hello. Where is the jail ward?"

"It's on six. But it has restricted access," said the old volunteer at the desk.

"Fine. *Danke.*"

Blücher headed for the elevators, punched six, and was relieved that the elevator actually started moving upward. Apparently the sixth floor did not require security key access.

As the elevator doors opened, Erich Blücher noticed an empty hallway to his left, but an unmarked set of heavy-looking, metal double doors to his right. These had to lead to the prisoner patients.

He walked over to the doors and looked through the small, reinforced window in one of them. He saw a uniformed police officer at a small desk. The officer had a phone, a pencil, and a magazine on the desk; nothing more.

First Blücher tried the doors. No surprise. They were locked. He knocked.

The knock got the immediate attention of the officer, who walked up to the doors without making any move to open them.

"Yes?" asked the cop through the doors.

"Hello, sir. I need to see Miss Milliken."

"Who are you?" asked Officer Spender. He was on tonight.

"I am her lawyer. Erich Schenck. I have received a call that she now wants to see me."

"I'll be right back," said Spender.

Blücher was perspiring. He figured he was going to be out of luck. He was wrong.

"Mr. Schenck, our nurse says that Milliken did make a phone call a couple of days ago. She must have called you. Come in and we'll try to wake her up."

"*Danke,*" said Blücher. He continued to appreciate small-town unsophistication. *This sloppiness would never happen in Austria.*

As soon as Blücher made it into the doorway, Spender frisked him. He found nothing remarkable.

Blücher said to the cop, "So she is sleeping? I want wake her myself, all right?"

"Sure thing," said the police officer. "She's right in there, and we've already unlocked the door. Don't be surprised at her restraints.

They protect her against herself." The cop pointed to the second door on the left, and Blücher walked quickly in that direction.

The idea that his prey might be restrained made things all the better. The horrible woman who had hurt his wife needed to feel his firm retribution in every possible way, and a sprinkling of extra fear would be icing on the cake.

Immediately after closing the door behind him, Blücher eyed Lisbath's sweating, fat neck. He looked around; there was nobody at the small, reinforced window near the top of the door. He slipped off his belt.

Milliken was restrained by thick, brown leather straps padded lightly with what looked like wool or fur. They had bright metallic roller buckles far from the woman's reach. At the foot of the bed he could see belts around the aluminum bed posts. At the head of the bed, the restraints were more obvious. Milliken's wrists were clamped to the painted, rounded vertical bed bars next to the wall. There was a half-foot-wide strap across her midsection. It was fixed under the bed.

He saw a blood-red bandage on one of her arms. She was breathing fitfully and immersed in sweat. Milliken coughed every few seconds despite being unconscious.

Blücher decided he would strangle her by standing between her head and the door. It would give him cover.

He slowly—almost ceremonially—looped his belt and began to bring it over her hair. A leather halo about to send her where there were no halos. He inched the belt down over her head. His teeth were grinding and he too was now perspiring heavily.

When the belt was nearing the bottom of its descent, Milliken's door banged open loud and hard. It was Officer Jake Spender, his gun drawn. He shouted, "Get back. Now! Let go of that strap!"

Erich's concentration was broken, and he looked backward toward the cop. At once his expression showed anger, surprise, and most prominently, deep sadness. He knew that he could not go through with this. Maybe if he hadn't been caught in the act, he could have killed the woman. Maybe not. It was now a moot point.

Blücher slowly released the belt so that it dropped around Lisbath's neck like a dog collar. He began to cry, his face beet-red and his body shaking like a leaf in a windstorm.

Officer Spender holstered his gun and removed the handcuffs from his Sam Browne. He threw Blücher to the floor and hooked him up.

Lisbath Milliken was off in some peaceful, warped sleep and had no awareness of what had befallen her.

🜄 🜄 🜄

Haberdeen's phone rang just as he had soiled his hands with the crystallized sugar from his Krispy-Kreme donut. He opened a thin, crinkly napkin and placed it on the phone receiver, then lifted the phone with his sticky hand.

"Haberdeen. Detectives."

"G-Man? This is Spender over at The Park."

"Yeah?"

"There's been an attempt on your suspect's life."

"On that nurse? Who the fuck tried to kill her?"

"We have identified the assailant as one Erich Blücher."

"Blücher? That son of a bitch! How did he get in to her room?"

"Well . . ." Spender was trying to think of an excuse. "Detective, he just sort of fooled us, that's all."

"*Shit*, Spender!"

"But listen: She's okay. She didn't get hurt. I don't even think she knew he was trying to kill her."

"Jesus," said Haberdeen.

"She's still sick as shit," said Spender. He was able to maintain some self-respect in this way.

"Is her doctor there?"

"I have no idea. Do you want me to ask the nurse?"

"No. I'll call his office tomorrow. This is enough for one day.

Protect that bitch with your life. We have a hell of a case here. I don't want her offed before she's convicted."

"Yes, sir," snapped Officer Spender.

💧 💧 💧

"Mr. Haberdeen, did you know that our Nurse Milliken was almost killed last night?" asked Dr. Howard on the phone.

"Yeah, I knew. They called me right after it happened."

"Listen," the doctor said. "I have some information for you. It's kind of strange. Where can I meet you?"

"Let's just talk on the phone. I don't have a lot of time."

"No. We have to meet in person for this. Once again: When and where can we meet?"

"All right. Shit. How about meeting at Borneo's? It's a bar on the waterfront—less than a mile from the station. Do you know it?"

"Well, no. But I'll find it."

"See you there at 7:00. That's in about two hours. Okay?"

"Seven."

💧 💧 💧

Haberdeen was on his second Budweiser when he saw the formal Dr. Howard enter the otherwise seedy backstreet bar. Howard had on a white shirt and tie and stuck out like a sore thumb.

"Doctor, over here," said Haberdeen.

"Glad to see you," said Dr. Howard.

"Hey, Lee! Give this man a beer," ordered Haberdeen. The barkeep nodded his head and reached for a glass.

"So what've you got, Doc?" asked Haberdeen.

"Are you sitting down?" asked Dr. Howard, sitting directly across from Detective Haberdeen. He needed to break the ice for what he had to say.

"Only my ass is sitting, Doc." At least there was some levity.

"Have you heard of vampires?" asked the doctor. "I mean it."

"Oh, God," said Haberdeen. "You know, Doc, this kind of stuff keeps cropping up, but it will never, ever hold up in court."

"I don't give a damn about court."

"*I* have to give a damn about court."

"*Listen to me*," said Dr. Howard. Then he explained everything he had been learning. About the Romanian doctor, about the p21 gene, about the red cataracts, about the need for human blood digestive products, about everything.

Haberdeen had a lot of trouble following the details (especially after his third beer), but what he did glean was this: The doctor actually believed that there was something behind this vampire stuff. More importantly, though, the medical man believed that Lisbath Milliken was one of them. A vampire. A scientifically verified, monstrous, weird, unbelievable, honest-to-shit vampire.

"We *cannot* do this in court," said Haberdeen. Even though he was leaning toward believing the whole fantastic mess, he knew the court system and he knew the judges and he knew just how well the lawyers would chop the crap out of any such argument.

"It doesn't *matter*," said Dr. Howard. "She's real, and we have to deal with it."

"No, we don't," said Haberdeen stubbornly. "We have her on murder one, and *it really doesn't matter whether or not she believes she's some fucking vampire.* You got that? *We don't need to give a shit* about whether the bitch chugs blood or bites people! If we can get her convicted of murder, then let the bitch bite every fucking one of the other inmates. It'd be a goddamn public service. *Got it?*"

Haberdeen's voice was getting louder as his blood alcohol content was rising. People in the bar turned to see who was shouting about vampires.

Dr. Howard shrank back a little, and Haberdeen regained some composure. The G-Man stared down some of the patrons—leered at them, actually—and they returned with no apparent sheepishness to their beers and conversations.

"Okay," said Haberdeen. "What if she is a vampire? So what? What do we do? Drive a fucking stake through her heart? Ask the ghost of Vincent Price if he'll take her in? *What?*"

"Are you sober enough to understand anything?" asked Dr. Howard. His intonation let Haberdeen know that he truly meant the question. It was not a joke, it was not demeaning. It was an honest question.

"Sober enough," Haberdeen managed.

"Okay. Listen. This woman has to drink blood once in a while to keep from dying. From aging prematurely. Human blood. Got it?"

"Bullshit."

"No bullshit. She drinks or she dies."

"Fuck her. Let her die then."

"I can't take that approach," said the physician. "I'm a doctor and I'm committed to extending life."

"By feeding a vampire human blood? *Give me a break!*"

"Well, maybe it can come from donors. Or a blood bank. I haven't worked it all out yet. The fact is, I'm not sure I'll be able or willing to give her any."

"Doc, this bitch is about to be convicted for first degree murder. She doesn't need any fucking blood. It would be wasted."

"We'll see," said Dr. Howard. "That's all I've got for you." He then rose from his seat, threw a $20 bill onto the table, put on his coat, and left.

Haberdeen just sat there, trying to digest everything he had just heard. After a minute, the G-Man figured his digestion would be better in the morning, so he paid the bill with Dr. Howard's $20, didn't wait for the change, and went home and to bed.

Thirty-seven

The next morning, when Haberdeen got to the station, he found a thick envelope and a well-wrapped box on his desk.

The police lab had limited facilities, and its biological analysis capabilities were virtually nonexistent. The lab director had forwarded the jars to the Connecticut State Medical Examiner for analysis. The report, which occupied the envelope, was straightforward. The jars were in the box.

The medical examiner's office had analyzed the contents of thirteen jars that had been confiscated from Lisbath's locked closet. All but one of them contained a foul soup of formalin solution (10% formaldehyde) and considerable dissolved blood solids. Actually, they held more of a stew than a soup because virtually all the jars also included a piece of someone. Human. The examiner had also analyzed what appeared to be a tissue-and-liquid sample that had been collected from Lisbath's Kitchen-Aid blender.

In ten of the jars were segments of umbilical cord that had matured over the years into brown, shriveled logs. They looked like motley, overcooked, wet sausages, and every one was a slightly different length. Two other jars contained chunks of placenta, the shared organ in which the fetus develops. The edges of each organ were so irregular that it appeared the pieces were probably yanked off the mother organ by hand. Or by tooth.

The last jar held an unusually dark and fragrant liquid. Ultimately it was determined to be a suspension of nothing but serum and red blood cells, many in clots, in formaldehyde. The remarkable thing about this jar was that it contained a multiplicity of human bloods. Painstaking analysis by the medical examiner found that it contained the bloods of a minimum of twenty-two different people. Coincidentally, the Medical Examiner noted that the lid of this special jar seemed to show the greatest wear, as if it had been opened and closed a great many times.

Eight of the thirteen jars had labels on them—masking tape written on by a permanent marker. The labels appeared to be codes, such as one labeled *S067980702*. Nobody in the examiner's office had any idea what the codes meant.

The blender sample included banana, egg yolk, egg white, and a bit of fetal tissue.

Haberdeen felt no need to look at the jars himself. He sent them to the evidence room.

The G-Man had asked Moraga to get supplementary statements and information, and a small pile of reports was brought to him as he was putting rubber bands around the lab report envelope.

Later in the morning, Haberdeen was putting the finishing touches on the package he wanted to deliver to Detective Sergeant Stevenson. One was a transcript of an interview with victim Wallace's next-door neighbor. The man was shown a photo of Milliken. Positive identification was easy. The woman sitting in the car with the murdered nurse was Milliken. And the guy would be happy to testify to that effect in court.

Originally, Peters of the health department had given Haberdeen the OK to arrest Milliken over the phone. This morning, at Haberdeen's request, he faxed in his original authorization to arrest under suspicion of endangering the public health. This guaranteed that the initial arrest hit on Milliken could be justified. So any potential false arrest charges could be beaten with ease.

It didn't bother Haberdeen that he had as yet nothing solid to bring to court from any of the women Milliken had made sick.

While originally the nurse-midwife's spreading puerperal fever was the main problem and complaint, Lisbath's murder of two people would be enough to send her up for life. The vampire stuff—and the childbed fever, for that matter—had been rendered of secondary importance as a criminal charge. All those women could file civil suits against Milliken once she was behind bars if they wanted to.

And if the bitch Milliken was some kind of vampire, all the better. Then she could suck the blood out of all those prisoners in the women's incarceration facilities with his blessing.

The G-Man loved it when things came together like this.

He continued polishing his work. It went something like this:

Lisbath Milliken was I.D.'d in the car with the murdered nurse in Shelton. Physical evidence such as hair samples clinched the identification. Later investigation by detectives assisting Haberdeen revealed that the suspect had argued with her job supervisor that one of the victims should have been her patient. Milliken was reported to be extremely, even angrily envious that the other victim got the call. So there was both motive and opportunity.

Items confiscated from her special closet included illegally-obtained canisters containing drugs consistent with the injections given to the Forman woman who died in the car.

A nice little package.

Haberdeen took a deep and easily-inspired breath, straightened up the papers and marched into Judd Stevenson's office with a slight smile on his face.

🩸 🩸 🩸

It was mid-morning, and Lisbath was more or less sitting up in her bed. She looked down through wet and unfocused eyes at her wrist restraints and saw red, wrinkled, chapping skin below the furry padding.

Her face looked as if she had been crying for a week, but in fact it was only last night that she had regained sufficient consciousness to understand her predicament. Her sheets were twisted around her; one of her legs was caught so badly it felt like a tourniquet. Lisbath's hair placed her into the Medusa category, and her bed stank of sweat and bodily wastes.

"Nurse?" she called weakly. The steel door to her room didn't let much noise through, and this faint plea wouldn't do the trick. Every few minutes she would gather enough strength to call out again, but her pathetic puffs of air were fruitless.

At 11:45, she finally heard her door unlock. It had been five or ten minutes since her last feeble call.

"So, Lizzie? You're awake, eh?" asked Sweetie the orderly.

"Who are you? Am I in the hospital?"

"You bet, dearie."

Lisbath raised her arms a couple of inches. "Take these things off," she pleaded.

"No can do, dearie," said Sweetie in an almost sing-song voice. He sure was in a good mood.

"Am I sick?" asked Lisbath

More than you'll ever know, bitch. But Sweetie's answer was more demure. "Tell you what, Milliken. I'll ask your nurse to come in. She can tell you *all* about it." He sashayed over to the sink, got a basin, and emptied the urine bag hanging down on the side of the bed into the metal bowl. Then Sweetie re-attached the bag to Lisbath's catheter tube, poured the stinking liquid out into the toilet and flushed, and briefly rinsed out the basin. He twisted around to face her, hands on his hips.

"Ta-ta, you nut!" He swished out the door and was gone. The door locked automatically behind him.

A drop of drool slid from the corner of Lisbath's parted mouth as she waited for the nurse.

"Honey, we need a *fan* in here!" said ward nurse Eulah Washington as she entered Lisbath's cell-room. Washington was a buxom black woman with a rear end twice the size of her head. She went straight for the window and, thrusting her hands between the bars, lifted the sash full up. No matter that it was barely forty degrees outside. She had her priorities.

"So you back with us?" she asked Milliken.

Lisbath nodded her head slowly and raised her wrists weakly, her request obvious from her tired eyes and quivering lips.

"Mmm-mmm-mmmm, vampire lady," said Washington. "You are not gonna eat yourself again. Orders is, they stay."

Lisbath was more taken aback by the word "vampire" than by the nurse's refusal to remove her restraints.

"What is this? Where am I? Why are these things on my arms?"

"Whoa. Slow down. I'll tell you," said Washington. "First, you're in the Park City Hospital prison ward. Second, you are under arrest for Murder One. Third, they are restraints because you tried to eat yourself."

"Eat myself?" asked a weak and basically uncomprehending Milliken. Tears fell.

"You were chomping into your own arms, honey," Washington continued. "Now you just take it easy, you hear? I'll clean you up and they'll bring you some food."

Eulah began her nursing duties as a key turned in the metal door. It was Officer Spender. Milliken was initially surprised to see a fully-uniformed police officer, but as her brain got more into gear, she began to understand.

"Ms. Milliken, I am Officer Spender. I am responsible for this ward. I need to ask you if you have a lawyer." Spender thought about that Blücher guy he had arrested for impersonating Lisbath's attorney. He decided not to tell Lisbath about the attack, though. Spender had a modicum of pity for the blisteringly ill woman.

"Lawyer?" asked a confused Lisbath. "Why?"

Spender needed to make his speech. "Lisbath Milliken, the district attorney has just filed first degree murder charges against you. You will need a lawyer. If you cannot afford one, one will be appointed by the court."

Ms. Washington interrupted, fast and loud. "Man, can't you let this woman eat first? Before giving her all that shit?"

"Sorry, Eulah. I have orders to determine her representation status, and it can't wait. Ms. Milliken? *Do you* have a lawyer?" he asked again.

"Well, no. Of course not."

"I'll let the judge know. A lawyer will be meeting with you pretty soon. I think they want to get this thing over with fast, so you might see someone today or tomorrow."

Milliken was just silent, beginning to deal with all the powerful assaults on her freedom, her body, her dignity, and perhaps on her own life.

Eulah brought over a steaming towel and began to lift Lisbath's sheets.

🌢 🌢 🌢

"Look at this shit!" said Stevenson as he threw the special edition of the local *Bridgeport Informant* onto Haberdeen's desk. "One day after we get the DA's OK for the Milliken case, that bitch Big T reporter is still stirring up the masses."

"Oh, Christ," said Haberdeen. "I'm not so sure I want you as my paper boy anymore, Sarge." He looked at the article's title. "That bitch reporter is already on this, huh? Crap. This is going to make things a lot harder."

"Read the article, G-Man. Your phone's about to start ringing. I told the switchboard that any calls that came in on this case go to *you*. Have fun."

"Terrific." Haberdeen settled in and lifted the paper to reading level. What he saw was little more than what that Big T reporter had already put out on the radio.

VAMPIRE NURSE, RED DEATH'S ANGEL, KILLS TWO IN BRIDGEPORT
May Provide Link to Scarlet Fever

By Constance Teitelmeier

Police have filed First Degree Murder charges against Lisbath Milliken, a nurse-midwife working in the Bridgeport area. As I reported recently, Red Death's Angel Milliken allegedly killed two people in Shelton.

Victim Doris Wallace had been giving birth at home when Milliken allegedly drugged her and drained her of blood. Most suspicious is that none of the drained blood has been found.

Victim Francine Forman, another nurse-midwife on the scene, was allegedly drugged as well to the point of death. She was found in her car parked in front of the victim's residence at 118 Front St. in Shelton.

Kevin Wallace, the husband, was found knocked unconscious in the home and remains in a coma. The newborn child was not injured and is staying with family members.

Unnamed medical sources link Milliken with the recent scarlet fever outbreak in Bridgeport. Authorities speculate that a woman who recently gave birth with Milliken's help may be the major carrier of the disease. The nurse-midwife's imprisonment may mean a major decrease in the number of cases reported locally.

Details are scarce at this point. Bridgeport Police Detective George Haberdeen is handling the case and has been unavailable for comment. Milliken's employer, Sharona Gomez, owner of the

Dickinson's Nurse Registry Service in Bridgeport, also refused comment.

Nurse-midwives handle simple home births. They are licensed by the State of Connecticut. They must employ the services of a physician if they suspect significant medical problems with the birth.

More in our next issue.

"Refused comment?" Haberdeen said to himself. "The bitch didn't even ask me." Then he remembered the phone message from Big T a few days ago. *Shit*, he thought. *Should've called her back.*

Thirty-eight

Prisoner Milliken's sleep was violent and tortuous. Bound in a prison bed, deeply ill, aging rapidly, bandaged, increasingly confused and under continuous, relentless stress, nothing about her mind or body was functioning normally.

Blood had leaked all over her covers, and its aroma was thick in the white, barred room. Lisbath's dreams were erratic montages of events that had no rhyme or reason. She dreamt of the ancient countryside; of spread legs framing a distended abdomen; of wooden crucifixes shoved into the rich earth moistened by dripping blood; of syringes; of medieval processions; of sanitary napkins; of bruised, sliced breasts.

Even in her unconsciousness, Lisbath needed an escape. Ironically, her retreat brought her full circle: She moved back to the time of the countess, but the noble's feeding frenzy was many days ago. Now, as the horror-woman slept high in her castle's sequestered chambers, Lisbath's dream vision saw the castle grounds from above, like a vulture awaiting its fodder.

For years, the women of the surrounding villages had been abducted by the countess, yet heretofore no person or group had felt empowered to take any action against her. The villagers were simple folk and felt powerless in the shadow of their noble.

Yet Jon Thust, a forester by trade, had been dreaming of a better world, where all the villagers were treated with at least some respect. And when he learned that his niece had been slaughtered in last month's torture-raids, he gained the strength he needed to assemble and lead a retaliatory attack on the countess and her minions.

What sounded from the interior like a mild and irregular thudding on the twenty-foot-tall, dense castle door barely caused a stir in the countess' slumber. Her bedchamber was on the third level of the citadel, far from the fortified entranceway. Soft feather pillows enveloped most every corpulent inch of the noblewoman as she wallowed in a sweaty dream world of red droplets and satiation.

The assault on the door was quite violent. The sound outside the building was a din of wood and metal mixing with an emotional human roar. There were more than twenty men, each brimming with anger and disgust. The peasants each had his own grudge against the countess, and the tall and powerful Jon Thust had finally mustered these pained folk to retaliatory action.

A steaming cauldron of tar and oil had been prepared perhaps ten yards from the door. One boy—the only young person in the group—remained back at the cauldron to stoke the wood fire. The entire area was pungent with the black, seething mass. The ancient posse seemed deeply energized by the swirling black fumes.

Armed with farm implements, sticks, knives, rocks, and whatever else they could pick up along the way, the gaggle of villagers was intent on destroying the vile woman who had taken and mangled their women for so many years.

One of the countess' servants, Gegoeh Pinzil, always had his bedding set up on the first floor near the rear of the castle. He was awakened at first by the dark stink of the tar. As he raised his head, Pinzil's ears picked up the pounding, softly belying the frenzy which mothered it. The man's confusion cleared quickly as he discerned some of the yelling outside the door.

Quickly, yet still clumsy from sleep, the servant shuttled from bed to bed, shaking and waking his cohorts as fast as he could. Clearly, if the countess—or the castle itself, for that matter—were under attack, then the Loyalites were in danger as well.

"Fast, men! Get up!" shouted Pinzil. "Outside are soldiers who would kill us all!"

As each man came to realize his plight, he went immediately to the arsenal for a weapon. There was such random, fearful excitement that no one thought to inform the countess of what was happening. But the shouts coming now from inside the citadel's walls broke her red reverie with a startling suddenness.

"What is happening?" she yelled into her chamber's darkness. As she edged rapidly closer to total, waking consciousness, the lady began to appreciate the foreboding tar and rotting oil aroma wafting in from beneath her door. This dank smell had a long and fearsome history for her and her ancestors. It always represented some kind of violent challenge limited in its viciousness only by the enemy's stealth and imagination. Her empire, limited as it was to just under 500 square miles, was in jeopardy.

Two floors below, a crude battering ram began pummeling the front door. With each increasingly larger smash, the Loyalites inside became more frightened. They could see the hinges begin to loosen and could actually sense the door's vibrations.

Thust's men on the outside were emboldened by the progress their ram was making. Shards of wood splattered off with every hammering shove. Jon Thust himself was infused within an adrenaline reverie. He visualized the propelling wooden tool as a collective penile extension, deflowering the bitch's abode and threatening her and her minions with violent, unforgiving death. Nothing would stop them now. And, he vowed, nor would the horrid lady stop any more fine hearts of the countryside's women.

All of a sudden the countess burst into the frenzied foyer. She began to yell commands to her simpleton Loyalites. "Add another bar across the door! Pinzil, you take five men to the roof and spear those animals from above! The rest of you—you chant now—loud and all together! The animals outside must hear this. You must strike fear into them. Hold your weapons at the ready and chant!"

"Chant?" one short-statured slave asked.

"Yes, you fool! Chant like this, over and over:

"DEATH UPON YOU ALL
BLACK AND FOUL
ENTER HERE AND
BLEED!"

The Loyalites took up the chant louder and louder, and it gave them a semblance of cohesion. Each faced the door as he yelled for all his life was worth.

The castle's foyer began to warm from the body heat generated by many hundreds of tensing muscles. The torches on the interiors of both facing walls were more than adequate for the dilated pupils of the fearful and increasingly violent Loyalites.

As the battering ram intensified its assault, an uneven hole began to appear from inside the door. The countess had gone to get her most powerful sword, and each of Pinzil's first-floor men was raising and lowering his weapon in time with their sinister death chant.

A swishing rain of spears and fresh urine from atop the castle caught Jon and his cohorts by surprise. Unschooled in battle methods, their ignorant focus was limited to what was directly in front of them. One spear smashed through the skull of Jon's brother, killing him instantly. The spear had been thrown so powerfully and with such fear-induced vehemence that it impaled the man's head fully two feet above the dirt.

Another spear, this one thick and heavy, shot through an older man's abdomen at an angle. He began screaming so uncontrollably that it sounded like two mixing voices emanating from the nether bowels of hell.

The startling attack disheartened the men for only a moment. Jon wrested control back quickly, knowing full well that if the assailment's momentum were reduced, the cause would be lost.

The countess was now in full fury and had re-entered the foyer, her sword drawn. Immediately she ran forward and thrust the experienced blade through the accreting hole. The lady knew it would have no human purchase just now; it was, rather, a herald of defiance and power. She moved it like a silvery taunting tongue and then withdrew the instrument quickly before the ram could attack it.

As she stepped back from this warped, metallic intercourse, a stream of boiling tar-oil mixture spewed inward through the hole. It was followed immediately by the muffled sound of a wooden bucket smashing against the door from the outside. Some of the black sludge flew hotly across the countess' right thigh, burning into the flesh, fat, and sinew deeply and causing the woman to grit her teeth. But she did not scream.

"Water!" shouted Pinzil as he descended the staircase from his rooftop station. "Put water on our lady!"

Pinzil realized quickly that the chanting Loyalites were too involved with their fear song to process his command. He ran to the washbasin in the eating chamber and carried the vessel to his lady. She had her eyes shut tightly, tolerating the pain and cursing the hated villager attackers. Gegoeh splashed the water over her thigh, at once cooling some of her pain and driving some of her raiment into the blackened gash. The liquid startled her, but she appreciated Gegoeh's attempt and felt reconstituted sufficiently to rejoin the battle.

A group of village dwellers who had earlier shunned Jon Thust's call to arms—a second wave, as it were—ascended the hill over which the countess' attacked citadel perched. Jon's small, enraged army at the front door knew nothing of this approach of the cavalry until one of the countess' roof-borne soldiers fell into the thick of them. He had an arrow through his groin, upward into his lower back, yet he was still alive. His body was a clump of broken bones and blood, a gelatinous splat on the ground with nothing more than the ability to moan and suffer.

It took a few moments for the men to deduce that the fallen bastard had been shot with an arrow from friendly forces stationed behind them. As an exhausted, surprised and somewhat uncomprehending group, most of the men turned around to see their brethren approach with resolve and fresh strength. And more weapons.

The attack became more fierce and certain now, with perhaps twice the number of troops and an increased collective motivation to end the horrid lady's reign of terror for good. Along with the battering ram, some of the fresh fighters began to throw their full weight against the entranceway. It was evident that the edifice door would not hold forever as it shuddered more with each new assault.

Eight of the men were competent, armed archers and engaged the roof-based soldiers with a virtually ceaseless barrage of arrows. This new threat to the castle keepers kept them completely involved with defending themselves, so they abandoned their attack on the main battering ram men. Freed to put all their weight and vengeance into the assault, the ground troops finally broke through the door. With a full battle-roar that needed no practice, the men stormed inside, knives and sticks and fists raging.

Thust had laid out an engagement plan during the trek up toward the castle with the first group of men. Upon gaining entrance to the structure, the men were to stream in with weapons blazing. In one swift, powerful movement they would bifurcate the warring denizens by pushing, smashing, and forcing them toward the left and right walls of the foyer. This would create a chasm into which the boiling threat of tar and oil would be discharged from the main vessel hidden outside. Immediately thereafter, each fighting man was to grab, trick, trip, or otherwise force his battle-foe quickly and without warning into the searing tar streak on the floor. This would kill few of them, but it would burn exceedingly painfully and continuously. More important, it would disorient the enemy. The "opening" in the defense thus created would make it relatively easy to overpower and destroy the simmering remnants of these horrible foes.

The flaw in Jon's plan was the unforeseen arrival of his own, unplanned second support team. The newer battlers had not been privy to the grand plan, and this could be their demise. As they blundered into the castle behind their brothers, many of the second wave stood virtually motionless in the center of the antechamber's floor. They were staring at the first wave, wondering what the tactical choreography they observed meant.

The lack of communication between the two groups of crude troops took its toll. The tar-tenders had been outside, hidden along one side of the castle, lest they be seen by a possible onslaught of the countess' men crashing out of the castle door. Having timed their delay carefully to follow the initial invaders' castle invasion, they sped around the castle side to the entrance and launched gallons of the black fiery liquid through the door as fast as they could. The near-lethal tar oil splashed onto fully half of the second group of villagers. Searing into the backs of these innocent souls, the liquid black weapon burnt into their limbs most severely and started fires on their exposed clothing.

The men began to shriek in pain and fall to the ground. But when a man would fall, he would splash into even more of the burning semi-congealed black liquid and it would do further damage to his body. Many were blinded or lost their scalps. This compounding of confused havoc and pain and burn rendered almost every one of the second group of villagers pitifully useless.

The first group of Jon's crude warriors had no knowledge of these war faux-pas. In the heat of battle, Jon's first wave continued to follow their battle plan precisely and with blind, almost military conviction. As they pivoted and threw their soldier-foes into the hellish mix of tar and oil and burning bodies, they were stunned to immediate tears to see that they were creating a boiling, tar-coated, suffering jumble of their brothers as well as of their enemies.

On seeing this tragedy, Jon Thust ordered his troops to pull out their brothers. Then he dropped to his knees and shook his head in self-recrimination. Yes, he had started an offensive that was critical to saving the village, but at what cost? And what else might go awry?

These questions brewing in Thust's mind swirled in Lisbath's as it cleared partially. She moved forward, to a more familiar place.

Milliken now dreamt of that dog attacking her in Avondale Lake those many years ago. She saw its approach and was deeply frightened. She felt frozen, as if she were trapped by some kind of spirit that just held her open for any kind of attack. She backed up against a cold, plate-glass window, feeling it shudder as her pudgy back made contact. She saw the animal's teeth revealed as the black canine lips separated. The hound's eyes almost glowed red in the distant afternoon sun.

Smack! Lisbath was startled awake by a crisp rap on her metal door. Something was different: nobody had knocked since she had been moved to this place, as far as she knew. The lock turned, and Officer Spender stuck his head in.

"Ms. Milliken, your lawyer is here." Then Lisbath heard the officer say to the lawyer, "Just knock on the door when you're through; I'll be sitting just across the hall."

The door opened more widely, and a handsome, blonde woman about thirty-five years old entered the room. She was dressed in a smart gray business suit and carried a heavy-looking briefcase.

"Hello, Ms. Milliken. I am Anna Windham. I am a public defender and have been assigned to your case."

The hygiene in the prison ward remained below the standard for the rest of the hospital. Anna was almost thrown back by the odors of the room.

"Do you mind if I open the window? It's not real cold today," said Anna.

Lisbath gestured okay weakly, and the attorney slid the window open halfway.

She took a chair from across the room and drew it up next to the open window. Mrs. Windham sat down, opened her briefcase, and removed a note pad. Bars of light fell across the yellow paper. She crossed her legs and poised herself.

Lisbath had been taking all of this in. She was conscious enough to understand what was happening. And she was grateful that her attorney was female. *Woman-to-woman*, she felt, there would be better communication. Lisbath even began to feel a little embarrassed about her disheveled appearance.

"Hello," said Lisbath.

"Ms. Milliken, do you feel up to talking now? I need a lot from you, and if you're not up to it, we can schedule another visit."

It took Lisbath a few seconds to get both her thoughts and her strength together. Then she said, "I am confused about what is happening. How I got here."

"You were in jail before. Do you remember that?"

"Well, yes. But then I got very ill. Next thing I remember is waking up in here with these leathers on." She lifted her wrists, showing them to Mrs. Windham like a child displaying a bruised knee.

"Can you make them take these off?" asked Lisbath. "They put cream on under the pads, but it still hurts terribly. They're on my legs, too."

"I don't know. I'll ask about it." Then Windham got right to it. "I understand from your file that you engaged in some self-destructive behaviors."

"I don't remember," Lisbath said. She truly had no firm recollection of what had happened, but still there was a dream-like image of chewing on her own arm that was swimming around in her brain. She was ignoring that image as much as she could.

Windham made a note about Lisbath's not remembering the episode. This could perhaps be used to advantage if they needed to use a mental-incompetence defense.

"Okay, Lisbath. Now, are you up to talking about all of this now or not?"

"Yes. Let's get it over with." She let her head fall back against the bed's bar-like headboard.

"Fine. Listen: I don't have time to beat around the bush. I need to know some things right off. What did you do to Francine Forman?"

"Who?"

"Francine Forman. A nurse-midwife with Dickinson's who was at Mrs. Wallace's in Shelton."

"I—I'm not sure."

"Well, let's do it this way, Lisbath. Did you inject anything into the neck of a woman in a car in Shelton? About a week ago?" Attorney Windham knew that talking about individual actions rather than the result of those actions sometimes made it easier for people to respond. And to understand a question.

"Well. . ." Lisbath let out a long breath. "Maybe. I have a hazy image of being in a car with a woman. Somebody I didn't like."

Great, thought Anna Windham. *This is going to be a tough one. Either she's uncooperative, or we have some mental problems that will double my workload here.*

"How about Doris Wallace? Did you take a lot of blood from her?"

"The mother."

"Right. The mother giving birth."

"Oh. I can't tell you! *Oh, no!* What do you know? *How* do you know?" Milliken was beginning to deteriorate. Yet she was able to see that all of her deeds were public now; that someone had let the bloody cat out of the bag. That she was in big, big trouble.

Lisbath began to bawl, shaking her entire body. She was writhing under her restraints and clearly departing whatever fleeting semblance of reality she had occupied thirty seconds ago.

It became obvious to Anna that going on with Milliken would be fruitless. Windham needed to wrap things up, being as helpful as her profession and time limitations would permit.

Feeling like she was going to be talking to a wall, Anna felt obliged to explain what was going to happen next. She turned toward Lisbath's contorted face and began to speak softly and in a very metered tone. Almost as if she were talking to a young child.

"Ms. Milliken, I am afraid that I will not be able to communicate with you—to talk with you—enough to learn the facts I need to defend you. You are not giving me the information I need. Even if you want to, it is not happening."

She continued as Lisbath seemed to be reduced to seizure-like movements. "Lisbath, I will need to call in a psychologist or a psychiatrist to talk with you. He or she will be a nice person, and it will be important for you to give that person all your attention and help. *Do you understand?*"

Lisbath was being thoroughly overwhelmed. She was desperately ill. She was getting older before her own eyes. She was in pain. She knew she was being held—incarcerated. She knew her life was on the line. She knew she had done some appalling things, even if she couldn't remember exactly what they were.

All these thoughts swam around in her head like cerebral tidal waves washing any semblance of sense away in small, irregular fragments. She had never been so decompensated; it was a mental and physical anguish that penetrated deep into her soul.

Then something inside of her began to change—to mutate: a switch being thrown in slow motion. It was something completely foreign to Lisbath's experience, and it wasn't anything she was doing deliberately. It was something happening to her, almost victimizing the poor soul. Something with its origins in a personal history buried in those secret outlying regions far below the bewildered woman's ability to comprehend.

All of a sudden Lisbath Milliken's body became calm. Her brow unwrinkled. Her muscle tone went from the tight, schizophrenic spasm of a seizure to the supreme serenity of the priest in the confessional.

Mrs. Windham saw this change come over the woman and stopped speaking immediately. Her back arched slightly and involuntarily as her mind oriented to this apparently non sequitur metamorphosis. Windham was fully captivated.

In a voice that had never made its way out of Lisbath Milliken in her entire life, she uttered, "What is this place?"

The strange sentence had come out so slowly it seemed to end long after Milliken's mouth stopped moving. The language was heavily accented and rather guttural, yet it was clearly English.

The question and its phraseology and execution reminded Anna of a séance she had attended in college even before she went to law school. A bunch of kids were playing at contacting long-lost relatives. They had the questionable help of a pseudo-Gypsy Armenian woman with more scarves and perfume than a French whore.

Lisbath's statement frightened the attorney, and she held extra still.

"*Again, woman: What is this place?*" demanded the delayed voice emanating from Milliken's restrained body.

Windham realized that the voice was in fact speaking to her, and that she'd better answer. She answered weakly, "This is the prison ward at Park City Hospital. But you know that already!"

"*Why am I here?*" inquired whatever was in Milliken. Lisbath's head spasmed slightly as she spoke, causing her disheveled, filthy hair to wiggle jerkishly with each word.

Anna Windham had heard enough. She began to push off from her chair, ready to sprint for the door. Never mind that she was a mature woman who had graduated at the top of her law school class—that she was a logician extraordinaire—that she was a mother of two who didn't even like sci-fi movies. She was scared shitless and wanted to get the hell out of there.

"*Halt, woman,*" ordered the Milliken voice. It continued its eerie delay, like a poorly dubbed foreign film.

Windham froze, half-up and half-seated.

"*Sit.*"

She sat.

Milliken—or whatever had possessed her—stared for fully ten seconds at the frightened attorney. The nurse's body twisted and rotated its head slightly, taking in the entirety of the suited, shaking professional before her. It then spoke again.

"*I am the Countess Elizabeth Bathory,*" said the bizarre voice. It splayed out loudly and seemed to echo in the small chamber. "*I do not belong here. You will release me.*"

Windham's hands began to shake uncontrollably, and she began to perspire heavily. Blotches of wetness seeped through her fine suit below the arms and in the center of her back. She wanted to run to the metal door and hammer on it with all her might, but she could not get up. Nor could she speak beyond a whisper, if that.

Lisbath's head was glaring at Anna, and the lawyer felt like the woman's gaze was eating through to the back of her skull. Windham's field of view narrowed so that all she could see were Lisbath's eyes, which appeared as glowing, blood-red, menacingly vibrating bull's-eyes.

"You will release me, woman, or my minions will defeat thee."

Anna's skirt began to absorb the urine she had just released when the hospital cell door burst open. Officer Spender had been knocking on the door, peering through the window, trying to determine if Mrs. Windham was all right, but there was no response. He made the decision to break in—despite attorney-client privacy laws—more from some supernatural sense of urgency than from police training. Regardless of the reason, he had done the right thing.

"Mrs. *Windham!* What's going on? Are you all right?" he asked.

The lawyer just sat spellbound, staring at Lisbath's body, sweating as if in a steam room and shaking like an epileptic in petit mal seizure.

Spender helped her up and virtually dragged her to the door. Windham did not resist, but as Spender moved her, the attorney's gaze remained fixed on Milliken. Her head was turned almost completely around by the time the pair got to the doorway.

As the door closed behind them, "Puzzle of Broken Hearts," Milliken's favorite song, projected from someone's car radio through the bars on the open window:

> I got all the pieces
> An' I know where they go
> But they just don't fit together
>   Any mo', any mo'
> They just can't fit together
>   Any mo'.

Lisbath's entire body remained motionless; maybe she could hear the music, maybe not. Moments later her body fell limp as a fresh corpse as it returned to deep, pervasive unconsciousness.

Thirty-nine

Officer Spender had brought Anna Windham into an empty hospital room on the ward and had lain her down on the bed. She continued perspiring and did not speak for several minutes. She stared straight up.

The policeman went to the door and called toward Nurse Washington, who had just entered the ward. She put down the chart she was holding and went right to the room.

"What happened to her?" asked Washington as she reached for a towel and began sopping Mrs. Windham's brow.

"I don't know," said Officer Spender. "She was in there with Milliken for a few minutes. When I knocked to make sure everything was all right, she didn't respond. Didn't even turn around. So I went in and found her like this." He motioned toward Windham's apparently catatonic body.

"She's Milliken's lawyer," added Spender.

Nurse Washington adjusted her stethoscope and began to take Mrs. Windham's vital signs. "Her heart's speeding: 150 per minute. I'm going to take her BP."

While Washington went for the sphygmomanometer (they weren't kept in the prison rooms for fear of hanging or their being used as weapons), Spender placed his hand over Windham's wrist. The woman looked pathetic.

Windham began to emerge from her cataleptic state. She turned her head slowly toward him and seemed to recognize the officer. She gave a slight smile, but her furrowed brow captured more fully what she was feeling. She had been through something terrible in that room, and she was far from over its emotional impact.

"She sounded so strange in there," Mrs. Windham said softly. "And she said she was someone else."

"Hallucinations?" asked Washington, who had just come in to take the lawyer's blood pressure.

"I don't know. She said she was Countess Elizabeth Bathory."

"Who the hell is that?" asked Spender.

"I don't have any idea."

"What else did she say?" asked an intrigued Eulah Washington. The nurse was taking medical notes, since anything unusual a patient says in a prison ward has to be written down.

It took Mrs. Windham a few moments to compose herself and her memory enough to piece together what else she had heard. Finally, "She said that I needed to get her out of there. That she did not belong there."

"That's what they all say," Spender chimed in.

"No, really. It was like someone else was in her body. And she *threatened* me."

"What kind of threat?" asked Spender. After all, she was in restraints.

"She said that her people —no, no—her *minions*—would get me if I didn't let her go. Or something like that. It was impossibly weird."

"That bitch is crazy," pronounced Washington. "At least your blood pressure is normalizing. I think you'll be okay."

"Thanks," said Anna. "I'm feeling a little better."

Washington saw and smelled that the lawyer had wet herself. She turned to Officer Spender. "Jake, let me clean her up. You can talk to her later."

"Okay, Eulah. Whatever you say." He left the room and Washington took care of Anna.

By the time Haberdeen got the call from Spender about what had happened, Anna was in a clean, dry hospital gown, resting under the covers, and some of her clothes were drying on hangers by the window. There was a knock on Windham's door.

"Come in," she said.

Officer Spender entered with a cordless phone flashing on hold. "Mrs. Windham, Detective Haberdeen, who's handling the Milliken case, is on the line. I told him what happened and he wants to talk to you." Without waiting for her to respond, Spender hit the talk button and handed her the phone.

"Y—Yes? This is Anna Windham."

"Mrs. Windham, this is Detective George Haberdeen."

"Yes, I know."

"I understand you had an interview with my prisoner."

"Yes. Although I wouldn't actually call it an interview. It was more like living in a horror movie."

"Tell me more."

Anna had to think for a moment. Even if her client was mentally incompetent, she still felt she needed to respect attorney-client confidentiality. How much, if anything, could she say?

Then Anna realized that, in her post-episode confusion and fear, she had already told either Spender or Washington or both basically what had happened in that room. Whether that was the right thing to do or not didn't matter right now. So why not let the detective hear it directly? She decided to go ahead and tell Haberdeen what she had experienced.

They spoke for about five minutes. Haberdeen keyed in on Milliken's apparent delusions. He asked, "What else did she say about this Countess Elizabeth Bathory?"

"Nothing," replied Windham. "She just identified herself as the countess and demanded that I get her out of there."

"What are you going to do?" asked Haberdeen.

"Arrange for a shrink for her. I'll talk to the judge. That's all I can do for now."

"Okay. Will you make sure I get a copy of the shrink's report?"

"Sure. The DA would get it in discovery, anyway."

"Right. Thank you for your cooperation." Haberdeen hung up without waiting for any further reply.

Well, thought Haberdeen, *this is a hell of a twist. Now the woman is having delusions?*

Slowly it all began to coalesce in the detective's thinking. Dr. Howard's claim that Lisbath was a vampire. The unusual, ancient disease all those women had contracted. The unlikelihood of an old nurse-midwife viciously killing people out of the blue. The dog's name and apparent bloodlust. Milliken's name change. Everything.

Haberdeen decided to pursue that expert Lisa had interviewed at her college. Now he wanted stuff first-hand. He looked up the college number and called.

Professor Cane wasn't in, the but Department Chair Dr. Andre Bodnir was. He answered the phone with his thick accent.

"Dr. Bodnir, this is Detective George Haberdeen of the Bridgeport Police Department."

Bodnir was surprised to get a call from a policeman. "Yes, Detective? Am I in trouble?" He was kidding, and Bodnir liked to play with people.

"Oh, no, sir. I need to ask you a few things."

"So a detective needs an anthropologist? Or is this about my ex-wife?"

"I need to ask you about some history."

"Detective, I am an anthropologist, not an historian. Do you want me to try to transfer you to the history department? I'm not sure there's anybody there at this hour."

"No, Doctor. This is history you apparently know something about. Or at least you might."

"Oh?"

"Yes. Have you ever heard of Countess Elizabeth Bathory?" hazarded Haberdeen.

"The Blood Countess?" Dr. Bodnir was honestly surprised to

hear that name, particularly from a policeman. "Where did you ever hear of her?"

"Let's leave that for later. So you have heard of her?"

"Of course. A vicious woman. Lived in the late 16th and early 17th centuries."

"So she's not around now."

"Of course not."

"Could she have a relative alive today? Maybe a distant one? Maybe even using the same name?"

"I don't think so. The entire Bathory line was destroyed a few years after the countess herself was killed. This kind of restricted genocide was common in that period."

"So Bathory didn't die of natural causes."

"No. As I remember, local villagers killed her out of revenge."

"Revenge?"

"Yes. Do you know why she was called 'The Blood Countess'?"

Haberdeen was intrigued. This blood stuff seemed to flow through almost everything his investigation was coming across.

"No, I don't. What did she have to do with blood?"

"Well, Bathory was known to bathe in the blood of young girls —poor peasants, of course—who lived in the surrounding villages. Somehow she thought it would make her younger, or keep her young, or something along those lines."

"She took baths in girl blood?"

"Precisely. You can imagine how pleased the fathers and brothers of these women were. That's why her castle was attacked."

"Shit."

"Yes. Exactly. Shit." With Bodnir's accent, the word sounded funny. "She cut them up, too."

"The girls?" asked the detective.

"Yes, the peasant girls. Swallowed their blood fresh."

"Vampire stuff," mused Haberdeen.

"Indeed."

Haberdeen was getting just a tiny bit sick to his stomach. But he figured he should get all the background he could on this woman since his prisoner somehow believed she was that very woman.

"Anything else?" he asked.

"The woman was pretty prolific."

"What do you mean?"

"At the beginning of the 1600's—the start of the 17th century—Bathory killed something like 650 girls, according to evidence collected by Count Fergo Ferzi. That, to me, is prolific."

"Me too."

"Right."

"Is that it, Professor?"

"I may be able to get more detail from my source books. Do you want me to check?"

"No. Actually, I'm sure I have more than enough. Thank you for your time."

"Detective?"

"Yes?"

"Why have you asked me all of this?" questioned Bodnir.

"You wouldn't believe it."

"Don't be so sure."

"Watch the newspapers, okay, Doc?"

"I saw something yesterday about a vampire nurse or something like that. And one of our former students came in asking some questions about Vlad Tepes recently. Is that what your call's about?"

"I really can't discuss that at this time."

"What *can* you tell me, Detective?"

"Watch the newspapers, okay?" Haberdeen sounded like an ingrate, but he couldn't risk making anything else public yet.

"As you wish," conceded Dr. Bodnir. "Good-bye."

"Bye." The detective stared at his phone. He had said good-bye, breaking the protocol.

Forty

Dr. Victor Burke, a frail, fifty-five-year-old frequent court appointee, was the psychologist requested by the judge (at Lisbath's public defender Anna Windham's urging) to evaluate Milliken. Burke's job was not to divine Lisbath's guilt or innocence, but merely to determine if she was competent to stand trial.

He was an agent of the court, and as a result had no vested interest in his findings. Before talking to Milliken, he was briefed by the PD, the prosecution, Anna Windham, and others as well.

The psychologist spent four hours with Lisbath Milliken in her cell/room at The Park. When Dr. Burke began his assessment of Milliken's identity and orientation responses, the nurse-midwife had no trouble stating who she was, where she was, and how she got there.

Lisbath had shown some apparent confusion about why she had been arrested, but Dr. Burke knew that anyone claiming innocence—whether honestly or not—would be equivocal about the reason for their arrest.

Lisbath "admitted" that she had served the several patients Dr. Burke enumerated. She did not, however, admit any wrongdoing with them. In this specific forensic psychological assessment environment, where competence to stand trial was the only question to be answered, Lisbath's reticence to discuss the women—let alone to admit guilt—was acceptable and even anticipated.

By the judge's order, the hearsay stories psychologist Burke had been told by lawyer Anna Windham and the ward staff could not be used in his findings except as context. He could only base his competent-to-stand-trial conclusions on what he observed during his own interview of the prisoner.

When the psychologist asked Milliken about Elizabeth Bathory, she admitted no knowledge of her and—more important, from the psychologist's perspective—she showed no body language change, intonation shift, or other sign of recognition.

Burke's twenty-page diagnostic report, half of it boilerplate and half of it meaningful, landed on Anna Windham's desk late in the day after his visit with Lisbath. It indicated that there was insufficient reason to find the nurse mentally incompetent to stand trial. Lisbath Juditha Milliken would be facing judge and jury.

Big T's intensifying radio and newspaper reports were sensationalist, as usual. Not surprisingly, they became the buzz of the town. To capitalize on the vampire theme, the local TV station ran hourly news updates about the case, often giving nothing more than inane pseudoscience from vampire movies. The station cheapened the news updates by playing scary organ music behind every one of them.

On Milliken's arraignment day, the courthouse steps were swarming not only with reporters but with hundreds of local townspeople. Everyone wanted to get a look at the vampire nurse, whom the press—primarily Big T—had labeled as "Red Death's Angel."

A shabbily-dressed couple had set up a card table by the sidewalk. They were selling coffee from a large metal container and blood-red bandannas that looked more like cheap shop cloths.

The hoard on the steps was ultimately disappointed. Lisbath was still very sick and stayed in her room at The Park. Only Anna Windham and the DA showed up, and nobody knew who they were. In absentia, Lisbath was ordered held over for trial.

The local media went crazy with Big T at the helm. "**VAMPIRE BROUGHT UP ON CHARGES**," and "**RED DEATH'S**

ANGEL TO FACE GOD AND THE COURTS," her articles touted.

The New York Times picked up the story from the national news services and sent their own reporter to cover Lisbath's trial firsthand. Inevitably, so did *The National Enquirer*.

◆ ◆ ◆

Haberdeen's phone rang. It was Big T.

"What do you want?" asked Haberdeen.

"Detective, last night I was covering the aftermath of a bad multiple car wreck on Highway 1."

"So?"

"So while I was at Q of A, one of the nurses asked me what was going on with the Red Death Angel case."

Shit, thought Haberdeen. *Now they're asking a reporter for the truth. That'll be the day.*

"So?" he asked.

"She said that one of Milliken's patients was in there—one Ilse Blücher."

"And? Is this going somewhere?"

"They said she—Blücher—had some rare disease and that maybe your Milliken was spreading it."

Haberdeen was deliberately silent.

"What's your comment on that?"

"I'm not a doctor, lady. You'll need to check with someone else."

"Detective Haberdeen, the nurse said that the health department was involved." She was laying her threatening groundwork.

Reporter Teitelmeier continued. "Do you want me calling them? Do you want me to announce to the public that we have a public health emergency due to the vampire? Or maybe instead you want people concluding that it's a terrorist act and starting a panic? Wouldn't that be cute?"

"*Shit*, woman! Haven't you already done enough damage? You are just making stuff up! Stirring up the public for no good reason."

"Well, Detective, I think there may be a reason. Now do you want to tell me about this disease, or do I call the Department of Health?"

"Okay, okay. Slow down." Haberdeen had to acquiesce; otherwise, this bitch would probably start a panic in the town. Nobody needed that. He was also experienced enough to know that Teitelmeier would probably call Public Health anyway, but he needed to appear as if he weren't withholding anything that could be made public.

"So spit it out," she demanded poisonously.

Haberdeen sat back in his chair and formulated his response. He knew that the press was not known for quoting people accurately.

"It seems that Milliken infected a number of women with childbed fever. It's some kind of *Strep* infection, and it's pretty rare." Haberdeen was careful not to refer to it as scarlet fever.

"Is Milliken sick with the disease?"

"I don't think so."

"So how could she spread it if she doesn't have it?"

"I don't have any idea. I told you, I'm not a doctor." Dr. Howard had not shared with Haberdeen the possibility, brought up by Dr. Fonescu, that p21-v confers immunity to bacterially-based diseases in particular. Even if the G-Man had known this, he would have kept his mouth shut rather than give the tidbit to this bitch.

"Are you withholding information from me? From the press? The public has a right to know, you know."

"I just told you, I'm not a fucking doctor. Why don't you go ahead and call her doctor directly?"

"I already tried. Dr. Howard. The man won't speak to me."

"Hallelujah," mumbled Haberdeen under his breath.

"What else can you tell me about Milliken?"

"Nothing. You know as well as I do that her trial is coming up. I can't give you anything else."

"Why do you think she killed those people? And why did she take all that blood?"

"Lady, talk to the DA. I don't present the case, he does. We're done for now."

"Nothing else to say to me?"

"Not that you'd want to hear."

Haberdeen hung up and breathed a sigh of relief. He detested talking to any reporter, but Big T was at the very bottom of his list.

♦ ♦ ♦

Big T called Dr. Peters of the health department immediately after she got off the phone with Haberdeen. The conversation was brief. She asked Dr. Peters, "What's the DOH doing about the childbed fever epidemic?"

Wary of reporters and with no political agenda of his own to protect, Peters would only respond, "No comment."

"If you don't give me what I want, I'll have to assume that there is grave danger, and that you don't have time to talk to me because your department is working on the problem day and night."

"No comment."

The following morning the Bridgeport Informant ran a lead article entitled "**RED DEATH'S ANGEL STARTED CHILD-BED FEVER EPIDEMIC, ACCORDING TO POLICE. HEALTH DEPARTMENT IS MOBILIZED.**" Haberdeen was quoted heavily and of course inaccurately throughout the article.

♦ ♦ ♦

Sergeant Stevenson called the G-Man in as soon as he had finished scanning the morning newspaper.

"What the fuck is this?" Stevenson demanded as he raised the newspaper almost to Haberdeen's eye level.

George Haberdeen hadn't seen the paper yet, so it took the G-Man a second to read the headline.

"Oh, shit," he said quietly. "I bet the story's all lies." He was livid.

"Lies or not, this affects public opinion," said the sergeant. His voice was gaining in volume.

"So what else is new?" asked Haberdeen.

"No more interviews with the press. Got it?"

"With pleasure, Judd. Thanks."

Stevenson winked at Haberdeen as the G-Man made his way back to his desk.

George's phone was ringing when he got there.

"Haberdeen, detectives."

"Detective Haberdeen, this is Brian Ogilvy with the district attorney's office. I'm handling the Milliken case."

"'Bout time you called," said Haberdeen.

"Yes, well. We're pretty busy around here."

"Okay, Mr. Ogilvy. Sergeant Stevenson gave you the file, right?"

"Of course. But we need to talk to you about the case. We expect to call you as a witness."

"Of course. What do you need?"

"Can you come down this afternoon? We've set up a temporary dedicated office at the courthouse. This case is big enough to merit that."

"Okay," said Haberdeen. "I can make it about 1:30."

"Fine. See you then."

The G-Man hung up and decided on a McDonald's lunch to be devoured on the way to the courthouse.

Haberdeen arrived at 1:25 p.m. and made his way around the metal detectors while displaying his badge. He was waved on by the attendants.

When Haberdeen opened the office door he saw a conference table with several boxes of files and papers. Two people were seated at the table. One, a man in his mid-thirties with a loosened, red tie and a white shirt, was obviously Ogilvy. Next to him sat a pretty woman with a clipboard.

"Mr. Haberdeen?"

"Yes."

"I'm Brian Ogilvy. Thanks very much for being prompt. This is Ms. Earl, my legal assistant."

"Hi," said Haberdeen with a slight smile and a nod of the head. He seated himself across from Ms. Earl.

"Ready to go to work?" asked Ogilvy.

"Always," said the G-Man.

"I don't need to ask you anything about what's in the files unless you think there's anything misleading in what the sergeant gave me."

"No. It's all pretty tight. I looked it over before he completed his report."

"Good." Ogilvy slid a copy of the *Informant* toward Haberdeen. "Have you seen this?" he asked.

Haberdeen said, "Yeah. This morning. It's all crap."

"So what's all this about? We're trying to decide whether there are elements to this murder case that we can fold into it to help paint Milliken as a monster."

Whoa, thought Haberdeen. *That's pretty direct.*

"What's this about?" Haberdeen repeated. "Well, the woman apparently infected lots of new mothers with this disease. It's . . ." The G-Man opened the file he had brought and looked up the scientific name again. "It's *Streptococcus pyogenes*. I learned about it from the health department."

"They knew about it?"

"Yeah. Dr. Robert Peters has been working on it."

Ogilvy asked, "Who's he?"

Haberdeen replied, "A deputy in the Department of Health."

"Got his number?"

"Sure." Haberdeen looked it up and provided it to Ms. Earl.

"That sickness? Same stuff as in scarlet fever," chimed in Haberdeen. He wanted to see Ms. Earl react, and he got his wish. He liked looking.

"Wow!" said Ogilvy. "Maybe we can use that. We'll see."

Brian Ogilvy scribbled a few notes and then continued. "Did Milliken admit anything at all? Even that she was at the scene? That she participated in the Wallace birth in some way?"

"Nope," said Haberdeen. "Claims she doesn't remember anything."

"Too bad."

"Yeah," said the G-Man. "Maybe it's not so surprising she doesn't remember. This is one weird chick."

"What do you mean?"

"Did the sergeant's report say anything about the Bathory episode at The Park?"

"No. What are you talking about?" Ogilvy seemed a little irritated that he had apparently been working with only partial information.

Haberdeen wasn't surprised that the "countess" claims Lisbath had voiced to her attorney Mrs. Windham had been excluded from the dossier given to the district attorney's office. Police reports are limited to stark, relevant information. The less muddy the report, the easier it is to defend it in court.

The detective proceeded to tell Ogilvy and Earl all about Lisbath's eerie episode with Anna Windham. The G-Man watched Ms. Earl's eyes through a glint in his own. He was having fun.

Haberdeen wrapped up his reportage of Bathory's appearance by saying, "The countess stuff is why they ordered the psych work-up in the first place. But Milliken came up clean. According to the shrink, she's competent to stand trial. Christ, I wouldn't use that guy again if you can help it. How could he ignore Windham's story? Does he think the public defender is lying?"

"You know as well as I do that the court appoints the shrink," said Ogilvy. "We don't have anything to do with it."

"Frustrating," chimed in Ms. Earl.

Surely, as Milliken's attorney, Windham wasn't going to mention Bathory's emergence during the trail, Haberdeen thought. And since this aberration had no obvious link to the alleged murders, there were no grounds justifying the DA's bringing it up. The judge would never permit it.

Over the next half hour, Ogilvy, Earl, and Haberdeen went over peripheral information that might contribute to the DA's strategy. Haberdeen left the meeting with a substantial sense of accomplishment. Even if Milliken wasn't going to be convicted of the unthinkable things she had apparently done to her birth-mother victims, at least she'd be locked up permanently with a murder conviction.

Ogilvy and Earl stayed in their temporary office, laying out their plan of attack.

Forty-one

Anna Windham tried several times to talk intelligently with Milliken. Sometimes Lisbath was communicative; at other times, she seemed to be in a world of her own. Her illness, whatever it was, got worse daily.

Windham also interviewed a number of Milliken's work associates and two of her hospitalized moms. None of the sick women had noticed anything wrong with Milliken's technique. Of course, none had enough knowledge to have criticized it effectively anyway.

Jury selection had been a difficult task. Virtually every local resident had seen Big T's television news reports or at least had read some of her yellow journalism in the *Informant*. Only a few knew Lisbath Milliken's name; most knew her only as "Red Death's Angel."

Due to this bad and predisposing press, Anna Windham had petitioned for a change of venue. However, Ogilvy argued successfully that this was a widespread news story (he cited the *New York Times*, for example), and that since people all across the United States would have heard of it, the venue was irrelevant. Also, of the array of crimes with which Lisbath was being charged, the two most felonious—murder and public endangerment—were local issues, having taken place in Shelton and Bridgeport, respectively. Both of these towns were served by the Connecticut Superior Court in Bridgeport.

The petition for change of venue was denied. His Honor Judge

Howard Franklin had limited each lawyer to a maximum of five peremptory challenges, wherein a lawyer could dump a potential juror for no identified cause as long as it was not for an ethnically-based reason.

During the jury selection process, Ogilvy had used only four peremptories. One was to remove a licensed vocational nurse. Another excluded an obese single mother. He also got rid of an animal rights activist. Finally, Ogilvy dumped a twenty-two-year-old male who wore filthy, pitch black clothes, had a necklace with a dangling silver skull with red plastic eyes, sported what appeared to be white-face makeup, and had a pierced lower lip. In hushed tones at the prosecution desk, Brian Ogilvy told Ms. Earl that he thought the guy looked like he had a pact with death and would probably idolize someone who stole blood.

Anna Windham also used four of her five permitted peremptories. During voir-dire, when all potential jurors were interviewed, two of the people referred to the devil and his minions. Talking out of the public's hearing at sidebar, Windham argued that anyone using the term "Devil" had been clearly biased by the press and should be excluded for cause rather than peremptorily. The judge disagreed, so Anna Windham used two of her peremptories to get rid of these people.

Another of Windham's peremptory challenges excluded a psychology senior on break from the University of Connecticut. Her fourth bounce was given to an old man who kept clicking his dentures. She simply couldn't stand the sound or watching the viscous, clear liquids slap between his uppers and lowers. Besides, she didn't have to tell anyone why she'd kicked him out. The jury that was ultimately chosen consisted of six men and seven women, along with four alternates.

On the first scheduled day of the trial, the courthouse steps looked less like The Stairway to Jurisprudence and more like a tiered circus with a random-act center ring. The number of drooling spectators dwarfed last week's crowd that had shown up at the arraignment. Several women had bought their preschool-age kids to see the spectacle, and groups of children were sitting on the steps chattering and laughing.

The bandanna people were back, this time with "Vamp" stamped onto the rags. The temperature was a little more tepid as February was maturing, but two more hot coffee and cocoa vendors had no trouble doing a fine business warming people up.

Bridgeport Police had blocked off the street in front of the courthouse. News vans with their towering antennas were interspersed with police cars in the restricted parking area beside the courthouse. Big T stood in a clearing by one of the building's exterior columns. The celebrity was surrounded by adulants; she was truly in her glory. The camera operator moved back to get the crowd in the background, and Big T began preaching about how we could all be safe now that Red Death's Angel was finally coming up for trial.

One Father Michael O'Herlihey was among the crowd as well. He came more to give comfort and reassurance to the gathered onlookers than to participate in the base spectacle before him. As an old friend of the rabbi's and in fact of the entire Shapiro family, the priest felt an obligation to be there in body as well as in spirit. The two clerics had had numerous conversations about the case since the rabbi's daughter Mandy was involved. O'Herlihey had called Chaim the night before the trial to let him know that he'd be out there, praying for them. Rabbi Shapiro said that he appreciated it; that perhaps they would meet that evening after the first day's proceedings.

Lisbath had been transported to the courthouse in an ambulance. Strapped to a gurney, she was brought in through the prisoner's entrance. It was at the back of the courthouse where no reporters were permitted.

The reporters who were seated at the far end of the peanut gallery stared at the spectacle rolling through the hallway's inner doors. Lisbath was lying on the noisy gurney, jiggling like a beached, fresh jellyfish as public defender Anna Windham moved the rolling prison out of the secure defendant area. She and a deputy rolled the gurney down the inner hallways leading to the rear doors of the courtrooms, into the Department VII court, and into position beside the defendant's table.

Windham began to ratchet Lisbath's back up to about sixty degrees so she could face the judge and witness box. The sheet began to work its way down toward Lisbath's lap. The crowd in the courtroom gasped as Lisbath's restraints and vomit-stained hospital gown were revealed in the wake of the sheet's descent. Milliken had been permitted to comb her hair and brush her teeth, but she was so obviously sick that it made little difference.

Public Defender Windham's thinking had been that Lisbath's pathetic presence might create pity in the hearts of the jurors. Successfully using the ploy that Milliken faded in and out of clarity, and that the nurse might be able to testify in her own defense if she were lucid, Windham convinced the judge to allow Lisbath's presence in the courtroom. But now this plan seemed be backfiring. Immediately, Windham returned the cover to its former position and tucked it in like a lobster bib. Milliken's face and wobbling neck, the only parts now showing out from under the sheet, were almost as red as freshly-peeled beets. Lisbath was staring off into space and drooling. She looked like she was eighty or ninety years old. Her head lolled off to the side. She was sicker than she had ever been and had no concept of where she was or what was happening. Mercy surfaces in unpredictable ways.

It was 8:45 a.m., fifteen minutes before the trial was due to commence. Inside the courtroom things were pretty quiet. The attorneys were all seated at their respective tables; bailiff Rufus Zink sat doing a crossword puzzle at his desk; and the court clerk was riffling through papers and typing on her computer keyboard. Most everyone in the courtroom just stared at Red Death's Angel. She was not aware of the attention.

Judge Franklin was in his chambers going over the jury instructions he intended to mete out at the beginning of the trial. He had already ruled that the press could occupy a maximum of ten seats; the judge had assigned his law clerk to distribute those seats randomly among the legitimate press representatives who had petitioned to be there. Court TV could occupy one corner but had to remain silent and refrain from showing any jury members. The remainder of the seating was to be limited to DA, police observers, the coroner, and families of the accused and any witnesses.

Lisbath Milliken had just one family member in attendance. Karlon Mire, the records clerk from Avondale Lake, had told Lisbath's sister Deborah about both the health department and the Haberdeen inquiries. Some time later, Deborah decided to find out what she could, called the Bridgeport police, and learned that her sister was going on trial. She made it to Bridgeport just minutes before the festivities were to begin. Lisbath had no awareness of her older sibling's fruitlessly supportive presence.

There was a smattering of angry, grieving Wallaces, Shapiros, and some people from their extended families as well. Even old man Manoff, from the janitorial service next door to Dickinson's, was there to get his fill of courtroom drama.

All of the subpoenaed witnesses were relegated to waiting out in the hallway so none could hear and thereby be biased by anyone else's testimony. The cold benches supported quite an assortment. Detective Haberdeen and Shelton PD's Ben Hawking sat talking at the very end of the benches. They had situated themselves to face the hallway as cops are wont to do.

Young Mandy Shapiro sat with her rabbi father and her mother Selma. Even though at age eleven she was barely old enough to be a believable witness, Ogilvy decided to call on the girl to justify the background investigation that had been launched against Milliken some time prior to the murders. Her testimony about seeing Milliken do her dirty work could prove valuable if she didn't crumble on cross-examination. Haberdeen had convinced the parents to let her testify by explaining that lawyers from both sides always take great pains to make their inquiries as low-stress as possible for children. The Shapiros felt it their family's civic duty to contribute to the woman's prosecution, so there they sat.

Dickinson's owner Sharona Gomez was there. Barbara Yoge had come to give Sharona moral support. They would sit together, the crook of Sharona's arm held protectively in Barbara's. Nurse Susie Rime from Dickinson's was there as well.

The DA was planning to use Sharona, whom he had interviewed three days ago, to testify about how angry Milliken had become once she learned that now-deceased nurse-midwife Francine Forman had been assigned to work the Wallace birth. And of course, Susie Rime was Haberdeen's "inside accomplice" as she gathered background on Milliken's activities. Rime had overheard the loud and stressful Wallace assignment argument between Lisbath and Sharona. Haberdeen was unaware of Susie's earlier visit with Milliken and the promises to Lisbath she intended to keep. He felt sure that he would have no trouble inducing the young nurse to testify against her "friend."

Ogilvy had also called six other people. One was Kevin Wallace's doctor. Wallace couldn't testify since he was still in a coma, but the doctor would be attributing Wallace's medical condition to cerebral trauma. He would also be corroborating the trauma claim with photos of bruises Mr. Wallace had suffered from being thrust back onto his home's brick hearth.

The next prosecution witness was to be the next-door neighbor who had identified Lisbath as being in the car with the slain Nurse Forman.

Linda Boating, the woman Mandy had seen giving birth, had been added to the DA's witness roster primarily so that Mandy could confirm her "sighting" of Lisbath's blood lust activities.

Gerald Turnbull, who had been present during Milliken's arrest in his home, was there as well. His wife Jackie had been too traumatized by the arrest to make a reliable witness. During every practice run with the attorney, Jackie began to scream and weep uncontrollably. The DA decided not to use her at the trial.

Kevin Ogilvy's expert witness—his "power" witness—was Professor Bernice Suddickton, an Amazon of a woman with more self-assurance than a cop. She was a specialist who taught midwifery at the University of Connecticut. Suddickton's job was to attack Lisbath's technique in every way she could, and the professor brought with her reams of studies, textbooks, and experience.

Lisa Ipple, looking thoroughly pregnant and rather uncomfortable, was also there. But not as a witness; her role was really peripheral, and the additional stress of a cross-examination was something that neither George nor Lisa wanted her to experience. She simply wanted to see what would happen, and the G-Man induced the judge to approve her presence as a "special case."

Defense attorney Anna Windham had only two witnesses to call. One was Dr. Victor Burke, the psychologist who had found Lisbath "sane" enough to go to trial. His report had indicated that the midwife saw her blood-taking activities as harmless. She also appeared to him to be penitent about having hurt Nurse Forman and Mr. Wallace. Since Windham had decided to forego any insanity defense, having Dr. Burke testify to Lisbath Milliken's penitence and her lack of malice during blood-taking should serve her case well.

The other defense witness Anna wanted to call was Karen Stade, the Dickinson's nurse, who would be a positive character witness for Lisbath.

Mrs. Windham had originally intended to add Joanie Perkins, the Yankee Pines Apartments manager, to her witness list. In an lucid moment during a Lisbath interview five days ago, Lisbath had told Anna that she and her manager were best of friends, so Windham figured Perkins would make a useful character witness. The attorney then learned that Perkins had been found near death in front of Lisbath's apartment. She had been hospitalized with what appeared to be dog or wolf attack markings. Despite being listed on the presumptive witness list, just like Kevin Wallace, this potential testifier was still unconscious.

Forty-two

Inside the courtroom, everyone seemed to be in place. It was 9:03 a.m.

Lisbath's irregular moments of consciousness provided her with unfocused snapshots of her surroundings. With each such vision, she felt the fear and pain of a kid peeking out from between her fingers during a scary scene of a horror movie. She felt like she was strapped down to a frying pan and had an audience to taunt her. Milliken needed an out.

The bailiff's signal light began to flash a five-minute warning of the judge's imminent appearance. Lisbath's squinted eyes picked up the rhythmic pulsations of light. Her eyes rolled partway up into their sockets.

In her viral delirium, Lisbath Milliken fled toward that warped ethereal world of centuries past. She could not distinguish whether it was dream or waking fantasy; it could have been her own creation —or perhaps, in some strange way, her own recollection.

The bailiff's light was hypnotic to her, and as she faded further into pseudosafety away from the courtroom, Lisbath saw the inside of the besieged castle. She perceived the pursuit of the countess and the woman's hunt for safety.

Although Jon Thust was being ripped apart emotionally by the horrendous scene of burning friends and enemies in the congealing glob of oil and tar on the castle's floor, the battle between his men and the countess' forces raged on.

"No! This cannot be!" shouted many of Jon's soldiers as they saw their suffering brothers writhing within the tar-oil mess. But Thust refused to reduce the vigor of the attack. He assigned most of his men to continue killing the remaining Loyalites, another three of them to work at saving their burning brothers as best they could, and he took two of his best warriors to follow him in pursuit of the sovereign herself.

She was nowhere to be found on the first floor, so the three ascended the stairwell, invigorated by the pursuit and the closeness of victory.

"You—check to the left. And you—look through there," Jon said to the other. "We kill her with no mercy and no delay. Understand?"

They agreed immediately. Reflexively. Satisfied that two good men were searching the main wings, Thust took off straight ahead, switching his gaze left and right as he hunted his prey like a hungry lion.

The countess had been observing Jon Thust's tasking from a perch near the third-level stairwell opening. She saw her chance for escape. As the three peasant warriors went their separate ways, the lady stealthily descended from the bedchamber floor, down both levels to the ground. Rather than run toward the warring factions at the foyer, the lady shrunk back toward the kitchens. Although the building was a true fortress, it had one small entrance at the rear used primarily by the food preparers to transport food in and garbage out. This human garbage was on her way out.

With the screams and cries of dying and burning men at the front of the building ringing in her ears, giving her some gratification even in her dire straits, the countess slowly made her way toward the kitchen door. What she had not expected was that one of Thust's men would have had the presence of mind to check for other entrances.

Rento Limit had stationed himself just beside the castle's rear door—the very door toward which the countess was headed. He had been leaning against the wall, crying like a baby as he heard his brothers inside the building moan and seethe in the heat of battle. Limit would learn later that his father's flesh had been literally melted by the thrown tar-oil mixture, but his tears would flow no more pitifully at that time than they did at this moment by the rear door.

A small, filthy dog emerged from the surrounding forest. It moved slowly up to Limit's legs and pressed its head against the man, rubbing almost as a bear would make his mark on a tree. His tail was moving slowly from side to side—not quite a wag; instead a clear statement that he was in a mildly threatening posture. Limit barely noticed.

The countess swung the door inward and began to move outside furtively. The startled dog jumped away and crouched in the tall grass.

The old door's loud creak immediately called Rento to action. He simultaneously raised his scythe and blinked his eyes hard to clear them of their tears. The man needed to see whether the target moving through the doorway was friend or foe before engaging his lethal swing.

The countess' corpulence made it instantly clear that this was the bitch herself fleeing her castle. Limit's first inclination was to slice off her head with one swooping executionary motion. He hesitated for a moment, however, thinking that perhaps Jon Thust and the others would want to be there when the countess met the demise she had earned so heartily.

Rento's vacillation cost him. The countess saw this peasant with his scythe raised and at the same time saw his hesitation. Knowing that she could not possibly outrun the fit man, the lady shoved her sword toward Limit's center of mass. She was not accurate, however, and the blade sliced smartly through his right thigh. The blood began to flow even before Rento realized he had been cut.

The adrenaline flashing through his veins blunted the pain almost completely, and he made his gut-level decision. As Limit fell toward the off-balance countess, the practiced farmer swung his curved blade forcefully across the woman's shins. He sliced completely through both legs perhaps a foot above her ankles, and the horrid woman toppled to the grass in a sick flurry of pain and disbelief. The black-and-white dog drew closer.

Now, his immediate task completed, Rento began to feel the searing pain in his thigh. He looked down at his leg and began screaming. Limit's voice mixed with the countess' lamentations in a sick, ululating opera of physical agony.

The battle inside the citadel was winding down. Jon and his two companions had completed their sweep of the second level and had moved on to the third. The level smelled heavily of garish, scented oils. The men knew this was the countess' private area. They searched quickly but without result. Satisfied that the countess was not hiding in any corner of her private floor, the three returned to ground level to rejoin their brothers.

Jon Thust's basic plan had been sound, and the remaining Loyalites were cut to pieces during the next few minutes. When the foes were all dead, Thust went to his wounded and burnt troops. All the hurt men had been collected and moved against the east wall. Jon held his formidable arms out wide, showing his community with his fellows, and he cried with them.

This somber moment gave some comfort to the wounded, and as everyone quieted down they heard the screaming coming through the kitchen door. Jon and five other unhurt men ran to the source of the sound, their weapons at the ready. They burst through the door and saw poor Rento Limit tying off his leg above the cut. But too they saw the countess, writhing on the grass perhaps a yard away from her severed feet and ankles. The dog had lain down in the bloody gap.

"You *witch*!" shouted Thust. "Finally we will stop your reign of death and terror!"

"You cannot stop me! No one can stop me! I am the Countess Bathory! You fools are *nothing*! You are all *less* than nothing!"

Everyone in the courtroom save Lisbath heard the bailiff's phone buzz. They shut up and watched what bailiff Rufus Zink was doing. He picked up the receiver, listened for a moment, nodded his head, hung up, and rose. Zink then faced the main seating area and spoke in a ludicrously booming voice far louder than it needed to be for a room holding at most forty-five or fifty quiet people.

"All rise. Department seven, The Honorable Howard Franklin presiding," he announced.

The courtroom fell eerily silent except for one juror's coughing fit and the sound of a magazine falling off someone's lap. The drizzling outside was muted.

Judge Franklin entered, sat down, and arranged the wide arms of his black robe over his expansive dais. Taking his time, he hit a few keys on his computer keyboard, pursed his lips, nodded his head, and opened a three-ring binder. Everyone in the courtroom —except for the experienced law clerk, courtroom secretary, court reporter, and Lisbath—was staring intently. Every finger's slightest movement was followed like an F-22 fighter's heads-up display.

"Good morning, ladies and gentlemen." The judge didn't even look up from his binder, yet he continued. "This is Case F01096635-2004, *The State of Connecticut vs. Lisbath Milliken*."

The court reporter's fingers silently smashed black buttons. She showed absolutely no facial expression.

"Clerk, swear in the jury, please," ordered the judge.

She swore them in.

For twenty-five minutes, Judge Franklin pontificated his jury instructions by reading from a carefully-prepared manuscript. He let the jurors know that they were the actual judges of the facts, and that his job was only to keep things fair and keep the attorneys in line. He spoke about the difference between "reasonable doubt" and "moral certainty." He told them that opening and closing arguments were simply opinions of the attorneys and were not to be interpreted as evidence. He explained what to look for, what to ignore, things that could be considered in judging a witness' credibility, and on and on.

Franklin's style was to gesture with a pen at the jury box each time he made a point. After the first ten minutes of admonitions, his gestures became almost comical. But no one laughed. The seriousness of the proceedings, particularly in light of there being a woman on trial for murder, hung over the scene like a thick, black tarp.

Judge Franklin then enumerated the charges against Lisbath Milliken. She was charged with several crimes:

—Two counts of murder in the first degree (for mother Doris Wallace and nurse-midwife Francine Forman);

—One count of assault and battery (for unconscious Kevin Wallace);

—Five counts of malpractice (one for each recently ill mother, including Ilse Blücher, La-TaKeisha Jeffers, Lucinda Smithson, and Jackie Turnbull, plus one for the probable abortion evidenced by the tissue sample found in Lisbath's blender); and

—Thirteen counts of larceny (based on the jars with their umbilici and other human contents).

As each charge was read, most of the audience gasped, sometimes silently, sometimes out loud. Big T's reports had been limited solely to the information she could get in public records and what little she could trick out of the authorities. As a result, her stories had left much of the gory detail out.

The reporters in the audience (one of whom was Big T) wrote feverishly as the charges were recited. Some of them grinned as they wrote, particularly when the last thirteen counts were enumerated, all of which surprised them. Their stories were going to be juicy.

"How do you plead, Ms. Milliken?" asked the judge.

Anna Windham stood. "The defendant pleads not guilty," she responded. Lisbath was staring at the ceiling, apparently not in touch with the proceedings. She may or may not have been awake. She was perspiring as if in a steam bath.

"Do you have an opening argument, Mr. Prosecutor?" queried Judge Franklin.

"Certainly. Thank you, Your Honor," said Brian Ogilvy. He then stood up and stationed himself at the lectern off to the side of the jury. This was the point where the district attorney would lay out the logic of his case and would plant suggestions about Nurse-midwife Milliken's guilt. All eyes in the silent courtroom were on Brian Ogilvy.

"Good morning, ladies and gentlemen," he began. Several of the jurors mumbled "good morning" replies as the attorney's gleaming smile swooped across them.

Brian Ogilvy began his speech slowly and with expansive melodrama. "The pathetic thing you see lying on that gurney," Ogilvy said as he pointed with a rigid, outstretched arm, "has performed *unspeakable* acts. She has murdered. She has stolen and *bottled* body parts. She has drunk fresh human blood. And that is just *part* of her disgusting, twisted story."

Lisbath remained in her deep dream-trance, oblivious to Ogilvy's verbal attacks. She was behind the castle, smelling the blood and the horror.

Two of Jon's men went to Rento and knelt in the tall grass to assist him. Thust continued his dialog with the woman-beast.

"You will die here, Bathory. And our women will be safe again. May you rot in hell!" Thust gripped his own sword tightly as he kicked Bathory's weapon out of her weakening hands. The kick broke two of her fingers.

"No, you fool!," shouted a weakened Bathory. "I am forever and you are nothing. *Nothing.*"

The countess continued. "Hear this before you move that blade. I will not die; I cannot die. I curse you and your families and your future issue forever! You will find me in your dreams and around every corner. You will never be rid of me. *Never!* I will haunt your souls for eternity! I will..." The countess's voice trailed off as blood pumped out her legs onto the grassy mound on which she lay.

Ogilvy continued his flamboyant presentation, referring to Lisbath over and over as "that *thing.*" Each time he mentioned the woman, Ogilvy pointed toward her in the same way. He was a ghoul divining his victim. The onlookers were eating it up. Most had the wide eyes of children, their mouths making small circles as their hearts beat faster and faster.

Mr. Ogilvy began describing for the jury what a nurse-midwife was. He spoke of the birthing specialty, the independence, and of what he termed a "lack of accountability for anyone with such little training." The thickly palpable courtroom tension began to relax a little in light of Ogilvy's somewhat distant, technical description.

Suddenly, the sounds of a loud commotion emerged from the hallway outside the courtroom. The jurors could hear yelling and unnatural animal sounds like barking and squealing and some kind of rumbling.

The uproar grew increasingly louder. Everyone in the courtroom was looking toward the closed double doors, wondering what was going on. Even Lisbath oriented vaguely in that direction.

The trial was at a standstill.

Bailiff Zink took it upon himself to get up to have a look. As he walked toward the rear doors, everybody felt grateful that *someone* was going to find out what the hell was going on. Judge Franklin nodded his head as his gaze followed Zink's progress toward the rear of the courtroom.

What sounded like bodies slamming against the door struck instant fear into some of the courtroom denizens. Many of the women grabbed the arm of whoever was next to them. Men were grinding their teeth and squinting.

"My God!" said one juror to another. Everyone stiffened further.

Zink took his last few steps quickly, drew his revolver, and peered out the small, framed window embedded in the door nearest him. He couldn't be sure of what he saw, but there was obviously trouble out there. Rufus Zink needed to take care of it. His training and instincts led him relentlessly to protect the courtroom and its occupants by any means necessary. He prepared himself and literally threw open the door and leapt into the hallway.

Zink had created an opening into the courtroom, and Lad charged through the doorway immediately. Bristling with malevolence, the dog that had escaped the pound had now somehow found his way to his mistress in the courtroom. He had bitten several people in the courthouse foyer and in the hallway just outside the trial room. Nobody dared touch him. People are naturally afraid to touch a rabid or attacking dog, and Lad appeared to be both.

G-Man Haberdeen and Officer Hawking, who had been sitting together outside the courtroom in the witness waiting area, saw Lad's menacing entrance. They ran in after him. Both men had their guns drawn, their weapons held in both hands, FBI style.

The creature was foaming and growling. His fur, up on end, was wet with not only the rain outside, but with blood from the people who had been in his way. Vlad the Impaler, no longer a partially dormant spirit in Lad, pounded its paws on the marble floor, and everyone cleared a frightened path for him.

Zink then burst back in through the door, his gun still drawn. He followed the animal's path as well, yelling "Halt! Stop! No!" His calls were foolish and fruitless.

Vlad ran straight for Lisbath and jumped up onto the gurney. His jarring arrival caused her to open her eyes. Milliken's illness had made her aging body weak and frail, but she was together enough to recognize her familiar. She began to crack a wry, uncomprehending smile.

"Good Jesus!" exclaimed Haberdeen. "That's got to be one of those goddamn *familiars* that Lisa was talking about!" He had been crouched in shooting position, trying to figure out how to approach this thing. He decided to try to throw the animal off Nurse Milliken, but his attempts to touch it were completely ineffective, as if the hairy thing on the gurney were made of steel.

The dog-monster began a vicious attack upon the Milliken body's face, unaware of Haberdeen's fruitless efforts to stop it. He bit and thrashed. He forced his teeth to tear across the visage, leaving deep slashes that bled freely. He punched at her old neck and chest with his forelegs. He sliced at her cheeks and lips. Lisbath's head was being flayed open before the entire courtroom.

Lisbath was trying to scream, but her weak sounds were muffled by blood and fangs and chunks of her own cheeks thrust into her throat. She gagged on her own tissues, involuntarily inhaling pieces of herself. This blocked most of her windpipe. The woman was beginning to suffocate with insufficient strength to blow out the clogs of her own flesh.

With her brain suffering from reduced oxygen, Lisbath began to lose consciousness. It could have been a blessing. But she did not simply fall into a dreamless stupor; rather, oblivious now to the tumult going on around her in the courtroom, she retreated again into her recurring vision of the countess and her plight.

As the blood leaked out of the Countess Bathory's severed legs, the crouched hound moved closer to the red source. Its eyes began a strange glow that belied its canine character. Apparently starving yet with more purpose than a simple scavenger, he began to lick and then to snap at the countess's bleeding stumps. She was in such pain and so fully engulfed in anger and vengeful mania that she barely noticed.

Thust yelled, "This is for all the women you took from us.

This is for all the decent people who will never again have to see your filthy countenance!"

He moved slowly and deliberately toward Bathory with his sword held high in both hands. It was pointed toward the ground, and its blade reflected light onto her corpulent body as the avenger arrived over her. As he stood there he saw her eyes open and close as she neared unconsciousness. He wanted this impending execution to take place while she would be aware of his actions. Thust needed the sweetness of revenge enhanced by Elizabeth Bathory's fear and acknowledgement.

Everyone in the courtroom was transfixed by the horrific scene of the dog attacking the nurse strapped down to her gurney. Onlookers screamed, and many were furiously working their way toward the door and out of the courtroom.

Hawking and Zink approached the animal slowly, thinking of backing up Haberdeen. Vlad turned immediately and began a deep, visceral growl that forced icy fear through the bailiff's veins. Through almost everyone's veins. The G-Man was virtually fearless, but he finally realized there was little he could do. He backed away. Maybe he could drag the animal off if it weakened, but that would rip chunks of skin off the woman. So Haberdeen just stood there, sweating and panting.

Officer Zink also knew that he could not fire a shot at the animal because of the danger of the bullet wounding someone else in the courtroom. He holstered his revolver and reached to his side for his baton. Vlad lunged off of the gurney and toward the officer. The force of the jump caused the gurney to roll back a couple of feet to the fence behind the lawyers' tables. Immediately, the animal captured Zink and crunched into his forearm with his powerful jaws. The arm snapped instantly. Vlad let his own body weight tear further at the man's shattered arm as he flailed like a Great White with its teeth still attached and slicing more deeply into its prey.

The screaming bailiff fell to the floor and tried valiantly but vainly to hit at Vlad with his free arm, but the dog dropped to the ground and buried every one of his teeth into Zink's fleshy abdomen. The man's piercing scream was so violent that the chandelier over the courtroom vibrated. Officer Zink was writhing in such agony that he couldn't see.

Haberdeen now threw himself at the creature, intending to body-blow it flat to the floor and then to fire shots at it from above. As if trained in combat, the animal simply shuffled back a couple of steps and let the detective fly by. When Haberdeen hit the ground, he was stunned. The animal jumped him, burying his ferocious teeth into the back of the man's neck. Haberdeen's head dropped to the floor, advertising his unconsciousness. Leaking blood began to collect in a pool below his face.

Vlad then sauntered toward the gurney, sweeping his large head from side to side and growling, daring anyone to come hear him. He knew he was in control, and so did everyone else. Nobody moved.

Milliken was unconscious and living 400 years in the past.

Jon brought the blade down to the countess's abdomen and very slowly pushed and twisted it into the bitch. When the sword's tip hit bone inside her back, she jerked. Thust began to walk in a circle around her slowly thrashing body. It was like spearing an eel on the deck of a ship. The dog began to eat at a leg aggressively, chasing its flailing, rough end as it would a thrashing enemy.

Lisbath arched on the gurney as blood leaked from her mouth. She was one with Bathory. She *was* Bathory.

The countess looked like a fat snake trying to wind around an invisible prey while having a seizure. Thust held the blade with both hands, moving nary a muscle in his hands, wrists or arms. As he paraded in a circle around her, the blade rotated slowly in the woman's abdomen and deeply into her back, grinding and pulling at her organs like a screw.

Bathory began to moan and scream with what little strength she had left. The strange, frightening dog stopped ripping at her leg and slogged toward her face. He began to groan and yelp, then became deadly silent. The glow in his eyes intensified. He brought his muzzle to the countess's contorted face and stared into her half-dead countenance. Bathory opened her eyes briefly and saw this filthy animal at her head. Something changed in her. She stopped flailing for a moment and brought her weakened arms over to the dog's neck. The animal did not resist. Somehow, he seemed to encourage it.

Finished with his self-protective attack on the pathetic weakling human men, Vlad leapt again onto the gurney. He almost lost his footing because of the blood pooling all over the table.

The animal placed his head, now seemingly larger than Lisbath's, directly over her face. Lisbath's arms rose toward Vlad's salivating countenance. The gurney straps resisted. The courtroom was transfixed.

Bathory moved her hands to the monster's head and then to the dog's ears and grabbed them, one in each hand. As she did so, the animal moved to her. In a shared effort, the dog pushed and she pulled the bloody muzzle toward her own face.

All of the villagers watched this bizarre ritual with uncomprehending eyes. Countess Bathory was bleeding heavily and almost dead, yet she was doing this strange thing with something resembling a stray dog.

Forty-three

In the courtroom, Vlad began his attack on Lisbath's body afresh, now targeting her throat as well. Her body began to quiver like a prisoner's frying in the electric chair. The straps binding her to the gurney made her movements fitful, the pitiful eel randomly slapping the deck in the throes of death. Vlad's tail was straight up as he gobbled into his mistress.

With no warning, the dog became still. Nobody would come near him, so the entire scene was frozen and silent except for the glops of blood splashing down Lisbath's trunk and off the gurney to the floor.

The animal opened its dog-mouth and an unnatural resonance emanated from his throat. Its black lips and tongue began to vibrate. The sound was at once gruff and insolid, force-fed through an irregular strainer. The vibration continued, a deadly and vicious reverberation frightening and moving every soul in the room.

Transfixed by that ungodly buzz, every onlooker experienced a brutal, eye-squinting headache coming on. As the pain began peaking, each affected soul perceived telepathically the messages the attacking animal was foisting upon the dying woman strapped to the gurney.

Slowly and uneasily, as if stretched over time, the four-legged monster on the table excreted on some telepathic level the utterance, "Bitch!"

Everyone remaining in the courtroom was spellbound by the enveloping surreality. And it did not stop. Vlad continued making his unearthly vibrating noises. The air around the creature's body became very dark, as if he were in a shadowed vapor, everything else in light. *"You have failed me!"* he spewed out psychically.

The standing courtroom residents were all holding their heads, in great pain, yet somehow thankful that these animalistic telepathic charges were hurled at only one victim: Lisbath. Milliken's eyes were at full-wide, revealing increasing horror as she was subjected to Vlad's admonitions.

The entire room became cold. The remaining onlookers breathed fog and shivered, yet were unaware of the change. Frost collected on the courtroom benches. The judge's glass of water froze and shattered.

The animal took another fast swath of blood from her neck. *"Bathory! You can no longer be feeder for me!"* The thing's mind-voice boomed directly and painfully into every head in the room. It had overtones of scraping wood and thudding lava.

The near-corpse on the gurney could do little more than stare at the vampire atop her. Lisbath's eyes wobbled in fear and helplessness. Vlad pressed his filthy forepaw into the center of her chest, dug in his long, sharp nails, and began a slow, powerful, irregular pumping action.

"We are Vlad Tepes. No mere human defies us! You will not prevail!"

Anna Windham stared at the scene, her hands pressed to her temples. There was something familiar about the silent mind-voice —or at least the feeling it cast over the entire courtroom. It brought back the unwelcome ghosts of Windham's first and only intercourse with the countess in Lisbath's cell.

"Bathory! You must die! You must live again as better flesh for me. To serve. To feed. To OBEY!"

The Impaler's forepaw now began a tortuous transformation into a reptilian claw. Its nails stretched to almost four inches in length, and each of the four dog-toes became scaled and turned a shiny, dark green. As each claw emerged, there was a discernable creaking coming from the paw area. The extension of claw seemed to give great pain to the harboring beast, and it cried out as if in torture. The foul buzzing that had been coming from the dog-beast stopped. As the claw completed its emergence, the only other sounds came from Vlad's heated breathing and the dripping blood all around the gurney.

Vlad the Impaler then drew his claw back. A deep, growling screech emanated from every orifice of his canine body simultaneously. He then thrust the claw toward the heart of the confined victim, burying it deep into her thorax.

Splayed partly on the grass and partly atop the heap that was Bathory, the animal's muzzle now went directly over her mouth. She began to extend her tongue and eventually began to lick her own leg-blood off of his mouth and snout. She stopped, coughing and spitting up blood from her own shredded internal organs, and then continued her gruesome meal.

When she was about to expel what would surely be her last breath, the demon female opened her mouth wide into an eerie gap. She used the last of her strength to accept the dog's lips and snout deep into her own blood-drenched maw. Her tongue helped lead the hairy canine protrusion inward by curling under the tip of the dog's mandible and drawing backward, inward. Bathory exhaled as hard as she could, which was really little more than a wheezing puff. As she did so, a thin, hot brown-green fog from the depths of her ravaged body egressed. The dog inhaled deeply. His eyes grew wide and the hound began to shake. He urinated involuntarily.

This beast-spirit, forced many years ago to assume canine form as it left Vlad Tepes' dying shell on the battlefield, now incorporated a second, soulless evil: the viral essence of Countess Elizabeth Bathory. The twin, wicked constellation would coexist for centuries into the future, sometimes in the same canine body, sometimes in a malicious dyad of the canine and its familiar.

In the courtroom, the grotesque animal atop Milliken began to twist. "**Aaaaahhhh ja morar schieh nok to-aht! Your master commands you! Back to me!**" reverberated in the brains of those who had not yet mustered the strength to get out of the room.

The Impaler moved his muzzle over Milliken's bloody mouth hole, almost touching her, tooth-to-tooth. Then his buried claw pumped again, shoving her internal organs back and forth.

A greenish cloud began to arise from the irregular orifice where Lisbath's mouth had been. She still saw kindred visions of the Countess Elizabeth Bathory's final plight: In the throes of her own demise, Lisbath saw again this same monster-animal stand over and draw the fog from Bathory—the very substance and spirit that he was now extracting from her.

The gas's dense, upward curl rose much more slowly than mere smoke. Vlad inhaled the substance deeply. His entire body became infused with the ethereal, dense spirit. Once again, Satan's world had a renewed, malevolent nexus.

Rather than pull back deliberately, the dog behind the castle appeared to fall away from Elizabeth Bathory's dying head.

While the villagers had been temporarily transfixed by this odd, bestial scene, the dog's retreat brought them back to reality. The Countess Bathory was on her death ground, and it was time to finish her.

Jon's blade had remained in the almost-corpse during the past few moments. Now he dragged his blade toward her head, creating a sickening wake of mixed blood and cut organs. He repeated his symbol-rich rotation about the corpulent mass below him three times, one for each sister he had lost to the monster. Thust then removed the blade and finally worked it into the bitch's mouth, now grinding, now pushing, now grinding again. Bathory's remaining consciousness was made to feel some of the horrors she had inflicted on so very many innocent women.

"Join me," said Thust to his five troops. Each came to the body and, as the countess lost ultimate consciousness, every man began to insert his blade slowly into her hulk over and over. Each visualized his mother's, wife's, or daughter's tortured death at this woman-animal's hands as he ground the sharp metal of revenge into the cask of her flesh.

As the animal on the steel gurney drew Bathory's evil essence into his foul lungs, host Lisbath Milliken finally expired. The nurse-midwife's body had been able to hold onto life the past few days despite a raging fever and relentless aging, but the Impaler's attack —and his extraction of Countess Elizabeth Bathory's spirit—left nothing but an obese, bleeding carcass.

When it was all over—when Bathory's reign over the countryside had apparently ended forever—the men stood around the immobile corpse and shoved their swords heartily into the earth surrounding it. Five swords plus Thust's blade encircled the bloody glob like prison bars. There the steel reminders and their hellish prisoner would remain for all to see.

With the Countess Elizabeth Bathory's curse ringing in his ears, Jon Thust exhaustedly headed toward the village. He would tell everyone that they were now safe; that Bathory was dead. He wanted very much to believe that it was so.

The dog-thing sulked off into the forest, no longer hungry. He was fulfilled. For now.

In the courtroom, content and bloated with the spirit he had just extracted, the monster withdrew his paw from the corpse's chest. Vlad spun to face the rear of courtroom, his reptilian claw spraying droplets of Milliken/Bathory's blood in a semicircle. He faced the few fools remaining there. He left the three-foot-high gurney and moved toward the floor in an eerie, slow-motion arc.

When he reached the floor, the ancient spirit panned its head slowly, taking in the visual environment. He saw the six remaining people virtually frozen in place, pumping steam from their warm chests into the frigid air. He saw chairs and benches strewn over the chaotic floor. He observed a brook of blood. And of course, he saw below him his former carrier—his former feeder-slave—ripped to shreds, beached on a rolling metal table, and useful no more.

Forty-four

Vlad the Impaler's lungs and body fluids were full of the vampiric virus he had extracted from the Milliken body. The virus that makes humans into blood-needers. The microorganism Dr. Fonescu had almost jokingly called p21-v.

The nether-beast loped through the courtroom doorway. Officer Hawking, who had made it to the back of the room during the final few moments of Vlad's attack, was able to follow the beast, gun drawn, waiting for a clear shot. The hall outside the trial area had been emptied of the general public; only police waited for the monster there.

With no civilian targets to impede them, Hawking and the others confidently opened fire at the beast. But their bullets were totally ineffective. Vlad the Impaler's soul, if it could be called that, had been formed into the dog-like corpus upon the original Vlad's death. It would remain imprisoned there forever, and it was *immortal*.

Virtually ignoring the gunfire, Vlad slunk out to the courthouse steps. They were still swarming with people. Nobody had expected the rumored "mad dog" to escape the gamut of police waiting for him within the confines of the building.

The animal scanned his environment arrogantly. He was now a dual being: Vlad Tepes, yes, but too the viral soul of Countess Elizabeth Bathory. His body literally vibrated with the evil power of the ages. He inspected the environment with the slow, menacing sweep of a reptile trolling for prey.

"My God! There's that dog!" screamed a tall woman in the crowd outside the courtroom. Everyone who could hear her followed her gaze to the monstrosity perched on the steps. In a strange orienting wave, as people saw others looking toward the steps, their necks twisted and their own gazes homed in. Eventually, there was an eerie silence as hundreds of pairs of eyes locked onto the beast.

Vlad's gaze came to rest on young Mandy, who was clutching her rabbi father's arm.

"Daddy! Oh, *no*! Daddy, protect me!" screamed Mandy as she saw the being's head rotate to the side, his ears extending straight upward, sienna saliva escaping his lower jaw. Mandy was pulling on her father's suit sleeve as he began to kick fruitlessly in the dog's direction.

Other people in the vicinity of the girl began to scatter. Some of those fleeing knocked down vendor stands at the curb. Parents dragged children by their upper arms to get them out of the monster's visual sweep.

Rabbi Chaim and daughter Mandy were so catatonically engaged in a mutual, frightened grip that they could not move away. Selma Shapiro was also frozen in shock and was unable even to scream.

The beast rose up on its toes, and every one of its hairs stood straight out from its body. Its eyes glowed a deep, undulating red. His head began to expand, and he screeched in apparent pain as his cranial bones extended, stretching the flesh over his head and distorting his vicious devil-face. He howled, then crouched.

The entire sky began to blacken as a fiercely cold wind rushed in from nowhere. Small pieces of the old flag over the courthouse sheared off and blew downwind. The few remaining leaves on the wintered trees sped off to their deaths.

The rabbi made a weak attempt to enfold his precious Mandy within his arms and the rest of his body. His coat tails were blowing so hard they flapped against Mandy's shoulders. Chaim's screams became muffled as he buried his face into his daughter's back. Mandy tucked her head down, protecting herself from something fully incomprehensible.

Everything became deadly silent. The spine-chilling wind stopped as quickly as it had begun.

Most of the people in and around the courtroom had run off, scared for their lives. A few had stayed, either because they were stupid or because they were too frightened to move. All of them, freezing from the hellish, cold wind of moments ago, saw the animal stir, then bring itself to its feet. It seemed to have trouble raising its tremendous head, but eventually it stood tall. Its eyes still glowed, but the monster blinked often, as if confused or in some kind of internal pain.

Vlad began to move his head again, but he fell down on his haunches. The onlookers felt somewhat less threatened. The monster's vile grip somewhat loosened, some started to wander toward the parking lot, looking back every couple of seconds to ensure that they were not being pursued.

Father O'Herlihey, who had remained because of an obligation to protect his flock, moved toward his good friend Rabbi Shapiro. The priest stared deeply at Mandy, his feet far apart. The holy man seemed to grasp on some plane unavailable to the general public that something was hidden and unfathomably foul here. The man began to shake his head, slowly at first, then increasingly more fervently. With each shake, his head twisted further and further, side to side. Chaim and Mandy stared at him, confused by his behavior and still shaken by the monster's presence.

The priest began to hold forth. His voice was fire-and-brimstone—the mode he used so often in his more heated sermons. He raised his hands and turned his palms toward Vlad, who was still down on his haunches. O'Herlihey quoted the Bible, from Nahum 3.5-3.6, following shortly after Ezekiel:

> Behold, I am against thee, saith
> the Lord of hosts,
> And I will uncover thy skirts upon
> thy face,

And I will show the nations thy
    nakedness,
And the kingdoms thy shame.
And I will cast detestable things
    upon thee, and make thee vile,
And will make thee as dung.

The air seemed to reverberate with these searing, damning words. The remaining mob in front of the courthouse were stupefied as they focused their attention on the priest.

Rabbi and Selma Shapiro were bewildered by their friend's pronouncements. All the rabbi could think of was to seek peace and safety for himself and his precious family. The rabbi put his arm around his daughter's shoulder and took Selma's shaking hand. The three of them began moving slowly away from the priest. Selma was weeping, and all three were perfectly stunned.

A few rogue reporters were gathering around O'Herlihey. Most of them were snapping pictures wildly and aiming their tape recorders at the clergyman as he held his hands high and continued his damning citations. He did not seem to notice the crowd around him; he saw only Mandy.

The young girl just stared blindly toward the pavement in front of her during the family's withdrawal to the parking lot. She was exhausted and trembling. Her eyes showed no emotion. Her father's protective grip felt unusually stiff.

Forty-five

Detective George Haberdeen was in a private room in the Queen of Angels hospital the night after the abortive trial. His painkiller-induced sleep was superficial and troubled. He had awakened several times throughout the night, unsettled about different elements of what had happened and too drugged to pay any attention to his surroundings.

As he awakened in the morning, his system relatively clear of drugs, George opened his eyes to see Lisa at his bedside. She was reading a paperback and didn't realize that he had woken up.

"Hi, Lisa," said George in a weakened voice.

Lisa lit up when she realized her man was back with her. She went over and hugged him, and his usually-serious maw broke into a grin that made both of them feel great.

This whole Milliken experience had actually brought George and Lisa closer together. She thought about the amazing span of dangers the cop's strength had had to endure. He had become much more protective of Lisa as he realized how vulnerable she was. And how much he'd miss her if she were no longer a part of his life. The baby growing in Lisa would have not only biological parents, but a married couple to bring him up.

Four days after Haberdeen was released from the hospital, he was permitted to go back to work on a limited basis: He was permitted to do desk work only. Even though he had been bitten deeply in the neck, nothing life-threatening had been severed. And with Lisbath Milliken now deceased and her case dismissed, Haberdeen's workload was temporarily almost nonexistent. He knew that Sergeant Judd Stevenson would be handing him a new case soon, but for now, he could coast.

But Haberdeen wasn't a coaster. This was his chance to dig just a little further, if for no other reason than his own peace of mind. Haberdeen decided that his first call would be to Dr. Mark Howard, who had gathered all that vampire information. He reached for the phone and dialed.

"Doctor's office," said the voice on the other end of the line.

"This is Detective George Haberdeen. Please put Dr. Howard on."

"He's just getting ready for his first patient. I'll see if he can talk." Thunder reverberated outside the doctor's office and made its way into the phone.

A minute later, the doctor picked up. "Hello, Detective Haberdeen. I understand there was quite a commotion at the trial."

"Yeah. That's part of what I'm calling about."

"Oh?"

"I'll get to that in a minute." Haberdeen paused. "Hey, Doc. I've got a question."

"Yes?"

"One of Milliken's patients didn't catch the disease. That's messing me up."

"And all the others had puerperal fever, right?"

"Right."

"Pretty odd. I am not aware of any natural immunity to *S. pyogenes*. As a matter of fact, now that I think of it, there's no immunity on record."

"So why didn't this one—her name's Boating—catch it?"

"How could I know? Unless she was already on some kind of antibiotic regimen. That's pretty likely."

"Okay. Great! That's put to bed. Now I've got more for you," said Haberdeen.

"Shoot."

"You asked about the commotion."

"Yes."

"Part of it was that bitch's dog attacking Milliken. He killed her."

"Wow."

"There's more. When he did it, he sucked some green shit from her. It was like fog. A green cloud."

"What are you talking about?" asked Dr. Howard.

"Just what I said. The dog sucked some kind of green breath from Milliken's dying body."

"This is nuts."

"No shit, Doc. But I'm telling you it happened. So what do you make of it? You ever heard of such a thing?"

"No. But . . . wait a minute."

"Take as long as you need, Doc," said Haberdeen. He sat back and began eating some Fritos from an emergency bag that had been sequestered deep in his desk.

Dr. Howard began to think. Most viruses are contagious by airborne transmission. The p21-v that he and Dr. Fonescu had discussed could conceivably be transmitted across space in that way. Also, viruses that made people sick—or killed them—often had no effect on animals. Like the Anopheles mosquito that carries malaria but never gets sick from it.

Dr. Howard formed an hypothesis and decided to tell Haberdeen about it.

"Haberdeen?"

"Yeah?"

"There's some small chance that the dog was taking a virus from Nurse Milliken. This doesn't make much sense, though. Like, I can't see how the dog could get it out of Milliken *en masse*."

"*On* what?" asked Haberdeen.

"All at once."

"Well, all the witnesses saw it just like I described it."

"It could have happened."

"Listen, Doc. I appreciate all your time. This helps a lot. Got anything else for me?"

"I don't think so, Mr. Haberdeen. Anyway, I must go now. Good luck, Detective."

"Thanks, Doc. Bye."

Haberdeen hung up and made some notes for himself.

Detective Sergeant Stevenson was walking by. In his typical style, he plopped the morning paper onto Haberdeen's desk. "Have a look at this, George." He shook his head in disgust and went into his office.

"Thanks, paper boy," George said.

On the front page of the *Bridgeport Informant* was another crowning achievement for Big T.

RED DEATH'S ANGEL KILLED IN COURT BY HER OWN MONSTER PET
Scarlet Fever Epidemic No Longer Threatened

By Constance Teitelmeier

Red Death's Angel was killed in a Bridgeport courtroom yesterday by her own dog, a monster that held an entire courtroom in frightened awe. This fiend will no longer threaten our fine community with her vicious deeds.

Not only did she murder women and drink the blood of her nursing clients, Milliken also spread scarlet fever microbes among her poor victims.

The three-column article went on to detail all twenty-two counts against Milliken. It went into great detail about Milliken's dog attacking and killing her. It included a confused mash of "information" on the dog's telepathically-sent admonitions.

The article then went on to describe briefly the subsequent scene outside the courthouse. There was little mention of Vlad's behavior outside the building since, as far as Big T knew, the animal had simply run away. Haberdeen was mentioned deep in the article, and George was glad that it glossed over his actually critical role in catching and stopping Milliken.

He put down the newspaper. Not surprisingly, the G-Man found nothing useful in the article. He continued putting details down on his pad from his conversation with Dr. Howard. As he was writing, he circled Lisbath's name. Then he remembered a couple of things that would come together shortly:

First, he thought about what Milliken had said to Anna Windham. About the strange voice that had come out of her in that room/cell at The Park. The one that claimed she was Elizabeth Bathory.

Second, he remembered what his colleague Hawking had said in a phone call they had yesterday. In the newspaper, the Big T article spoke of the telepathic messages the animal had spewed around the room, but the article's report was jumbled and contained little actual quotation of what the dog had "sent." During their phone call, Hawking told Haberdeen that in one of the transmissions, the animal had referred to Milliken as "Bathory."

Elizabeth Bathory. Lisbath. Lis-Bath. It fucking couldn't be, he thought to himself. *Too ridiculously obvious.*

Nevertheless, Haberdeen decided to check into his Milliken file. He began to put two and two together. He realized that Lisbath had changed her name from Claire just after that dog had attacked her back in 1961. It must have been at that moment that the animal—clearly it was Vlad the Impaler—infused Countess Elizabeth Bathory's soul or spirit or virus or whatever the hell it was into Milliken's body. Milliken must have been a "familiar."

Where did Vlad get Bathory's soul in the first place? he wondered.

Haberdeen could never know of the violent attack on the Countess Bathory's castle. Nor would he know of the "stray" dog's strange activities—sucking vapors from over the writhing, dying woman. Yet Haberdeen could continue his analysis despite his being partly in the dark.

Things were beginning to gel in the G-Man's thinking. Every piece of the puzzle that began to fit made for an increasingly bizarre final picture. Haberdeen decided to try to figure out what those labels taped to the containers in the woman's closet meant. Obviously they had some type of code to them. They had things like *S077980702* and *S082990914* on them.

The lab identified that the one of the "younger" of the jars had *S064000310* on it. These provided the key Haberdeen needed. He figured the last six digits—in this case, 000310—were likely the date of the collection. That would mean March 10, 2000, if he were right.

That left S064. What could that be? It didn't matter for now. His current guesses were close enough for government work. If Haberdeen were to be assigned some kind of related task like finding other "victims," he could use these possible date codes for correlation against Milliken's birthing assignments.

The G-Man felt he had solved another part of the mystery. He was feeling pretty powerful. This much closure felt great. He wanted more.

Within the next week, Haberdeen had amassed considerable information on the fates of Milliken's most recent patients. With the help of another officer, Haberdeen learned that the tremendous La-TaKeisha Jeffers had required enormous doses of antibiotics—five times the normally-prescribed amounts—but had recovered successfully. She and her daughter Ma-Chondra, who had been staying with La-TaKeisha's sister during her mom's hospitalization, had been brought back to the woman's apartment without incident. Since Jeffers was somewhat ambulatory, they were able to use a van for the transport.

Dr. Coop Gold's patient, Lucinda Smithson, had been diagnosed with *S. Pyogenes* early in the game. She too was given antibiotics and recovered fairly quickly.

The initially comatose Kevin Wallace eventually regained limited consciousness three weeks after the trial was over. Unfortunately, he had sustained considerable brain damage and had to be cared for by his extended family. The upside was that he did not remember being married, and so did not miss Doris or his children.

Jackie Turnbull, the woman Milliken was servicing when she was arrested, had been given an antibiotic regimen immediately on her admission to the hospital. That had saved her. Her baby Henry was healthy and unharmed.

Unfortunately, Jackie had witnessed all the up-close tumult of Milliken's arrest, and that experience left a deep psychological scar. To have seen the police burst into her sacrosanct birth room and drag her health caregiver away in handcuffs was sufficiently disturbing to send her to therapy. Haberdeen had spoken with her husband Gerald. Mr. Turnbull told Haberdeen that Jackie had been diagnosed with Post-Traumatic Stress Disorder. Turnbull blamed the whole mess on police incompetence. He hung up on Haberdeen.

Herr Erich Blücher was being held in the city jail pending his trial. As a result of his planned and partially-executed attack on Lisbath while she lay in her hospital cell, he had been charged originally with attempted murder. But in a soft moment, Haberdeen, who had seen the horrors the Milliken woman had foisted on so many families, convinced the DA to reduce the charges against Blücher to mere assault. No battery was charged since Blücher's belt was never actually put around Lisbath's neck. Of course, Erich's deception—his impersonation of a lawyer to gain entrance to Lisbath's hospital cell—would be mentioned in his trial. Haberdeen would have no role to play at Erich Blücher's day in court, but he intended to be there anyway. He knew that his attendance would give him just that much more closure.

Ilse Blücher was healthy and back with her extended family

and her new daughter. She visited Erich in jail daily. The man was still quite angry to have fathered a girl and refused to discuss a name. Ilse named her daughter Regina.

Forty-six

The neighborhood boys Perry and Jim had a fun plan. Every time a car would start to come up the road, one of them would roll a water balloon out onto the asphalt. Then they'd run back into the bushes and watch the balloon explode if the car hit it. The one who had the most hits at the end of the day would have to buy the candy.

It was Perry's turn next. He went to the soggy cardboard box the two had hidden in the bushes and chose a full, bright yellow balloon. As he bounced it in his hand, Mandy Shapiro came down the street. She was smiling and suspected what the boys were doing.

"What'ya doin', guys?"

"The balloon trick."

She knew it well. Roll out the balloon just before a car gets to it, and watch it splatter. Startles the driver sometimes.

Mandy asked, "Can I watch?"

"Sure. But you gotta stay in the bushes the whole time. You can't hide fast enough."

"Can too!" said the girl.

"Can not. You wanna play with us or not?"

"Okay. I'll hide. Who's winning?"

"Jimmy has four and I have five. And it's my turn," bragged Perry.

An old Ford had just turned the corner at the end of the street, and Perry positioned himself near the curb. As the car came closer, the boy rolled the balloon out like a cylindrical bowling ball and ran for the bushes.

The driver was a slick-haired teenager with his date, and he had seen Perry roll the thing out. When he was a couple of feet from the balloon, he slammed on his brakes, deliberately making a frightful sound. He didn't like people messing with his date—or his car.

"You little bastards!" he screamed. He looked directly at the bushes where he knew the kids were hiding. When they saw him beam in on them, they ran as fast as they could to the alley entrance just by the bushes. Then they sped down the long, wet pavement.

"Hey! Come back here!" yelled the teenager. He really had no intention of going after the little delinquents, but he did want to scare the shit out of them.

His scream almost doubled the running speed of all three kids. They were a block and a half away when Jim, who was ahead of the other two, slipped on a wet patch. He flew several feet before sprawling onto the asphalt like a floppy doll.

Jim's right knee and elbow were scraped badly. Perry and Mandy ran up to him and immediately looked down the alley to be sure that the driver wasn't following them. Then they stopped to help Jim.

Jim was crying as he rubbed his knee. Mandy stared at Jim's arm where the blood was dripping. She was fascinated. Mandy came from a Kosher home, where the meat was always drained of blood even before being brought to market. She had never seen more than a few drops of real blood before that fateful day at the Boatings' window. Mandy knelt down beside the boy and began cleaning his scraped knee, working her fingers and a Kleenex all around the fresh wound.

At the far end of the alley, a black-and-white animal with a short-haired coat was watching. The animal had been drawn to the site by recognizing the scent of one of the children. It watched her remove the blood. It saw her poise.

As the animal continued to observe this scene, its eyes began to take on a red glow. His head grew slowly and painfully in girth, and his body began an unmistakable, low vibration.

On all fours, Vlad the Impaler stared at Mandy Shapiro with ravenous eyes. He seemed to imagine her future. The virus that was Bathory was eating away in him. It needed sanctuary. It needed somewhere to grow.

WITHDRAWN